THE BERLIN GIRL'S

Leah Moyes

Production by eBookPro Publishing
www.ebook-pro.com

THE BERLIN GIRL'S PROMISE
Leah Moyes
Copyright © 2018 Leah Moyes

Edited by Irene Hunt

Previously published by SpuCruiser Media as
"Berlin Butterfly: Deception"

Leahmoyesauthor@gmail.com

Facebook @BerlinButterfly

Twitter @authormoyes

ISBN 9798301608186

The Berlin Girl's
Promise

A Historical Fiction Novel

LEAH MOYES

To my children (and borrowed children)

Taylor for your adventurous spirit and example of strength.
Ryan for your boundless heart and honorable service.
Harlie for your selfless love and grace.
Jace for your influence and willingness to serve.
Alex for your testimony and perseverance.
Chad for your kindness and wit and Bubba for your
eternal smile and positive influence.
I could never be prouder or feel more blessed. I love you.

ReadMore
Press

Sign up for **Readmore Press'** monthly newsletter and get a FREE audiobook!

For instant access, scan the QR code

Where you will be able to register and receive your sign-up gift, a free audiobook of

Beneath the Winds of War
by Pola Wawer,

which you can listen to right away

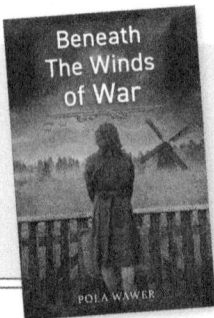

Beneath The Winds of War

POLA WAWER

Our newsletter will let you know about new releases of our World War II historical fiction books, as well as discount deals and exclusive freebies for subscribed members.

PROLOGUE

Berlin, 1966. Separation of the two countries of East and West Germany endures as the Cold War enters its nineteenth year. Tensions continue to rise in the Soviet sector with Communist control, shrewd espionage, and clear deficiencies of rights, freedoms, and choice for the people of the Deutche Democratic Republic. Friends, family, and neighbors no longer trust each other as Stasi detainments and unaccountable disappearances threaten daily life. The wall itself has become nearly impenetrable with double partitions enclosing a death strip filled with razor wire, spike mats, tank traps, motion detectors, and soldiers ordered to shoot on sight. Despite the risk, East Berliners continually test ways to escape to the West.

Twenty-year-old Ella Kühn, in five short years since the rise of the Berlin Wall, has experienced more than her fair share of incomprehensible pain and heartache. The separation of her brother Josef and only friend Anton to the West, burying her father, the disappearance and death of friends, fear, torture, and loss—culminating in the forced departure of her love into military service. Stefan's ten-year sentence with the *Nationale Volksarmee* came after his protective efforts to keep Ella from the clutches of a colonel with malicious intent turned fatal.

With Ella's own failed attempts at freedom, the survivor's guilt she bears is a foremost burden on her mind as the victim toll continues to escalate around her. Only Stefan's love, his promise to return, and the belief that someday she will be reunited with her family keep her alive.

ONE

WHY PETER?

March 1966

The crisp, scented leaves of *Buschwindröschen,* and the fragrant yellow buds of the *Scharbockskraut* bush, scarcely masked the rotten smell of foul feces from the nearby duck pond. While my legs met some relief stretched into a thicket of long grass, the ground beneath my chest remained firm and cold. The dense hedges overhead provided decent coverage against a shroud of darkness as I scooted painstakingly forward on my elbows. My slow and tedious combat crawl had progressed very few inches within the hour.

My companion's patience grew thin. I held my breath as a bright light flashed across Wrede Bridge. Our bodies remained still as the powerful beam lingered on the neighborhood of *Sorgenfrei* before finally moving on to the canal.

The darkness gave us a few precious seconds. I glanced at Peter who returned the look. His smile arched candidly, similar to the day we met.

"Ella, come." His hasty whisper came as he eagerly hopped to all four limbs and scampered closer to the wire. My throat constricted, unable to eject a response. He was moving too fast, too confident . . . my heart raced with fear when the shouting began. I could no longer see his silhouette in the shadow of the new moon.

Gunshots pierced the silence. Ducks squawked in panicked flight, flapping louder than the cries—cries from an unknown origin. They could have been my own. By the time I reached Peter, he hung lifeless. His back pressed weightily against the razor-sharp points of barbed wire. Thick, dark blood pooled beneath him. His mouth, that moments ago curved upward, now gaped open. Scrambling for composure, my trembling fingers tugged until the wire released him. His immortalized expression stared back at me while I cradled him in my lap.

"*Nein, bitte nein!*" Dissenting screams shook my core as another round of bullets penetrated the cold night air.

My eyes burst open as my hands frantically patted my body in search of wounds or blood. Wisps of heavy breathing expelled with every move; I could hear the thump of my heartbeat. *A heartbeat . . . my heart is still beating.*

I glanced around. Familiar objects greeted me—Stefan's painting of Cochem hung on the wall, Mama G's padded chair in the corner with the bookshelf above, the worn pages of my favorite book Immensee spotted next to a stack of undelivered letters.

Muffled sobs of relief came swiftly as I fell flat on my back. With my legs pulled tightly to my torso, I curled like a baby. The dream seemed so real . . . frighteningly real. Sweat, mixed with tears, dripped down my face. The emotions were conflicting—loss and pain, yet somehow that sorrow became fused with gratitude. I hadn't been shot trying to escape East Berlin nor had I held a dying Peter in my arms.

The unforgiving surface felt icy beneath me. Winter lingered in the walls of this old apartment building despite March being the doorway to spring. The dust-covered radiator in the corner offered no relief. I shivered. My cheek momentarily rested against the wood slats before I realized I no longer lay comfortably in my bed, but below it. *When did I fall?*

A bluish light appeared through the small window above as the darkness started to dissipate. A man's voice, coming from the antiquated radio on my night table, interrupted my confusion. I must have forgotten to turn it off before I fell asleep.

Nachrichten für heute!

As the newsperson spoke, a recollection of the previous night's bulletin resurfaced. My heart sank. Tears welled up once again remembering the report's details of yet another violent, incomprehensible murder at the wall.

19 Mar 1966 Berlin-Treptow

Two children shot dead by machine pistols used by People's Police near the Planterwald S-Bahn border. Ten-year-old Jörg Hartman and thirteen-year-old Lothar Schleusner, both residents of Friedrichshain. Full denial by Communist Party Security Division and Defense Council Leader Erich Honecker—

Silencing the radio, my legs mustered the strength to stand despite the weakness in my knees. As I hovered over the kitchen sink, the imagined faces of those frightened children filled my mind. Snatching a handkerchief from the rack, I moistened it to cool my heated face then paced the room anxiously. The newspaper, spread open at the foot of my bed, drew my attention even though I had read it multiple times the day before.

"Der Stolz Deutschlands"

German military pride occupied the print. Page after page was lined with pictures of soldiers in uniform both home and abroad. I scanned them repeatedly. Endless stories of the *Nationale Volksarmee* and their -country-wide accomplishments appeared, yet—despite my daily hunt—I had yet to find any news or photo of my beloved Stefan.

As I dressed for the day, I reflected on the nightmare. *Why Peter? Why now?* Our meeting nearly four years ago in the pub had been so brief. I barely knew him before he was killed at the wall; and as disturbing as those images were, the ones of me vividly at his side trying to escape were nearly as devastating. I promised Stefan I wouldn't leave. Getting to Anton and Josef in the West had been something I had tried before— before committing myself and my heart to Stefan at the train station where his ten-year sentence began.

I grabbed a paper and pencil, my only solace during times like this— the tragic death of the two small children, the nightmare, and my excruciating loneliness.

20 Mar 1966
My dearest love,

I paused. Sharing this sadness would only make his heart heavy—*no, I must keep my correspondence positive, even though he may never see it.*

> *I hope when you read this letter you keep it close to your heart, and if there is ever an ounce of doubt in your mind, read it again and again. I LOVE YOU STEFAN! I will wait an eternity for you if I must.*
>
> *I miss you. I miss seeing your face, your smile, the way you look at me, our first dance, the art room, our moments alone. I have tried to walk through Volkspark and the butterfly path without you, but it's too difficult. Everything I see is a reminder of us and our past.*
>
> *I often think about that night. If you hadn't come and risked your life and freedom to save me from the colonel, I would not be here. I owe everything to you and waiting for your release is a small sacrifice in comparison.*
>
> *When that day comes and your requirement is complete and your sentence served, I will be the happiest woman in Berlin. We are meant to be together.*
>
> *I hope you are healthy and safe. Not a day goes by, I don't think of you. I see your face when I go to sleep, and it's the first thought when I wake up. I will wait for you. I'll be here when you come home.*
>
> *All my love, Ella*

I set it down on top of the pile of letters that had been written over the last thirty-three months, none of which I could send, not knowing where he was or where they could be delivered.

On her visits home, Katharina made multiple requests to the liaison staff at the NVA main headquarters for an address but was told his specific regiment was mobile. Writing was the only way to express my feelings for him, and somehow seeing those words on paper strengthened my belief that he was mine. Someday, when we were together again, I would be able to give them all to him, and he might see how much he meant to me, even in his absence.

I warmed a cup of tea and went to the window, a daily routine: watching the sun rising above the concrete rubble that used to resemble a church, children excitedly bouncing hand in hand with a parent on their way to kinder school, Herr Köhler across the way sweeping the walk in front of his *Brezel* shop—meticulously clean, people would come from all over the city for his pretzels.

Wait. Max-Beer was filled with people, more than I had ever seen before.

Suddenly, I realized what the dream had tried to force me to forget. My mug nearly crashed to the floor as I sprinted to the mirror. The small number in the corner that counted down Stefan's return remained in the thousands, but in larger characters, written in bright red wax was today's date—Sunday, 20 March—with the word *PARADE* boldly circled.

It was the day I had been waiting for since the announcement was made. Nothing, not even a horrible nightmare, could keep me from getting to downtown Mitte this morning. Grabbing Mama's sweater, I fled out the door.

TWO

KARL MARX ALLEE

"Come on, Lena!" my cries amplified as she stepped off the bus, "I don't want to be late!"

"There are thousands of soldiers, Ella. How are you going to be able to pick him out?"

"I don't know. I just have to!" Grabbing her hand, we raced through the crowd to find a higher perch that faced the boulevard. After an anxious step onto a bench, I pulled Lena up next to me. The moment I caught sight of the neatly formed ranks of soldiers, I had to remind myself to breathe. He was out there somewhere. The mere thought of Stefan being in the same vicinity caused my heart to flutter with anticipation.

Despite the time that had passed since we said goodbye at the train station nearly three years ago, he was my every thought. Reflection of his face, his voice, and his touch made me blush as though it were yesterday.

Scanning row by row, the soldiers marched in perfect alignment. Even though I knew it would be nearly impossible to see him, I still had to try. Many young women in similar circumstances joined me. It was if we were part of a strange, exclusive club—one I would rather *not* be a member of.

Celebrating the tenth anniversary of the creation of the *National Volksarmee,* the parade brought all the military units not detained back to Berlin. There hadn't been a parade of this size marching down Karl Marx Allee since Hitler was in power—of course back then, the same boulevard was known as *Stalinallee* and served *der Führer* for a very different purpose.

This overwhelming display brought every possible citizen living in the Soviet sector to the streets, and this was the happiest I had seen the people in years.

The legions marched briskly and in full precision. They were all nearly identical with their gray parade dress tunic, black or silver belt depending on rank, matching-color gumdrop helmet, black riding boots, and the ceremonial dagger or saber at their side. Their meticulous, stiff steps appeared as though they were wind-up toys focused in one direction and not distracted by the large assembly in the least.

As the end of the soldiers came in sight and the rows of tanks began, my face caved in disappointment. I knew it was an unrealistic wish, given the size of the ranks and the indistinguishable physiques. However, the moment the parade announcement had been made, it was all I could think about. A glimpse of his face, brief as it would be, could carry me for another three years.

My thoughts went to the platform of the Friedrichstraße station where I said goodbye to Stefan. It was at that moment I vowed to give my whole love and affection to him, promising to wait as long as necessary regardless of his duty, his family, or anything else that would stand in our way. He sacrificed everything to save me; owing Stefan my life and my future, I was his and I was sure of it . . . until a letter arrived last autumn and then doubt seized a small portion of my heart.

25 August 1965

Dearest Ella,
This is a very hard letter for me to write. Two of my comrades were killed by undetected landmines in an area close to the southern border. I cannot tell you specifics since this letter can be compromised, but my heart is heavy.

Jonathan had a wife and two children and was only twenty-eight years old. Philip wasn't married and was so young, only nineteen, and had been assigned to our company barely two months ago. I wasn't far from these men and received some shrapnel in my upper torso and down my leg. I'm fine, but Ella, I should've been killed. It was by pure circumstance I was behind them. I got a piece of loose barbed wire wrapped around my boot as we were scouting, and I stopped to untangle it. Because of this momentary delay, my life was spared. I cannot stop thinking about why it wasn't me. Why was I randomly chosen to survive?

If I had died, you would have waited for nothing. It is unfair and selfish of me to continue to ask you to wait. I know the years will be long and the loneliness can be weary. It would be naïve of me to assume you are not approached by available young men. If you choose to be with someone else, I cannot expect you to refuse. I will understand. It's an impossible request for me to ask you to wait seven more years. The first three years without you have nearly driven me mad. Please know I will always love you. However, I cannot in good conscience presume you should remain obligated to me.

Forever, my love, Stefan

"Ella? . . . Ella? Are you well?" Lena tugged on my sleeve as the crowd thinned. She draped her arm around my shoulders. She knew nothing of the letter. It had been delivered by Katharina while on holiday and read nearly a hundred times since. Yet, with no way to respond and no correspondence since, uncertainty slowly crept in.

Questions that never entered my mind before the letter suddenly emerged. *Why is he speaking this way? Does he believe in us as much as I do? Or does he know or see something about our future that I don't?* Everything I held onto for assurance felt as though it was slipping from my grasp. Even now as I craned my neck down the boulevard, the last of the soldiers faded away and moved completely out of sight. I was thoroughly discouraged.

"I'm sorry, Ella!" Lena sighed, "If I had caught the earlier bus, we may have had a better view. It's all my fault!"

"No, Lena, it's mine." I readjusted my hat to stop the springtime wind from nipping at my ears. "I just get foolish thoughts in my head and erase all reality. I should have known it would be too difficult to pick him out."

We walked silently arm in arm down the street.

"Wait, do you hear that?" I pulled Lena to a sudden halt.

"Hear what?"

"That noise." I realized with the increase in pedestrian chatter on the street I needed to clarify. "There's an echo, like a speaker. Do you hear that?"

Lena tilted her head as if that position aided in better hearing.

"*Dem anständigen Soldaten . . .*"

"It sounds like an announcement of some sort, but where's it coming from?" I asked.

"Over here, Ella. Look." Lena pointed past a shorter part of the wall off Zimmerstraße. The roof of a Volkswagen bus could be seen with a row of six speakers mounted on top. It was parked near the wall on the west side."

"What are they saying?" We stepped close enough to listen but not appear as a threat.

"*Dem anständigen Soldaten danken alle landsleute Dem Schützen dankt nur die SED . . .*"

"There is too much noise, I didn't hear what it said." Frustrated, I turned to Lena for clarification.

"All Germans thank the honest soldier, only the SED thanks the marksman," she repeated back to me.

I passed her a puzzling glance as she continued, "I overheard a soldier complaining at the Franke house that the West has increased their propaganda against the East. There's a fleet of buses just like this one dispatched all over the border. They're called "Studios at the Barbed Wire.""

The thought warmed my heart. "At least there are people who haven't forgotten us."

The announcements continued at a rapid pace with seemingly no intent to stop. "*Auf den zweiten Mann kommt es an.*"

"It all depends on the second man?"

"Yes, haven't you seen all the posters and the messages on the zipper?"

"No, I haven't." Not much had changed in the way I kept to myself.

"They're angry about the refugee shootings and demanding an end to the *order to shoot.*"

"Good," I concurred, "Someone is standing up to the SED." A similar bus pulled up next to the original one. Together they timed their announcements to reach more people. This conspiracy seemed to agitate the border guard who had been quiet up until now.

"Standing up, yes, but not making much progress." Lena pointed to additional reinforcements of the People's Police. A half dozen soldiers jumped out of the bed of a truck and hustled towards the wall. The two soldiers originally there had picked up rocks and threw them at the vehicles. Another soldat shouted incomprehensible statements their direction.

Afraid of getting caught in the altercation, Lena grabbed my arm again, and we quickly hustled away from the area.

"Never a dull moment in the East." I chuckled once our distance felt safe enough.

"No, never, but let's not waste another minute of this beautiful Sunday afternoon before we both have to go back to work tomorrow. We haven't seen each other in months," she reasoned. "I do believe there is a cafe near here that I went to with Christoph once."

Christoph. It seemed like ages ago. Four years since the awful day when my failed escape ruined more than one life. While Lena seemed to have forgiven me and recovered well on the outside—the scars on her wrists barely visible—her eyes revealed deeper wounds, and she hadn't been with another man since Christoph's disappearance.

"What a wonderful idea." I tried hard to make my response genuine, although I was a terrible fake.

"Come on, Ella." She tugged. "*Streusel* is calling."

I laughed at her attempt to entice me with treats. She knew me too well. It almost always worked.

We stopped at a place called *Bäckerei Balzer*. Lena said they had the best *Streuselschneken* she had ever tasted. Before Lena and Stefan entered my life, I had no concept how deeply my body craved flavor. Now, the smallest details brought me joy. The jelly slipping out the crease of a *Krapfen* when I took a bite, the salt that stuck to my tongue from a fresh, warm pretzel, or the wafting aroma from the steam of a newly roasted *brat*. I had no idea the world offered so many pleasures, and as usual, she was right. Barely getting past the confectioners' sugar, I was smitten.

We sat on the small patio out front and watched people on the street. Despite the permanent darkness that seemed to hover over the city, today felt different. Everyone appeared to have an extra lift in their step or smile on their face. The parade gave us all a strange sense of pride and comfort.

I beamed, thinking that despite my inability to pick Stefan out from the rank, he was there. His foot touched the ground I walked on, his mouth yielded breath from the same air I did, and his beautiful blue eyes shared my same vision. It seemed to be such a reach, but my soul felt closer to him right now than it had in years.

"I've seen that look before, Ella."

I blushed. "Do you think he's here?"

"Yes." Lena matched my smile. "Yes, I do, and you know what else I think?"

My grin widened.

"I am certain he is thinking of you this very minute, as well."

My desire to believe her more than anything swelled while I sat back and savored the moment.

It was briefly interrupted by the waitress who brought fresh cups of coffee to our table. As the steam swirled above, I studied Lena carefully. She was quite beautiful. Her flawless white skin accented by her blonde curls matched nearly every toy doll I had ever seen in a store window. Only the small lines that circled her eyes were new, but as always, she still turned heads everywhere we went.

"Do you believe you'll ever love again?" The question had a life of its own. I had pondered it often but never imagined it would reach my lips. My own expression rivaled her surprise. "I'm sorry." My shoulders cringed. "I shouldn't have asked something so personal."

"It's fine. I've thought it in my mind many times." She laughed softly, except it was a tormented laugh. "I guess since we never learned if Christoph was actually killed or not, my hope is that he *will* reappear someday." She shook her head. "It's a silly thought."

"No," I spoke up, "No, Lena, it's a delightful thought. There shouldn't be a time limit for love." My mind wandered to Stefan. "Don't ever give up on him." Reaching for her hands, I squeezed softly. Her smile contradicted the sadness in her eyes.

"When was the last time you heard from Anton and Josef?" She shifted the conversation quickly.

I stiffened. My hands instinctively met my face.

Since our separation on that August night five years ago, the memory of Anton and Josef disappearing around the corner had been etched deeply into my heart. At the time, it was the greatest pain I had experienced without death involved . . . until I met Stefan.

"Did something happen?"

Tears formed at the corners of my eyes. I couldn't keep them from falling.

"Ella?" Lena's voice rose with alarm.

I reached into my purse and pulled out an envelope. My fingers trembled as I handed the letter to her. It was dated over a month ago.

8 February 1966

Dearest Ella,
I have urgent news and struggle to put the words down, but this news can't wait any longer.

Josef has taken ill.

It began with fever and chills, then rashes appeared. By the time the doctor arrived, his breathing was short and faint. He is in the infirmary now, yet little is known. Oh, Ella, I'm sorry. You trusted him to my care, and I feel like I have failed you. I wait by his side daily, but he is weak. The doctors are unsure he will live through the month.

I know the post can take time but all I can hope for is when I write again the news will have changed for the better.
Please forgive me.

Love, Anton

"Ella, . . ." Lena tried to say my name with confidence, only concern crept across her face. "I'm sure Josef is well. I'm positive Anton would have found a way to reach you if . . ." her voice trailed off. My eyelashes fluttered quickly, fighting the tears. I couldn't bear the thought of losing Josef.

"Lena, I don't know what to do."

She brushed my cheek with her finger. "What have you tried?"

"Everything I can think of. I wrote a letter immediately, only it takes too long, so I went to the border and begged. Of course, they only laughed at me. I went to emigration, and they handed me the same forms I've filled out for the last five years." My gasps came sporadically from speaking so fast. "Lastly I went to Mr. Brauner's apartment . . . but he's gone."

"What do you mean gone?"

"Just gone. His neighbor came out when he heard me knock several times."

"Does the neighbor know where he went?"

"No, he knew nothing. He said they'd been gone for quite a while."

"When did you see the Brauners last?"

"About a year ago."

Lena was silent for a while before she spoke, "I'm sorry, Ella. I truly am."

The excitement of the parade had momentarily paused my fear. Nonetheless, it was all I could think about now.

"Maybe . . ." Lena's eyebrows curved downward then suddenly lifted. "Wait! What about reaching the hospital where Josef is being treated?"

"I thought about that," my mumble surfaced with weak enthusiasm, "I don't know which hospital, nor do I have access to a telephone."

"The Frankes have one."

My face went still as I recalled the black rotary phone I'd seen on the desk in the mortuary office the time I was in there with Stefan. It was brief, and I didn't care much about it back then, although now . . . now it could be of great use. My mouth curved upward then instantly frowned—the house and mortuary were beyond my reach.

Lena seemed to read my mind. "Ella, I can try to get to the phone, but Herr Franke rarely comes out of the mortuary now. It would be difficult to enter undetected."

I eyed her curiously. "Who meets with the dignitaries?"

"*Frau* Franke." Lena leaned in and whispered, "If women were ever allowed to be part of the SED party, she would be insufferable. Things are much worse with Stefan gone."

I nodded, understanding very well the significance of his absence.

"Katharina will be coming home soon. She could help. I know she would do it for you."

I forced a smile. I hadn't seen Katharina since she delivered the letter from Stefan last November, and though she knew nothing of the contents, her very presence brought a familiar sense of ease.

"We will find out about Josef. I'm sure of it."

I silently sipped my coffee as Lena talked about the new maid at the Franke's. I barely heard her chuckle regarding the poor woman's first serving experience, as my concentration remained elsewhere. The tussle to keep Josef's lifeless form out of my head was torment, the fatigue nearly consuming me.

"Lena, I must say goodnight." It was well after 6 o'clock when we hugged our goodbyes.

"Maybe next time I could come see your new flat." Lena smiled and kissed me on the cheek.

"Yes, of course." I tried to match her grin. "Thank you, Lena, and I will stay in touch better this time."

As I waited for the bus, a crippled boy resting against a street lamp in front of me caught my attention. He appeared to be around Josef's current age. I paused, considering that I, too, was almost sixteen when he and Anton left five years back. It seemed like a lifetime ago.

My thoughts centered on Josef . . . in pain or suffering. The image of him calling out for me or for Mama and Papa was distressing. He was too young to die.

I needed to get news, and for the first time in a very long time, the temptation of escape flared up again. Could it be why I dreamt of Peter . . . the news about the murdered boys, the letter from Anton—was it a coincidence . . . or something more significant? I stared hard. Everything about the boy seemed familiar. *How can I do that to Stefan? I promised to stay, but his last letter was so confusing—almost like a sort of farewell message. Maybe I no longer belong here. Maybe I'm holding onto something that can no longer be held.*

Shaking my head to clear it, my hand slid impulsively into my purse to retrieve a coin. I held it out as the teenager's eyes met mine.

"*Danke*," he whispered. Our fingers briefly touched. My jaw tightened as I fought my emotion. This boy belonged to somebody at some time . . . yet, here he was alone. A solemn reminder to me that nothing in this life was ever certain.

THREE

4ᵀᴴ Msd

The next morning, I rolled over in bed, although I could not encourage my body to leave the warmth of the quilts.

What did I have to look forward to? Another day at Gustav's only brought with it another day of demands, complaints, or worse . . . watching happy couples nuzzle up on the benches as they focused on nothing but each other. All while my heart suffered in silence. I grabbed the pencil and paper from the nightstand.

21 March 1966
Stefan,
I miss you!

Too difficult to continue, I pushed it aside and got out of bed. I reluctantly washed my face. Scanning my appearance, I was grateful my skin no longer appeared ashen or my eyes hollow, and although my hair still craved its freedom, there was no reason to wear it down. I pulled my dark curls into a tight braid.

After buttoning my tan uniform dress, I reached past Anton's tinnie pin to get my name tag off the shelf. The shield pin stared back at me, rejected. It hadn't been worn since Captain Scharf returned it after the attack, and since then, its role had shifted.

The trinket no longer felt like a friend. It had become a bristle, a reminder that if I continued to keep Anton's pin close to my body, I couldn't let him go. I loved Anton, only it seemed that to love Anton would be to refuse Stefan, and I couldn't comply.

I clipped my name tag to the left breast of my dress with a loud exhale. My heavy discouragement was for more than Anton or Josef, but for Stefan, my parents, my work, Mama Genau . . . the list seemed never-ending.

Glaring hard at my mirror, I was angry I had been dealt such a difficult life. *What did I do to make God hate me this much? Why does it feel as though his wrath culminates towards me?* I splashed cold water on my face once more with a murmur . . . *Why do I even speak of a God who doesn't exist? No one could be this cruel.*

I reached for my towel. The need to pull myself out of this slump was dire, nothing good came from feeling sorry for myself. After patting my cheeks dry, I pinched the corner of the towel and rubbed the number off the end of the daunting *'2674'* in the corner of the mirror. The stump of red wax squeaked irritatingly as I replaced it with a four. I sighed glumly. Time strangled me.

The last countdown I displayed on my mirror was for the days I served in the Franke home, but the current enormous number represented how many days before I could be with Stefan for good. It was easy to get discouraged looking at it, but my misery didn't change the fact I still had to work to survive. I could not afford to live and operate in such a depressing trance. *Wake up!* I slapped my cheeks briskly until my brown skin topped a slight shade of pink.

The move from Mama Genau's to this small apartment hadn't quite sunk in. Stefan's painting was the only décor on a very blank wall. I paused longer than normal as my fingers swept over the hardened curls of the water then brushed across the greenery, upwards toward the castle. *Cochem has to be the most beautiful place on earth,* I imagined, but its indisputable magnificence truly depended on whether Stefan would be there with me.

Oh, how I miss him! My heart ached as I reluctantly pulled my eyes away and glanced around the small space. I had only kept two things from Mama G's apartment after I moved—my bed and her chair. My throat stung sorely as my eyes flashed to the empty chair. She was always in that chair when I returned home. I would kneel on the floor next to her armrest so we could talk, sometimes for hours. The only two mamas I had ever known both left after such a short time in my life, yet both left lasting impressions.

Time grew short, my shift at the cafe was to start in less than an hour, but I just wanted to feel her near me. I collapsed in the chair and pressed my ear to the backside, hoping somehow to suddenly feel her arms drape around me, soft and secure. I contemplated all the things that happened in the three years since Stefan was taken from me—the worst being the night I lost her, eight months ago.

"The heart attack was swift, and she didn't suffer." The doctor's words should have brought some comfort, yet selfishness consumed me. She was my family, and with Anton and Josef across the wall and Stefan somewhere in East Germany, I literally had nobody. It was like losing my loved ones all over again.

The small clock on the counter ticked loudly as I wiped my face with my sleeve. Mama G's smile appeared on the inside of my eyelids. I missed her laugh, her loyal ear, and soft shoulder that cradled my tears more than once.

I always knew the day could come when she would leave me, however, I never fully prepared for it. Mama G's youngest daughter Khloe had married in July of '64, then for nearly a year it was just Mama and me, and I was okay with that. I patted the arms of the chair as if patting the real person and grabbed my sweater. The bus ride to the checkpoint wasn't as far as the Franke's home had been, but the walk from the bus stop to *Leipziger Strasse* was half a kilometer, and the chill in the air would remain for at least another two months.

As I arrived at *Gustav's*, I realized the attraction of yesterday's parade created an unusual frenzy. I started work here a little over two years ago and was familiar with a steady stream of soldiers, although they were generally Border Guard, being as close as we were to Checkpoint "C" or "Charlie" depending on who you talked to. This morning, however, was different.

Immediately overwhelmed by the number of patrons bearing the patches from the outer divisions of *der Volksarmee*, I had to stop myself from staring. Every step taken brought me face to face with different detachment members, and with each one, the hope I would somehow find *my* soldier.

In one of the few letters I received, Stefan had mentioned the name of his company, the *4th MSD*, which I later learned to be *Motorisierte-Schutzen-Division Erfurt*. The customer who explained this told me the *MOT*, the more common name for MSD, had a key role in protecting the country as a motor rifle tactical unit, and I should be honored Stefan was selected for this division. As proud as his words made me feel, it was still hard to be happy hearing he might be good at being a soldier.

The idea Stefan could possibly still be in the city somewhere made me smile. Then the sad reality hit me, he wouldn't be able to find me even if he wanted to. He didn't know I had moved or even where I worked, since the letters I received in his absence were hand delivered by Katharina when she was home from school. This time she wouldn't be home for another two weeks.

"Ella! You're late!" Gus' voice shook roughly above the customers. I really wasn't tardy, but I could see the owner of the cafe was stressed under the unusual circumstances. Hilde, his wife, had already seated four separate parties and was showing another two to their seats.

The soldiers, for the most part, were respectful, generally in good spirits, and not offensive in any way. We didn't serve alcohol at the establishment, so I rarely had to deal with a drunk, and that was one of the best parts of this job. Since the incident with Colonel Anker, anytime I caught a whiff of liquor, the memory of that man's heavy body trapping mine on the cell floor, his scarred face, and foul breath was forever engraved on my brain.

"*Fräulein?*" A soldier from a nearby table called for my attention. I tied my apron, waved Hilde off, and headed toward them.

"Yes?" I briefly glanced at each of the squaddie's faces. An innocence mixed with untamed eagerness faced me back. I couldn't help but smile.

"May I help you?"

The four men seated in the booth spoke simultaneously.

"Whoa, gentlemen," I laughed, "one at a time, please."

Something unusual on their uniform jumped out at me. I gasped and pointed to the shoulder patch that bore the identification *4th MSD*.

"Do you serve in that company?" I faced the highest-ranking officer.

My understanding of the military hierarchy only increased with this job. My voice cracked unexpectedly as I spoke.

The man immediately swelled with pride. "*Ja*, I am the commanding officer for this unit." He smiled and winked.

I could hardly breathe. My hands shook as I steadied them against my pounding chest. I leaned in but could barely get the words out.

"D—do you, um . . ." I stuttered, " . . .do you happen to know a soldier by the name of Stefan Franke?"

The officer did not appear surprised, his stare unnerving as he tilted his head with what appeared to be careful calculation. He then glanced at the others around the table and finally answered slowly, "*Ich mache . . .*"

My heart fluttered wildly at his positive response. After all the times I had served soldiers, this would be the first time someone knew my Stefan! Smiling wide, I resisted the urge to throw my arms around his neck in happiness.

"Now, just calm down, Fräulein." The officer was brash, though kind. "Is there something I can help you with?"

"Yes!" I nearly shouted. "Please!" Tears started to run freely down my cheeks. "Please tell him, the next time you see him, I love him and miss him."

"Oh!" His eyes went wide with my candor. He glanced at my nametag and pointed.

"Are you . . . ?" He paused and winked at the other soldiers who all seemed to know something I did not. "Are you Ella Kühn?"

I nodded, unable to speak.

"Well, nice to finally meet you!"

The whole group broke into loud laughter.

A different soldier spoke, "We can't get Stefan to stop talking about you!"

I half laughed; half cried. The commander stuck his hand out to shake mine. I eagerly met it.

"Ella! There are other customers!" Gus' loud cry from the back didn't budge me.

I ignored him as the officer continued, "Well, one thing's for sure," The man's eyebrows rose. "Stefan didn't exaggerate one bit!"

My face immediately went hot as I peered down to my hands.

". . . and humble," he snickered.

"Just please," I faced him again as I fought back more tears. "Please tell him I miss him."

"Oh, *scheisse,* Fräulein!" The officer slapped the table and pointed to the door. "Tell him yourself!"

FOUR

THAT FELT REAL

I spun around to where the officer pointed but could not move. My eyes took in the sight of a man resembling Stefan, his height, his posture . . . even his features. I was paralyzed.

"Ella."

My name drifted through the air as my body tried to remember basic functions—thinking, breathing, speaking—it was as if I had forgotten how to do any of these.

Then he smiled.

The simple curve of his lips jolted my heart, granting life back into my limbs. While I somehow reached the center of the restaurant, each second felt like an eternity before we touched.

His fingers brushed my cheeks on their way to my neck, and without hesitation he pulled me to his lips before our bodies even collided. Met with familiar taste and tenderness, the kiss lengthened until breath became necessary, and even then, our bond slipped to an embrace. Long and tight.

I wept.

Even with Stefan's arms securely around me, I still questioned the belief that he was really here. *Can I possibly be imagining this? Can it be another dream?*

When our lips met a second time, all my doubt and insecurity disappeared. He kissed me as if we were the only two people present and continued until the audience of howls and whistles finally subsided. Tears flowed easily.

As I hesitantly pulled away, I took in his uniform. Stefan's long hair was cut quite short, the blond barely noticeable under his diamond-shaped cap. His skin was tan and a bit weathered. Instead of his parade uniform, he wore a traditional brown jacket, secured loosely by a wide belt of similar color. Thick black boots completed his appearance.

It was strange to see him in a soldier's uniform; yet he was as handsome as ever. He lifted me up and twirled me around then kissed me again as my feet hit the ground.

Gus slammed both his fists against the kitchen counter. "Ella, get back to work!" the grumpy old man huffed aloud.

From the other side of the café, Hilde's countenance beamed with delight. There wasn't a person here who didn't understand the significance of a military reunion . . . well, except Gus.

"Gustav, dear." She was a good wife to him even though he didn't deserve such a sweet woman. "Ella is taking the rest of the day off!"

"What?" he cried with exasperation. "*Scheisse!*"

I looked to Hilde in a panic. Her hands were full on her own. "I can't leave you with it this busy."

"Yes, you will." She tried to appear serious, except her smile broke through. "Now go!"

I ripped off my apron as fast as my hands could move and gave Hilde a quick squeeze before tossing it behind the counter. Returning to Stefan, I slipped my hand into his but pulled my body tightly against his side as we walked out.

When we stopped just outside the doors, I paused, trying to comprehend who stood before me. My fingers released from his grasp and skimmed along his jawline then caressed his cheek as if I was testing an illusion.

"How is this possible?" I cried. "Is it really you?"

He smiled, then without a word, his hands gently reached for my arms and swept me away from the door and up next to the brick siding. As he leaned in, his lips pressed with all the passion his absence amassed. Every nerve within me stirred, and I willingly conceded.

"That felt real," I whispered in between the measured gravity of his lips. Unable to move—nor desiring to—I wished for this moment to last forever.

He paused an inch from my face. Small lines had formed outside his deep blue eyes that regarded me with captivating adoration. I considered the last time I saw them and what his eyes had witnessed since—the pain and heartache he encountered as a soldier and the devastation of watching his friends die.

"Really, Stefan, how? How is this possible?"

He rubbed his palm against my cheek; I sensed there was much to say, but he just regarded me in silence.

"How long are you here?" A question I hesitated to ask.

"Three days." Stefan's face lit up. "In celebration of the anniversary, we all get three days respite in Berlin!"

Tears sprang to my eyes. "When did your three days begin?"

"This morning."

My heart swelled at this news while I reached for his face. Gliding upward, my fingers caressed his short hair, knocking his cap to the ground. His eyes rolled back as his head pressed softly into my hand. *He missed my touch as much as I missed his.* He reached for my wrist and kissed it. His lips brushed against my skin so lightly the tease sent an electric surge through me, confirming the truth. We were in love.

"How did you find me?"

"Lena."

"Lena?" I gasped. "When did you see her?"

"I visited my parents this morning and found Lena."

The moment lost some of its magic the instant he mentioned his parents. Yet, I knew that if I could never let him go, I would have to find a way to accept them as well, whether they wanted me or not.

"Thankfully, she told me how to find you." His grin only reached halfway; it was the old Stefan. "Otherwise, I would have had to spend the entire time searching," he muttered through a kiss on my forehead. "I would have never given up."

"But—" I paused, unsure of how to form the right words. "—your last letter—" I choked, unable to continue. His hand cupped my cheek.

"Ella, I was in a tough place. My only intention was to give you a choice."

"I've made my choice." The confidence in my voice waned. "Do you still want me?"

Stefan's intensity held me hostage. "More than anything in this world."

My eyes closed as his lips brushed over the lids. "I can't imagine life without you, Ella. You're all I think of every day."

"Please, don't ever ask me to leave you, Stefan. You're my life."

He responded with a kiss—one I could barely describe in words. The passion that coursed through our attachment paled against anything I had ever felt before.

When we parted, my entire body felt faint—dizzy and slightly unstable. Stefan's arms fell around my waist to secure me, but instead of drawing me close, his stance now held back. The way his eyebrows curved, and his shoulders dropped, anguish replaced elation.

"I'm sorry to hear about Mama Genau. I'm sure that was incredibly hard for you." I laid my head against his chest. It felt both different and familiar at the same time. "I should have been here for you," his voice vibrated against my ear. With each breath I felt his body rise and fall, reaffirming he was alive and next to me.

"I miss her immensely."

"I'm so sorry." The angst in his voice was unmistaken.

"It was difficult," I whispered. "I live alone now, in *Mitte* once again."

"I would take away all your pain if I could, my love." His hands glided from my waist up to my shoulders. In the chill he had become my only source of warmth.

I leaned back ever so slightly, searching for the simple gaze we shared before our paths diverged. Remnants of the old Stefan, now interwoven with the new, mirrored back. We had been altered by a world that swallowed our youth, neither one of us naive to its cruelty. Yet, instead of longing for a past that could never be retrieved, my spirit leapt towards the present, which clutched this tangible gift. With a renewed hope, I chose not to waste another minute on sad memories.

"Your comrades seem happy for you." I smiled with recollection of the morning's events.

Stefan laughed out loud and wiped his forehead. "I actually planned to come see you alone. Well . . ." —he chuckled again— "there isn't much you can do alone in the military . . . and they all wanted to see your reaction."

"Your commander was in on the plan?"

"Yes, they all were." He beamed. "And Ernst was honest when he said they can't get me to shut up about you . . . and, of course, the part about you being *die schönste Frau der Welt bist*."

"Most beautiful in the world?" I questioned.

"Without a doubt."

My insides felt as though they would bust open, like there was no more room in my body for the happiness I felt. "Can we be together the whole time?"

"Every minute until curfew."

"Curfew?" I choked out the word. I had been familiar with the subject off and on through the East coinciding with various uprisings, but nothing recent.

"The soldiers are restricted after ten o'clock at night. If we are out on the street, we face serious consequences."

"Where are you staying?"

"At my home . . ." Stefan's warm breath exhaled slightly. "unless . . ."

I watched his expression, he tried to say something, but it seemed hard for him. "Unless what?"

"I'll stay with you if you want me to."

My heart thumped rapidly. I was sure he could hear it through the silence.

"You don't have to decide now—" The moment was relieved with a distracting kiss to my cheek that effortlessly slid to the curve of my neck. Skin that had not felt the touch of a man in years tingled with anticipation; his entrancement skills hadn't changed a bit. His whisper tickled, "—but, if you don't want me to leave you tonight, I won't."

Despite the chill in the air, a warmth washed over me, soothing the bitter crests that grief had created over the years. An unparalleled tranquility hovered between us and made it easy to forget time still passed whether we moved or not. With obvious reluctance, Stephan released my body and held both hands in his.

"It's still hard for me to believe you're standing here in front of me," I whispered as he kissed my nose.

"I know, Ella. Three years is a long time, but we still have a longer time ahead of us."

"Stefan," I mumbled, repeating my earlier plea, "please don't ever ask me to leave you."

His eyes diverted, and his head lowered. *What is he hiding?* I reached up and gently pressed my fingers against his cheek and forced him to see me. "Please?"

He pulled me in tight once more then reached for my hand and led me away from Gustav's. With no clear destination, we meandered casually down Friedrichstraße. The air carried a wave of bliss, awakened not only with my own emotion but the sight of others who had similar reunions. Soldiers with pretty girls intertwined passed us by the dozens. No words exchanged, but simple smiles confirmed our shared good fortunes.

As the peaceful waters of the Spree came into view, beautiful pink clusters from the cherry trees rained over us and across our path. I marveled at the colorful "snow" beneath my feet. Stefan led me to a nearby bench where I scooped up a handful of blossoms and held them to my nose; the sweet scent was euphoric.

Once he was seated, I curled up on his lap. My lonely, aching arms now filled with the very man I longed for. My head resting comfortably against his shoulder, I imagined the Greek statues his grandfather had sent to the house for that first *Fasching* dinner, and a sense of jealousy arose within me at their frozen state. If I was to be immortalized, it would be exactly like this.

"I've missed it here," Stefan uttered quietly.

From my view, a guard paced systematically, his dog on high alert. The newly reinforced wall—stronger and more restrictive than ever—was dotted with looming towers and intimidating spotlights, but that wasn't what he meant. He missed his life, and we both yearned for what we had before the colonel took it away.

The silence floated around us like the caress of a feather as I pulled his hand to my lips. The roughness of his fingers lingered while I kissed each one. *When had his palms become so callused? Where did he get these scars across his knuckles?* He was a fighter now—crouching in bunkers, trudging through fields, battling in combat—part of a different world.

"Do you miss the mortuary?"

Stefan smiled. "Yes, I do. It sounds strange. You would think it was the leisure life I grieve for. I really like being a soldier, aside from the death. The kind I see now is different, not peaceful like at the mortuary. It's much more brutal and uglier." A frown momentarily pulled at his lips then fled.

"You know what I really long for?" He winked.

"What?"

"I miss walking through the house and seeing a stunning, dark-haired beauty with big brown eyes, long eyelashes, and irresistible lips." He kissed me again—slow and sensual.

"Can't we just stay like this forever?" I sighed.

He grinned, his lips touching mine as he spoke. "Marry me, Ella."

I drew back. My eyes searched to see if he was joking. "What did you say?"

"Will you marry me?" The lines that had appeared on his forehead previously, completely disappeared. With no humor detected, the sincerity in his voice seized my breath.

"Don't think, Ella . . . don't try to argue it in your head . . ." Stefan's eyes pierced mine. "What does your heart say?"

The nod started subtly then grew from there. "Yes," I whispered, ". . . it definitely says yes!" My eyes filled with happy tears. "Yes, Stefan, I will marry you."

Entwined in each other's arms, the sun gradually moved across the cloudless sky; the morning turned to afternoon. It was the only time in my life I was completely content having accomplished nothing.

Stefan reached into his pant pocket and retrieved a beautiful gold pocket watch, its chain dangling loosely around his fingers. It was the only part of him that revealed a prosperous background. I placed my hand over my mouth to keep from giggling at the contrast. His eyebrow raised with intrigue. "Are you laughing at me?"

I barely had the chance to oppose when his hands flew to my waist and squeezed. I tittered in delight as he tickled me to the grass. The soft blades cushioned my fall while Stefan's arms straddled my shoulders, his proximity hung temptingly close. Although the blue in his eyes appeared light and content, a sliver of unfamiliar intensity smoldered.

No words were spoken.

His lips brushed my forehead with a tender touch before he stood to his feet. As Stefan reached for my hand, he lifted me upright like I weighed nothing at all. His strength was admirable.

"My mother has arranged a small gathering this afternoon . . . in celebration of my return." He brushed a twig off his uniform. "Would you come back to the house with me?"

I understood Frau Franke's definition of small even better than Stefan did. The entire upper elite of the DDR would be present. He reached for my hand. "We can tell them the good news together."

I grinned, picturing the look on their faces. That alone might be worth the visit. With the announcement of our engagement, I could almost predict the conspiring that would follow. I kept my pessimism hidden; Stefan was still the optimist, but I knew better.

"Why don't you go home, share the news, and I'll go freshen up." I was dying to get out of my work dress. " . . . and we can meet at Dafne's at six to celebrate. That still gives us just over three hours before your curfew."

"Dafne's it is," Stefan conceded. His arm draped comfortably around my waist as we walked towards my flat. I loved the way the *soldier* Stefan never shied away from displaying affection in front of others. He seemed quite comfortable today showing the world we were together. I hoped that confidence endured through his parents' visit.

Once we reached the door, I snuggled up to him again. His embrace swallowed me lovingly. He tilted his mouth to my ear. "Do not be late, love. It'll be hard enough being without you for the next couple hours, don't punish me past six." He sealed his words with a soft kiss before parting.

Unable to tear my eyes from him, my sight watched his silhouette until I could no longer see the brown on his jacket or crease on his cap. My mind tried to comprehend the day—*Stefan is here . . . here in Berlin*—the realization seemed implausible. With a wide smile and an eager step, I rushed inside to prepare for the night.

FIVE

WHERE'S ANTON?

At five minutes past six o'clock, I walked into Dafne's, and suddenly an overwhelming feeling of déjà vu consumed me. Despite the
familiar essence of inviting cuisine and fresh baked pastries, catching
sight of Stefan immobilized me.

Somehow, still in uniform, he made the military dress appear more
alluring than I ever thought possible, and to be here with him in this
place where we first fell in love—the moment was beyond remarkable.

As I removed my sweater, he was immediately by my side. Placing his
hand at the curve of my lower back, he led me to his table. Once again,
it appeared as though he wanted everyone to know we were together.

"You are lovely, as always!" Stefan gripped his cap then set it on the
table. The weight of his stare could be felt as he proceeded to pull out my
chair. Reaching for his own chair, he scooted it as close as possible without sharing my seat. His proximity forged an intensity I was unprepared
for. My yearn arched to his whisper, "I have dreamt of seeing you here
like this for so long."

I met his smile as he reached over and touched my hair, which fell in
a full wave down my back. His fingers tenderly brushed across the wide
neckline of my sapphire-colored dress then rested at the edge where it
barely tipped my shoulder.

"This color makes your skin glow." Stefan leaned in. The warmth of
his breath lingered long after his lips brushed my cheek. His countenance

radiated as he spoke. "Ella, you're stunning, absolutely breathtaking."

"You've obviously been around men too long." I laughed out loud.

"No. Well, yes, but look at you! If you were a man, you would be missing you too!" I wrinkled my nose as I attempted to follow the logic in that. He laughed. "Three days are not long enough!"

I nodded in agreement.

"After this respite" —I cringed even as the words came out— "when will I see you again?"

Stefan shook his head. "I don't know. We never know where we'll be ahead of time—they change direction often, and the way things are heating up with Czechoslovakia, I could be on that border in less than a month."

I bit my bottom lip.

"In a battle?" The strain on my throat compounded with images of hostility escalating in my mind. He leaned over and grabbed my hands.

"This is what I have been trained for, Ella."

My eyes became moist. Stefan rubbed my skin with his thumbs. "Most of the time we've been on standby for the Soviets. The greatest action I've seen thus far is angry farmers in the east and stubborn factory workers in the north." He chuckled, perhaps in an attempt to lighten the mood, but my mouth still pulled downward.

"This is a celebration, sweetheart." He squeezed my hands tighter. "Champagne!" he cried.

"Oh, Stefan, I don't . . ."

"That's right." He laughed again. "I forgot." He kissed one of my hands, then yelled, "and sparkling water!" We giggled. There would be a lot of remembering tonight.

The time seemed short as the clock ticked closer to 9:30, the latest we could stay and still be home by ten, his curfew time. Stefan glanced at me with his irresistible stare; the blue eyes I saw in my head every night were real and looking back at me.

"We must go."

The time had come. Stefan would want to know which home he would go to upon departure. We moved to the street.

At the curb, I slipped my hands up underneath his arms and around his firm back. The solidity of his muscles lured me into indecision. My chest involuntarily pulsated with a clear longing to be with this man.

Why shouldn't I invite him home? We love each other and plan to marry. I don't ever want to leave his side again—but am I really ready? Stefan seemed to sense my confusion.

"Ella, I love you," Stefan whispered. "I love you enough to wait forever." He kissed my cheek and slipped his arm around me as no other words were said. Every step towards the bus stop was trying. My heart wrangled my head, making an obvious choice over the matter nearly impossible.

As we walked down *Pappelallee* towards *Eberswalder*, a group of raucous men approached from the opposite end of the street. Between the tousled hair and shabby clothing, a brashness emerged typical of most Berliners who lived in the back alleys and vacant buildings.

I felt safe and secure in Stefan's arms as the distance between us and the men shortened. The closer we got, however, that reassurance gradually slipped away. Suddenly, memories of an earlier time surfaced.

They were older now, like me, but there was no mistaking Anton's old "friends"—the ones he hung around before I made it difficult for him.

I wanted to look away, but my eyes were drawn to the leader. The charred skin across his right cheek reminded me of the night Anton fought for me. I stiffened. Stefan peered down at me. In silence, my hope was to pass peacefully, and in the end there would be nothing to tell.

Nonetheless, it was obvious the boy—now a man—had *not* forgotten. Jurek puffed his chest out a little further as he gestured to his two friends and whispered. Their attention immediately fell upon me. Stefan did not miss this. He quickly pulled me partially behind him and kept a solid lock on my arm.

"*Sie!*" Jurek acknowledged me with a pointed finger. He stopped a few metres away, but his body swayed with antsy agitation.

Stefan held me tightly as we halted, yet said nothing.

"You," Jurek's voice filled with irritation. "Yes, you." He shook his hands at his side as if prepping for a fight.

Stefan's muscles tensed beneath my hands, expanding underneath his clothes. "Be on your way," he spoke calmly.

Jurek snickered and eyed his friends. "I'm not talking to you, *arsch*, I'm talking to the girl." He glanced around Stefan in an attempt to glare at me, but his insult only enflamed the situation. Stefan's grip intensified.

"Where is he?" I knew who he was asking about but didn't respond.

"I want to know where that boyfriend of yours is hiding. Where's Anton?"

My eyes grew wide. Anton told me Jurek was searching, that he wanted revenge, although I knew he could never find him. Anton was too cunning for him.

Stefan spoke up, "You need to leave now."

Jurek sneered, sweat rolled down his cheek. He wiped it with his sleeve, took several steps closer and spit near Stefan's boot. "What are you going to do if I don't, *Soldat junge*?"

The slur to Stefan's military identity was a foolish choice. However, Jurek had never been bright.

"I'm giving you a chance to leave without getting hurt." Stefan's voice was level, but I sensed his patience growing thin.

"You're giving *me* a chance?" —Jurek pumped his fists, he wanted to fight— "And what is it about this black rubbish that has guys—" Stefan's right hook caught him square in the jaw. Jurek fell to his back while I stumbled behind Stefan, his body solidly between us. Although surprised, Jurek quickly jumped to his feet with both arms extended. His attempt to get his own punch in failed. He didn't stand a chance.

"Move back, Ella." Stefan's hand gently pushed me farther away. Jurek swung but connected only with air as Stefan swiftly struck him twice in the gut. Jurek doubled over in pain, and when Stefan followed up with a rapid kick from his boot, Jurek was flat again.

Stefan took a threatening step towards the other two who didn't even consider helping their friend, running down the street like scared little schoolgirls. Had it been any other time, I would have giggled. Instead, the taillights of my bus flashed in my side view. I gasped and pointed to the bus as it disappeared down the street. Engrossed in the skirmish, we didn't even hear it approach.

"*Scheisse!*" Angry, fist raised, Stefan turned towards Jurek who was still squirming on the ground. "Get out of here . . . now!" The blood vessels in his hands and neck protruded simultaneous to the gasps of a small crowd that had gathered. This was a side of Stefan I hadn't seen before. His presence was commanding, fearsome, yet reminded me of what it felt like to be protected again.

Jurek stumbled to his feet and glared my direction. "This ain't over!"

Stefan took a threatening step closer. "Go! Now!"

Jurek spit blood then wiped the trickle on his sleeve without taking his eyes off me. His twisted expression frightened me, not simply from the scars but from his warning as well. He turned quickly and vanished around the corner.

Stefan grabbed my hand as we walked briskly towards a different bus stop. I checked the time on my watch, 9:50. He wasn't going to make it, and I knew he wouldn't leave me alone, either. Unsettled, my eyes scanned all directions before they centered on him. Though he didn't reciprocate my look, his movements indicated an urgency to get out of harm's way.

"I'm sorry, Stefan," I mumbled as we walked. Responsibility weighed heavily on my shoulders.

"You don't need to explain." His eyes darted about. I knew he risked much by breaking curfew.

"What will happen if you're caught?" My query signaled my fear.

"For starters, I'll lose my leave, then I—" His answer ended abruptly. "I won't be caught."

"I'm sorry." My sniffles failed to remain suppressed. "I feel awful."

"Ella," Stefan's quickened pace came to a sudden stop. The crease in his forehead disappeared despite the strain. Gently, he lifted my chin to meet him as he whispered, "I understand you had a life before me and withstood some tough times. I don't judge you."

"I know, I just don't want you to think there was more between me and Anton than I told you. We were close, but we weren't together."

Stefan grabbed both my hands in his and held them up to his chest. His heart beat faster than normal.

"If you say you are mine now, then nothing in the past matters, right?"

I smiled, slightly relaxing. "Yes, I'm yours." I squeezed his hands back. "Only yours."

We started to walk again, but after a short distance, Stefan froze. Following his gaze, a military truck approached from the end of the street. He grabbed my arm and pulled me into the closest alleyway; our bodies tight, I felt his hurried breath against my cheek. Anxious, he tugged roughly on my arm to hide behind some garbage cans. His finger slid to his lips for silence as we crouched as low as we could get.

The steady hum of the truck closed in, idled, then finally passed. Stefan leaned his back against the building and exhaled loudly. The lines in his forehead deepened, coinciding with a rigid jaw. My eyes dropped to the cap twisted tightly in his fist, obliging my soul to ache for him and his status. There was much I didn't understand about his life now, yet from his reaction, I knew this was serious. Getting him home would be harder than we thought.

"Can we try to catch another bus?" I whispered.

He responded negatively. "Too risky."

"Where are we exactly?" Even though I was present on the street as we walked, I wasn't aware of my surroundings, my thoughts centered only on Stefan and his emotions.

"Too far to get you to Mitte," he replied. After what happened, I knew he wouldn't let me out of his sight. He stood and paced.

"You can stay in the guest bedroom."

I choked out my response. "Your house?"

Stefan nodded.

Images of Lena on the floor, her arms covered in blood, filled my head. Horror surfaced. "I—I can't stay in that room."

Stefan nodded again, desperation evident. "Then Katharina's."

"That's the room right next to your parents." I could barely get the words out.

"Ella, please. It's the only option right now. I have to get off the streets." His pleadings made me realize how selfish my comments sounded.

I grabbed his hand. "Okay." I inhaled sharply. "Let's go."

It was a dangerous trek. Although it wasn't unusual to see military vehicles everywhere, somehow, that night they multiplied. Several times we sought shelter behind structures or landmarks and many times for several minutes. It took nearly an hour to move two kilometers to the Franke's, and after everything we had already been through, anything that kept Stefan safe was more than worth the struggle.

When we entered the dark house, my hesitation pulled Stefan's arm back. Even in the blackness, visions of being dragged away in handcuffs stifled me. With little exertion, a gasp preceded the tears that simmered at the corners of my eyes. Despite his inability to see my emotion, he reached for me with a softness I hadn't felt since the encounter with Jurek.

"I'm sorry, Ella. I'm sure it's hard for you to come back here."

My hand covered his. In the tenderness of the moment, we conversed without words, both acutely aware of how our final moments together here, years ago, had ended.

With continued silence, he guided me down the hall and gently up the stairs. Instinctively, I pressed my lips tightly closed as we passed the master bedroom to reach Katharina's.

"I'm positive they've already gone to sleep," he whispered once we were safely past. "They won't even know you're in here."

"What about tomorrow morning?"

Stefan paused momentarily. "They need to get used to seeing you—Ella, you will be my wife someday." Somehow, when he said this, it sounded truly believable.

That night when Stefan tucked me in, he sat at the edge of the bed. I knew he wanted to stay, only we both knew that was impossible.

"I love having you here. You belong here." His fingers traced my lips then slid down my neck and rested softly on my shoulder as he leaned in. My eyes closed to the warm sensation of his touch that intensified into a clutch once his lips met mine. As the kiss extended, deep and slow, his hold moved to the back of my head, gently pressing me into him. My desire to feel him, all of him, amplified. The yearning that burned within seemed unquenchable. I could taste his hunger mixed with my own.

When Stefan pulled back, I inhaled, winded. As the passion slowed to a purr, his forehead rested wearily against mine. When he spoke, the strain in his voice was unmasked. "I can't live without you, Ella."

My eyes blurred while my lashes fought hard to keep still. This man before me was my very existence. "I belong with you, Stefan, and will go anywhere you want me to."

With one last brush of his lips across mine, he breathed, "I will never let you go."

SIX

OBDACHLOS

Somehow, the light from Katharina's windows was more beautiful than the sunshine had ever been from mine. The brightness bounced from wall to wall before it landed on the fluffy white quilt I had curled up under. It was quite possibly the best sleep I had ever had.

Before he left last night, Stefan opened Katharina's closet doors and told me I could wear anything of hers. Both of us knew Katharina would be delighted to comply, but merely touching the material felt foreign to me. I had never worn such fine fabrics before, even for a day dress. A simple green one was chosen with a cream-colored sash at the waist.

I tied my wayward curls into a loose bun before I carefully cracked open the door. Relieved to find the hallway empty, my eyes instantly swung to the far end where the art room was located. The happiness cultivated there was a pleasant memory. I tried to walk toward the stairs, but turned, physically drawn the opposite direction. My smile entered the art room before I did.

The room was empty. Nothing had changed. My half-painted butterfly still sat on the easel splattered with faint-colored drops. The short walk to the canvas stirred a significant fondness—only possible from a favorite memory. My hand glided over the image. It was long-dry, nevertheless, I wanted to touch something that brought me such great joy. A neighboring easel displayed Stefan's completed painting from the Elbe River valley. Watching him paint had been a thrill. The artistic talent he possessed was unparalleled.

A loud creak startled me. I whipped around to find the door ajar. My breath stuck in my throat—there were very few people I was prepared to see here. Lena's face peered through. Pleased, I lunged to open it wider and pulled her towards me. Even though I had just seen her at the parade, it was because of her I was suddenly indescribably happy.

"I saw Stefan in the kitchen." Her smile radiated. "He told me I would find a surprise upstairs. He didn't say what."

"Oh, Lena, can you believe it?" I hugged her tightly. "Who would have thought a few days ago I would see him and be with him and . . ."

She zeroed in on my face, ". . . and what?"

"We are going to marry."

Her pallid complexion lost what little color she owned. This was not *quite* the response I expected. "Does his mother know?"

"I . . . I think so, assuming he told them yesterday." My eyes narrowed. "Why?"

"I don't know . . ."

"What do you mean?"

"I don't think he did." Lena's eyes studied me carefully.

"What makes you say that?"

"Things . . ."

"What things?" I grabbed her hand and pulled her into the room farther to let the door close shut.

"Oh, Ella," she tried to put a lift in her voice, "it doesn't matter. Stefan loves you and that's all that matters."

Disheartened, I slumped onto the nearby stool. "It matters to Stefan."

"He would marry you even if they told him not to."

"Did they?" My voice was weak.

"Did they what?"

"Did they forbid it, Lena?"

She stumbled with her words, then exclaimed clearly, "I'm sure everything is fine." She held my hands tenderly, but my countenance remained heavy.

"I don't know why I believed there was a remote possibility they'd suddenly welcome me with open arms," I mumbled as Lena wrapped her arms around my shoulders.

"I'm sorry," she whispered in my ear. "I shouldn't have said anything."

"I knew it wasn't going to be easy. I only hoped the idea wasn't completely repulsive in their eyes."

"Don't let anyone, including me, take this from you," Lena retorted. "Stefan has such little time, don't waste it worrying about his parents. Everything will work itself out." She lifted my chin. "Go and enjoy the time you have with him. Do *not* let his family discourage you."

I grinned with resolve. *Yes, the only thing that matters at this moment is him and me.* Lena kissed my cheek.

"I need to get back to work. Can I get you anything?" She smiled slyly. "You are a guest after all." I matched her smile and shook my head no. As she closed the door, I reflected on her words. *Who would have ever believed I would be a guest here?*

Sauntering about the room, I finally reached the cupboard. "*La Vie en Rose*" was still on the turntable. I flipped the knob to ON and set the needle. Once the music started, I moved to the floor, leaned my back against the cupboard, and closed my eyes as it played. Edith Piaf's vocals had healed my fragmented spirit more times than I could count.

When the song ended, I opened my eyes, and instead of feeling sad, the recollection of where I was and who was waiting for me downstairs caused me to jump to my feet and hustle out the door.

Somehow, I managed quite luckily to never see Herr or Frau Franke in my journey to the kitchen. In fact, the house seemed unusually still, not even Johann crossed my path.

"Where is everyone?" I whispered unnecessarily as I entered, since Stefan was the only one in the room, and the way he beheld me made me glad he was. He wasted no time in wrapping his arms around me. Although on hiatus, his duty still required him to wear his official uniform, but there was something about it that instantly put me at ease—that and his affectionate embrace.

"You are beautiful." He tightened his clasp. ". . . even in my sister's dress," he joked. I giggled and playfully pushed him back.

"Your sister happens to be one of the prettiest girls in Berlin, and as her brother you should be proud of her."

"I am!" Stefan quickly defended, ". . . but what kind of big brother would I be if I didn't tease her as well?"

My smile confirmed my agreement as he closed the gap between us once again. The laughter ceased the moment our lips became one. Every time he touched me, it was as if I melted into a dream, a place I never wanted to wake up from.

As we parted, Stefan announced excitedly, "We have a busy day today, young lady."

"Oh?" I questioned, completely unaware of his plans. "What makes it so busy?"

"We are going to see the city together, all the places we love."

My smile grew as I imagined them briefly in my mind. "I will have to convince my work this is a good plan, as well." We laughed together.

Stefan and I arrived at the café once more, but only long enough to talk to Hilde again. Quite perceptive and kind-hearted, she'd already asked Geri her married daughter to cover for me while Stefan was on leave.

"Oh, Hilde, thank you!" I hugged her tightly.

"Now go, Ella. Don't waste your time here, love." She shooed me away with her dish towel. Now there really wasn't a thing standing in the way of spending the next two days with Stefan.

We rode the *Oberleistungsbusse* to the open plaza at *Alexanderplatz*. A wide web of streets converged to this center, only recently under reconstruction.

With the parade, the soldiers returning to Berlin, and reunification of lovers or families, both cars of the O bus were filled to capacity with many passengers unable to get a seat. Stefan swooped one arm around my waist, and with his other hand he held tightly to the strap above his head. Each bounce and jostle could have been uncomfortable under other circumstances, but because it was Stefan I bumped into, it was more of a pleasure. Once we were safely off the bus and away from the crowd, his grip loosened, and we easily fell into step side by side with our fingers softly intertwined.

Although the air was crisp, the sun smiled generously down upon us through scattered clouds. The smiles, giggles, and gladness were plentiful. If it weren't for the military trucks that lined the road, the *Volkspolizie* guard, and dogs, it could almost feel like the war or the wall had never existed. *Almost.*

Without time commanding our every move, we meandered along the walkways. Only steps from the bank, *Sparkasse der Stadt*, laborers were actively removing rubble that had remained untouched since 1945 or before. All around us, residents of the DDR emerged, curious to see any premature construction of both the *Urania-Weltzeituhr* and *Fernsehturm.*

Crowds maneuvered near metal barriers to catch a glimpse of the posters promoting the enormous turret-style world clock designed to display the current time of hundreds of cities around the globe simultaneously.

We continued along the footpath under the Bahnhof rails and towards a large cordoned off section nearly a kilometre north of where we started. Production had already begun on the concrete foundation and cylinder base of the television tower and observation deck estimated to rise over 350 metres high, all part of the government's master plan to reconstruct Alexanderplatz to its original pre-war vision.

"The news report on the radio this morning suggested that both are being constructed for the twenty-year anniversary celebration of the DDR." Stefan's face lit up with excitement. His enthusiasm reminded me how intimately entrenched he was in this culture. "Both of these structures are unlike anything in the world!"

"It appears to be quite an undertaking," I exclaimed, peeking through the crowd. "According to the pictures, these structures will take a long time, maybe years."

Stefan folded his arms around me from behind and whispered in my ear, "Yes, projected for autumn 1969. Think of how the world will view Berlin when we have the tallest tower in Europe."

"Are you sure the tower is for broadcasting?" I implied espionage on a whole new level.

"Well, dear," —Stefan chuckled at my expected pessimism as he guided me from the masses and towards the Neptune fountain— "we do need to protect our assets."

With our focus on each other, we both tripped over a large crack in the asphalt. Catching ourselves from a humiliating tumble, we laughed aloud in consideration of his last comment.

"Our assets do need a bit of renovation," I giggled.

Stefan clutched me tight. "I love it when you smile." He kissed me tenderly in the middle of the turn-about without regard to anything or anyone around us.

The honk of a car drove us back to the sidewalk and towards the few farmers' carts nearby, attempting to benefit from the high numbers of patrons in the plaza. Although they struggled to make their small inventory appear greater than it was, the presence of color was refreshingly appealing. The baskets of Brussels sprouts, parsnips, and kale had been intertwined with a handful of flowers from a spring bloom, the scent from the tulips superseding our steps. Stefan held a handful out in front of me while I delicately drew a single stem from the bunch. I inhaled deeply as the yellow petals tickled my nose.

We strolled hand in hand through the streets as if years or towns had not separated us. By early afternoon we had circled back around the outskirts of the plaza and reached the *Haus des Lehrers,* a building that had been completed in the last couple years with a giant mural wrapped around the exterior face depicting life in the DDR. Fascinated with the colorful creation, I was drawn to its unique illustration.

As I maneuvered around the building and searched the art for the most obvious depiction of East Berlin . . . the wall . . . I nearly stumbled upon a pile of debris. Stefan reached out to catch me before I fell to the walkway. Once upright, I glanced over the wooden boards resting precariously against a nearby building. In my inspection, two tiny bare feet extended out one end. I gasped. It wasn't too long ago that I had been reminded of what life on the street was like.

"Stefan, it's a child." My palm pressed lightly against my quivering lips.

He peered around me. Frowning, his eyes flickered between me and the child, his hand squeezed tightly as I stepped closer. A young girl not older than six or seven lay inside. Suppressing a heavy sigh, I knelt down next to the small opening. The feet retreated. Pulled in tightly, the child's legs curled up against her body on the far end. I tried not to visualize the images that her frightened eyes may have witnessed in her young life. My hand extended tentatively, yet she did not take it.

"Are you alone?"

She stared at me and said nothing. Carefully choosing my words, I knew their impact could either frighten her or appease her. My greatest fear was that she might run away.

"Are you hurt?" I recalled my own distrust of strangers as a child, especially on the streets.

Stefan left my side momentarily, I assumed to make it easier for me to converse with the timid child.

"What's your name?" I sat down on the dirty sidewalk, refusing to go about my day and walk away from this child. "My name is Ella." My hand extended once more. Again, it was not met.

Stefan returned with a pretzel, slipped it to me, and stepped away again. As I glanced back at him, my heart leapt with gratitude. He met my smile then pretended to be sightseeing.

"I bet you're hungry." The warmth of the pretzel melted against my cold fingers. The child's eyes widened, the fresh scent of baked bread and cinnamon salt filled the small space. Her head lifted.

"Here, I want you to have it." I held it out farther. The girl sat up a bit more. "It's yours."

She reached forward . . . hesitantly . . . then swiftly grabbed the food, her fingers nearly as black as her hair. Despite it being twice the size of her hand, she gulped it down quickly, possibly afraid I would change my mind and take it away.

"Can you tell me your name?" I whispered while she licked the salt off her dirty fingers. I glanced back at Stefan as he watched from afar. He smiled then pointed to his heart and mouthed, *I love you.* My grin, in return, couldn't nearly convey how much I adored this man.

The girl was nearly finished but had curled back up into her protective position.

"May I know your name?"

Her face softened. The food had brought a light glow back to her pale cheeks.

"Mari," she whispered.

"Mari. That's a beautiful name." I sighed, fighting discouragement. *What can I do to help her?* "Do you live here alone?"

She paused again then nodded yes.

"I used to be alone, Mari. I know how scary that can be."

My finger tapped easily on my lips. *The Waisenhaus. If it's still operating, I can take her there.*

"I will be back, please wait for me to return." I jumped to my feet and ran to Stefan. "The Waisenhause! I need to get her to the orphanage."

Stefan's eyes went wide. "Do you know if it still exists?"

"No," I cried anxiously. Concerned Mari would disappear, I kept my eyes glued to the boards. She didn't move. "I can't leave her, Stefan!" Tears formed easily. "I can't leave her."

Stefan's palm cupped my cheek. "We won't. I promise."

We walked back to the shelter together, and I bent down once again. "Mari, this is my friend, Stefan. May we please help you?"

She shook her head back and forth heatedly, visibly scared. The thin blanket that covered her fell to the ground as she shook.

"I know a place where you'll be safe. Will you please come with me?"

She refused again, but this time I reached in, determined to help, only to find large open sores exposed on her thin legs. I pulled my hand back as my eyes trailed the lesions up her arms and neck as well. She was infected.

"We need to get her to a hospital."

I scanned the neighborhood. "There." I pointed to an apparel store across the street. "Let's get a fresh linen to wrap her in and get her to a clinic."

Stefan knew me well enough to realize I wouldn't be able to think of anything else. Mari's safety was now a priority. He hastily purchased a new blanket. Mari cried and whimpered while we wrapped her in it. Although she did not fight us, she seemed terrified.

We asked the shop owner where the closest hospital was, and he directed us several streets away. Again, Mari whimpered with every touch while Stefan carried her as gently as possible.

"Please! Please, help us," I announced the moment we entered the doors. A nurse rushed over to me. "This child is in pain and needs medical attention immediately."

The nurse scanned Mari's condition and curled her nose. "*Sie ist obdachlos.*"

"That doesn't matter." My cheeks instantly enflamed from her apparent homeless prejudice. I glared hard at the nurse. "She needs help."

"*Es ist egal, sie wird sowieso sterben.*"

My eyes constricted like daggers over her complacency. Even though Stefan balanced the child in his arms, he immediately freed one hand to hold mine back. He sensed a fire stoking the moment the nurse alluded to Mari's impending death. Stefan didn't know my past in detail, but he knew me well enough to know I was seconds from responding with my fist.

He turned to the doctor who had stopped due to the commotion in the hallway. "I will pay for all the medical care of this child." Stefan spoke to the man, but his eyes returned to Mari. "Whatever she needs to heal."

"*Ja*," the doctor consented.

My face relaxed despite the nurse's frown. Finally, the woman called for additional assistance.

"*Was soll's, tut sie da rein.*" She pointed to put her in a side room. There were two other patients present and only one available bed. Stefan carefully laid Mari down. She hadn't stopped crying since we left her little home. I couldn't stop sniffling either but knelt to her side and rubbed her knotted hair.

"You will be safe here. You will get help, and I'll check on you very soon."

When the doctor approached, Stefan handed him his grandfather's pocket watch. The gold alone was far beyond the man's annual income. "Please, do whatever is necessary to care for this child."

The doctor's expression rivaled my own. I could not believe he was giving up his family heirloom. The man slipped the watch into his pocket and nodded agreement.

I peered over to Mari one last time and whispered, "You will be okay."

Stefan's arm went around me and led me away from her. I didn't notice the smell before, yet once we stepped outside, the fresh air consumed us. My torso convulsed in a sob, and I nearly collapsed to the ground.

"I'm sorry."

"You don't need to apologize." Stefan held me securely against his chest. My tears stained his perfect uniform. His hand gently rubbed my head as he whispered next to my ear, "I have never loved you more than I do today."

As Stefan guided me away from the clinic, I had difficulty balancing the thoughts in my head. *Why do I feel strongly about helping this child when we pass dozens just like Mari in the streets every day?* I waited three years to spend every moment with Stefan, yet found myself easily distracted by a child? But this was not *any* child.

The second, I laid eyes on her, my thoughts went to Anton. His mysterious childhood, his life on the street. What did he see? What did he experience? What happened before he arrived at the Waisenhaus? The questions peppered me relentlessly, followed up with instant shame. In the arms of the man I love and still, memories of Anton haunted me. The possibility that our historical bond might be greater than I understood frightened me.

By late afternoon, we found our way to Friedrichshain Volkspark once more to the fairy tale fountain and its healing waters. The times I had come alone grossly dwarfed the chance to be here with Stefan. Colors seemed to blossom naturally brighter, bolder, and more beautiful because we were there viewing it together. Although few flowers actually bloomed this early in the year, it was if my vision was enhanced by Stefan's presence.

The water—even with small slivers of ice—danced, the birds sang, and the statues seemed to laugh alongside us. Spring had never appeared so perfect, and East Berlin had never felt so alive.

Except in the private butterfly garden, where all time stood still.

The silent flap of the wings around our heads, on our clothes, and closing the gap between us was revered, almost sacred—a voiceless celebration of our decision to unite as one.

"Please come home with me, Ella."

"Why must we go anywhere?" I stretched both arms out to my side, allowing a simple perch for the butterflies if they chose to rest.

Stefan's hands cupped my waist. "If we could be together every moment, that would be my only wish." He burrowed his face in my neck.

"... and I can't think of a more perfect place than here," I affirmed.

When he laughed, the tickle from his unshaven chin against my skin caused me to giggle with him.

"Are you going to join me, love?" His eyebrows rose with the return of his serious inquiry.

I hesitated, then smiled sweetly. "How can I possibly look my best for you tonight if I'm unable to prepare?" It was a tease, although it masked a deeper notion, afraid to let on that I knew his parents did not want me there. I also didn't want Stefan to know what Lena had inferred about their feelings towards us. I refused to allow anything or anyone a chance to ruin our time together.

Before I stepped on the bus an hour later, Stefan kissed me on the cheek with a simple request, "Six o'clock sharp, sweetheart, not a minute later." I matched his grin while boarding then maneuvered to a window seat. I wanted eyes on him as long as possible.

Waving goodbye, Stefan's half smile arched amusingly and matched the joy that reflected from his scintillating eyes. I had to restrain myself from leaping off the bus and back into his arms. *What is wrong with me? Stefan is right there, and I'm leaving him!* I knew it was selfish to not want to go with him only because of my fear in facing his parents, but I simply didn't want anything to interrupt what was possibly the most perfect day.

Before we reunited again that night at Dafne's, I rested and felt whole again. Finding Mari and seeing her frail body experience this much pain for such a small child made me realize how lucky I had been that even though my birth mother and father gave me up, they did not abandon me to die on the street.

Rifling through a drawer, I located the picture that was brought from the orphanage. It was difficult to find a similarity to me and the woman in the photograph. *My mother.* Even in black and white, I could see that her skin was fairer and the curls circling her face were lighter than mine. My fingers even appeared in deep contrast to her as I held it, but for the first time, a profound feeling of gratitude emerged. My mother loved me enough to leave me at the orphanage, knowing I would be safe there. I didn't know her name or anything about her, but instead of feeling discarded or castoff, a strange appreciation surfaced. I moved her picture to the shelf next to where Anton's tinnie pin, my father's pipe, and his medal rested—a place of hallowed reverence.

As I made my way to the café, I reflected on Stefan's role in Mari's welfare. I could not have accomplished it alone, and it was apparent the staff would not have conceded had he not offered his precious pocket watch. My love for Stefan was immeasurable, an unbreakable connection no matter what our separation.

Once again, in our little corner of the world, we nuzzled together like all the lovers I had jealously envied in the last two years. **Finally**, I was the one doing the cuddling with the only man I desired.

"Tell me what your basic day is like?" I asked in between bites of my *Rhubarb Streuselschneken*. The crumbly cake, topped with cinnamon, flaked disorderly against my lips.

"You don't want to know about my day, El."

"I really do," I disputed. "I want to look at the time and think . . . my love is training right now . . . or eating right now. I want to know about everything."

"Well, it's definitely not as exciting as depicted in those books you read." He smiled. We both knew that was one habit I could never give up. "I wake up at six each morning, eat breakfast, then depending on where we are—a stationary camp or transitional camp—I could be in instruction for hours; weapons training, hand-to-hand combat, or endurance drills . . . like I said, not really interesting." He heaped a spoonful of sugar and dumped it in his coffee. I forgot how much he loved sugar. He responded to my reaction, "You forget, love, I don't have these luxuries when I'm away." I smiled; it was hard to imagine East Berlin as having "luxuries".

"What has been your favorite part of the military thus far?"

"Weapons training." His sly smile appeared again. "I'm a marksman now, which means I'm an expert shot with the G3."

"What's the G3?" I sipped my tea.

"It's a battle rifle, widely used by the *Volksarmee*. I hope I never have to use that skill, but if I ever do, you can be assured I won't miss."

I pictured Stefan behind a gun. It was a difficult image. He had spent much of his adulthood valuing the human body. I couldn't imagine how hard that would be for him if he was the one responsible for taking a life.

Near the end of the evening, the waitress brought matching strawberry tarts to the table. As if we hadn't had enough sweets already, I nearly protested, but something held me back. Instead of Stefan diving into his like normal with another spoonful of sugar, he hesitated. I watched the lines on his forehead deepen while he moved his hands off the table anxiously.

My pause was joined with a grin. It was a rare moment to see him nervous. "Are you well?"

He chuckled, partially out loud, but mostly to himself. Wiping the moisture that built on his nose, Stefan slid to one knee at the side of the table. My eyes followed his next movement with profound attentiveness. He reached for my hand, which I easily surrendered.

"I asked you to marry me, but I want to do it properly." In his other hand he held an open jewelry box, a round gem centered a silver band, the most beautiful thing I had ever seen. "Ella, will you be my wife?"

I struggled to move—even speak—paralyzed by the ring, the man, and the reality. I wasn't dreaming. *Stefan wants to marry me!*

Skipping heartbeats, my trembling hand flew to my mouth. I

attempted to speak but only air escaped. My eyes flashed between the jewel and the man holding it. His countenance beamed with a light only conveyed through him. Tears filled the corners of my eyes as both my hands reached for Stefan's face and softly cupped his cheeks. My lips, irresistibly drawn to his, pressed fervently and affectionately with more love than I believed was humanly possible.

Without parting, the word finally came forth. "Yes!" I said it three times to be sure he heard me. Stefan reached for my hand and slipped the ring onto my finger. Unbelief surfaced as I stared at its new home. It was the only jewelry I had ever held, and it was the finest thing I had ever seen, but even then, it paled in comparison to the man before me.

Suddenly, Stefan lifted me from the chair, and with both hands securely clenching my waist, he twirled me. My skirt swept precariously high, but I only thought of him.

As he set me back down, one arm stayed snuggly attached while he glanced eagerly around the café.

"She said yes!" he bellowed loud enough for every patron in every bar along *Pappelallee* to hear. East Germans, desperate to find joy in between their gloom and desolation, instantly raised their glasses with festive shouts of cheers, enthusiastic slaps on their tables, and congratulatory cries.

Rounds of liquor still flowed in celebration an hour after the proposal and even up to our departure. A permanent smile refused to leave my lips as we said our goodbyes and strolled hand in hand down the street.

As the bus stop neared, apprehension surfaced and pinched a piece of my happiness away. The weight of a ticking time clock etched deeply in my mind and across my fragile heart. Every step, every second, every move fell behind us and into an irretrievable past. The more I tried to hold tightly to what I had, the more I felt it slipping away. The imbalance overwhelmed me.

While we waited for my bus, Stefan kept a defensive watch, only this time no one interrupted us. Standing behind me, both his arms wrapped lovingly around me, protective and pleasurable, I almost willed the coach to stay away.

That night when I arrived alone inside my dark and empty apartment, the shadows nearly suffocated me. Collapsing to my bed, sobs racked my body knowing my countdown had begun. As much as I wanted tomorrow to come, to see Stefan and feel his touch, the day also represented forthcoming pain. I buried my head under my blanket, tormented with the idea of having to say goodbye to the very breath of my soul.

Tears soaked my pillow cover. *Why didn't I invite him here? Why am I so scared?* My self-berating continued until the moon rose directly outside my window. Its limited brilliance seeped through and cast a dramatic glow on my new diamond ring. I gaped at its beauty. The irony of my conflict was unquestionable . . . *how is it possible to be completely happy and desperately lonely at the same time?*

My thoughts strayed to the excruciating future and reality of what lie ahead, destroying what little hope I hung on to, leaving the devastating question behind . . . *how will I survive without Stefan?*

SEVEN

ALWAYS IN MY HEART

The next morning, a messenger appeared at my door with a letter. Stefan's penmanship identified me as the recipient. When I reached for the envelope, my hand trembled slightly. Despite the knot in my stomach—which anticipated bad news—my fingers couldn't open it fast enough.

> *Dearest Ella,*
> *I am momentarily delayed with a family obligation and a handful*
> *of guests. Uncertain of my required length of time here, my only wish*
> *is for you to join me. The messenger awaits, and the driver is at your*
> *command.*
>
> *Love, Stefan*

Glancing at the boy, it was apparent from his stance that he had been informed of his duty.

My clenched jaw may have been the only outward indication of my frustration, but an agitating burn quickly expanded from my chest to my limbs. *I can't go . . .* facing his parents for the first time since my arrest frightened me, and I was convinced they believed Stefan's military service was entirely my fault.

"Please wait here." Grabbing my paper and pencil, I scribbled an absurd response . . .

Stefan,
Enjoy the time with your family, I will wait for you here.

Love, Ella

. . . then handed it to the boy. He peeked at the name. "You're not coming?" His brows lifted, surprised.

"No. Please get that to Stefan."

"Yes, Fräulein."

The click from the door could be felt in my head. *How come I'm so verdammt obstinate?* Stefan asked me to come, practically begged. I flew to the window in time to see the black car pull away from the curb and roll down the street without me. Would Stefan meet it, hoping I'd emerge—disappointed in my absence? *Had I made a mistake?* He wouldn't have asked me to be there if he felt I would be humiliated or mistreated. *Foolish woman! What if he doesn't come?* Our final day could be wasted from my complete selfishness. So, I waited . . . very impatiently.

Tick, tick, tick, the second hand movement repeatedly pulsed in my brain.

Shifting my eyes from the counter clock to the window, I noticed the birds above Herr Köhler's rooftop flapped their wings with each second . . . *tick, flap, tick, flap, tick, flap. Twenty ticks, twenty flaps. Twenty cracks in the sidewalk below me. Twenty leaves attempting to sprout from the oak branch nearby . . . why twenty?*

Time had become my enemy. The miniscule timepiece that rested near the sink had never received this much attention. 1:43 p.m. *Maybe if I count people, it will speed up time . . . one, two . . . eleven, twelve . . . maybe just children . . . one, two . . . five. Wait, I counted the one in the blue coat twice.* My fingers pressed against my temples. *Stop, Ella, stop!*

The thunderous scolding in my head lessened the farther I moved from the window. 1:44 p.m. Grabbing a book off my shelf, an intensity arose to hold something tangible in my palm, anything to swing my cognizance away from senseless idiocies. I fell into Mama's armchair and pressed my cheek against the back, her scent was fading. 1:45 p.m. *Tick, tick, tick, one, two, three . . . nine loose pieces of thread extended from the hole in the upholstery near my right knee.*

Even with my favorite words peering back at me from the open pages of *Icarus*, the numbers in the corner expanded with each tick. Letters of the alphabet blended as I hastily skimmed each page . . . *three, tick, four, tick, five, tick, six, knock, seven, knock . . . wait . . . knock?*

Restricting even breath, my body held completely still . . . *knock!* I scrambled to my feet, the book easily discarded in my rush, landing distortedly on the floor. With sudden exertion, I jerked the door wide and instantly became winded at the sight of Stefan standing before me.

His uniform was neatly pressed and creased in all the right places. His hand scrunched his cap in a juvenile fashion. The illuminating blue from his eyes exploded as they peeked from underneath his eyelashes, and his smile . . . curved as if he possessed a secret. My fingers gripped the wood frame to steady my vaulting heart.

"May I come in?"

"Yes, oh yes, I'm sorry, I—" Flustered, I muddled around, searching for my mother's sweater. I barely noticed the case he carried in his other hand.

"Relax, beautiful." Stefan had a keen sense of emotion. He lifted my abandoned book off the floor and replaced it on the shelf. "We have plenty of time."

Despite the many hours to prepare, dense pressure built in my chest as I paced the room. Blankets, newspapers, and dresses were flung in random directions in an effort to locate the sweater. Stefan met me next to the bed and placed his hands softly around my wrists, forcing me to be still. His touch, soothing and tender, instantly appeased my agitation. However, my distress was never really about clothes. My grief was rooted in his looming departure. I would give anything to have another day or two—or all of them—with Stefan.

He stepped closer, the spicy scent of his aftershave reached me before he did. Closing my eyes, I inhaled deeply, the need to imprint that smell in my mind signified his impending departure. Tears bubbled on my lower lashes, threatening to spill over as Stefan's hands moved from my wrists to my shoulders then around to my back. Veiling my sorrow, I buried my head deep in his chest, as close as physically possible—even then, I felt him slipping away.

"We don't have to go anywhere, Ella." Stefan lifted my chin with one hand and dried my tears with the other. "We can purchase some food, bring it back here, make dinner, and be together."

I sniffled hard and nodded with big pouty lips. After a morning of endless waiting, sharing him with anyone, even a waitress or a clerk, stirred restless pangs of jealousy. My only want was for the world to swallow us whole and make us disappear somewhere together and alone.

Unsure of a clear destination once we stepped outside, we discovered a Geschaft three streets away. Slightly embarrassed with the little knowledge I retained of my neighborhood in the six months of occupancy, my ignorance came with a confession. It was intentional . . . the more time I spent at work, the less time I counted days—anything to keep my mind off Stefan's absence.

Only now, right now, I didn't have to think of anything but us. With a smile, a bag of groceries, and my arm intertwined with his, we made our way back to the flat within the hour.

"I'm sorry, Stefan," I apologized as two cups of tea were poured. "There's no table for you to sit at or a television for you to watch."

"Why would I want to watch that when I can watch you?" I'd forgotten how smooth he was with words. Stefan's back leaned comfortably against the counter. He made my impoverished setting much more appealing. I set the steaming mug next to him, but he stepped away and retrieved the case he'd brought with him.

"I have a surprise for you," he declared cheerfully. I peeked at the brown leather box that seemed vaguely familiar. Placing it on the countertop next to the stove where dinner was cooking, he unlocked the clasps and opened it wide. I literally felt my heart skip a beat.

"For me?" I uttered through a gasp.

"Yes, for you." Stefan planted a quick kiss on my cheek as he set the record on the turntable. Instinctively, I guessed which song he was about to play then swiftly flipped the stove knob to low. Dinner could wait.

"It was only gathering dust in the art room, although the moment I caught sight of it, a most pleasant memory emerged." He chuckled and slid his hands around me. "But it belongs here with you."

By the time Edith Piaf belted out the first words to *La Vie en Rose,* my body snuggled contentedly secure against Stefan's chest. My head naturally rested on his shoulder while his arms sheltered me. Our sways were slow and steady, deliberate in our attempts to halt time.

When the last note played, his breath warmed my ear. "I know this song meant something to you before we met, but I hope when you listen to it, you think of me as well."

I nodded subtly. With or without a song, I would think of him every moment.

Stefan's lips grazed my forehead faintly then landed on the tip of my nose. "I believe the *Rouladen* is ready, love" He stepped to the stove and lifted the lid where a wisp of steam escaped a perfectly sautéed filet. The smell of bacon, onion, and pickles filled the room. It had been well over a year since I had eaten such delicacies, but Stefan was a charmer and managed to persuade the store owner to sell him his rarest assortment of edible treasures.

I grabbed a small quilt from the bottom of my bed and lay it across the floor. Stefan laughed as we recreated the art room picnic, including the picture of Cochem centered on the wall right above our heads.

"Katharina once told me that you wanted to take me to Cochem." I pointed to his painting.

"I still do." He settled on the floor with two plates and forks.

"But . . . I can never leave East Germany."

"Well, the plan from before . . . you know, before I became a soldier . . ."

My head dropped a bit at the mere mention of *before*. His fingers immediately went to my chin and lifted it to meet his gaze. "It isn't your fault, Ella." I bit my lip and fought the urge to cry. The responsibility of his circumstances felt like a noose around my neck.

"I'm a good soldier. I didn't know I had that in me." His voice reflected a sense of pride. He cut the meat roll and placed half on my plate. The aroma nearly distracted me as he continued. "I contacted my grandfather for advice. He's a well-respected man in Soviet Russia, and we have a fine relationship. I told him about you and how we needed to be together. He's my mother's father, but unlike her, he truly understands. He sent money that very night." Stefan reached for both my hands and squeezed. "It's in a safe place, and when I'm done, we will leave someway, somehow. I promise we will be together far from here."

I grinned at his confidence. My heart lifted enthusiastically with the possibility. As we resumed our meal, a calm had finally settled in.

"Can I ask you a question?" Stefan's tone was kind, yet it was the hint of obscurity that worried me. I nodded. "Why didn't you tell me about Josef?" He lifted his glass to his lips but listened for my answer before he drank.

A few seconds passed in silence, although I knew the reason instantly. I didn't want Stefan to think about Anton. "It's not good news." My eyes lowered to my plate. My fork had been fondling the same piece of meat over and over.

"Lena told me of his condition this morning." His hand raised to my cheek, I moved inevitably into his touch. Despite the delicious feast, I now wished for dinner to be done. "My heart breaks for you!" he whispered intensely then leaned over and rested his forehead next to mine. With his skin so near, I delayed interruption, but I wanted to share—a need to talk of my only brother's fate took precedence.

I kissed Stefan on the cheek, letting my lips linger. Everything about him was perfect, and now he longed to share my pain. I stood and retrieved the letter. The worn edges made this parcel's fragility a risk. No matter how many times I read it, the words never changed. My fingers trembled as I handed it to him. I studied how his features reacted the further he read. Stefan's pleasing buoyancy turned acutely dark.

"This was sent six weeks ago."

My teeth pulled my bottom lip in and gnawed gently with agreement. "But it only arrived ten days ago."

"I'm sure you would have heard something by now. . . if the result was . . ." He paused and the next word came out a whisper, "tragic." Stefan's eyes swiftly swung my direction then brightened. "I'm certain Josef is fine."

I knew he aimed to be encouraging, but his trepidation, Lena's response, and my gut displayed the gravity of the situation. It was dire.

"Lena mentioned the idea of using the mortuary telephone to call the hospitals in the west." Stefan's gaze absorbed me. "Why didn't you ask?"

Disappointment burrowed within me. We were past simple courtesies; he was to be my husband. *I should be able to share anything.* "Yes . . .

I should have. I'm sorry," I whimpered as I stopped chewing on my lips and pulled my mouth tight. I did not want to cry this last day with him. "I'm afraid there's nothing more I can do."

"Well, I spoke to my father . . ." Alarm transpired within me. Herr Franke may have been getting older or more reclusive, but he was still dangerous. "No, it's not what you think." Stefan set his plate aside and scooted closer. "I arranged for Lena to clean the office again, once a week like she used to. He won't be anywhere near it during that time, and she can use the telephone to try and locate Josef."

A subtle sigh of relief slipped through. Instantly, I felt ashamed of my thoughts. He wouldn't hurt me or my family. I hugged him tightly. "Thank you, Stefan. Thank you."

For several hours, Stefan spoke about his regiment; his commander—who I found more likable than he did—and his closest comrade Edgar Weitzner, a cabinetmaker from *Lichtenberg*. He shared Edgar's story of how he'd been sentenced to serve as well. He left a wife and small child, one year of age. I felt a twinge of jealously that despite their separation, they were still married. "I can't wait for you to meet him one day," he added with a chuckle as if he remembered something only he and Edgar would understand. "You would really like him."

"Why is correspondence limited?" I tried to ask in a way that didn't sound resentful.

"Post is difficult. We don't receive many letters in the field due to the risk. We also rarely send. I have an address for central post now, but I've been advised by my commander not to rely on it. Please, Ella, . . ." Stefan reached for me. "Please know that even without a letter, I think of you nearly every minute of the day."

I stood up again and retrieved the stack of letters off the shelf, the ones I had written him, including the most recent one from two days ago—not knowing he was so near.

"This is where I poured my heart out." Kneeling beside him, I set them in front of him on the linen. Stefan reached for me with one arm wrapped around my waist then pulled me gently to his chest. With his other hand he held the letters, reading each one slowly and quietly. Occasionally, his touch constricted and released, three years apart can bring about a wide range of emotions.

"May I please keep these?"

I smiled. "Of course, I want you to have them." It was like a part of me would always be with him.

As that insufferable clock chimed nine o'clock, a pang in my chest sent a maddening reminder the night was nearly over. Stefan's departure was scheduled at six-thirty tomorrow morning.

I picked up our plates and moved them to the kitchen counter. When I sat back down, I rested my head against his chest once again. I fit perfectly under one arm and against his side as he reclined with ease.

My eyes followed the glide of my hand as it skimmed his upper body, its distinct slopes lifted and fell along with his breath.

It wasn't my imagination, Stefan was here at this very moment. My fingertips tingled as they traced along his arm, up his shoulder, and over his shirt to his neck; he had removed his uniform jacket hours ago. His skin warmed to my touch. As my hand reached his face, he closed his eyes, and my fingers moved along his cheekbone to the temple and forehead and then through his hair. I wanted to remember every detail. He appeared completely at ease until my fingers reached his mouth. Lightly tracing his lips, they parted enough to release a faint exhale followed by a soft moan.

Stefan's head tilted my direction with fixated intensity, the azure tint in his eyes that illuminated earlier now deepened. He rolled to his side and leaned only on one elbow. His other hand guided me flat to the floor. Fragmented air seeped from my mouth with anticipation.

"My turn," he said.

Stefan's choice of weapon became his lips. Leaning in, he raised my hand to his mouth, his lips lingered leisurely on each finger before they slid to my wrist and along the length of my arm. At my shoulder, the fabric of my dress should have slowed the thrill, but his skim only increased it. His lips finally arrived at the hollow of my neck. Although the distance to my jaw was short, this touch created the greatest sensory delight. By the time he reached my ear, I was nearly winded. As he swept across my forehead, eyelids, and nose, I awaited his objective, and within seconds his determined lips melted against my own. The weight of his body now pressed against my side fervently. He had won the battle, and I willingly surrendered.

When he paused, our lips remained close but no longer touched. Several tears escaped. *How can I let you go?* My heart stirred restlessly. My hands reached for his face and drew him back to me. Fervor from the kiss blazed through my limbs and seared my toes. I knew the answer. *I can't.*

"Stay," I whispered.

Stefan pulled back, his eyes searching mine.

"Please . . ." I pleaded as my tears increased. "Please don't leave me tonight."

Concern filled his eyes. "Ella, are you sure?"

I nodded. My hands abandoned my sides and glided up the front of his chest, tightly intertwining my fingers in the folds of his shirt before pulling him to me once more. His lips didn't hesitate. The next kiss surged with all the passion we had suppressed during our long separation—an intoxicating release.

He slipped his hands underneath me and lifted me as if I weighed nothing at all. I felt the bulge of his upper arms as he carried me to the bed. The gentleness with which he laid me down was felt with his prolonged touch. His hand caressed my cheek then retreated.

An eternity passed as he unlaced one boot at a time then set them aside. When his fingers finally reached the buttons of his shirt, I had to shove my trembling hands underneath my legs.

Motionless, my body froze in stark contrast to the heat of his gaze. As he stared, the lump in my throat expanded. *What am I supposed to do?* I tore my inexperienced eyes away momentarily and scanned my dress. *Do I take it off?*

Flashing back to Stefan, his shirt had disappeared, revealing the contoured muscles I had felt earlier. My breath came in shallowed gasps. He was beautiful. The pale disparity of his chest to the golden-brown of his sun-kissed forearms was only marred by the sight of a dozen small half-inch scars on his left side, presumably where the shrapnel had pierced him. The thought of him in physical pain wrung my heart.

He hesitated next to the bed. "Are you sure?"

"Yes." I tried to sound confident, but I wasn't. I simply couldn't watch him leave.

Stefan's hands moved to his belt, and with a quick flick his belt vanished. His pants dropped to the floor, only his underclothes remained. The room suddenly grew very warm. My eyes scanned the length of his form, every part of his body appeared stronger. I bit my lip as I viewed the additional injuries that trailed down his leg. I wondered if when he saw his wounds, he saw his friend's faces as well.

I still hadn't moved when Stefan placed one knee on the bed then eased to my side. I hoped the subtle chatter of my teeth was louder in my head than outside.

I pulled my hands from underneath me and clasped them across my stomach, clenching them tightly in an attempt to stop the quiver that seemed to grow with his proximity.

I closed my eyes.

I wanted Stefan here, I wanted him to be with me, but I suddenly felt overwhelmed—almost claustrophobic. Remembering the intensity of that last kiss and how I wanted him to take me at that very moment brought forth a smile. *I can do this. I want this.*

His fingers delicately brushed my lips then slid down my neck to barely above the bodice of my dress. They tickled my skin with a faint tap before they moved, a tug indicating the release of the top button. I remained still, yet inside, my head grew dizzy. A bead of sweat rolled off my forehead, the liberation of the second and third buttons was confirmed with another pull.

I peeked to see a portion of my slip exposed . . . *my chest is exposed!* I was no longer on my bed, but a cold concrete floor surrounded by white walls and splattered blood.

I gagged. My heartbeat hurdled into a sprint as air struggled to reach my lungs. Light-headed and faint, my head swayed from side to side. A voice cried . . . *was it my voice?* Stefan was gone, and my eyes widened at the appearance of a jagged scar. The ghastly zigzag abrasion robbed my sight and replaced it with an angry bald head. Cold, vengeful eyes penetrated me harshly.

I screamed, "Stefan help me!" Shrieking, my voice escalated to sheer panic. My arms swung defensively, crashing against warm flesh. Through tear-blurred vision a hand reached for me once again, and I thrashed wildly in resistance.

"Stop!" I cried, wrestling the fiery constriction in my throat. "Stop, stop, stop!"

"Ella!" Indistinct familiarity arose.

Panting desperately for air, I punched the bed with rolled up fists and cried, "No, no, no!" My legs pulled in tightly against my shaking torso. Even as I buried my face in my hands, tears slipped through my fingers. *Why is that wicked man here? He's supposed to be dead!*

"Ella, It's me . . . Stefan." A considerable amount of alarm arose from a voice nearby.

My eyes opened fully. The person in front of me *was not* the callous façade of an evil man . . . it was an adoring, perfect man. *Stefan! He came! He's here to save me!* Stefan's anxious paces shifted awkwardly before me. *Why isn't he coming to me?* My eyes flickered past him to the kitchen counter the . . . clock, the ticks . . . my breath continued in exasperated puffs as I recognized the outline of Mama's chair in the corner, its silhouette deepened in the shadow of the sole lamplight. *Oh, no! I'm home!*

My body wilted in shame, sobs racked my strained throat. My hands crossed tightly against my mouth in an attempt to control more cries. The space between my fingers allowed for intermittent air, but my brain was still suffocating.

"I'm sorry, El." Stefan's voice cracked with regret. One hand anxiously massaged his head, no more loose bangs to brush through, yet he rubbed it as if there were. Our eyes met, his intense gaze thick with anguish.

My hands dropped to my lap and clutched my skirt. *This can't be happening! Stefan can't believe it was his fault!*

"I'm so sorry." Despite his attempts to sound calm, it belied the distress in his behavior. "I'm sorry I scared you."

I shook my head vigorously. "Please, Stefan . . ." I fought the tears again. I couldn't imagine his remorse. "It's not you." I held out my hand. "Please . . ."

He hesitated.

"Please . . ." I begged again. "It wasn't you. It's that man." I slid my legs off the side of the bed. "I can't stop him from appearing. He's always there . . . haunting me." My words trailed off while my fingers unbuttoned the last two buttons of my dress. I fumbled for the hem of my slip. Stefan approached cautiously, carefully sitting next to me.

"No, Ella."

My hand gripped my slip tightly upward to reveal the scars on my waist. A permanent circular discoloration bordered the two-inch crude mark on my hip. Stefan's breathing slowed right before his fingers delicately traced my damage.

"Colonel Anker's always a part of me." The reality of those words was crushing.

Stefan's hand slipped over mine and guided my slip down. Kneeling before me, he carefully rebuttoned my dress. Lingering only momentarily at the top, his hands slid down my arms and rested at my waist.

"I truly am sorry." His voice weakened as he repeatedly apologized, "I should have never let you leave my house that night. I should have stopped him."

We both knew how unrealistic that was. Stefan's fate could have been much worse. I glanced up at him, my eyes puffy and tired, my cheeks saturated.

"You saved my life."

He lowered his head and whispered, "I was nearly too late. I don't know what I would have done had he killed you. It's all my fault."

Angst squeezed my heart while tears continually slid down my cheeks. The need to persuade him of his innocence worried me.

"No, it was him. Only him."

"Are you sure I didn't harm you?"

My palms cupped his cheeks and lifted his head towards me, Stefan's light-hearted countenance defeated "You could never hurt me."

My eyes momentarily drifted across his uncovered body before I continued. "Both of us scarred . . . but not broken."

Stefan's arms wound around my back and drew me close. My cheek pressed against his bare chest, and although the same closeness moments earlier had stirred our thirst for passion, now it soothed an open wound.

I knew it was Stefan that touched me. I knew this in my head, but for some reason I could not stop the image of that devil from emerging. I hated the intrusion. Would I ever be able to forget the colonel?

"I'm sorry I pushed you away." I sniffled hard, replaying the events in my head, my entire face wet. Humiliated, I tried to bury my face, but he tugged my chin upward and leaned in. His kiss, extraordinarily different than the passionate ones we had shared, carried an element of empathy that I needed more than ever. Mixed emotions shrouded my thoughts. I wanted Stefan to touch me; I'd dreamt of feeling him against me. One more thing Anker had seized from me.

"Don't leave me," I mouthed softly.

"I'll never leave you," Stefan assured then stood to his feet. His hands gently guided my head to the pillow. Tugging the blanket from the end of the bed, he pulled it close to my neck, and with a safe distance between us, he crawled to the other side and lay nearby. I could sense that he didn't want his closeness to frighten me again.

Blinking incessantly, my tired eyes fought to stay awake. I watched Stefan across from me. Despite his protective reasons, the separation saddened me. I literally ached for him. *Things can't end this way.*

"Hold me?" I whispered.

Troubled, Stefan remained fixed.

"Please," I pleaded. "I need you."

He slid under the covers and inched himself over until he was next to me. I curled into him, my arms snug against his muscled chest, my face resting comfortably against his arm and groove of his shoulder. The faint fragrance of sweat and musk lingered on his skin. Warmth from Stefan's body emanated a necessary calm to my anxious soul while the fingers of his free hand slipped repetitiously through my hair, tenderly soothing, until I fell into a peaceful sleep.

I awoke to Stefan sitting on the side of the bed dressed in full uniform. One palm lightly caressing my back. In frantic desperation, my body shot upward, the morning light from the window barely cracking the hazy darkness. *Why did I fall asleep?* Slinging the blanket aside, I clambered towards him. The fabric trapped my ankles and landed me awkwardly in his lap. I didn't care. The only thing that mattered was Stefan. His touch, his kiss, his existence. My arms flung around his neck while my lips eagerly sought warmth. His affection conveyed equal determination.

Anxious, my lips skimmed his. "I'm sorry." Pangs in my chest surfaced with a sudden recollection of the night. Disappointment tainted the moment. I had let him down.

"Ella," he reassured, "please don't be sorry. I was with you all night, exactly where I wanted to be." He leaned back, the deep-blue tempest in his eyes begging me to believe him.

"But . . ."

His fingers glided across my cheek and over my lips in attempt to stop my protest. I conceded and kissed them softly. When he replaced them with his own lips, a familiar desire consumed me.

As we released, he carefully slid me off his lap and back onto the bed where my feet dangled off the side next to his. He gripped my hand tightly. "We still have seven years to go. I can't force you to wait—"

"I'll be here, Stefan," I cut him off. We had been through this, but he needed to know with absolute certainty I was his. "I love you. I promise I'll wait for you."

His smile went wide. "That's all I need to know."

His other hand reached into his coat pocket. A faded blue ribbon emerged, tangled playfully around his fingers.

"Oh," I gasped. It was the ribbon I had given him at the train station. Its condition confirmed it rarely left his side.

"I will always have a part of you with me."

I rested my hand over it, the heat from Stefan's skin combining with my own sent contrasting chills through my body. I tilted forward, electricity coursing through our lips as they met one last time.

No kiss would ever be long enough for goodbye.

As we released, my eyes followed his long walk towards the door. Suffocating, my heart shattered. Springing from the bed, I ran and leapt into him, my arms clinging to his shoulders, my legs linked around his waist. If he had to leave, I was determined to feel him— all of him— once more. His hold tightened, his head buried in my neck before we reluctantly let go. Standing before me, he smiled his half grin, kissed the ring on my finger, and walked out.

Stefan was gone.

I dashed to the window in time to see him step out the front door into a gloomy rain. He slung his bag over his shoulder, adjusted his cap then hesitated. In between the drizzles, he circled around to face my window. My heart leapt as I reached for the glass, my palm pressed against it as if I was touching him personally. He tipped his hat, blew me a kiss, and disappeared down the street.

Collapsing on my bed, my eyes stared harshly at the ceiling. An old water stain portrayed exactly how I felt, brown and dismal. These last three days were filled with the most dramatic extremes of emotion, and the exhaustion—both physical and emotional—overcame me.

I rolled to my side and closed my eyes. Pulling my body into itself, I wanted to freeze life in this very position for seven years. To wake up in 1973 with Stefan lying right here. With reluctance, I opened my eyes again. Next to me on the pillow that cradled Stefan's head, the indention still visible, lay a simple piece of paper. I reached for it then gazed upon a beautiful pencil sketch of a forget-me-not flower and the words:

Ella, you're always in my heart. Stefan.

My fingers softly traced each petal of the flower then followed the words his fingers had created. My mind fought to hold on to the miracle of this moment. *He touched this last! He was here. He touched me, kissed me, and held me* . . . yet once again, the romanticism vanished.

I shivered. The room suddenly fell empty and cold. No love. No laughter. Sadness threatened to consume what had been three days of utter joy. Now that Stefan was gone, it felt as though my heart was crushed all over again.

EIGHT

IS IT REALLY YOU?

27 March 1966

Dear Stefan,

I'm so grateful you were able to give me a communal address to write to. I know you said you might not receive the letter for many months, if at all, but any attempt is better than nothing.

Lena stopped by yesterday. Thank you for arranging for her to clean the mortuary office. Her first day was two days ago and the operator was able to connect her to three local hospitals found in the Allied sector. She can only leave her name since we can't risk them calling back. She will follow up on what information they find in a week. It has been a difficult waiting process already. I haven't heard from Anton or Josef for six weeks now.

You will be happy to know I have checked on Mari. She is healing well. I plan to visit the Waisenhaus in the next month. I hope they'll accept her, she's only six — practically a baby — yet no matter what, I won't let her return to the street. I'll find her a home. If you were here and we were married, we could have adopted her and cared for her as our own.

Every night as I prepare for bed I'm reminded of our last night together. While it didn't go as planned, I cherish the very thought of you being here with me and I cannot stop thinking about it. Your forget-me-not drawing and sweet message remain on your pillow.

I read it every night. I'm so fortunate to have you in my life.

I gained much but lost so much at the same time. I feel like the luckiest girl in the world to have spent three wonderful days with you, just you and me. I can't wait until we can do that forever. Until then here is the photograph you paid the man at Alexanderplatz for, he delivered it yesterday. I now wish he had taken two, so I could look at your face as often as you can mine.

I want you to have it. Please do not forget me Stefan; you forever hold my heart in your hands.

Your love, Ella

I sealed the envelope and carried it as if it was everything I owned, and in a way, it practically was. The only thing I could remotely feel sure of was the love Stefan expressed to me, my love for him, and the ring I proudly wore on my finger.

"Oh, darling Ella!" Hilde squeezed my hands as she admired the jewel. "He must love you very much!"

My smile rivaled hers.

"I believe he does." My face beamed.

"Enough gossiping. Back to work!" Gus was his usual self.

Hilde ignored him. "Do you have a wedding date?"

"Not yet." My lips curved downward. "He has several more years of service left." I failed to tell her exactly how many.

"Well, congratulations, sweetheart." She kissed me on the cheek and handed me an apron. I smiled . . . *yes, back to reality.*

It was another four days before I saw Lena again. She showed up at the café as I was closing for the night.

"Ella! I have news!"

I ran to her side, and we slipped into chairs at the closest table.

"Josef?" My eyes expanded with anticipation.

She nodded.

"Oh, Lena, tell me."

"Sorry, I'm winded. I was afraid I would miss you."

Nearly out of breath, she must have run from the bus stop. My patience stretched. A better friend would have attended to her panting first. "What do you mean miss me?"

"I don't know where your new flat is."

My face wrinkled in regret. "Oh, I'm sorry." I reached for her hand. "That will change."

"Wait!" Her sudden halt alarmed me. She grabbed my finger.

"That . . ." she stuttered, "is that . . . an engagement ring?"

I exhaled in relief at first then paused. Her previous reaction caused apprehension. "Y-yes."

"Oh, Ella." She squeezed my fingers. "It's beautiful."

"Really? You really like it?"

"Of course! I've always wanted happiness for you. I just worry . . . like a big sister would." She smiled. "Speaking of big sisters . . ."

I grinned in return. I hoped her light mood was an indication that her news was equally optimistic.

"The person I spoke to at the fifth hospital on the list recalled a boy with Josef's description. I explained the approximate date, the symptoms, and Anton as well. He thought he might still be there."

"Still there?" I cried. Lena's breath remained irregular. I retrieved a glass of water for her.

"If that's true . . ." I paced the floor. ". . . then he isn't . . ."

"No." Lena smiled wide after two large sips. "He hasn't passed."

"I need to know. When will we know?"

"I can't try again until next week," Lena then added, "but he gave me a nurse's name who might know more."

I rubbed my head. "No, I have to know sooner."

"How? The public telephones the city's installing will not be in use for another three months."

"What time do the Franke's retire to bed?"

"Ella! You can't! If they see you, you'll be arrested." Lena stood up to join me.

"I have to know."

She glanced around and shook her head.

"Please, Lena. I need answers."

Lena muttered, "They generally retire to their room by seven when there's no guests, but I don't know if they actually sleep. The television is left on occasionally." It sounded as if she were trying to discourage me, but I was determined.

"Can the mortuary door stay unlocked? Or a window? I can climb through a window."

"There has to be another telephone somewhere," Lena suggested, knowing full well they were scarce and controlled. "Even if you get to the telephone, the nurse might not be there when you call."

I ignored her deterrents. "What's the name of the hospital?"

"Ella . . ."

"Please, Lena, tell me the hospital name."

"*DRK Klinikin*. I'm worried for you. If you're arrested again, you might never be freed. Think of Stefan."

I ignored her pleas. "I'm thinking of my brother."

The next evening, I arrived at the Franke's at half past seven. Lena had left the servants' door unlocked. It made the most sense—the one door to go unchecked. Fortunately, when I slipped in most of the house was already dark for the night. According to Lena, Johann stayed on full-time now but retreated to his room the same time the Frankes did.

I hesitated at the entrance of the staff room and was instantly flooded with memories. Many of them were pleasant, some not as much.

Glancing at the shelf, my name had been removed, but my hand reached into it anyway. It was empty. Recollection of the times my hand returned with a simple gift from Stefan warmed my heart and generated a brief hallucination. His handsome features, fresh on my mind, nearly delayed my purpose. I quickly refocused and snuck silently from the room.

The beam from my small flashlight barely cracked the darkness as I tiptoed towards the mortuary doors. My last entry found myself in Stefan's arms on the other side. My hand reached for the handle, expecting it to be cold; everything had turned chilly without his presence.

The stench of burnt flesh overcame me. Immediately, my sleeve was raised to cover my nose. It seemed much stronger than I remembered, or I had forgotten how awful it was in the years since my absence.

When the door creaked a little louder than expected. I held my breath then stepped through and watched them close shut from the shadows. My ears, actively alert, waited for any sound of movement.

Silence.

A slight exhale escaped my lips as I wiped my moist brow. Lena was right, this time if I was detained I would actually be guilty, and with Frau Franke making political decisions in the home, there would be no mercy. The result would most likely be a Stasi prison camp. Of course, she had the means right here to make me disappear altogether.

The deep red and brown patterns of the mortuary created dim visibility, but I had never been in here at night. Contrasting elements of uncertainty and familiarity clashed. On the left, silhouettes of foreign objects appeared. On the right, the room with the containers—with the names written above. *How many bodies are in there now?* I trod through temptation as I passed. *Does Herr Franke stay in the mortuary because there's more work to be done? Or is it because it's his personal sanctuary?*

Once I reached the office, my palm skimmed the width of the door before it rested on the handle. My fist gripped the metal with an unnecessary tightness and braced for another memory to strike upon entry, one that started out beautiful and ended quite sad. It was the last argument Stefan and I had.

My light naturally flashed from the couch and his kiss to the desk where he deliberately shunned me. A false accusation that involved Anton, and yet here I was in a way still bringing his name forth.

I chastised myself. *This isn't about Anton. It's about Josef!* Yet every step I took further into this room, the less I could concentrate. With limited sight, my other senses became heightened *Is that Stefan's cologne I smell?* My hand waved the torch nervously about until it centered on the black item I had come for. Tiptoeing towards the desk, my hand deliberately brushed the arm of the couch. Confidence swelled within from its acquaintance. *I can do this! For Josef!*

Immediately, light flooded the room. I spun to find someone standing behind me and dropped the flashlight to the floor. The thud and my consequent yelp immobilized me. Adrenaline pulsated through my body while attempts to slow my quickened heartbeat were unsuccessful.

"Ella!" his voice quaked. My breath hastened.

"Johann?" I cried, momentarily grateful it wasn't a Franke, but the butler's face quickly flushed to anger.

"What are you doing here?" he demanded, grabbing my wrist and snatching the flashlight off the floor. Speechless, I cowered.

"Come with me." He squeezed harder. "You will need to explain yourself."

I shook my head and raised my other hand in defense.

"No. Please. I didn't come to steal anything."

"You can explain it to the missus."

"Please, Johann. Please!"

His grip was nearly as tight as the cuffs. He seemed to have no intention of letting go and any attempt I made to get loose, the restraint intensified. With my other hand, I clenched the frame of the door and dug my heels into the carpet. Lena came rushing forward.

"Johann," she whispered. His eyes widened, and his body stiffened. Instantly, he released my arm. "Ella only came to use the telephone." She touched his shoulder tenderly, her calming presence always amazed me.

"Please, it's the truth," I begged. He eyed me with doubt then glanced back to her.

"Why?" he questioned. We all stood still.

"My brother is really sick."

"You don't have a brother." Johann placed his hands on his hips.

"I do." My mouth felt as though it was stuffed with cotton balls. "I never spoke about him because he escaped to the West . . . without me and . . . if the Franke's found out . . . you know what they are capable of."

I grabbed his hand. "Please, Johann, please let me phone the hospital. You can listen to the call. I just need to know if he's alright."

The wrinkles that circled Johann's mouth deepened then relaxed. The silence was torture as he contemplated the facts.

"Alright," he huffed. "Make the call quickly and then leave."

Withdrawing the piece of paper Lena had written the hospital name on, I stepped over to the telephone, unsure what to do next. The night of the Cuban crisis, the phone had been brought to the main house and I had seen Herr Franke place it to his mouth and ear. I mimicked the motion timidly, the black handle heavy in my fist then awkwardly against my head. Lena moved over to help me.

"Place your finger there, at the '0' then turn it all the way around".

A woman's voice filled the handset at my ear. "*Welche Nummer wollen Sie anrufen?*"

My eyes went wide. I nearly lost my grip. "She wants to know my destination," I whispered to Lena.

"*Hallo?*" she repeated impatiently.

Lena pointed to one end. "You need to speak into that part. Tell her the hospital name."

I forced out the words. "I . . . I want to talk to the DRK Klinikin in West Berlin."

The woman repeated my request. "DRK Klinikin, West Berlin? *Bitte bleiben Sie in der Leitung.*"

Amazed, I pulled the handle away. "She asked me to hold." Lena smiled at my ignorance and placed it back to my ear.

"DRK Klinikin, *Wie kann ich Ihnen helfen?*"

"Uh . . . yes, yes, you can help me. I am looking for someone."

"*Patientenstatus, halten bitte.*"

"Patient status," I repeated and leaned the handle outward and encouraged Lena to listen with me. I bit my lip.

"Patientenstatus?"

"Um, yes, I'm looking for a nurse . . ." I pulled the handle back once again. "Lena, what was her name?"

"Gertrude."

"Gertrude," I said into the phone. "Is Gertrude available to speak?"

"Halten bitte."

My head felt light. *Was that a good sign?* A few minutes of silence passed.

"*Hier ist Gertrude.*"

"Yes!" I spoke excitedly, "Yes, um, I am Ella Kühn. My brother Josef Kühn was ill many weeks ago. Do you know who he is or his condition?"

"Josef Kühn?"

"Yes." My cheeks grew warm with anticipation. "He is sixteen . . . uh, probably tall and thin, brown hair."

"You are Josef's sister?"

"I am."

"From the East?"

"Yes!" I cried. I heard her make a muffled call away from the telephone. Some inaudible noises followed.

"Ella?"

My fingers froze in their grip. The male voice on the other end was familiar but distant. I stumbled to say the word.

"Anton?"

"Yes!" the voice cried. "Yes, Ella, it's me, Anton!"

My mouth opened, but there was no air in the room. Gasping, blood drained from my face as the handle slipped from my grasp. Lena reached for the phone. "Anton, this is Lena, a friend of Ella's. One moment, I think she's in shock. She was very worried about Josef. Is he alright?"

"Yes, yes, Lena. He was very ill for a long time, but he is now recovering. Can I please talk to Ella?"

"Ella," Lena cried, "Josef is going to be fine. Here, Anton wants to speak with you."

I couldn't believe what I was hearing. *Anton wants to speak with me.* I reached for the handle again and pressed it against my ear tightly as if that would bring him closer.

"Anton, is it—really you?" my words sputtered out choppy.

"Yes, yes, it's me. We have missed you so much! I . . . I have missed you."

I whimpered, "Your voice, Anton, you sound older."

"You too."

"I . . . I miss you, and . . . and miss Josef very much. He is well?"

"He is still weak, but he'll live. For a while the doctors had little hope. How did you find us?"

"I had a lot of help." My thoughts instantly went to Stefan who started the process.

"Ella, when are you coming; when will you join us?" Anton's question came out like a plea.

"I . . . I don't know. I . . . Oh, Anton, I can't believe I can hear your voice."

Johann huffed near the door. Suddenly, his finger went rigid to his lips. His face completely still, his beady eyes doubled in size.

Lena and I exchanged frightened looks. Anton's cry continued.

"Ella, Ella, are you still there?"

Johann's head shook side to side, and fear constricted my throat. The creak from the main mortuary doors sent a chill through the air. Panic paralyzed me. Lena reached for the telephone handle and hung it up on Anton mid-sentence. With her other hand, she pushed me down and inside the cavity of the desk at the very moment the door flew open.

Through a crack from the back of the desk I could see Herr Franke standing face to face with Johann and Lena; his face teetered between surprise and anger.

"What are you doing in here?"

Neither one spoke immediately. If it came down to it, I knew Johann would turn me in to save himself. His darting eyes told me he was pos-sibly considering this.

"I asked you a question." Herr Franke appeared tired but determined.

"It's my fault, sir," Lena spoke up. I held my breath, imagining all the times Lena has had to pay for my many mistakes.

Herr Franke's stare turned to her, his forehead wrinkled simultane-ous to the fire in his cheeks.

"I . . . I left my key in here when I cleaned last. Johann was kind enough to allow me to retrieve it. See, I found it," —she held up her apartment key from where it had been in her pocket the whole time— "and we were just leaving. I'm sorry to have disturbed you."

"Most apologetic, sir." Johann bowed low. "Is there anything I can as-sist you with tonight?"

"No," Herr Franke mumbled. His countenance had softened. "I came to retrieve my book." Lena's eyes followed his pointed finger as he moved towards the desk.

"Oh, sir," —Lena was swift— "let me get that for you." She quickly reached for it before he could refuse.

"Fine," he said as she handed it to him.

He gazed at her suspiciously then stepped towards the door. He held it open and waited for both Johann and Lena to leave with him. I heard their steps fade away, and the clasp of the heavy mortuary door close once more.

I let out a sigh of relief and rested my head against the wood as I pon-dered the night. *Josef is alive and recovering, and I spoke to Anton! I ac-tually heard his voice, and he heard mine!* The deep tone was more like a man . . . not the teenage boy from five years ago.

Crunched below the desk, I waited what seemed to be forever be-fore I felt it was safe to depart. I was sure Johann got Herr Franke tucked back in before he allowed himself a reprieve from the night's events. I could picture him scolding Lena, letting her know exactly how disap-pointed he was in her. He too must believe my negative influence was far reaching.

I quietly slipped out to the mortuary hall, only this time using the de-livery doors in the back. The risk of going through the house once again was too great. As my hands skimmed the outer wooden doors, despite the recent fright, I reluctantly dwelt on the idea that this could be the last time I would ever be at the Franke's. Even with a ring on my finger, it was possible I would never be accepted. The reality was bitter sweet.

As I rushed away from the house, I spied Lena rocking nervously on a street bench a half block away. She had waited and once she caught sight of me, jumped up and ran towards me. Her arms hurled tightly around my neck, and when she squeezed, I felt a dampness from her cheeks.

"Please, Ella, promise me we will never do anything like that again . . . please?"

I nodded my head. Although it was frightening and I risked much, in the end it was worth it. I not only learned of Josef's fate, but I heard Anton's voice. My dearest friend, Anton.

NINE

KLEIN MAUS

May 1966

His fingers brushed across my back with barely enough pressure to tease. My skin reacted sensationally to his touch while his fingers trailed my spine to my shoulders. I attempted to focus on the painting in front of me, but when his lips skimmed my neck, my thoughts diverted with very little effort. My heart beat rapidly, eyes closed, imagining his next breathtaking move. By the time his arms cradled me, my smile radiated with gratifying pleasure. A gentle turn brought me face to face with my love, my . . . I opened my eyes . . . *Anton!*

I choked. There was no air. A coat of sweat on my skin leaked into my eyes and blurred my vision as I stumbled out of bed searching for the light. Pain shot through my leg as my thigh hit the night table in the corner. The fingers of my left hand rubbed the knot that had formed as my right-hand anxiously fumbled around the base of the lamp until I found the knob and twisted. Desperate for much-needed oxygen, I staggered to crack the window open. Frantically I scanned the room. Nothing. No Anton . . . no Stefan.

The back of my hand brushed against my clammy cheek then made its way across the rest of my face. My drenched nightgown did little to collect the tears as I dropped to the floor beneath my window and buried my eyes in the damp fabric. *It was a dream!* I insisted vigorously to calm my racing heart. *It was not real!* Although, it wasn't a nightmare either, and up until I realized it was Anton . . . it felt . . . nice. I slapped my cheeks. *No! I can't allow myself to take joy in this!*

I walked to the sink and splashed cold water on my face. *You love Stefan!* I paused, completely still. Anton's face appeared again. I tugged at my nightgown until it fell to the floor and turned the shower to *cold.* I needed a deeper shock, anything to drive these thoughts from my head.

Wrapped in my robe, I walked to the bookshelf with a renewed sense of stability. As I reached for Stefan's last letter, I gazed at the ring on my finger and smiled. There was no question where my heart lies. *I will marry Stefan.* I gripped the paper tightly and curled up in Mama's chair to read it for the tenth time since it arrived yesterday, despite being dated over a month ago.

27 April 1966

Sweetest Ella,
You cannot imagine my delight when I received your letter. Afraid it would be years before contact, I have reread all the ones you gave me our last night together at least a half-dozen times each. Some I have already memorized.

I could never forget you, and now I can look at you every single day. Thank you for the photograph, it is my greatest possession. You are the reason I get up every morning and move forward. Another day behind me is another day closer to you. My profoundest desire is to be by your side.

Ella, I have been promoted. I have received the position of Stabsgefreiter. I will receive the patch with two stripes of Lance Corporal in the next advancement ceremony. I never believed I could do this well as a soldier. I thought the only path I could know is one of the mortuary. If I continue to do well, I can make a respectable career of this, and this would possibly be the answer for us to leave Berlin. We might not have to wait seven years if we are granted another respite. We could marry the next time I see you! If you are willing, the possibility of our union could happen prior to the fulfillment of my sentence and my commanding officer would recommend me for an alternate post with my wife at my side. I'd have to commit to a lifetime in the military, but just think about it, Ella. We would no longer be separated. I would be able to come home to you every night. I know the life of a soldier can be difficult at times, but the NVA are moral people. They protect and serve the goodness of Germany.

I hope you are well. I too think of our time together and hold onto the vision of you in my arms every single day. I know it seems so far away, but we will be together soon. We are meant to be together.

I love you!

Your fiancé, Stefan

I read it again and reminded myself it was Stefan's touch that I yearned for . . . Stefan's lips I thirsted for and only his companionship that I ached for.

Unable to fall asleep, I dressed and set out early for the *Waisenhaus*. Today was the first day in weeks I wasn't scheduled to work at the café, and Mari was close to making a full recovery and being released from the clinic. I was determined to make arrangements for her, although I didn't know what to expect when I arrived at the orphanage.

As I stood at the bottom of the steps, my bosom filled with unforgettable memories. The last time I stepped out this door, I entered the Kühn's automobile and started a new life, one I never intended to lead me back here. I flicked the bell.

Various noises and commotion erupted from the other side, but no one came to answer. I rang the bell again. A child's face appeared at the window. I knocked heavily.

"*Was wollen Sie?*" A young nurse appeared, much younger than I would have expected. When she asked what I wanted there was a hint of annoyance in her voice.

"Is Nurse Gitta available?"

"*Wer?*" she snapped impatiently.

"Nurse Gitta."

"*Es gibt hier niemanden mit diesem Namen.*" The woman forcefully denied knowing anyone by that name. I sensed she wanted to close the door, so I quickly stuck my foot in the way. The door bounced back, surprise covering her face.

"*Entschuldigung, ich habe Arbeit zu erledigen,*" she quipped impatiently.

"I have work to do as well, may I please speak to the nurse in charge. It is urgent."

"*Warum?*"

"Why? Are you the nurse in charge?" I countered.

She responded by opening the door but flipped her hair in my direction and walked farther inside. From the way she left the door open, I assumed this was her way of inviting me in.

The scent of old wood and some combination of vegetables cooking, lingered through the long hallway. I did not recall it ever smelling this good.

"*Warten Sie hier,*" she barked for me to wait.

I waited. I scanned the white walls, the wood floors, and the crooked light above my head. Heat flooded my cheeks, this was my childhood! Years of running through these halls, hiding, laughing, fighting; it was all a part of me. Within minutes, the silhouette of a woman filled the back doorway. My eyes lifted as the familiar amble approached. The wide hips and broad shake of the shoulders brought tears to my eyes.

"Nurse Margret!" I cried.

Her eyebrows pinched then raised as her frown curved the other direction. *Is she smiling?*

"Adela?" Her stride increased until she stood directly in front of me.

I nodded, grinning like a toddler.

"Oh, dear!" She clapped her hands and pulled me in. I remembered her being much taller and larger, but her grip was like before, nearly suffocating. "Oh, how I have missed my mischievous *klein Maus!*"

I giggled at the nickname. The only other person to call me that was Anton . . . I hugged her back and kissed her on the cheek.

"Are you well? Where is Nurse Gitta, and why are you in charge now?"

She patted my head and pointed to another room. We moved to a couch. It was evident she sauntered much slower than before, and the gray on her head rivaled that of Gitta from long ago.

"Nurse Gitta passed away three years ago." Her eyes grew heavy. Although there was little affection between them, their association spanned decades, and the pain of her loss was reflected in her mournful countenance.

"I'm sorry."

"I am the head nurse and will probably be here until they bury me as well. I know no other trade. This is where I belong."

I listened to her words, but my thoughts shifted to my childhood. Nurse Margret had played a much larger role in who I was today than I gave her credit for. A tough old woman, she didn't desert us, and she didn't leave us to die on the streets.

I reached for her hands; they were cold. "Nurse Margret, I owe so much to you; my life, my past, everything I am today is because of you, and for this I'll always be thankful."

Her square jaw jiggled enough to let her mouth curve into a partial smile. I was sure she hadn't heard from many of the children who left here.

"How's that scamp Anton doing? I assume you are together? You were inseparable here."

I stumbled on the words, "Not together . . . no." I hesitated. Why was he suddenly foremost in my thoughts? "He's actually in the West." I smiled. "He is free."

"Well, I assure you child," Margaret's chin shook when she spoke. "You will not be apart for long. You two are meant to be together."

The comment left me speechless, almost afraid.

Her head tilted, and her eyes scanned me as if she had a truth probe. My eyes shifted towards the door.

I quickly changed the subject. "I have actually come here for a favor."

Her lips tightened in a straight line, but her eyes didn't move.

"I found a girl on the street—"

"No!" She waved her hand fiercely.

"Nurse Margret—"

"No, we are full, Adela. We cannot take any more children, and the streets are still bursting with them."

"Please," —I leaned towards her— "I know about the secret room and the hidden Jews." She offered no expression. "I *know* you care more than you want people to know you do. Like when you took Anton in when we were full, and stopping the government from taking our home."

She remained silent.

"This girl is only six, no family, and no options. My friend paid a hefty price for her recovery at the clinic. She is healed, and she will not be a burden. I will pay what I can as well, but she needs a home. She needs you."

Nurse Margret sighed heavily. "Oh, Adela . . ."

"You are her only hope."

As the silence between us grew, the sound of giggling children amplified from the day room. A generous improvement since my departure nearly ten years ago, which could only be attributed to the woman who pondered before me.

"Bring her next week, but no more. Don't go out searching for *straben-kind*." She grunted as she stood. "There are just too many."

I jumped to my feet and hugged her tightly. "Mari will do nicely here. She will be a good girl . . . much better than me." Grinning, I rushed to the door. "Thank you, Nurse Margret! Thank you very much!"

Hurrying to the hospital, my body barely kept my excitement contained. I had been incredibly worried about Mari and her future. If circumstances were different, such as a better position or married myself, I would have insisted on caring for her. Yet given my small income and status, raising a child could not be done on my own.

"Mari!" Beaming, I entered her room. She was coloring a picture with the wax cubes purchased a month ago, and every time I visited they were attached to her little fingers; something I could not complain about.

"Ella, you look happy." She smiled with full pink cheeks and shiny eyes. Her legs and arms no longer bore open wounds—only faint scars. The teeth peeking through her grin were cracked, but in time they would fall out and be exchanged with new ones, healthier ones if Nurse Margret had anything to do about her hygiene!

"I have found you a home."

Mari's fingers paused, the yellow wax cube she used to draw the sun dropped against the paper as she folded both arms tightly across her chest and grunted. "I don't want a new home. I want to be with you." Her face crunched like a raisin, and tears flowed easily.

My hands reached for hers. "This was the home I grew up in." My thoughts swayed to its many imperfections, one of course being the lack of education, but anything beat a life on the street. "You will have food and be safe, and I will visit you often."

Mari paused in her grief. "How often?"

"Every week."

"Are there other children?" Mari set her coloring aside and climbed onto my lap.

"Yes," —my arms wrapped around her— "lots of other children and a woman who will care for you as if you were her own child."

"What's her name?" Mari leaned her head against my shoulder.

"Nurse Margret."

As I walked home that day, my heart was full. For the first time in a very long time, deep gratitude overflowed. I couldn't save all the children, but I saved one; like someone saved me. Placed on a step twenty-one years ago, they chose to save my life by that action, and it wasn't until Mari entered my life, I recognized the depth of it.

TEN

Yesterday

16 June 1966

Dear Josef,
I cannot express entirely in words how I felt when I learned you were
no longer in harm's way. The fear of the unknown after that first
letter from Anton was enough to break me. You are my only family, I
don't know what I would do without you. Please take care of yourself,
do everything the Doctor orders and continue to follow your studies.
You are becoming a man and one day will find a wife and provide for
a family of your own, thanks to Anton, our friend.

I hesitated as I wrote the word *friend*. Was I trying to convince myself
that's all he had ever been? I continued.

Please tell him I will always be grateful for his role in your upbringing
and welfare. His friendship is invaluable.
Write when you are well enough, and I will continue to keep you in
my thoughts as always.

Love, Ella

I sealed the letter and laid it on the table. It seemed the only way I could force my mind to forget Anton was to not acknowledge him or his role in my own life . . . at least until my heart was stronger.

The dream I had experienced was extremely vivid and emotional, and I struggled to focus for days after it occurred. If that wasn't enough, Nurse Margret's assumptions and inquiries regarding our relationship laid the foundation for additional doubt. Together, they confirmed—in some ways—that my confidence in Stefan's relationship was clouded by Anton.

I shuffled over to the mirror begrudgingly and smeared the last number off the glass to reduce it by one. The digits seemed to choke me. Staring at the streaks, my finger struggled to pick up the wax. Instead, a stiffness grew from my legs up to my jaw then out to my clenched fists. I pounded the ceramic basin, which accomplished nothing except to bruise my hands. Upset with my juvenile wavering, I ran the faucet and splashed icy cold water across my face.

Stefan's life is on the line because of me. Everything he experiences is because of me. My faithfulness to him hinged on ceasing my correspondence to Anton. I knew this to be true, though my heart clashed with the idea, even if my mind couldn't fully comprehend why. The thought of ending our friendship was devastating, but the evidence was clear if I didn't do it, I would always have him somewhere in my head. Someday I might not have the strength to keep him from reaching my heart.

* * *

12 July 1966

Dear Ella,
I was concerned when our telephone call ended suddenly. The letter
I wrote you back in March was returned without reason, whether
by you or the ministry it remains unclear. When Josef received your
letter yesterday, I was relieved. However, it left me confused. I hope
I didn't offend you somehow. Your reference to Anton "our friend"
seemed distant. I guess I always assumed there was a potential for
more. Could I be wrong?

Hearing your voice — after so long — it's hard for me to describe what it felt like. Something inside me stirred, which I haven't experienced for years. You said I sounded older. I am, but you have grown as well. You're no longer the child I used to play with. You're a woman now. I know I have asked this before, but are you still trying to reach us? Are you trying to get to the West?

If only you could see what they have to offer here. The universities and state libraries with more books than you could even count, large museums with all types of art and sculptures, theatres where actors sing and dance, discotheques and street fairs. It's a vibrant and lively place where I know you would find happiness and comfort.

Please know Ella, you are missed more than you can imagine.

Love, Anton

17 August 1966

Dear Ella,
It has been too long since your last letter. Are you well? The last correspondence you shared was too short. I know you well enough to know something must be wrong. I ache to hear from you. Please write more. I am terribly jealous it was Anton who got to hear your voice on the telephone. If only I had been stronger, I could have joined him.

I wish you were here. There is so much I miss, but a lot I don't. Anton took me to a festival yesterday. There was music and art and I watched a woman draw and she reminded me of you and your butterflies. We bought Nussecken and the chocolate melted in my hand before I could eat it all. On the way home we stopped at a market. You should see them here! You know how back home, the same can of beans would be on five different shelves? Here, there is a store called KaDeWe and there are many rows of different kinds of foods! Its where Anton bought my birthday present, a Haller futbol jersey. He is my favorite on the West German team. People say we have a good chance at going far in the World Cup this year.

Can you believe I'm 16? Anton said if we save our money we can go to Denmark for Christmas this year. I have seen pictures in my geography books at school, and it is a very beautiful place. I've never been outside Germany before! I hope you will be with us by then. I never thought I would say I love school, but when I was sick and in the clinic, I missed my friends and my books. It is because of you I missed my books.

Anton misses you. It has been too long, 5 years is too long to be separated. Maybe you should write to Anton and let him know you are still trying to get here. You are still trying, aren't you? Please write back.

Love, Josef

1 November 1966

Dearest Josef,
I have been a terrible sister, please forgive me. I received your letter over a month ago, yet I cannot use the excuse of work because I'm home alone most evenings. I no longer go out with friends, and I spend most of my time reading or visiting Mari in the Waisenhaus. Mari! I just realized I have not even mentioned her to you before. Stefan and I found her on the street, a small child, near death and now she lives in mine and Anton's old orphanage. I hope you will meet her someday. She is a sweet girl and more like the younger sister I never had.

There is no reason why I didn't write earlier. There is nothing wrong; in fact, I have good news. I'm engaged! I never mentioned Stefan to you before because I wasn't sure where the relationship would lead, but while on leave in March he asked me to marry him and I said yes. He is a good soldier, like papa, not like border patrol. He is quite good to me, but because of his service we have very little contact. In fact, I may not see him again for years, but in my heart, I know this is right.

My sweet Josef, you are growing up too fast. I feel awful I am not there to look after you like I promised Papa I would. I'm very proud of you and your great accomplishments. Soon you will attend the university and learn more than I can even imagine. If you had remained here in the East you would be forced into conscript. You get to lead a better life than I could have ever hoped for you. I hope you thank Anton every day for the role he has been tasked to play in your life. I know Papa is watching over you and pleased. You are becoming an honorable man.

I'm sorry I missed your birthday again. I love you. Even if I'm not there, I think of you every day. I don't know if I will ever be there. Stefan serves in East Germany and that's where I must remain to receive him when his service is complete. I know you may not understand now, but someday you will meet a woman who will make you happy and you will love her and then you will know.

I wish the very best for you and Anton, you both deserve to be happy. Anton will always hold a special place in my heart, my childhood is filled with happiness because of him, but it is impossible for people to be together living such different lives in different countries. Please give him my best.
I will write again.

With Love, Ella

***

"I'm forcing you to come out with me tonight." Lena appeared in the café at the close of my shift.

I was truly happy to see her, only I felt less like celebrating. "Lena, I don't think so. I don't feel up to it." I glanced out the window at the mid-December flurry and shuddered.

"I won't take no for an answer." She brushed my response off with a wave of her hand. "I would venture to guess the last time you went out was when Stefan was on leave nine months ago."

My lips flashed a tired grin. Being with Stefan remained a pleasant memory. "You may be engaged, but you're not dead. Stefan would understand." Lena removed her coat and helped me clear the dishes from the last tables.

"Um, I—"

"Nope! I'm not listening." She placed one hand tenderly over my mouth and grabbed my arm with the other one."

I groaned, defeated. "Let me at least remove my apron."

"Yes." She laughed. "*That* you should do."

I folded it and placed it on the counter.

"Goodnight, Hilde." I waved to her as she swept behind the counter.

"Goodnight, dear, and have a good time." She winked to my groan.

"Why would anyone possibly want to be out on a night like tonight?" After clasping the buttons on my coat, I wrapped my scarf tightly around my neck.

"Because there is more to life than work. You're only twenty-one, live a little." Lena linked her arm through mine and pulled me in tight for added warmth as we stepped outside. With only my eyes exposed, snowflakes accumulated on my nose and eyelashes, and the farther we walked, the more we looked like two snowmen waddling down the street.

"To Dafne's?" I conceded as a steamy mist blew from my lips. This had to be the coldest day of winter thus far.

"No, to *Zum Schusterjungen*. They play rock music late."

"Rock? *Amis*? At "The Cobbler Boy?""

"And Brits," she added slyly.

"When did you start listening to that?"

"Greta introduced me to it," she giggled. Despite the thick clothing between us, her excitement surged through to me. The pink on her cheeks was not only from the weather. "There's this band called The Beatles; I can't seem to get enough of them."

"Beatles? Like the bugs?"

"Ha, yeah, but they don't look like bugs. They're rather handsome."

"How do you know?" I studied her reaction.

She blushed. "I have their album."

My eyes went wide. "Are they permitted?"

"Not likely." Her dismissive demeanor surprised me.

"Since when did you start becoming the rebel?"

"Shhh, I'm not a rebel," Lena chortled. "I just like their music."

Even though I wasn't too thrilled about going to a bar, I eagerly entered for the heat. Everything about this establishment dripped warmth the moment we stepped in: red-brick paneled walls, oil lamps at each table, and two burners on opposite ends. Even the strong scent of hazelnut somehow masked the mandatory use of the chemical *Wofasept* around coal.

As we located an empty table near the back, my expression didn't hide the shock of the high number of patrons out for a bitter winter night.

"Why so many people?" I scanned the room. *What in the world are they doing here?*

She answered with a nod. "They come for the music."

My eyes spun with concern . . . I truly believed the youth of today had somehow lost their minds. "It can't be that good."

"You'll see." Lena grinned widely as the lively beat echoed from a nearby "dance" floor—created by pushing several tables against a wall. The vocals almost sounded like young boys. I missed their initial appeal but enjoyed observing Lena's reaction to it. In between her bouncing shoulders, her mouth mimicked the words to the song, perfectly in tune. The lightness that suddenly swirled in my head made this moment somehow magical—mostly because I hadn't seen Lena this happy in an incredibly long time.

Once the song ended, she flagged a waitress over but tipped her ear to the new beat, which had only begun. "Oh, Ella, don't you love this rhythm?" She clapped her hands and turned to the barmaid. "I'll have a *bier.*"

Again, my glance in her direction seeped disbelief.

"*I can't hide . . .*" She sang the words, loud and confident. She had changed a bit since my departure from the Franke's. Not only had I never seen her sing out loud like this, but she rarely drank anything more than brandy.

The waitress impatiently turned to me and mumbled, ". . . you?"

"Um . . . tea please."

She rolled her tired eyes and rushed off.

"Are you well, Lena?" I nearly had to shout.

"Yes." She stared back at me with a strength I hadn't seen in years. "Listen, this part's my favorite."

I studied her as she sang about holding hands.

"What's his name?" I questioned boldly.

Lena's eyes flickered. "Who?"

My grumble was low and irritable. "The man who's turned your life upside down."

She knew she couldn't hide it from me, but her hesitation to divulge was apparent. Perhaps she thought I would assume Christoph was no longer on her mind. I waited and finally a simple grin broke through.

"Freddy."

"Freddy?" I gasped. "And where might Freddy be on this fine evening?"

"Over there." She pointed to the bar. "He's the barman."

"A barman?"

She nodded and waved as he glanced over. He somehow knew we were talking about him.

"He's cute," I confirmed. He was tall and thin, with long chestnut hair and nearly as long sideburns. "How did you meet?"

"A friend arranged it."

". . . and you are . . . okay?"

"Yes." Her answer was short.

With my mittens removed, my fingers rubbed briskly together for warmth as I soaked in the surroundings. Despite the music and chatter, the ambiance was surprisingly serene. Vines snaked through lattice partitions that separated the tables, and the windows imitated a game board with colorful glass squares. It had been some time since I enjoyed a relaxing night out.

"Du bist ein Idiot!" The insult startled me. I twisted my body around to find three teenagers in a heated conversation.

"Anyone who even considers joining *FDJ* is outright stupid!" One boy slammed his fist down on the table in front of the others, apparently unaware he was drawing attention.

A momentary glance towards Lena confirmed she was still immersed in the music, humming effortlessly along. My eyes skimmed the room. I was no expert in spotting a spy, but I did have a smidgen of knowledge on the Stasi, and this was precisely the conversation they would be looking for.

"There's no way you would ever find me involved with a communist organization. You know Schumann forces the belief it is the only path for a German youth!"

"It might become mandatory."

"Yes, being brainwashed is essential to their goals, Jonas."

I tried not to listen, but it was hard to ignore.

"Karl, you know the Vopos are following you right? The ridiculous stunt with the Vietcong donations was like walking into the SED and announcing your intentions of defecting."

"Yeah, I received a post about reporting to the youth work yard in a week, which I won't be doing."

Unable to sit still, I inched forward to the edge of my chair until my feet were flat then impulsively traveled their direction.

"Hey." I faced the boys directly.

"What?" The loudest of the three spoke up, the lines in his forehead falsely aged him.

I squinted past them then behind me before I slipped into the one empty chair at *their* table. In my side view, Lena's eyebrows scrunched with the tilt of her head.

"I just think you should keep your voices down."

The same loud ring leader snorted, "Oh, I see, boys . . ."

The waitress appeared with my tea.

The loudmouth, who couldn't have been more than eighteen, snickered again, "We are upsetting the *princess*." The others joined his tease with snorts. "Let's let her get back to her fantasy world of rainbows and glass slippers and drinking her high society tea."

My eyes dropped to my clothes. My dress wasn't made from the finest fabrics, I didn't wear much makeup, and my hair was still in a bun from work. *Why would he assume I came from money?* The flash from the diamond on my ring reminded me.

In a quick check, I noted both his jacket pockets had been torn, one still hanging by a thread, and his pants were thin with several patches and no hem.

"Look!" I snapped back. "I don't care what you may think of me, although it's untrue. I also don't care what your political beliefs are. What I do care about is coming here to enjoy a little music and a chance to leave the world outside and not have some slighted teenage boy alert every communist devotee between here and Friedrichshain to his careless stupidity!"

With audacity I stood, disregarding anyone around us who had now stopped to listen. "Shut up or someone will shut you up . . ." I leaned close; my eyes enflamed. ". . . and believe me when I say it's a real game of Russian roulette you're playing, and your odds don't look good."

I returned to my table where Lena's curious expression had remained unchanged. She quickly closed her mouth.

No words were said as I clutched my tea with both hands and sipped with satisfaction. The warm liquid wove a soothing path down my throat.

A figure appeared at my side. Only my eyes moved. It was the receiver of my rant. His face no longer distorted in unbelief or ruddy from the turmoil he stirred. It appeared much brighter now.

"My name is Karl-Heinz." He held out his hand to shake, but I didn't meet it. "I . . . I'm—" he struggled to find the words.

I cut him off. "If you insist on making this acquaintance, Karl, sit down. Your hovering is bothersome." He laughed out loud then took a seat across from us.

"You are tenacious." He smiled widely then continued, "Are you familiar with the anti-revisionist movement?"

I stared at Karl hard, my cup resting against my lips. "Did you really not hear what I just said?"

He chuckled again. "Yes, every word, which is why we need a person exactly like you to join our cause."

"Karl," I fought to keep disdain out of my voice, "you are a child, playing a dangerous sport for amusement."

"What's your name?" he inquired slyly.

"Helen." I didn't skip a beat. Lena giggled. Her swollen cheeks indicated she nearly spit her beer onto the table.

Karl peered back and forth between us. One eye lifted higher than the other, doubt appearing across his countenance. Suddenly, he angled his ear towards the speakers.

"This is a great song."

I rolled my eyes. *Not you too! Like a child . . . easily distracted.*

"Want to dance?" He held out a hand. "Of course . . . only if your fiancé will allow it."

I peered at Lena, her grin matched his. She nodded. "Oh, go have some fun."

"Yes, *Helen,*" Karl snickered, ". . .isn't that why you came in the first place?"

I didn't grab his hand, although I stood to join him. Having never danced with anyone but Papa and Stefan, I hid my trepidation well.

"What is this song called anyway?" My lip wrinkled to the slow, depressing manner in which it started.

"It's called *Yesterday.*" Karl led the way to the small dance floor. People joined together all around us. *Oh no . . .* it instantly struck me this would remain a slow song. My muscles tightened as Karl turned to me.

He placed one hand on my hip, only to be immediately brushed off. His reaction was playful as he extended both hands out for me to join them. I beheld his open palms, then my gaze flashed up to his face. His intentions emerged through the innocence of his youthful features. In this brief moment he reminded me of Josef. I met his hands. "The lyrics are about a break-up," Karl shared. "A lover who misses what he had." As we turned about, the words affected me more than I planned on.

My attention wandered to Stefan. "*Yesterday*" was amazing, *today* not so much! My eyes flickered between my dance partner and my hands. How I wished they were intertwined with Stefan's, his were the only ones I longed to hold.

With a quick release, I drew one finger up to scratch my eye, an intentional cover-up. My whole body seemed to recognize the delusion, and the building emotion converged on my throat then slid upward as if the only possible release could be through my eyes. My finger pressed harder. I didn't want this stranger to see my vulnerability—he was already borderline irritating—yet he was much more intuitive than I gave him credit for.

"Ah, there is a sentimental side to the tough exterior," Karl whispered, thankfully only within my earshot.

I didn't respond.

"I apologize if I annoyed you earlier," he said genuinely. "Can we be friends?"

I nodded with agreement; there were relatively few these days.

At the end of the night, we had combined tables, and even Freddy, Lena's *friend,* joined us. He was witty and comedic, entirely different from Christoph but likeable all the same.

"Helen . . ." Karl reached for my hand to kiss it goodnight, although I pulled it away before it reached his lips. He had drunk a lot in a short time. "Would you be kind enough to tell me your real name?" He winked.

I laughed. "Ella."

"Well, Ella, to you and your future husband." Karl held up yet another Obstler and swallowed in one gulp. "May you have a long, happy life together."

After placing a coin on the table, I secured my scarf around my neck. Chances are it was twice as cold as it had been before we arrived.

"This will be our adieu, for tomorrow we will be liberated," Karl mumbled and hobbled to his chair where his own tattered coat hung. His friends doubled over, equally intoxicated.

"Karl," I quickly twisted around and reached for his arm. "What do you mean by that?"

"Oh . . ." He laughed again. "Did I not tell you?"

My stare absorbing him hard, I quickly pulled him away from the others and into a corner for privacy.

"We are leaving tomorrow. It's all planned."

"What's planned?" My tone became serious.

"Do not worry about me, princess," Karl hooted, "I will no longer be bound by the communist inhumanity and their collectivist agenda."

I shook my head and gripped tighter to his arm. "Please don't."

"Oh, sure, you were quite insistent I leave earlier, only now . . . now you want me to stay. I'm sorry I cannot love you."

Karl's dramatics got a degree louder at the last of his sentence. He enjoyed the fact I was nearly begging.

"Stop it!" I growled. "You know what I mean!"

"Ella," Karl seemed sober for one short minute. "There is no life here. I have made my choice. I choose freedom." He handed me a small folded paper.

"What's this?"

"Where you belong." Karl joined his friends at the door and waved to the small cluster of patrons as they departed.

My breath caught—every inhale bristled my throat. I retreated to a stool, stunned. Images of Peter and Helmut walking out of the pub resurfaced, and I did nothing to stop them.

Lena and Freddy joined me, but I couldn't disclose the conversation. Although my trust in Lena was unquestionable, I barely knew Freddy. Lena wrapped her arms around me, instantly recognizing the grief in my countenance.

"What happened? Did he offend you?"

"No." My head quavered with a heavy heart. "No, he didn't."

Once home alone, behind closed doors, I coiled in Mama's chair with a quilt draped securely around me before the note was revealed. It was simply the contact information for the anti-revisionist party leader Karl spoke of.

Find Darek Mayer
Prenzlauer Berg
-KH

When I sighed, a feeble cry escaped as well. *Why didn't I run after him? I didn't even try to stop him.* Several teardrops wet the paper. Crinkled tightly in my fist, I tossed it across the room with no intention of entertaining any fanatical idea while survival was still a top priority, especially since Stefan's sentence was incomplete.

Yet within minutes, I shrugged off the covers, and dashed over to retrieve it. Somehow, a connection to Karl and his idiotic devotion surfaced. I recognized myself in him—his desire to be free and have choices—and despite the warning bells signaling, the paper was placed in my drawer.

ELEVEN

LENA AND FREDDY

2 January 1967

Dear Stefan,
Another year begins and all I can hope for is that it flies by quickly. I met a boy . . . not what you think. He was actually barely tolerable, but he had plans—you know—to leave. I couldn't stop him. I didn't even try very hard and although I never planned to see him again, his fate haunts me. Every day people disappear from here, sometimes on their own and other times not by their choice. There are days I fear walking out my door and then there are days I know I cannot let such dread control me. I know I can manage on my own, but I look forward to the day when I can conquer my fears with you by my side.

Each day without you is a trial. I know I can wait for you as long as necessary because I love you with all my soul, but now I know what I'm missing, and that's the hardest part. I dream about waking up in your arms and never letting go. It is a wonderful dream. Thank you for the phonograph. I have two records now in my collection and both by Miss Piaf. I have listened to other popular music but have yet to acquire anything but her.

Josef is getting stronger and healthier. Once again thank you for your part in helping me learn of his condition. It was strange being in the mortuary again and definitely felt empty without you.
Mari too is happy and safe. She asks about you, like how we met.

I told her how we fell in love. It is my favorite story. She is a bright girl and will have a suitable future because of your kindness.

I read in the newspaper your regiment has moved North. The farther away you get, the more painful the sting, but you are part of me and I will never let you go. Be safe my love and come back soon.

Your love, Ella

8 January 1967

Dear Ella,
I heard the good news, although it seems strange I didn't hear it from you directly. I thought our history together deserved more. I'm not angry only surprised.

It's hard to believe anything good should come out of the East, but your engagement proves differently. I hope to meet Stefan one day. Your affection would be the best thing to happen to any man. I hope he recognizes his good luck and treats you well.

I'm happy for you, Ella. It's just getting used to the idea you might not come to the West that's so hard. I think Josef and I had a different future in mind.

I would be lying to myself and you if I didn't confess my hope that you would have joined us here. Every day I live with regrets from our past. This is not meant to upset you or disrupt your life. I only wanted you to know.

Josef's letter also mentioned a girl you took to our orphanage. Please tell me the story. When I think about our time together at the Waisenhaus I can't help but smile. You were so stubborn klein Maus! Even now thinking of the first day we met, watching you try to outrun Nurse Margret makes me laugh out loud. That day will always be one of the best days of my life!

Please keep us updated on your celebration and future. We think of you every day and hope for the best.

Love, Anton

El,

I'm quite happy for you! Engaged? My big sister is engaged! I wish I could be there when you wed. Maybe the wall will be down before then, and we can all live together as a family is meant to be. Please tell Stefan I welcome him to the family! Write and tell me more about the man who has swept you off your feet.

I have very little effects from the illness now. My lungs continually grow stronger while I ride my bike every day. The delivery job I have been hired for allows me to be active many hours. At first I tired after two and three, but now I can work until late afternoon. It has also helped me learn the neighborhoods and streets and earn spending money. Occasionally I pass the wall and it saddens me as I wonder where you are at that very moment. Do you think we can try to see you at the viewing posts? I've passed the one on Bernauer near our old flat but there are others. I just want to see your face, sister.

Yes, I am preparing for University. I have decided to study law. I hope to understand government regulations enough to get you free. It is time, Ella. I miss you!

Love Josef

I should have felt relieved. All the thoughts and emotions that had built up previous to my disclosure to Anton about Stefan ought to have brought a considerable amount of peace, but it didn't. Much more needed to be said, but in the end, was it for Anton's sake or mine?

When Stefan was by my side on leave it was easy to feel right about our future, but each subsequent day apart brought trepidation. Outside of the few letters, read dozens of times, I lacked Stefan's daily reassurance. My love for Stefan was not suspect, it was the external pressures that couldn't be controlled I feared the most. *What if our absence somehow alters his commitment or even changes his future aspirations? What role does fate play in our lives anyway?* Then my thoughts disobediently strayed . . .

Is it possible Anton and I would be together had I left with him that night? Truly together? The question was valid, but what good did it honestly do to even wonder . . . I never left . . . and *of course, I would have never met Stefan.* A simple smile emerged . . . I couldn't picture my life without him. He was everything to me now.

I tapped the pencil against my lip and glanced up from the table. It was a cold but clear spring morning as I attempted to write Anton a response from the patio of *Bäckerei Balzer.* Four wadded pieces of paper lay next to my cup of mint tea; each effort seemed worse than the first. My feelings for Anton were complicated, even more than I believe I understood. My love for Anton was real, but was it the love a wife would have for a husband, or was my love out of dependency or protection?

Even as I attempted to analyze my thoughts and feelings, I knew being with Stefan was my true desire. After our first encounter at Friedrichstraße station—where a spoiled, immature boy tormented and humiliated me—who knew he would become the one my heart longed for, but he was, and I could not allow myself to be the one to doubt.

17 March 1967

Dear Anton,
Please rest assured I would never refuse your letters. I am unsure why it was returned. Another mystery to plague the East.

Mari, the child I found, had been abandoned on the street — left to die. After her medical attention I made arrangements for her at the Waisenhaus. I saw Nurse Margret — she is nearly the same yet aged. Nurse Gitta passed away a few years ago and Margaret runs the home now. She asked about you. She was always fond of you. It was strange being there after so many years and yes there are good memories for me as well. I passed the closet and wondered if our secret place had been found by other curious children.

I'm sorry. I should have written you sooner about Stefan. You're correct. You have been my dearest friend and I shouldn't have been afraid to tell you anything. Even about my love for Stefan. I do not regret the decision I made to stay with Papa to the end, but I'm sorry I had to say goodbye to you and Josef.
I know there's a small part of us that wishes we had never been

*separated. It's hard living lives completely apart. Your world holds
so much hope and happiness and for many years mine lacked even
decency and civility, but somehow through it all I found hope and
then I found happiness and love. I could never replace what I had
with you Anton. You were the only reason I survived my childhood.
It's because of you I am breathing today. I will never forget it or you.
We may never be in the same place, but my thoughts of you will
always bring joy to my heart. This isn't goodbye, just moving forward.*

Your best friend forever,
Ella

I addressed the envelope, knowing it would be weeks before Anton received it. The average time for post carried nearly a two-month delay,
but even with it lying before me, its release provoked a struggle. *Am I
being selfish or cautious? Why can't I have both . . . the love of my life and
my best friend?*

Anton's presence was missed immensely . . . yet, there is little doubt
this letter needed to be sent. If he was waiting for me, his wait was empty. I had no desire to leave the East without Stefan.

"Ella!"

Lena and Freddy appeared before me. Her arm wound comfortably
through his. Recognition of this generated an indisputable smile.

"Lena, please sit—both of you, please join me." Sweeping the
scrunched papers towards me, a spot was cleared. "Sorry, I've been
writ—"

"Writing letters!" Lena laughed as Freddy held out her chair for her.
The way his fingers lingered on her shoulders brought a sparkle to her
eyes. It warmed my heart to see her happy.

"Yes." The fresh tingle of spearmint tickled my nose with the next sip
of my tea.

"To Stefan, Anton, or Josef?" Lena inquired openly.

Freddy's eyebrow lifted as if I had three lovers.

"Freddy, remember I told you Josef is her brother, Anton is her best
friend—both live in the West—and Stefan is her fiancé in the military."

My smile broadened when she said the last part.

"What is new with them or you?" She waved the waitress over and ordered *kaffe* and a pastry for them both.

A flash of guilt came over me. Falling into unsociable routines between work and hiding in my flat had become a grim habit of mine.

"I . . . I'm sorry," I reached for her free hand, Freddy held the other. "Please, forgive me. I'm a terrible friend."

"Oh, Ella, you aren't a terrible friend. I simply worry about you being alone."

"I'm not entirely alone," I insisted. "I do see Mari regularly at the orphanage."

"How's she doing?" Lena had always been fascinated with the story.

"Remarkably well. No complications from the disease."

"Such great news. I would love to meet her someday."

"Yes, you'd find her rather intriguing." This brought forth a chuckle.

"And the men in your life, how are they?"

Lena instantly noticed my brief glimpse at the envelope in front of me. "Freddy, love, do you mind giving me a moment with Ella?"

"Anything, sugar." He kissed her on the cheek and disappeared around the corner.

"You didn't have to send him away, Lena. Anything can be said in front of him. I'm quite aware of your attachment." My mouth curved up warmly.

She scooted her chair closer. "Be honest. I always know when something's wrong."

My lips formed a tight line as I looked down at my hands. "I told Anton he and I aren't meant to be together and that I loved Stefan."

The silence seemed uncommonly loud. She waited until I peered up at her then grabbed both of my hands in hers. "Ella, love, I understand you care for them both dearly in very different ways. You have a big heart with a lot of love to give, but in the end, you cannot belong to both."

"It was hard." Moisture welled along my lower eyelashes.

"If it wasn't, I would question your humanity." Lena sighed. "Are you sure about Stefan?"

I nodded my head. "Yes. I'm sure."

"Then you need to be okay with letting Anton go." She glanced at the letter. "It was the right thing to do."

My confidence grew in agreement. Lena's mindfulness was precisely what was needed. Many times her wisdom somehow surfaced at the exact moment my spirit tumbled to its lowest points.

Lena lifted her drink and motioned for me to do the same and clinked it gently. "To our futures; may they be exactly the way they should!"

"Speaking of futures . . ." My eyes flashed to the approaching Freddy. "Yours seems to be progressing extremely well."

Lena beamed widely. "Oh, he is a gift from God."

Freddy leaned in with a kiss to her cheek. "Did I stay away long enough, love?" His affection and the way he doted was charming.

"Too long." She grinned, and he readily met her lips with a quick peck.

"Ella," Freddy turned towards me. "Would you like to join us for *Walpurgisnacht next month."*

"Oh, I don't—" Lena shot me a stern look. My mouth literally stopped midsentence as I watched her face twist in different directions, "I . . . would . . . love to . . . Freddy." I corrected myself.

Lena nodded satisfactorily at my sudden change of heart.

"I wasn't aware people still celebrated Saint *Walburga* anymore." My mind recalled Nurse Margret teaching the history of several saints. This one, however, fascinated me only because its observance had a fiery conclusion.

"I'm not really religious or into witch folklore," Freddy confessed, "but my mates and I have been gathering lumber for weeks. Our bonfire aims to be the largest in the East. Our goal is for the West to feel the heat!" He chuckled with his ambition.

"I've never actually attended one in person. I watched from a window once."

"Well then, it's settled. We'll expect you there." Lena hugged me as they stood to leave.

"Where, exactly?"

"Are you familiar with the shoe factory in Treptow?" Freddy pulled Lena in close.

I grinned. It was less than a kilometre from Mama Genau's old apartment. "I am."

"The 30th of April, 6 o'clock." He leaned down and kissed my cheek. "Nice to see you again, Ella."

"You too. Both of you."

TWELVE

KLAUS

Summer 1967

Since going out to Freddy's Walpurgisnacht bonfire, I had joined him and Lena for dinner two additional times over the summer and once met them at his bar to prove I was not the complete recluse Lena believed me to be. Other than that, I kept working, reading, and walking like before.

Anton's response arrived in early August, close to the sixth anniversary of the wall.

8 June 1967

Dear Ella,
I would be a fool to assume you wouldn't win the affection of another man in my absence. Although my heart will always ache for your companionship and desires to be close to you, I would never stand in the way of your happiness with this Stefan. When will you marry? Have you given up the idea of joining us in the West? Even if he comes with you, I know you belong here. I want you to know what it's like to be truly free. It is indescribable.
I've been offered the opportunity to manage a small construction division. It's on a job farther from the border and closer to Schöneberg,

but it will be a profitable opportunity. I wish you could see it. You might not recognize the changes in me.

I don't know how much news you get from the West and its possible because of what I say this too may not reach you, but something sensational occurred here. Less than a week ago an unarmed student was shot as he protested. He was only protesting, Ella. Killed here by a man who had historical ties to the SED and Stasi. It happened here, in the West where fascism is discouraged! This has stirred quite a disturbance among many —especially the youth. Even Josef's friends have marched. I warned him to steer clear for safety's sake, but he's passionate about his beliefs. Do not worry about him though, he is a very smart young man and uses his head wisely. I will keep you updated. We are safe. I know you face a great deal more harm than we do. You are in our thoughts daily.

Love, Anton

13 July 1967

My dearest El,
Thank you for your letters. Sometimes I don't get post for months, yet every time it has come there has been a letter from you. It is the precise thing I live for. My men know all about you, and like before, can't get me to talk of anything else. You are the best part of my life, and I can't wait until you become my wife.

I have news — it is bittersweet. I have been chosen for special training. I am honored to be selected for the task. Unfortunately, I can only take part of my command with me. The details haven't been disclosed, but I am sure this will assist us in the objective to possibly make a strong future move. Edgar and I, along with six others, leave on the train tomorrow at sunrise to an undisclosed location. I am grateful Edgar is with me, and we will continue our service together. He has become like a brother to me.

What an honor it has been to have my hard efforts recognized. I do not know how long it will be before I can write again, but continue to send your letters to the same address as before. They assure me they'll

attempt to get them to me.
I carry your photograph in my front pocket, the one closest to my
heart. You are the source of my strength, and I take every breath
because of you. I love you, Ella, my wife-to-be.
Please never forget or doubt I am yours.

Love, Stefan

"Breaks up, Ella," Gus hollered from the kitchen. "Lunchtime run is about to begin."

Stefan's last letter, worn and tattered, was carefully placed back in my apron pocket for the second time today. Each time I read it my heart skipped a beat as if it was the first. One correspondence every couple of months was torture. This one arrived five weeks ago, late August, shortly after Anton's. From Stefan's new assignment, I was sure the next one could take even longer especially with no standard protocol regarding the post. Other *NVA* soldiers whom I'd met at the diner said it depended on what company he was with, what training he'd received, and what duties he was assigned. In some cases, letters didn't come at all, so I was lucky to get any.

Retying the sash holding my hair back, I sighed miserably before approaching a table. If only there were more assurance of when I'd see Stefan again, it would make these mundane days seem like nothing at all.

"Are you ready to order?" The smile that found its way to my lips was manufactured. Over time, my skills to produce artificial cheer had become a necessity.

"*Currywurst* for me, *sauerkraut* for her . . . oh, and two *kaffe* please." I scribbled their order on my small paper pad.

"Sweet and cream?"

"One, the other black."

I nodded politely and collected the menus as the man inched closer to his date. The routine had become predictable. *One . . . two . . . three,* I counted with each step toward the kitchen then twisted my head back precisely at the moment he slipped his arm around her shoulders. With glossy eyes and an envious heart, my expression remained unhindered by the time the food order was slipped to Gus.

The flash of my diamond ring in the galley lights presented a tender mercy and silently reaffirmed Stefan's love. The next smile was genuine as I hustled to get the coffee and seat an additional five guests at their table.

In the last several months, Gustav's location had gathered growing interest from the military personnel and visitors allowed to cross into East Berlin, mostly because of the recent changes to the tourist visa and its proximity to checkpoint C. But part of me believed there was an element of curiosity . . . to gawk at the *creatures* behind the fence, like exhibits in a zoo.

Even though the leadership from the East didn't make their motives public, once they opened the border for approved visitors, the locals knew it was a desperate effort to boost our weak economy. The DDR arrangement imposed a minimum exchange of 25 Deutsche Mark to the East German Mark at the time of the crossing with a strict regulation forbidding East German currency returning to the West. With the limited time the visitors were allowed, Gustav's became a convenient stop to spend any unused money from their holiday venture . . . although, over time, people returned on their own for his *Grünkohleintopf—the best kale stew in the borough.*

Rarely, the appearance of any government elite found its way to the diner, which was precisely why I loved working there. It wasn't exactly the type of place confidential political business would be handled. Unlike the strategizing in the Franke home, the conversations here were merely hearsay and gossip. Relatively safe and, to an extent, quite boring.

Another group of four entered. Changing to the afternoon shifts at Gus' had proven to be more beneficial over time, and although my work week consistently averaged over fifty hours, the few tips I received somehow doubled between noon to three.

"Ella, after Eberhard cleans the corner table, seat the new customers over there." Hilde rushed about, an incredibly hard worker at her advanced age.

"Ella! One and two!" Gus was quick but cantankerous today . . . and every day, come to think of it.

I retrieved the first order as Hilde cried from another table, "The *bulletin* is to go; can you take care of it please?" She pointed to a man reading a newspaper on a nearby stool.

"Of course." With the food packed tightly in plastic wrap, it was then placed in a paper sack.

"Sir, your food is ready." I held it out to the man who ordered it.

"Ella?"

Surprised to hear my name, my eyes slowly examined the customer in front of me . . . a man from my past, someone I had thought was possibly . . . dead.

"Klaus?" I gazed around nervously, an annoying habit. "Is it really you?"

"Ja," he said, appearing as stunned as I was.

"It's been a long time," my words choked out.

"Over five years."

". . . and Fritz? Where is he?"

"With me."

"So, you're both . . . okay?" My eyebrows bent, everything seemed surreal.

Klaus shrugged his shoulders.

Gus growled from the back, "Ella, three . . . now!"

I glanced his direction briefly then whispered, "What happened that night?" As close as we were to the border, I should've known better.

"Ella! *Jetzt! Jetzt!*" Gus' face had turned nearly purple.

"I'm coming."

Klaus watched the interchange. "Yeah, I wondered the same thing about you."

He waited for my return then removed his hat and rubbed his head. "Fritz and I are meeting friends tonight at a place called Patz on *Markusstrasse*. I'm sure he'd like to see you."

He appeared much calmer than I remembered. Maturity maybe or fear?

"I . . . I don't know."

Curiosity forced me to pause, yet I couldn't shake the memory of our last visit. *Could they really have gotten away without consequences?* The only real reason *I* wasn't detained was because Herr Franke kicked the police out of his house.

My heart wanted answers, my head saw warning signals. I could not let anyone—or anything—jeopardize my plans of being home when Stefan returned, and somehow seeing Klaus made me feel as though anything could happen.

"Thank you, but I don't think so. It's good to see you, though, and tell Fritz hello."

"It's good to see you too!" He shook my hand. As much as we had been through, we were still strangers.

By the time my shift ended at eight, my inability to get Klaus and Fritz off my mind led me straight to Patz. It was more about answers than anything else. *Where did they disappear to? Did they ever see Simon again? Are they still trying to leave?*

Still in my work dress, I shoved my name tag into my pocket, retied the sash from my hair around my neck so my dark curls would fall across my shoulders to appear more casual, and quickly swept a brush of gloss across my lips. I may not have prepped for a night out, but I also didn't want to appear entirely dull before I stepped inside a pub.

Klaus stood at the bar, his flirty demeanor was uncommonly carefree, a side of him unseen from before. Next to Klaus' female friend, Fritz appeared in serious conversation with two other men. My eyes quickly studied the room on approach. For some reason, my chest burned with the prospect that our conversation could turn risky. With that possibility, my scan for obvious eavesdroppers was tested. The establishment was completely packed. It would be hard to identify an informant . . . they no longer stuck out.

Fritz noticed me immediately and grabbed my hand to join them. This was such an awkward reunion considering our last encounter we were all running and hiding for our lives.

"Ella," —Fritz lifted his drink— "when Klaus told me he saw you today, I was quite relieved. We thought you had—you know—when you didn't return to your house that night."

I nodded, silently reflecting the awful day at the Franke's.

"Yes, I stayed with Lena."

"Christoph's girl?"

"Yes."

"Mmmm," Fritz sighed, "I heard about Christoph." For a crowded bar, the silence that lingered between us seemed deafening. A hasty change to the subject was warranted.

"What about Simon?"

"Don't know. We never heard from or saw him again."

"*Auf Freunde und auf Leben und Freiheit!*" Klaus held up his glass attempting to alter the mood with his tribute to friends, life, and freedom. Others randomly joined in. His "date" giggled with delight. Unclear if they were attached or if they had just met, she seemed smitten either way.

"Oh, Ella, you need a drink." He turned to the bartender before I could refuse. "Another round of Schnapps."

"Oh, not for me. Thank you." My lips pressed together tightly before whispering, "I don't drink."

His eyes grew wide. "Don't drink?" The others stopped talking.

"Uh, yeah. I don't." The response was always the same . . . complete disbelief.

"Okay." He turned to the bartender. "One *wasser,* bitte." Klaus handed me the glass and finished his toast.

"What happened to you?" I inquired again at the first chance. Brassy drum beats from a nearby speaker trounced my words. Moving closer to keep the conversation semi-private, I repeated my question. "Where did you go?"

They glanced at each other and leaned in. Fritz spoke first. "We hid for a long time, first with friends, then strangers, then several months in the basement of an abandoned industrial shop—"

"How did you survive and get food?"

"It was difficult." Klaus was less forthcoming.

Fritz continued, "Once it seemed like they had stopped looking for us, we started over with different names, identities, everything. I'm Lamar, by the way." He smiled and shook my hand, pointing to Klaus. "This is my brother Rupert."

"What about you, Ella?" The old Klaus momentarily reappeared. Trust was a rarity.

I contemplated how much to share. It could have gone altogether differently. Well aware of my timely fortune, I muttered, "I was spared."

"How?" Klaus pushed.

Pain, anguish, grief . . . the list was long . . . memories started to surface. Everything about those days I tried to bury. *Why did I come here to unleash such agony?*

"Painfully." My glare at Klaus was unmasked.

Fritz lifted his glass.

"*An Familie und Freunde.*" Another toast to loved ones prompted others around us to respond cheerfully, instantly lightening the dark mood.

"*Auf das Leben.*" I raised my water glass *to life.*

I excused myself to the water closet. Once inside, my heaving amplified in the stall. Tears fell rapidly. *I shouldn't have come.* The guilt of Christoph's disappearance weighed heavily, a burden I knew would never be relinquished. His fate was solely on my shoulders.

Several women came and went before I could restrain my emotion. In spite of my desire to slip out of the bar undetected, a splash of cold water facilitated my ability to re-join the brothers for a proper goodbye.

"It was good to see you." I kissed Fritz on the cheek, shrouding my inner torment. "I'm grateful you are safe . . . *Lamar.*" His smile preceded an equally congenial hug.

Klaus leaned casually against the bar holding an unlit cigarette. The target of his flirtations was no longer nearby, so it seemed reasonable to place my hand on his arm. "May we part as friends?"

He rotated to face me with dark eyes. A tingle rippled the skin down my spine.

"Of course." His voice was solemn. "Why wouldn't we?" He shook my hand goodbye then returned to rolling the cigarette in his fingers.

With the long walk home, I tried not to think of that fateful night, but it lagged heavily on my mind. *Had they not stolen a van, had the police not shown up for Simon, had it gone as planned . . . would I be in West Berlin? Or would I be dead?*

One thing was for sure though. With either of those outcomes, I would not have gotten to know Stefan. Thin threads it seemed . . . thin threads of chance.

The next morning, in preparation for work, a slight bulge in the right-side pocket of my work dress dew my attention. A small, crumpled napkin had been tucked in next to my nametag. Confused, I unfolded it. In sloppy and hard-to-read handwriting was an address—numbers and an unfamiliar street name. Nothing else was written.

From Fritz or Klaus? They were the only ones close enough without me noticing, and of course, the only ones who knew me. Not Klaus, his suspicion was transparent. Why Fritz though? Could this be a personal address? He could have handed it to me . . . no this was too odd. *Maybe this napkin holds the key to something else . . . something less legitimate.*

Either way, my interest was subdued and the napkin tossed on the shelf. In the past, I would have done anything for a chance to leave the

East. My acquaintance with Klaus and Fritz had come at such a time, an anxious time. I still missed Anton and Josef immensely, but when Stefan's sentence ends, fulfilled, the only place he would find me is here in Mitte, East Berlin.

THIRTEEN

Sᴀɴᴋᴛ Nɪᴋᴏʟᴀᴜs

30 November 1967

Dear Stefan,
Please, be careful. I know you are safe. I have to believe you are
safe, but where you are I do not know. I found solace in a most
unusual way. I stepped into the Marienkirche two weeks ago. The
old cathedral we passed off Karl-Liebknecht-Straße when you were
on leave. I felt peace the moment I entered the front doors. It was an
unusual experience. I moved to a bench and listened to the music and
watched people come and go in prayer, and they would light candles,
hundreds of candles lit near the back. I saw this once before as a child,
but I don't know why, maybe you do. Too afraid to speak to anyone,
I sat there for hours. I have now spoken to a God I am unfamiliar
with twice at home, but I am willing to do whatever it takes to keep
you safe. I don't even really know how to pray. I did not hear thunder
shake or lightning strike, but a calm seems to come over me each time
and it's what I desire with you away from me. The one companion I
yearn for with your absence.

I walked to Alexanderplatz yesterday and although it was far from
the wonderful visit I had when we were there together, you would be
pleased with the progress on the television tower. I sat on the edge of
the Neptunebrunnen fountain for nearly an hour marveling at the
sight. It now extends a good 80 metres or so. Just like you said. The
ministry insists it is meant to bring power and respect back to the

DDR. It will be complete when you return, unless by some miracle I get to see you before 1969. I can't wait for us to be there together once again.

Hold my photograph tight against your heart, Stefan, so I may feel your closeness from here. I look forward to your next letter whenever it will come.

Your love, Ella

I had almost forgotten it was first Sunday Advent until a father present-ed the calendar gift to his daughter over lunch the first day of December.

Upon refilling the man's coffee, I peeked to get a look at the wintry cover. *Sankt Nikolaus* was surrounded by elves, animals, and angels singing atop a snow-covered cabin. The brightness in her eyes rivaled the twinkling stars in the scene and brought similar sentiments to mind when Papa had presented Josef and me with our own, the first Christ-mas we were all together. Anticipation of what would be found behind each door was unparalleled. It didn't matter if it was chocolates or trin-kets, the experience became a fond recollection.

The orphanage honored the Advent countdown, but with only one *adventskalendar*, sharing one chocolate amongst thirty children was not easy. It was while at the Kühns, my individual worth became more ap-parent, gifted with my own calendar and wreath. Papa even let me light the candles by myself.

"Ella, dear, will you be celebrating *Heiliger Abend* with family?" Hilde noticed my interest peak with the customer. She knew of my engage-ment but nothing else about my personal life.

"No, Frau, I have no plans. Stefan is still away."

"You must join us then."

"Oh no, I couldn't. It's meant for family."

"You are family," Hilde insisted sweetly. "Gustav, write down our ad-dress for Ella dear. She will be joining us on Christmas Eve."

Although his reaction was blocked from my view, I pictured his brow scrunched in a wrinkle. It was hard to imagine him being festive over anything but steady financial means.

Since the Kühns passed and the wall went up, this time of year was nothing more than another cold season to me. I kept the Advent wreath from Mama G's house and generally lit the candles in her memory but did little else to separate it from the rest of the year. Hilde's invitation tempted me.

"Are you certain it's not a bother?" My question seeped with reluctance.

"No bother, love. We are happy to have you." Hilde placed her hand on my cheek. She had three grown children, but only one daughter lived in Berlin with her family. Hilde had always shown affection for me above that of only an employee. Her kindhearted touch went back to work, clearing tables.

"Would you mind if I brought someone?" This sudden request surprised even me.

"Anyone, dear."

It could be I missed Stefan or grew weary of being alone. Either way, my agreement to attend resulted from a persistent tug on my heart strings, and it felt good.

The night of Heiliger Abend arrived.

With Special permission from Nurse Margret, Mari appeared at my side. Although not typical for the Waisenhaus children to have such an arrangement, Nurse Margret finally relinquished her permission. My constant needling may have played a part.

As we approached the door of the flat, the sounds of revelry came alive. Mari pressed her ear to the wood. Her expression lit up with anticipation of what was happening on the other side. Despite my gentle knock, Hilde answered quickly and threw her arms around us both.

"*Komm herein! Komm herein!*" She wore a bright red turtleneck sweater with a matching flower in her hair as she sang her enthusiastic invitation inside.

"I'm thrilled you have come," she cried as she swooped up a glass off a nearby table and drank the contents in very few sips.

"Everybody is here!" She waved her hand in the direction of the crowd. It seemed apparent she had not only invited family, but all the odd and lonely she could find. Their home was overflowing with merriment. She motioned for us to enter, and we were immediately met with the strong scent of pine.

"Oh," Mari softly uttered as we caught sight of the festive evergreen

branches, which delicately hung over every doorway. As her gasp graduated to squeals of delight, she scanned the considerable room and pointed out the Christmas tree garnished in the corner. Covered with incan-
descent candles, the flames lit up the ruby colored apples and ginger-
bread ornaments spread throughout.

Floral arrangements covered each table, but the *adventskranz* demanded the most attention. It was the largest wreath I had ever seen,
decorated with pine cones, berries, and a variety of colored ribbon. The
four red candles were already lit with a pile of roasted chestnuts in the
center.

On one side of the room, a small keyboard was being played by an older man with a white beard. He could have portrayed Sankt Nikolaus but
wore a green suit. Two women stood arm in arm singing the words to
Oh Tannenbaum, swaying with full mugs of *Glühwein,* the spiced mulled
wine. The traditional holiday drink was being poured by a girl who appeared to be no older than thirteen. *Maybe she is Hilde's granddaughter.*

"Look, Ella." Mari stopped next to a large display of carved, wooden
angels playing musical instruments. "I like this one the most." She held
up a figure who shared her similar features . . . a child with long brown
hair, brown eyes, wearing a white dress, and holding a large shiny star.

"She's beautiful, exactly like you." One arm wrapped around her petite shoulders. She celebrated her eighth birthday a month ago but had
progressed a great deal in the two years since we met.

We were drawn to the kitchen by an array of delectable foods and
scents. A plump goose centered the main table, flanked by red cabbage,
apple and sausage stuffing, potato dumplings, sautéed mushrooms, and
backfisch. A variety of specialty sweets and confections decorated one
end, and not only one Christmas Stollen but two stretched several feet
across, filled with nuts and fruits. I had not seen a display of food like
this since the Franke house. I imagine being in the food trade helps to
find otherwise unattainable indulgences.

"Hilde, thank you for inviting us." I reached for both her hands and
squeezed. Only days before it had crossed my mind to cancel, afraid we
were imposing, but now after being here for only a few minutes, I knew
we had made the right choice. "Hilde, this is Mari. She's my little sister."

Mari's fingers tightened with the introduction. A glance her direction
revealed her cheeks had turned a rosier shade. We really looked nothing

alike, but nobody questioned. Hilde let go of my hands and reached for Mari's cheek with a small pat and a soft squeeze.

"You are a precious one, my dear."

Again, Mari smiled shyly.

"Mari, dear, did you celebrate *Sankt Nikolaus tag*?" Hilde referred to the traditional December fifth festivities.

"No."

"Well, we can't let that be." She handed her a small boot and pointed her over to a table. Trim it over there and set it under the tree before Sankta Nikolaus arrives." Hilde then added grimly, "And beware . . . *Knecht Ruprecht* will be making his rounds later to make sure nobody has lied to Sankta Nikolaus."

Mari eagerly obeyed. Every child in the orphanage became familiar with Knecht Ruprecht. The demon in our holiday dreams, his job was to frighten children into good behavior.

While Mari decorated her boot, Hilde introduced me to her family and their neighbors.

"This is Ella, our best worker at the café," she announced repeatedly. Of course, there are only five people employed at the café, so the odds of distinction were highly in my favor.

"This is my brother Heinrich, his wife Julia, and their children Jonathan and Clarissa. Our neighbor, Frank, and his wife Donna. Gus' two sisters Henriette and Brigitte on the couch with my nephew Georg. Georg's wife and daughter are across the wall." Hilde said it quite matter-of-factly—I would have missed it if I wasn't listening carefully. My eyes shot his direction while my lips parted to speak. My intention was to say I understood what he felt, only the words didn't come. And even on a night like tonight, when it should be easy to find happiness in the façade of celebration, the familiar void behind his expression was apparent. His thoughts were frozen elsewhere.

After several hours of eating and singing Christmas carols, a loud, abrasive knock on the door had Mari running my direction. The folk myth was about a devilish crew who went door to door to frighten children away from misbehavior. Mari cowered behind me as the door was slowly opened. Three figures with long fur coats, black clay masks, and jagged horns appeared. They were terrifying even to me, an adult.

Hilde noticed all the children had fled in fear. In response, she offered the unwanted guests a hot mug of *feuerzangenbowle*. When presented with the flaming wine as an alternative, they readily accepted it in lieu of tormenting our occupants and moved onto other homes and other families. The moment the door closed, Mari's small hands loosened their grip on my leg.

"You are safe," I whispered, "Now go and see if Sankta filled your boot." While the demons distracted, a very different Gus than the one I see at the café, slyly filled the children's shoes.

"Ella! Look!" Her squeal confirmed her discovery of the small toys and candies. I smiled at Hilde and Gus as they glowed in the corner. All the children giggled in delight at their good fortune of not finding coal in their boots but gummi bears and chocolates instead.

"Thank you," The words were whispered with immense gratitude, pleased I had not given in to my desire to cancel and especially tickled for Mari. Such joy was scarce when I lived at the orphanage. Mari already experienced a better life since the day she had been discovered.

"Mari, please thank Hilde and Gus for their invitation." I pointed them out. "Thank you both, but unfortunately, it's time for us to leave. The last bus for home departs in thirty minutes." Their hallway cuckoo had recently chimed 9:30.

Goodbyes were said to all present, but when we reached Georg, the careful placement of my hand over his was intentional.

"My brother and best friend are in the West. I don't know the depth of your pain, but I have an idea. If you ever want to talk, I would love to listen."

Georg's eyes lifted. A smile appeared for the first time I had seen this evening.

"Thank you, Ella, thank you."

As Mari and I rushed to catch the bus, we both felt rejuvenated. Her with her tiny hands full of gifts and me with a knowledge that someone other than Stefan still cared for me. Gus and Hilde were good people, and I was extremely blessed to have them in my life.

FOURTEEN

"INTO EACH LIFE SOME RAIN MUST FALL"

10 January 1968

Dear Stefan,
Once again a new year has begun without you. My days all seem to
run together, and my dreams are dark as of late. I know I shouldn't
worry, but naturally I do. You are my world and all I can think about is
you returning home safely. I read that the Soviet Union selected some
special troops for elite training at an Artillery Technology Academy.
I don't know if that's where you are, but if so I hope you are safe and
enjoy the training. I pray that it remains training and you will not be
privy to any actual fighting. I understand that relations with China
are strained. Thankfully, nothing seems to have come of it yet.

The Americans and North Vietnamese are involved in a dreadful
conflict. You're probably already aware of this with your military
connections, but I happened to see some horrible images last month in
the press. The villagers had been tortured and persecuted by the Amis.
Women and children included. It frightened me. I never believed
they had such disregard for the innocent. Josef insists it is inaccurate
propaganda, but I don't know what to believe.
I saw Katharina last week — my only delight without you here. I
hoped she had somehow received post from you, only she hasn't as well.

She is stunning and so intelligent; I am sure she will have an offer of marriage within the year. If that happens, I hope you will be able to attend. More for my personal reasons than hers. That sounds quite selfish, but I have never felt such a yearning in my lifetime until you became a part of it.

The tower has reached an unbelievable 170 metres. When I stood in its shadow, it was difficult to imagine its final height to be more than twice that size.

If you get a chance, please try to write me a short note so I may know of your well-being. I love you with all of my heart.

All my Love, Ella

15 Mar 1968

Dear Stefan,
I know I shouldn't write to you about this, yet I have no other outlet for my grief. A customer I had become friends with lost a family member, his cousin Elke, in a tragic shooting in the Spree. My friend could barely speak of the event without losing control. It broke my heart to hear the story. What is equally devastating is the love of Elke's life was also killed by her side, they were shot by the border guard. A man and woman in love seeking a better life were gunned down. How do these men who shoot for sport live with themselves? They are evil, and I only hope they will meet judgement one day. I know this is more impacting in your absence, but I could not bear to survive this world without you. Please come back to me Stefan, please don't leave me alone.

I purchased another album for the phonograph. I stumbled across a jazz singer a week ago when Lena and I went out. Yes, I went to a dance hall although I did not dance. The song is called, "Into Each Life Some Rain Must Fall" The vocalist is a woman named Ella Fitzgerald — great name — with an equally great shade of skin color. She is an independent black woman who sees no shame in who she is or what she stands for. Her lyrics touched my heart deeply. She speaks of the similarities between rain and tears and how this is something we must all experience though some more than others. It is in her words that I am able to find comfort knowing I am not alone in my sorrow. Please don't be disheartened by my loneliness, be encouraged for it is you who I yearn for. Though my days seem dark and gloomy now, it is when you return Stefan, the sun will shine for me.

All my love, Ella

6 April 1968

Ella,
Please do not read all the things that are placed before you in the East. I won't elaborate for fear you won't receive this. You must trust me and Anton. We would not lie to you.

My university classes are challenging. I think of you often when we study passages from poets or orators that I'm unfamiliar with. I am sure you could explain the meanings without hesitation. Next semester I'm taking a philosophy class, and to really enhance my university experience, an accounting class as well. I'm not skilled with numbers. Thankfully Anton's ability to measure and calculate in construction has proved to be his strength, so he has offered to tutor me. His employer has been quite pleased with his abilities, and his small team has now grown to over twenty. He continues to ask of your welfare but other than that he seems immersed in his work.
I look forward to hearing from you soon.

Love, Josef

10 May 1968

Dearest Katharina,
I hope this letter finds you well at school. I know I haven't written you often and I'm sorry for that. It has nothing to do with you, it is a social disorder of mine. I'm afraid I am too willing to let others do all the work in a friendship and that I know is unacceptable. You have always been so good to visit me when you are home for holidays. I'm sorry your duties kept you away this most recent one, but thank you for the stationery gift, it arrived just days before Christmas and was a wonderful surprise.

How are your studies? Have any boys or should I say men now, swept you off of your feet yet? Speaking of men, I have not heard from our beloved Stefan in quite some time. Many months have passed without a word. Maybe he has found the time to write you and if so would you be so good as to fill me in. I worry for his safety, he is as you know everything to me. Enough of my wants, I do wish you the very best in all your accomplishments. Write if you can.

Much love, Ella

24 May 1968

Dear Stefan,
I hope you are well. I hope you are learning much and becoming the soldier you desire to be. I'm sure they see what I see, an amazing man! The common hop has sprouted again, and a woman was holding an arrangement of forget-me-nots in her hands when we passed on the street today. It made me think of you and all the times you not only brought me some, but the picture you drew our last night together. It continually brings me joy as they are my most favorite flower to see in the summer. I plan to visit our secret garden this weekend, the one in Volkspark near Friedrichshain. I can't wait to see the butterflies again. I have been painting as well. Hilde has offered to purchase a few of my butterfly paintings for the diner.

Three days ago, I was approached by a businessman about working at his restaurant called Zur letzten Instanz in the old district of Mitte. It's possible you have been there, but I have not and understand it to be a well-liked establishment. I'm not sure why he would come to me although he has become a regular at the café in the past few months. He is a nice man and offered to pay me more than Gus can pay. He said in tips alone I could make my monthly wage in one week . . . and it's fairly close to my flat. I have considered this. Gus and Hilde are good to me, well mostly Hilde is, but it might be time for change. Let me know what you think, sweetheart. Your opinion means more to me than anyone's. I have so much to tell you, I can't wait to see you again.

All my love, Ella

1 June 1968

Dear Ella
You are perfectly fine. I know you have adult responsibilities and do not expect you to cater to my query needs. I do miss you, I miss our visits in the library, sharing books, stories and secrets. I have not met anyone here remotely close to my Ella, no one feisty or daring enough. While there is much I miss at home, I absolutely love school, I am involved in many activities and have found quite a skill in the sciences, Physiology is my favorite, I suppose that is a family trait. I have dated several men, but nothing serious has come of it. I do not expect that anything will unless I happen to cross him in the laboratory hovering over a microscope classifying blood cells . . . my medicinal prince charming!

I have not heard from Stefan myself for quite some time, but Ella, do not fear his absence, love, or devotion. It is unequivocally centered only on you. When he is able, he will write to you, I know he loves me as his sister, but you are the only woman that has possession of his heart.

Do not be a stranger, sincerely, Katharina

5 September 1968

Stefan,

I'm unsure if you are receiving my posts. I haven't heard from you in over a year. I read that the NVA has been involved in a few riot control skirmishes and border conflicts, nothing too serious. I don't believe you are there since you might have been called elsewhere due to your secret training, only I can't help but worry. It's built in I'm afraid. You are the love of my life and I could not live without you, so I hope your health and safety are of no concern.

I also read that many young men here in Berlin were pressed into military service for Moscow's response to Prague. So maybe you are there training these new soldiers. Wherever you are, I know we are meant to find each other again when your service is complete.

I'm no longer at the diner—I took the position at Zur letzten Instanz. Established in the 1600's it's one of the oldest restaurants in Berlin and although nestled tightly behind a church and accompanying graveyard, it commands quite the patronage. The clientele is a wide range from soldiers to officials and even American or British diplomats who cross the border just to eat here. It's rumored that Napoleon, the great French Emperor himself, frequented our little establishment. The food is some of the best I have tasted in my whole life. I receive a free meal every shift. It has been quite some time since I have been offered so much, aside from you my love. I will continue to save for our dream after we wed, the one we talked about. It will happen, I know it will come true. Please just send me word that you are well.

All my love, Ella.

24 December 1968

Stefan
Merry Christmas, my love. We may not be together, but you are all I think about. Please send me word of your safety. Nineteen months have passed with no word, yet nothing has led me to believe you are

in harm's way, The NVA has moved towards Berlin and I hope there is some truth to the rumors of another parade and respite.

Mari sends her love to you — I share my memories with her and it brings all those happy days forward as if it were yesterday. She knows you are the reason she is alive. You would hardly recognize her now. She is growing like a weed. At nine years old, her beauty is astounding, and her strength continues to improve.

From the restaurant I have become friends with two local NVA soldats who are familiar with the inner workings of the Volksarmee. They have offered great council and comfort while I await your word. They continue to assure me that the privation is normal and not to be alarmed. Yet as the silence grows, I cannot help but worry. I miss you, Stefan.

All my love, Ella.

25 March 1969

Stefan

Please write to me. I'm afraid. I miss you more than words can express. I watched for you at the parade. I arrived hours before and remained late, well after the last remnant of anything military related rolled away. The next three days I roamed the streets from dawn to dusk. My heart leapt each time I saw a man in uniform — which was nearly every minute of the day, but you were nowhere to be found. I even went as far as sitting on a bench across the street from the Franke home to see if you would appear, but nothing happened. I still live in the same flat in Mitte for the very purpose you will always be able to find me, yet with no sightings, your absence now terrifies me. Were you here? Has something happened? Please, Stefan, please write to me.

All my Love, Ella

27 April 1969

Stefan
Another shooting at the wall and another 3 medals of valor, only this
time the soldiers received accompanying promotions as well. I know I
should be careful about what I say, that these letters are probably even
read by some who believe the killing is justified. It's revolting and
heartbreaking and only compounded more with your silence.

Please write to me. Please assure me of your health and welfare. I
can think of nothing else each day. Please don't make me suffer with
no word. Just one short correspondence would bring an immeasurable
amount of peace to my soul. Just one.

All my Love, Ella

12 May 1969

Stefan
Fear has taken control. What I had believed to be real no longer
comforts me. If you have changed your mind about us, please tell me,
please just share your intentions so I may at the very least know you
are alive.
Please?

All my Love Ella

2 July 1969

Stefan
Do you still love me?

Ella

My hand trembled with restlessness the moment I set my pencil down.
Those words, ***Do you still love me?*** somehow coursed through my veins
like a poison, dousing any kind of vitality along its path. I reached for my
purse and scrambled for the door.

A desire to be in a place that filled me with life and breath consumed me. I practically ran to Volkspark. The pathway that led to the fairytale fountain felt narrow and stifling, yet the closer I got, the more unrestricted my tears came.

Children happily giggled and danced near the clear cascade, but my only focus was the lane behind them. My pace quickened under the arch and rashly I maneuvered through the foliage, but once I reached the opening of the butterfly garden, my hesitation prevailed. Will this bring the resurgence I need or the torture only a bygone memory can offer?

Pushing a wayward branch aside, I stepped through. The sensation of entering a different realm was triggered by the familiar flurry of colorful wings. My eyes closed to the subtle waft of movement all around me. The soft kiss of their touch, mixed with the warmth of the sun, brought a peace to my soul I was sure had perished. I crumpled to the ground, fatigued, while my ever-growing fears surfaced, uninhibited.

"Where are you, Stefan?" My cries grew louder with each word. "What has happened?" My shriek diminished to a whisper. "Are you alive?" Each of my limbs extended freely outward as if the world did not exist on the other side of the shrubbery. The beauty of my isolation was filled with flowers, leaves, twigs, and the full weight of rumination.

The unknown had become a slow, torturous descent into the darkest crevices of my mind. I remained subdued on the ground for hours, the soft grass beneath me turning cold once the sun slipped away, its light reduced to only a glowing sliver of orange through the oak leaves that swayed timelessly above me.

Despite my desire to never stand up again—to just relinquish all I possessed—I knew life carried on with or without me. And while without me seemed so much more appealing, I forced myself upright, left the shielding protections of the private garden and reluctantly returned home.

18 September 1969

Ella,
We haven't heard from you in over a year. Our posts have gone unreturned, so I can only hope they are reaching you. We heard of another brutal escape attempt that failed and worried momentarily that you had changed your mind and decided to try but I recall you had resigned to never leave the East because of your beloved, yet we haven't gotten word of your marriage or anything else. Please Ella do not turn us away. We think of you every single day.
How is your fiancé, Stefan? Does he realize how lucky he is? He must know. He would be a fool not to. I cannot help but feel envious of his position.
Josef has nearly completed two years of university. He is bound and determined to find a legal way of getting you here. Please consider coming home to us. It will never be the same without you.
We see the tower over there in the East. It doesn't matter where we are in Berlin we can look up and see its shadow over us. It must be 300 metres high! At first, West Germany believed it to be another source of infiltration to the allied sectors but later learned it was for broadcasting — although I hope they are not so naïve to believe it doesn't have other unspecified duties.
With as much as you read, I am sure you have heard the news about the rocket ship reaching the moon, but I just have to say I am still in shock. An astronaut actually walked on the moon! Of course, the Soviets pushed to be first but in the end it was the Amis! The excitement here was unbelievable. People were tuned in all over, gathering in stores, homes — even churches brought radios out for everyone to hear the words, "That's one small step for man, one giant leap for mankind!" Of course, the greatest "leap" would be for someone to tear down this wall.
Please Ella please write and let us know of your well-being.

Love, Anton

I let the letter fall to my floor, then let my head fall to my hands. He speaks of Stefan . . . *Stefan. Does he even remember me?*

FIFTEEN

HE LOVES YOU!

Fall 1969

It has been twenty-eight months since I last had contact. Could it possibly be that he was killed, and I was never notified? His comrades knew me—they would not have failed to find a way to tell me of a tragedy. Katharina would have informed me. Therefore, it must be worse than I imagined, and he no longer cares for me and did not have the strength to tell me himself.

I pulled my jacket over my blue uniform dress and walked to the bus stop. My shift at Zur began in less than an hour, but as the 109 approached, I hesitated; answers were needed.

Instead of waiting for my own bus, I boarded the 109 and rode it straight to Pankow. When I saw Katharina last, a little over a year ago, she mentioned that she was leaving school to help her father with the duties of the mortuary. As I approached the back entrance of the building, I hoped that was still the case. If Herr or Frau Franke happened to appear, I could not retreat. Inhaling sharply, my legs stiffened and bolstered my shoes into a determined stance atop the cement stairs. Nothing could stop me now. *I need to know.*

I knocked firmly, but with thinning patience, the wait lasted barely a second before I knocked again.

When a strange man in a white physician's coat opened the door with little room to spare, I huffed in surprise. He stared at me blankly. "Yes, may I help you?"

"I—I'm here to see Katharina, is she in?"

"She is . . ." His eyebrows curved skeptically. "May I ask who is calling on her?"

"Ella Kühn."

Instantly, those same eyebrows lifted with surprise. "Ella? You are Ella?" As he reached out to shake my hand, the door flung wide open.

"Katharina!" he cried, "Katharina, come quick. Please, Ella, come inside." I was slow to move, taken back by this unusual response.

Katharina came around the corner and gasped at the sight of me. It had been too long since I had seen her last, yet she didn't wait another moment and lunged for me, her arms wrapping my shoulders tightly as she buried her face in my hair.

"Ella!" she whimpered. "Oh, I have missed you."

After several seconds she released her clasp. Her eyes gazed lovingly on mine then she reached for my hand. "Please come." Her quick steps led me down the hallway towards the office—the office Stefan once occupied. The same room we kissed, we craved, we argued . . . and where I spoke to Anton last on the telephone. This room, even the little time I had spent here . . . somehow became the site of many significant events in my life, and despite Katharina's personal touch, memories of Stefan leaked from every corner.

"Please sit. Tell me everything. Where have you been? What are you doing here? Where are you working?" She hardly took a breath in between questions. It was strange looking upon the woman Katharina had grown into. At twenty-two she was so beautiful and seemed quite strong.

"I'm a waitress at Zur Letzten Instanz," I finally spoke.

"Zur Letzten Instanz? What a wonderful place!" Katharina stole a quick breath and called for the man who had opened the door. "Love, come here, meet one of my oldest, dearest friends."

"I know," he laughed. "You talk about her so often it's as if I already know her!"

"Ella, this is Edmund, my husband!"

"Husband?" I choked out.

"Yes, we married three months ago. I gave Lena your invitation."

My lips pulled into a tight line. I had withdrawn from everyone in the last year, including my closest friends . . . even Lena. We hadn't spoken in over nine months and I'd never informed her of my job change.

"Nice to finally meet you, Ella." Edmund extended his hand once again.

I met it with a planted grin. "Where did you meet?" I asked with feigned interest. I truly cared for Katharina's good circumstances, but had trouble focusing.

Edmund chuckled. "In the laboratory."

Recollection of Katharina's own words in the letter describing her ideal man came to mind. She had found him! Fighting the bitterness, my eyes observed the way she longingly regarded her husband. As he leaned in to kiss her, it appeared as though they forgot I was present. They were the snuggly lovers I was jealous of.

"Was Stefan at your wedding?" I interrupted anxiously.

"Stefan?" Katharina's face scrunched unnaturally. "No . . ." She scrutinized me carefully.

"Not even a letter?" My cheeks grew warm.

"No."

"Why wouldn't you hear from him for your wedding? You are very close."

Katharina glanced at Edmund. He squeezed her hand.

"I haven't heard from him since the last time you asked, but even then it had been much longer . . . 1967, June, I believe." She let go of Edmund and reached for me. Grasping both my hands in close to her chest, she stammered faintly. "Are you telling me you haven't been in contact with him either?"

My head shook dazedly as tears lined my cheeks.

Katharina squeezed tighter. "Nothing?"

I wiped my nose on my sleeve just before Edmund handed me a hand-kerchief. "No, Katharina, no word since his letter dated 13 July, 1967."

"We assumed he had cut off all ties with us." She led me to the couch and directed for me to sit.

"Why would he do that?" I cried. "You're his family."

Katharina stared at her hands. "Because . . ." she stopped herself.

"Katharina, because why?" I demanded.

She straightened her skirt; her hands shook nervously in her lap. Edmund slipped out and left the two of us alone.

"Please tell me why."

"Because my parents would not accept your engagement and commanded that he break it off at once." Her words were straightforward, but her face showed signs of anguish. "They were adamant about the separation, especially if he wanted an inheritance."

"He never told me," I whispered. My eyes closed, but the tears still dropped at a steady pace. *Why didn't he tell me?*

"Stefan is a gentleman, and the last thing he would ever do is break your heart."

"Yet, here we are." My lips quivered. Katharina rubbed my cheek as I mumbled, nearly incoherent, "I assumed your parents wouldn't be happy, but—"

"Oh, Ella," —she cut me off— "*I* was happy. I was thrilled when I received the news from my mother, despite—"

I buried my face with my hands. This was more than I could bear.

"You have to believe me when I say he never cared about the money. It was always about you. *He loves you.*"

My sobs accelerated with those words, the increased wetness weighed the handkerchief down as my fingers squished it tightly in my fist.

Katharina stood and moved about the room. "What do you suppose has happened?" she muttered. My eyes followed her movements with growing alarm. She noticed and quickly reworded her statement. "I'm sure nothing has happened, and they just have him very, very busy." She pushed some papers aside on her desk and located a newspaper. "I did read that a select group of Special Forces soldiers were sent to the Soviet Union to train. He could be there."

"Yes . . ." A sudden surge of energy lifted my face. "Yes, in his last letter he mentioned a special training. Maybe that's it. He's not even in Germany and can't get word to me." My deep breaths brought little relief as my thoughts filtered to the possibility of treacherous conflicts in the Soviet Union.

"Yes, I'm sure that's the case, because I know Stefan nearly as well as myself, and your love is the only thing he lives for." She walked back over to me and wrapped one arm lovingly across my shoulders.

Guilt, mixed with relief, washed over me, especially knowing that I wasn't the only one who hadn't heard from him. His own family knew nothing as well.

"I was just worried, Katharina. It's been too long; I didn't know what to think."

Katharina jumped up and hustled over to the desk. Fumbling around in the center drawer, she finally pulled something out.

"This should erase any doubt you could ever have." She handed me an envelope although it was addressed to her.

28 June 1967

Dearest Katharina,
I do not know when I will be able to send post again, but it is imperative I tell you how much I love you. You have been the greatest sister one could ever ask for. Please care for mother and father and the mortuary as I would, had I been there. With time they will need more assistance, and I cannot predict when I will be privy to return to my duties at home.

Being a soldier has been an honor, and although I arrived at this position by challenging means, I do not regret my actions the night I found Ella. I would do everything all over again if it meant she was safe. She is the very reason I draw breath. It's her face I see in my dreams and her arms I hunger for. I know this might be difficult with your distance and school but visit her when you can. She is the only future I see.

With Love, Stefan

To see Stefan express his truest feelings to someone other than me suddenly immersed me with foolishness for suspecting his devotion.

I carefully folded the paper and attempted to hand it back, but Katharina held up her hand. "No, please keep it. Read it every day if you must."

"Thank you," I whispered, embarrassed. "I'm glad I came here today."

Katharina squeezed my hands. "I know without a doubt Stefan loves you and will be home soon." With a giggle, she continued, "You'll marry, and we'll both have squirmy little children who will play together daily."

I forced a grin.

"You will see, Ella, this is nothing at all and please forgive me for not visiting you. Stefan would be disappointed in me."

"I believe you have been a bit busy." My insinuation forced her to laugh out loud. "Besides, you are the only reason I had any of his letters before his respite, and we are indebted to you for that."

I hugged her tightly again then opened the door to leave. Edmund was unloading some crates in the hallway and stopped to say goodbye.

"You're a lucky man, Edmund." I patted his arm. "She is a beautiful *schmetterling*."

His radiance could not be rivaled. "Yes. Yes, she is. Nice to finally meet you, Ella."

He and Katharina walked me to the door. "Please, Ella, please do not stay away long!" Katharina pleaded. "Anytime you need me, come to the mortuary. Neither one of my parents step foot in it anymore, and you will always find me or Edmund here. We will always be here for you!"

"Please visit me as well," I added readily. "I'm often at the restaurant." We kissed each other on the cheek and agreed to meet soon before we said goodbye.

I meandered slowly towards the bus stop, and while I wasn't as distraught as before, the question still arose . . . where was Stefan? Two and a half years and no word. It seemed impossible to imagine an affront in light of our time together, his declaration of love, and even a proposal.

Stefan asked me to marry him, to wait for him . . . where could he possibly be?

SIXTEEN

FAMILIAR FACES

The next day, I arrived earlier than expected for my scheduled shift at Zur and quite apologetic. In all the time I had labored at either restaurant, I had never just not shown up for a shift, so I was unsure as to whether I would even have work when I returned. Employment was unpredictable in the East—many vacancies, yet equally as many dismissals.

Conrad, the manager, had always found me to be a very hard and responsible worker. The threat was evident, however. If I ever repeated such reckless behavior, he would not hesitate to release me. Eagerly, I accepted his warning and immediately went back to work.

For an unusually warm day in late September, the increase of patrons in the afternoon hours confirmed the belief that the food at *Zur*, even in the garden, always outweighed any unpleasantly-high temperature. Nearly all of the *biergarten* tables in the patio were filled by noon, and the shade from the large oak tree and its copper-colored leaves provided minimal relief from the cloudless sky. Whether I was sweating from the humidity or the rush, I found myself constantly seeking relief in the form of the cold closet or linens. Still, I was a mess.

"Ella," Conrad called to me at the end of a very short break. "I have a specific request for you."

I paused. I knew I couldn't refuse anything due to my recent actions. His eyes carefully glanced over my harried appearance.

"We have some special guests arriving for a two o'clock lunch, and I would like you to be their waitress."

My brows tapered with slight confusion. I had no trouble serving anyone who was sent to my area.

He continued, "They'll be dining upstairs. I need you and Angelika to trade places." *Oh, now that made sense.* Angelika was a good worker, although she was a little rough around the edges. She spoke like she worked in a bordello rather than a sophisticated restaurant like Zur, yet many patrons loved her sass, so it was generally not a problem. *This group must be government.*

"I mean no offense, . . ." he stumbled on his words, ". . . but do you think you could appear a bit more presentable?"

Definitely government. Laughing, I nodded and side-stepped towards the bar. "Is there still an extra uniform in the back room? I'll change immediately."

When I approached the table shortly after they were seated, familiar faces greeted me. My countenance carefully hid an internal cringe. Of all the people in the DDR, it had to be these three. Seizing a quick breath, I moved around the table taking their requests for drinks.

"Ah, it's the Grist twin," Herr Mielke announced with delight. As the other two peered up from their menus, Mielke continued, "You know, I met Fräulein Grist once after her performance in *Ariadne auf Naxos*. She was spectacular . . ." He was speaking to the other men but made sure I heard him. "Do you sing my dear?"

I shook my head. "No, sir. May I bring you a drink?"

"Vodka. Vodka all around. We are celebrating!" It was obvious I was supposed to respond, but I was afraid to know the details of what he considered a celebration. "It's a beautiful day, we have a beautiful waitress, and we are about to dine on the best food in Berlin." He was so loud that all patrons within earshot reached for their glasses as if he was making a toast.

"Koen, what is your maid's name?" He could have easily asked me, but I was accustomed to the way women were treated. It didn't surprise me.

"Her name is Fräulein Kühn, Erich."

"Kühn, huh?" He smiled wide. "Why in the world would you let her go, Koen?" He leaned over to Herr Wolf. "I would very much like to see her cleaning my home every morning." Herr Wolf chuckled, contrasting Herr Franke's frown.

I excused myself to get their drinks, but what I really needed was some oxygen. Down the stairs, I stepped outside and leaned my pounding head against the corner of the sole red brick wall in the courtyard. It was damp and cool. Angelika came to my side.

"You alright?"

I nodded then sighed.

"You look like you could use a pint!"

My eyelashes lifted with a giggle. Angelika could always make me laugh.

I couldn't really place my reason for not drinking before the incident with Anker, it just never seemed appealing, but after the attack, it was more revolting than ever. Yet, there were times I wondered if I drowned my sorrow in a bottle of liquor, could it possibly help me forget?

"Look, El, if you want me to take care of those *stickig* politicians, I know exactly how to handle them."

I laughed again. It would be our ticket out of here, but it would be a pleasure to watch.

With a shake of my head, I patted Angelika's arm. "I've got this. Thanks, though."

Balancing the tray of drinks up the spiral staircase, I inertly approached their table.

"Yes, Wolf they are meeting in two days." Mielke didn't acknowledge my return as he leaned inward to speak to his comrades. I placed his drink in front of him and moved around the table, trying to ignore their conversation.

"Do they know it's an arrangement?" Wolf responded.

"The informant insisted they have no knowledge of our awareness."

"Then we will proceed as planned."

Herr Franke interrupted. "Thank you for the drinks. I believe we are ready to order." His eyes remained on the menu.

"Chicken vegetable soup and squirted beignets for me," Mielke declared.

"An order of Pork knuckle with lamb sausage," Herr Wolf followed.

"Make that two," added Herr Franke.

"Oh, and we cannot overlook the caramel-stuffed cream puffs . . . for all, please." Mielke chuckled, removing his eyeglasses.

I scribbled quickly, anxious for my time at their table to pass.

"Do you listen to music, Fräulein?" Mielke reached for my arm.

I wasn't quick enough. My skin prickled at his touch.

"Yes, some."

"What musicians do you fancy?"

I glanced up. All three pairs of eyes were waiting for my answer while Mielke's fingers remained curled around my wrist.

"Edith Piaf."

"Ohhh," Mielke snickered. "Yes, her voice is quite soothing."

His companions nodded in agreement.

"The *Republik* finally got those *Scheisse* Beatles banned." Mielke let go of me and shook a finger at Herr Wolf. "Their devotees were uprising. It should have happened much earlier."

"Would you like some more vodka?" I attempted a smile, anxious for an excuse to leave.

"Yes, keep it coming, dear. Wait . . ." Mielke continued to talk to his party despite his request. "Can you believe that Arsch, Biermann? Awarded the Fontane prize, then publicly passing it to the *Außerparlamentarische Opposition*."

"Just like Schneider," Wolf conceded. "These musicians think they can say or do anything. They believe they're outside of our reach."

Herr Franke noticed me lingering. "What is it you needed from Fräulein Kühn, Mielke?"

"Ah, yes." He turned to me with a grin. "Make it two orders of beignets, please."

Making my way back to the kitchen, I found Angelika smoking a cigarette halfway outside the back door.

"What are you doing, Angelika? If Conrad sees you, he will be irate . . . smoking near the cooking?"

"I'm mostly outside," she chuckled. "Loosen up, Ella. You're too uptight."

My mood instantly lightened; she was one of a kind. "Hey, Angelika." Although the space was already narrow, I leaned a little closer. "Do you know what the *Außerparlamentarische Opposition* is?"

She stared at me shrewdly. "The APO? Why?"

"I just heard it mentioned and didn't know what it was."

"Of course." She wrinkled her nose and tapped her cigarette. A piece of ash hit my shoe. "Your government boys up there probably have quite a distaste for it. It's a growing opposition group, mostly students in the West that fight everything the SED stands for."

"Why would musicians be a part of it?"

"They're artists. They put their frustrations into their lyrics, like *Chausseestraße 131*. *Liedermacher* had to record that in his flat with a smuggled microphone and a tape recorder. He had been blacklisted from the *VEB Deutsch Schallplatten* because the Socialist Party did not agree with his choice of poetic words."

"VEB Deutsch Schallplatten?"

"The state music publisher. *Gott*, Ella! You read all the time, how do you not know anything about music?"

I shrugged my shoulders. "It's just not important to me."

"I will change that." She tossed her remaining cigarette butt to the ground and stepped on it. "Next time I go out, you're coming with me."

Out of fear, my pupils doubled in size. Visions of Angelika forcing me out of my safeguarded existence emerged.

"I'm going back to work." I thanked her with a kiss on the cheek and grinned shrewdly on my way back to the dining area. Angelika somehow had that effect on me.

Two hours later, the men stood to leave, Mielke motioning for me to come over. Per Conrad's request, they were to be my only customers, and because their meal was on the house, I didn't expect to be tipped as well.

Arriving with a plate of apple cakes for their departure, I set it down before them and proceeded to clear the empty dishes when Mielke reached for my hand once again. My teeth bit my lip as he raised it to his fat lips. A crumb of bread hung at the corner, and I tried not to cringe as his mouth rested against my skin.

"A pleasure, Fräulein. Please compliment the chef for us. He outdid himself this time." Mielke smiled then walked away.

Wolf tipped his hat and departed with his comrade. Only Herr Franke lingered.

My eyes attempted to divert but caught peripheral sight of his hand leaving his pocket and extending my direction. I glanced at a bill tightly rolled like a cigarette. He shook it towards me then nodded consent for me to accept. As my fingers retreated with the bill, it unraveled and the numbers 50 peered back at me. It was a fifty Mark. I had never been tipped that much by any table in one night. With each passing second it felt heavier in my hand. My eyes stumbled from the money to the man.

"For you . . . and Stefan," he mumbled and reached for his hat.

Tears came quickly to my eyes. *Why?* I wanted to scream. *Why would you say for me and Stefan? You don't even want us together.*

As he moved farther and farther away, I grew antsy then gave in and rushed after him, catching him at the bottom of the stairway.

"Herr Franke?"

He paused.

"May I speak with you?"

He considered the other men, who nodded and walked ahead.

"I just thought you might want to know . . ." My hands trembled at my side. ". . . I haven't heard from Stefan since 1967."

Emotionless except for a small wrinkle that suddenly appeared on his forehead, Herr Franke questioned quietly, "Two years?"

"Over two, sir." I stopped myself from chewing my bottom lip then continued. "His last letter said he had been chosen for special training, but he never said where. I haven't heard from him since."

Herr Franke's hand slid up his cheek to his balding head.

"He isn't angry with you, he has . . ." —the words choked out— ". . . disappeared."

Although the news wasn't good, Herr Franke appeared relieved. His lips pulled together after releasing a small sigh. It's possible he had been carrying a great deal of regret believing Stefan *chose* to disassociate.

"Let me give you the Marks back." The bill was now folded around my fingers.

He held his hand up. "No, it's for you." Replacing his hat, he joined his party outside.

That evening, when I stepped out of Zur and onto the cobblestone street, the strong scent of pine from the nearby burial ground drew me close. The wrought iron gate was ajar and enticed me to stroll uninhibited in tranquility until the bells rang precisely on the seven o'clock hour, reminding me of the bell tolls from home. Not the flat I lived in now, but my Bernauer home, so instead of walking to Max-Beer, I caught the tram in Alexanderplatz and rode it straight to Acker.

Lured by the sights, smells, and remembrance of the happier times with the Kühns, Anton, and Josef, I meandered towards our flat, but instead of finding the five-story apartment building we called home, a ragged pile of shattered concrete, metal, and brick faced me.

Our place had been demolished, along with two others nearby.

Struggling for breath, I hobbled towards a bench across the street, my eyes shifting painfully from the pile to the reinforced wall. Images of our life in that home materialized; the window Anton and Josef left through, the books, toys, phonograph, and cuckoo clock, as well as the couch Papa died on . . . all gone. Only the shadow of the church of reconciliation remained, even Friedhof Sophien had been altered. The entire front of the cemetery had been cleared.

This ugly concrete divider had taken so much from me and continuously tore a hole in my heart, yet as I watched from my perch, it had somehow become just another part of the city.

My astonishment grew when several school girls not more than twelve or thirteen years old skipped past the barrier as if it were a row of trees. Not a glance its direction, nor a cower or shiver when the soldier with the black rifle walked past them; in fact, they giggled and smiled in flirtatious acceptance. *Have we become so accustomed to its sight that it no longer affects us?*

The life of the wall now spanned eight long years, seven years longer than I ever believed it possible.

I studied the tower—one soldier carelessly shifting his weapon around as he tried to roll his cigarette, the other motioned to three women as they walked by, whistling at their shorter than normal skirts . . . a third and fourth soldier whooping over some amusing tale. Only one squaddie narrowed his attention through binoculars towards something in the *sperrzone*.

I remembered the day when the sound of gunfire was as steady as the flock of birds that left the spree every winter. Now, the barrage of bullets happened only on occasion, but when it did, you knew it was for one sole purpose.

My stare prolonged. Somehow, we allowed this evil edifice in, and by some means it had become a natural monument in our lives. The very thought shook my core. If we remained this tolerant, it might never vanish.

SEVENTEEN

ASSAULT!

3 January 1970

Ella,
The other day I stood next to the wall in front of the church of reconciliation. My only memory inside that place was when Papa and Mama took us there for Christmas Mass the first year you were adopted. Do you remember how mad you were that they woke you up for it? So mad that you blew out every candle you passed and stomped all the way to our bench. Then you spent the entire sermon moaning so much that we left before it was over. I'm not sure if that's the reason we never went back, but my guess is that it was. I have so many great memories with you. You made my childhood unforgettable.
Near the church is a viewing platform. I've stood on it before, but it has been years. Could we please meet? I know it's hard to plan with the unpredictable post, but I'm going to go there every Sunday at 12 noon for as long as it takes to see your face. If you can, please come, sister. I miss you!

Love, Josef

The paper felt heavy or more likely my conscience added the extra weight as I read Josef's letter. I no longer wrote to anyone. Despite my heartache and desperation, I stopped my attempts for answers from Stefan. If he was alive, it seemed apparent a choice had been made that no longer included me. Yet, this new year marked the emergence of his three-year mystery and nothing to confirm his existence.

If he really does still love me, like Katharina insists, wouldn't he try to reach me somehow?

While my heart and soul fought the confusion, it also strived to block out others I cared for, especially Anton and Joseph. With so much emotional turmoil, it was easier to ignore correspondence than pretend all was well. I envied their lives, their opportunities, and their constant bliss. I shut myself off from the world despite their constant pleas for answers.

29 January 1970

Ella,
Are you well? We haven't heard from you in a very long time. I — we — are very worried for your safety. Please, Ella, we need to know if you are alright.
How is Stefan? Is he good to you? Please write.

Love Anton

"Ella!" Conrad called for me. The tone in his voice indicated he wasn't pleased. With no recollection of any particular slip-up lately, I heeded his request and approached his office quickly.

"Yes, sir?"

"You have a letter here." He pressed it roughly into my palm. "Please do not have your personal correspondence sent to the restaurant. We are not your postal box!"

"I—I didn't give it out." I bit my tongue. Arguing with Conrad was not wise. His door slammed near my face.

The handwriting was familiar. My curiosity battled my reluctance and eventually won. As I stepped outside, the temperature was below freezing, but I didn't want others to know my business. My thick gloves prevented a speedy removal, and eventually I reached the simple note.

13 February 1970

Ella,
Why do you shut me out? I am worried about you. I am sorry to bother you at work. I was afraid if I showed up in person you would refuse me.
Katharina told me of your visit and where you now work. She also told me the terrible news that you had not heard from Stefan in quite some time now. That must be heartbreaking.
Please, Ella, I am your friend, please let me comfort you. I miss being a part of each other's lives. Please, I need to know if you are okay.

Lena

The last time I had seen Lena, a year and a half ago, she and Freddy had announced their engagement. Characteristic of their unusual unification to begin with, it was celebrated at the *Kulturpark Plänterwald* Amusement Park. Of course, the key word was *amusement*, something that had become quite foreign to me. I was truly happy for Lena but failed miserably as a supportive friend.

My attendance spoke volumes of my selfishness. I craved relief from the guilt borne over Christoph, hoping Lena's new love could offer this, yet on the other hand, witnessing her and Freddy's open affection was a clear reminder of the ongoing happiness I mourned.

I had become a thorn on her rose and the pebble in her shoe, incapable of laughter, joy, or even common decency, and after an hour of miserably attempting to fake enjoyment, I skipped out on the anticipated thrill of the new Ferris Wheel and left without even saying goodbye.

7 March 1970

Ella,
Josef is worried sick and I as well, please reach out to us soon. We
cannot bear this absence of word on your safety. You are my best
friend. Please Ella, please write to us.

Love, Anton

Having remained unopened for over a month, I piled Anton's letter with
the others then located my stationary in an unused pile of its own on the
shelf. As I pulled it down, something small fell to the floor. A crumpled
fabric layered in dust landed on my shoe. Assuming it was garbage, I
reached for it. Bits of black ink appeared as I flattened it against the arm
of Mama's chair.

Recognition of the mysterious address I received the night I met up
with Klaus and Fritz materialized. Although partially faded from two
years ago, the numbers were still readable. Grabbing my pencil and paper, I slid to my knees and leaned against Mama's seat for use as a table
and began to write.

19 June 1970

Dear Anton and Josef,
I am fine. I'm sorry I stopped writing. It was selfish of me to be so
childish. Stefan and I are no longer together. I don't even have a
reason for it, but I will be fine.

I paused. *I was not fine.*

I believe I detached from everyone because I struggle to understand
where I belong.
I continue to work at Zur, I read when I am home and do little else
now. Do not be concerned. I have been through tougher times before
and survived. I miss you both immensely.

I studied the napkin as I held it loosely between my fingers . . . *why did Fritz and/or Klaus give this to me? Why didn't they just talk to me about it?* It had to be something secretive they were involved with. A foolish thought . . . and what was equally ridiculous was assuming they would still be there. If they had found a route to the West, they would surely be gone.

Josef, please forgive me for being self-centered. I look forward to hearing more of your progress and the wonderful things you are experiencing in school. I miss you. I hope to see you soon.

Love, Ella

The letter was placed in my purse. The napkin too, regardless of how irrational it was to hold on to.

That night I went to a bar with Angelika and Felix *the cook*, the man she was currently dating. Although my bitter mood about socializing hadn't changed over time, I yielded under Angelika's grating insistence. She was like that annoying windup toy dog that yaps until it runs out of turns.

"I ordered you a Pilsner." Felix proudly set the bottle before me. He was just trying to be nice but didn't know me well enough to know about my aversion to alcohol.

"I don't drink." This sentence had become an exhausting staple over the years. I really needed to develop a better response.

Angelika spit her mouthful all over the table. "At all?"

"No," I said matter-of-factly as I snatched a napkin and wiped my arm. Tired of telling people why, I had no intention of elaborating.

"You just might be the only woman I know who doesn't drink," Felix snickered as he grabbed the bottle and gulped it quickly before I changed my mind. He wiped his mouth with his sleeve and laughed. "Even my twelve-year-old niece can down a pint pretty quickly."

Shrugging my shoulders, I twisted my back towards them. I didn't like him much at work, and it was apparent I wouldn't like him much away, either.

The music suddenly seemed louder. My watch displayed 9 o'clock.

The lively beats of what I was becoming familiar with as rock and roll filled the room. Despite government manipulation to regulate it, the music brought many patrons to their feet and to the tiny dance floor. Resentment consumed me. Stefan promised to take me dancing. I tuned everyone out and swayed to the rhythm as if I were all alone.

My solace was short.

"I want to set you up with my friend, Kalin," Felix mumbled in an unsettling voice. I glanced back to a disturbing smile. His eyes betrayed him as he scanned my figure. I placed my palm against my forehead and groaned. *What am I doing here?* Felix had asked me on a date the first time we met, but I refused three times holding my ring in his face. He finally turned his attention to Angelika. I never mentioned this to her.

"No, thanks!"

"He's your type," Felix tested me.

"Excuse me? What's my type?" I questioned, irritated.

"Men with money." He grinned slyly, his tongue licked his upper lip.

My nose crinkled, lips pursed, and I held back what I really wanted to say. "I'm engaged."

"So, you say . . . but I've never seen you with anyone."

"That's none of your business."

"He's a member of Congress, a *neue Politiker*." Felix's gape hung below my neck. I wanted to slap him.

"Who?" I snapped.

"Kalin!"

"Then definitely, no. I want nothing to do with politicians!" I tried to concentrate on the music. *Am I still engaged? Can you be engaged when there's no contact? I shouldn't have come. I'm not good in places like this . . . or around people like this.*

"The Rolling Stones!" Angelika cooed to the newest song reverberating in the background. "Ella, did you hear about the concert they were going to have in the West?"

Their beat was energizing but I had never heard of them before. I motioned no. This should not have come as a surprise to her after our last conversation on music.

"Yeah, the people's police reveled in detaining hundreds of teenagers near the border just because they showed up on *Leipziger Strasse* to try and listen over the wall."

My eyebrows curved downward in confusion. "Just because they wanted to hear music?"

"Yeah, but the Stones never showed, so basically the people were arrested for waiting to hear a concert that never happened."

"Arrested?"

Anjelica pulled out a cigarette and lit it. "They threw the kids in trucks and some still haven't been freed after eight months." She didn't even bother to ask me if I was okay with the nauseating smell of smoke. I tried to ignore it. Puffs blew out her mouth and nose as she continued. "My youngest cousin Axel was sentenced to two years in prison—he's only 16!"

"Two years for standing on the sidewalk?" I didn't think there was much that would still amaze me in the East, but this news definitely did. If the government was that aggressive when the music didn't play, how much worse would they be in a place that *actually did* play the restricted music. I shifted uncomfortably while my eyes darted around the room, yet everyone seemed quite relaxed here.

"So, how should we celebrate your birthday?" Angelika changed the subject easily. It was apparent she cared little about any music ban.

"My birthday?" Her question rattled me.

"Yeah, next week."

"H—how would you know that?" My eyelashes fluttered wildly before they froze in suspense.

"Really, El?" She inhaled effortlessly. "There are no secrets at work. I slept with Yan from the office." Felix gawked at her, his shock matching my own.

"Look, that was a month ago, okay?" Still holding her cigarette in her fingers, she grabbed the long neck of the bottle for another swig.

I hadn't had many friends outside of Lena and Katharina, therefore, her openness about her sexual freedom was astonishing. Despite Stefan's absence, I still held on to the belief that someday he would be the only one I'd give myself to.

Angelika found her way over to Felix's lap. She boldly straddled it and kissed him seductively. I tried looking everywhere except at them.

Angelika giggled as she came up for air. "So, what are we going to do?"

"For what?"

"*Scheisse*, Ella! Your birthday, *um Gottes willen*! How old are you going to be anyway?"

"Twenty-five," I muttered. She was referring to the date the Kühn's gave me—it was just a day. It didn't mean anything to me.

"Twenty-five and a virgin," she proudly announced. Anyone within earshot instantly tittered.

Heat flared my cheeks and slipped out my open mouth in less than a second. Even though her brazenness was typical with others, I'd never been her target.

Maybe I really don't need friends.

"Verdammit!" rolled from the tip of my tongue as I tossed a Mark on the table. Heatedly, I yanked my purse off the chair and headed for the door. What I really wanted to do was throw something, even break something. My hair stood erect on the back of my neck as I shoved the door open, nearly hitting an incoming customer, and although it was Angelika's ludicrous comment that got me riled, the wrath came from deeper within.

Very few people appeared on the now-darkened street. I fumed irritably against the nearest wall. *Why did I even come?* Angrier at myself more than anyone, I pulled my sweater tightly across my chest as a warm summer rain started to fall.

"Ella!" Angelika busted out the door.

I hustled around a corner.

"Ella! I was just joking!" she yelled, although from the sound of its distance, she made no attempt to follow.

Being that Angelika lived only a few streets away from me, I had hoped to not walk all the way home alone, but she wasn't worth the wait. My previous path was chosen knowing that, most of the time, police presence meant there was always security.

Shuffling along the walkway near the wall, my movements appeared trancelike. My feet had followed these same steps many times. Sometimes alone, sometimes—in happier times—with Stefan and even with Anton before the wall went up. *Anton! Josef! The letter.* I meant to send it today. Reaching into my purse for it, I felt the napkin from Patz. Moving closer to a nearby street lamp, I pulled it out. Using my head to shield it from getting wet, my fingers slowly rubbed over every word then number.

The diamond in my ring reflected the light and sparkled like new drawing my attention from the napkin. Conflicted, I glanced back and forth between my two hands. One held the possibility of a new life and the other . . . a life I no longer recognized as my own.

The band spun slowly as my thumb moved methodically against it. Closing my eyes, I slipped it off my finger. My mind justified the move painfully, but the moment the ring landed in my purse, it echoed a simultaneous assault on my heart. A nearby cement wall became my ballast, cold and rough against my forehead, the napkin held tightly between my fingers. *Do I have a choice? If Stefan no longer wants me and there is the remotest possibility I could make my way to the West, shouldn't I find it?*

With determination, I set out immediately to locate the address. I knew logically it was a ridiculous quest. At least two years had passed, an impossible inquiry, but I could think of nothing else as I made my way towards the unknown neighborhood in Friedrichshain.

Well after 10 o'clock by the time I reached the particularly run-down neighborhood, only the smell of rain remained in the air. The drizzle had stopped, but my hair hung heavy and wet against my shoulders. With my eyes alert, I passed numerous neglected buildings that reflected bygone eras of usefulness, both factories and office buildings alike appeared fragmented and dark. My resolve to unravel this mystery outweighed the truth of my vulnerability. Each step I took, echoed both a cheer and a scolding.

My brown oxford shoes maneuvered through rubbish piled ankle high along the streets and spread well into the weeds and rubble. Bundles of fabric sacks lined broken, deteriorating benches. Brief glimpses into the hollows of the cloth revealed faces and bodies of the vagrant poor.

All the times I'd walked alone, I never felt so uncomfortable. I was lost. Guardedly, I slipped into a small pub unlike those closer to home, but its bustle provided an element of comfort. Slightly cautious, my decision to ask for help outweighed wandering the streets for hours. I stepped to the counter and presented the address to the barman.

The man's brow raised. His wariness apparent upon my approach.

"I'm looking for someone; can you direct me the correct way?"

"You aren't from around here, are you?" His bushy mustache shrouded most of his mouth, his grimace appearing only on his lower lip.

"No." I didn't want to share anything else. "Can you direct me to this address?"

He drew a map of the streets on his own napkin then added, "You should get on home girl, this is no place for your kind."

I wasn't quite sure what he meant by that. My skin color, gender, maybe the way I dressed? My outfit, a light blue woolen sweater with knee length pencil skirt, was stylishly modest, but it proved I should be out socializing and not strolling alone in a strange place.

Thanking him I left, my carelessness evident, yet I couldn't resist. I was angry with Angelika and Felix but mostly Stefan. The sting of rejection, even assumed, currently outweighed any concern I had for myself.

The location wasn't far, although once I arrived at the supposed correct address, it still seemed wrong.

Surprisingly, only two streets from the border, the building seemed to be an abandoned, ramshackle structure. *This must be mistaken, or I'm too late.* Klaus and Fritz may have lived here once, but no longer. I scanned the two buildings surrounding this one, and they too appeared empty and unkept. Frustrated, I hustled across the street. Maybe there would be some indication it had life from a different view. Atop a decent pile of cinder blocks, I attempted to see past the overgrown shrubs blocking many of the lower windows, not even sure what I was looking for . . . a light possibly . . . or movement.

Clank! A noise immediately pulled my attention to the blackness of a narrow alley. Squinting, my eyes struggled to identify the source through the darkness. Goose bumps formed on my skin as a small shadow—perhaps a dog—swelled in size. Even though everything in my head told me to run, I tiptoed on to the street. It wasn't until the figure stood completely upright that a startling chill descended down my spine. The silhouette of a man now faced me from the shadow.

Glancing down the empty street, I staggered backward. The barman's words pulsing like a beacon in my head. This is no place for your kind. Unable to get my limbs to move fast enough, my foot hit the curb, and I tumbled backwards to the concrete, leaving one shoe in the gutter. For a brief moment, the only sound I heard was my heavy breathing then suddenly a low grumble emerged and swiftly graduated to a full laugh. It came from him!

Paralyzed, I cowered as the man got closer. Everything seemed to move in a slow spin, and despite the repeated cries in my head to move, I froze.

"Well, well . . " The sneer of a vindictive tone crowed loudly. "What a lucky find!"

The crude flesh of an old wound appeared as he turned his face towards the sole streetlamp. Panic smothered my chest, instantly cutting off my airway. When I found my breath, it spurt erratically.

It was Jurek! He was alone, but so was I.

His confidence surfaced in the way he paced his approach, slow and purposeful as if there was no one to challenge him and he had all the time in the world. My fingers frantically scratched the ground at my sides, desperate to gain steadiness.

Now, completely in full view, the smirk on his face widened. Keeping my eyes fastened to his every move, my peripheral vision caught the rapid rise of my chest. My mind hysterically whirled with an impossible prospect of escape. Even if I somehow coerced my body to move, it wouldn't be fast enough.

Just as I got my legs to scramble upright, Jurek leapt my direction. His icy hands caught both my arms, his grip clenching fiercely. With Stefan he cowered, but with me he dominated.

"Oh no you don't," he barked. "Not this time!" His laugh filled the silence of our surroundings. "And this time, there's nobody here to stop me. Anton's not here and neither is your soldat junge!"

My mouth opened to scream, but only a weak gasp escaped. I tried to slip through his fingers, but he only held tighter, causing my arms to lose circulation. My leg swung wildly attempting to make contact anywhere it could, but the blow to his shin was weak.

He yanked me closer. His deformity only inches from me, I tried to turn my head, but he released one hand to firmly grab my jaw and force my eyes forward. "Look!" he screamed. "Look at it!" I squeezed my eyes shut. This only angered him further. "What? Afraid?" Saliva sprayed me as he spoke. "You think you're better than me because you're not scarred? Anton thought he was better than me too.

Shoved to the ground, the pressure from Jurek's boot pinned me flat. With a flick of his wrist, my eyes flashed open to a metal blade . It was a knife! My mouth formed a cry for help but inaudible, it only emitted weakness.

"Let's see how you like having people stare at you!" he shouted. My body wriggled laboriously side to side, channeling all the strength in my torso towards my hands. My fingers fought fervently to pry his boot off me until his free hand strapped my neck down as well. His grip choked me. Flashes of black and white images flickered behind my eyelids.

A shrill screech sounded in the distance. My mind wanted to believe it meant something, but clouded and confused, consciousness was slipping fast. The shriek repeated, followed by a shout. Jurek's grip on my neck loosened long enough for me to push his hands away. I scooted frantically backwards on my butt, putting little distance between us. I followed Jurek's glare from me to someone rapidly approaching. His lips arched with repulsion then his body shot upward. His final glance my direction told me this would never be over.

"*Stopp, sofort!*" The demands to stop came swiftly as two men rushed the scene, their whistles blowing long and brash. Startled, Jurek hustled back into the shadows and rapidly disappeared. One of the men made a feeble attempt to follow but stopped and returned.

Placing my hand to my throat, it felt strained and sore. Besides my torn stockings, a quick examination of my legs and arms proved the bruises and scrapes were only superficial. I refused to imagine what Jurek had initially intended.

"*Geht es dir gut?*

Stunned, I peered up into the faces of two border patrol. I was alright but too frightened to answer their question. Instantly I clambered to my feet and raised my trembling hands high into the air. My eyes flashed to the guns slung over their shoulders.

"Fräulein?"

My body quivered.

One soldier stepped forward and gently pushed my hands down. "We aren't going to shoot you." His voice and subsequent smile were soothing. "Despite what you may think, we're not all hungry to kill. We—"

"This area is off limits," the other soldier, not as friendly, cut off his comrade. "You must remove yourself at once."

"I'm sorry," I stammered. "I think I got lost looking for a friend. Then . . ." my voice trailed off as my eyes flickered back to the alley where Jurek had both appeared and disappeared.

"Yes, Fräulein, this is not a safe place for a woman alone." The calmness in which the first soldier spoke was conflicting. On one hand, he put me at ease. On the other . . . he reminded me of Stefan.

Tall with a rugged build and broad shoulders, his appearance should have been intimidating, but when he grinned, the curve only reached halfway. *Breathe!* Just like Stefan, only the emergence of a deep dimple on his left cheek separated them. Blinking repetitively, I couldn't stop staring. It *wasn't* Stefan, and I knew that, but it took everything I had to look away.

"Are you alright?" He retrieved my lost shoe and knelt to replace it on my foot. My movements were mechanical at best, dazed by what was happening. When he reached for my hand, I easily gave it, and he led me away from the dark alley and the direction Jurek had fled.

As we passed the original building that brought me to Friedrichshain in the first place, the flutter of a curtain, partially-hidden beyond an overgrown bush of Bishop's weed, caused my eyes to do a double take. *Did they see that? Did I see that?* The subtlety of the fabric's movement could have been imagined, but my gut told me otherwise.

"Where are you headed? Maybe I could show you the way?" the handsome one offered. I pried my eyes from the distraction and back to the border guards escorting me out.

"I will be off my station in ten minutes, and you really shouldn't be alone in this area."

Sensing the weight of his eyes upon me, I tried to ignore his persistence. He didn't know me well enough to make assumptions. I used to live in Treptow for heaven's sake, accustomed to being alone on rough streets. Yet, the confrontation with Jurek proved it doesn't matter where I am, alone is risky, and if they hadn't come when they did, I don't know what the result would have been. I shuddered at the thought then quickly released my hand from his clasp and shoved both my hands in my skirt pockets.

"Please allow me to walk you home." The kind soldier repeated his offer to assist, "I want to be sure you really are alright." I studied him carefully; his complexion remained smooth and free from the wrinkles that dishonesty seemed to produce when concealing something. My pause may have given him hope, but my hesitation came more from astonishment than consideration.

"Um, no, thank you. I'll just head home now." What I actually wanted to do was return to the building and see why it appeared abandoned and occupied at the same time. Only that was currently impossible.

"Where is home?"

I hesitated. There are positives and negatives to sharing too much personal information with anyone, much less border guard. He seemed innocent enough, but so did many of the informants who sell their secrets.

"Not too far."

He stopped walking and smiled again as he faced me. He might have thought this was a game, but staring back at that familiar smile, my heart confirmed. This was no game.

"Where?"

"Mitte."

"Really? I do too," he responded, pleased. "What street?" The friendly soldier pursued, although the other guard grumbled with opposition.

"*Max-Beer*"

"I live on *Rosenthaler*. We are practically neighbors."

"Hans," —his fellow soldier shifted uncomfortably— "we need to finish our rounds. She needs to leave."

"What's your name?" Hans ignored his comrade.

"Ella."

"My name is Hans." He reached out and shook my hand. It was a firm handshake. "I'm leaving soon, I should walk you home. This is no place for a respectable woman."

His willingness to help was a bit unnerving, especially since he happened to be my least liked soldier of all the military. My thoughts shifted to the two young border patrol back at the Franke's who had earned medals of valor for killing an innocent man. I could never have any respect for border guard.

"I will be fine, thank you."

He tipped his hat and grinned again. His resemblance to Stefan irritated me, mostly because he was border guard but also because it forced me to think of him. Shame crept in as my eyes reluctantly swung to the indent on my finger where the diamond ring had rested only an hour earlier.

I waved goodbye then hurried down the street to board an approaching bus. It didn't matter if it was the one I needed or not. Anywhere but here was an improvement.

That night as I laid in bed, there was much to ponder . . . the movement in the "vacant" building, Fritz and Klaus, Jurek and his vengeful threats, my future, and even Stefan . . . confounded now with the interference of a border soldier who happened to resemble him.

Out of thousands of soldiers, how is it that the only one I encounter tonight happens to have a minor resemblance to Stefan? *Is this my answer?* Should I not be pursuing whatever it was in Friedrichshain? With heavy eyes I turned to imagine Stefan watching me from the other side of the bed, his voice whispering sentiments in my ear and his touch caressing my hair. Somberly, my fingers inched towards the pillowcase. I knew very well it would be found empty and cold but caressed it longingly just the same.

EIGHTEEN

ELLA, YOU MUST BE CRAZY!

"Why do you need a knife, Ella?" Felix questioned from the kitchen. His grating voice rose a bit louder than I wished.

"Shhh, Felix, please."

"Just tell me why first."

"I want to feel safer . . . you know, walking alone at night and such."

His eyebrows pinched together. "That's it?"

"Yes, for personal protection only."

"Why so hush then?"

"I just . . . I don't want everyone to know, that's all."

"Alright." Felix shrugged his shoulders. "I can get it to you by Monday, but if you get caught with it, don't tell anyone it was me."

"Okay, thanks."

On my way out the door, he added, "and I'm willing to accept payment . . . other than Marks."

"No." I didn't even turn around. If there were other options, I would have gone to someone else, but my acquaintance list was rather short, especially those who might have access to restricted items. Getting any kind of personal weapon was difficult, and since I intended on going back to that neighborhood and the vacant building again, I would not be unarmed this time.

After three days of carefully watching the evening border patrols off *Melchior* and *Engel* in Friedrichshain, with an added alertness for Jurek, I finally found the nerve to approach the questionable building myself.

Pressed against the nearest alley wall, everything about this moment brought a heavy ache to my chest and tears to my eyes. My thoughts overwhelmed me, even maddened me—the memory of Jurek in the shadows, the border guard who came to my rescue, even the idea that I was pursuing the possibility of escape—but not enough to force me to retreat.

With my senses wary, my ears remained vigilant for sounds from behind and in front. Tension mounted while waiting to hear the steps of the next patrol pass. Once the solid sound of boots against the pavement closed in, the familiar strain on my throat constricted. It could have been anyone . . . even Jurek.

Imprinting my lower lip with my teeth, my breath halted as if under water. Nothing in and nothing out. A small bead of sweat on my brow trickled down my cheek and hung on the edge of my jaw before dropping to my dress. Another one began the same path as whispering voices grew near. With limited view, I labored to discern the topic of conversation, hoping it would shed some light on the identity, yet their low mumblings prevented it.

Once the steps moved farther away, I finally exhaled. The rapid thump of my heartbeat took longer to recover. As I patted my face with my sleeve to remove the excess wetness that had formed, my sighs seeped weakly. *How many chances will it take to learn it's not a good idea to be alone in such places?*

My naked wrist reminded me I'd forgotten to wear my watch today. Counting silently to a hundred before extending my head out, the street was devoid of movement, so I daringly crept my way to the front. The handle of my newly acquired knife reassured me as it pressed firmly in my grip.

The old, rusted door moved easily under the gentle push of my palm. For something quite worn, it should have made more noise. Its condition piqued my interest. Touching the hinges, a small amount of oil residue soiled my fingers. *It's been maintained recently.*

I wiped the grease on my skirt then reached into my purse to retrieve a small flashlight. In a hallway similar to my old flat, the recognizable scent of rotten wood and mold satiated my nose.

The small beam of light revealed peeling plaster, cracked tiles, and massive cobwebs that slowed my progress through the initial entry.

Shuffling hesitantly forward, my thoughts wandered to my Bernauer apartment in Mitte and was reminded of its deteriorating condition before it was demolished.

In the next room, my miniscule light hardly reached the ceiling or the back wall, its size stunted me. Fragmented machinery dotted the floor along with piles of wood, concrete debris, and a heavy layer of dust. Nothing seemed to separate this particular building from every other abandoned structure in the city. *The address must be wrong.* Discouraged, I headed back towards the front door when faint voices erupted down a narrow hallway.

Images of Jurek and his friends suddenly filled my mind. This was precisely the type of place Anton used to take refuge in when he lived on the street. Trembling, I flipped my light off. Through an upper window's distant moonshine, I tiptoed behind the silhouette of a large pile of debris and crunched low to my knees, berating myself repeatedly for my foolishness and the risks taken for answers.

Although controlled, the mutterings echoed in the hollow space. Afraid to look, I kept my body curled tight and covered my head with my hands, not that it would prevent discovery but was more about feeling terrified.

The intense conversation slowed to a purr the closer it got.

"What's the time?" an older raspy voice questioned.

"10:45"

The two conversing were clearly male, but the second one sounded much younger than the first.

"Jonah had overnight, what do you think happened?"

"Don't know"

"Is it clear outside?"

"It should be, the inspection time was nine minutes ago, let me check the window."

Between the rustling and heavy breathing, their movements paralleled mine. Something seemed amiss here, their conversation didn't sound like Jurek's type—homeless or destitute. Why else would they be in an abandoned building late at night?

After what seemed to be a safe amount of time—well after their footsteps moved away and the door closed shut—I emerged to an even darker room. The moon was either hidden by clouds or moved high above the building. The thought of what might have happened had I surprised them with my presence made me shiver. I was well versed in what happened to those who were suspected of being spies or informants.

I flipped the flashlight on again and snuck down the back corridor, careful not to flash the beam anywhere near the windows. Two rooms on the right had been caved in, one had boards leaning in the opening that created a small, dark pocket. The room on the left was completely empty, and the space at the far end was filled with old tools, but no other exit was found.

Where did those men come from? They appeared from back here somewhere, but everything seemed to come to an end.

Wandering the rooms again—poking around the equipment, cabinets, and tables—nothing seemed out of the ordinary. Frustrated, my steps led me back to the empty room, scanning for any kind of irregularity, still nothing. As I turned to exit, my light beamed on the room behind—the one with the small, open space underneath what appeared to be unsteady boards leaning against the frame. It was big enough for a person to get through.

I hesitated. *Ella, you must be crazy.* Crouching to my knees, my light flashed through but could not reach the end. Blackness strangled my tiny stream of light. *What if someone is still here?* I tried not to think of the consequences, driven with a curiosity to know what these people were up to. My suspicions were probable, yet I needed to know.

With the flashlight tightly between my teeth, I crawled on all four limbs underneath the boards. Surprisingly, I managed it easily with room to spare, not even touching what appeared to be fragile wooden slats. It was a good ten steps before another room appeared, filled with debris though not a cave-in as assumed. I stood upright. Concrete blocks and rubbish challenged another small entry but didn't completely obstruct it.

Maneuvering past and down that hall, a circular stairway came into view. Again, the blackness was impenetrable with my torch, yet my step to the first metal rung was without hesitation. My fingers clutched the railing as if I would plunge to my death. Each subsequent step, a chill nipped upward, and a slight breeze fanned my skirt as I descended. Emotion swelled my chest. What would I find? What lay ahead?

When my foot reached a dirt floor, I spun around to behold a few chairs, a table, and an unhinged door lying against the wall. Rubbing my cold arms, I stepped closer to the door. My fingers reached out and ran along the edges, but as I gripped it, they turned ice cold. I pulled the door carefully towards me as a frigid draft escaped. With a wider rift, a black corridor appeared, blocked by a small cart filled with dirt. My heart nearly stopped.

A tunnel!

Overcome, my pulse raced fervently, and despite the colder temperatures, sweat emerged above my nose and lips. I pushed the door back to its original position and turned to the table. My light revealed pages of plans including a complete schedule of the border patrol checks and posts. There was no doubt this was an escape plan, and if Klaus and Fritz were somehow involved, this could change everything.

As I backtracked my way out, my contemplation of the discovery grew more perplexing. Questions surfaced that hadn't been asked in years. Could I really leave? If I was involved, could I actually take steps to leave Stefan and go to the West? Then a troubling notion developed . . . was I really leaving him, or had he already left me?

Once I reached the main hallway again, I paused. Even though there was access to the notes of the soldiers rounds from below, without a concept of time, the information did me little good. If I got caught, the secret would then be at risk.

With the door propped open only a sliver, I scanned the obvious direction . . . all clear, now came the hard part: the blind side. I twisted and listened. The street sounded empty, but within seconds, shadows appeared with heavy footsteps. I assumed the movement belonged to the patrol, but out of view, it could be anyone. It could even be Jurek. Gently, the door was closed and my back pressed solidly against it. *How am I going to get out of here?* Even if I were to slip out undetected, I would still be in Friedrichshain well into the night—something I had already learned could be quite risky.

After contemplating my predicament, my resignation was clear. I would spend the night. It wasn't the worst place to camp—thinking back to the time I slept in the closet after the Bernauer apartment was raided.

With a quick examination of that first vast room, I located pieces of loose plastic wrap. Laying it flat against the cold concrete floor, my search began for something soft to lay on top of it. Underneath what appeared to be a sewing machine of sorts, shredded pieces of stuffing were piled ankle high. When I reached for it, a mouse scurried between my legs.

My scream caught before it reached my open mouth. Rodents were not scarce in my building, but I had managed to keep them out of my flat. Sitting atop the closest table, it took several minutes to bring my heart rate back to normal. It wasn't necessarily out of fear, merely uninvited freedom to crawl on me at night.

I weighed my options, which were basically only two. Stay here and face whatever night crawlers there were or leave and face whatever lay beyond those doors. I stayed.

The only three metal chairs I could find with all four legs and a seat bottom were retrieved then lined up like a bench. Taking the plastic and fabric, a new bed was built, one that was not against the floor but risked open vulnerability.

Once horizontal, my sweater pulled tightly around my torso, sleep eluded me. Not because of the shadows that danced or the strange noises that creaked through the walls, but because of the energy that suddenly flowed through my veins.

The idea of finding this tunnel, a channel to the West—back to Josef, back to Anton—played over and over in my head. Yet simultaneous to the images of a long-awaited reunion, another vision gradually edged itself in. Stefan. Seeing his carefully concealed emotion, I struggled to discern his reaction. Was he happy or sad for me? Speculation governed until my eyelids grew heavy . . . then dark.

NINETEEN

You Aren't A Spy, Are You?

"Get up!" A sharp object poked my shoulder. My eyes opened to two men hovering over me.

I shuddered and fell off the chairs to the ground. Stealing quick glances about, recollection of the night's events resurfaced. My sights settled back on the men as I jumped to my feet. I shrewdly studied the offenders. They were regular men, not strabenkind or border patrol. A quick breath of relief slipped from my lips.

"What are you doing here?" The man with the graying beard was gruff. "You are trespassing!" He continued to poke. I yanked the stick from his grasp and held onto it.

The other man, noticeably younger but sharing similar features, spoke with a much nicer tone.

"You shouldn't be here, Fräulein." He held out his hand.

I carefully considered the two then grabbed it and allowed him to hoist me to my feet.

"Thank you," I mumbled brushing cotton strings off of my skirt. I stretched my back until it cracked; the makeshift bed had not been too comfortable.

"Get out!" The older man, near my height, stepped up and tilted his face clearly too close. "Leave! Go find a shelter or something!" he demanded seconds before I shoved him backwards. Surprised, his fists curled, but I stood my ground.

"I'm looking for my friends, Klaus and Fritz. I was given this address."

The younger one stepped between us. "We don't know anyone by that name."

I rubbed my aching head . . .*what are their new names?*

"Rupert!" I cried, remembering how Klaus' name reminded me of a character in a book. "Rupert."

They passed a look that confirmed I was right. Butterflies began to dance in my stomach.

"He did not!" Graybeard nearly shouted while he paced. The younger one had difficulty suppressing a smile. I handed him the small napkin with the handwritten address then added, "I'm not lying. I'm sure you know them. Where are they? Where are my friends?"

Graybeard's complexion turned nearly purple as he spit, "Leave or I will contact the authorities."

"No, you won't," my counter came swiftly, "I know about the tunnel."

Both men's expressions showed varying degrees of panic. "*Scheisse!*" the older man huffed angrily and paced again, then glared at the younger one. His finger shook aggressively. "Leave it to Rupert to want to bring on another woman."

"Is he here?" My eyes lifted.

"No!" he shot back.

Biting my lip, I swallowed my desire to insult him. Whispering with restraint, I turned to the nicer man, "Will he be here today?"

"He doesn't arrive until dusk," he answered but was abruptly interrupted by the older man.

"Who else have you told of this? Friends? Family?"

"Nobody!" I hollered.

"Shhhh, please?" the younger man pleaded. "Please lower your voice."

I conceded for him and continued, "I only found the tunnel last night. Besides, I don't have anyone to tell. My family isn't here. That's why I want to leave."

We all stood still as the light began to shine through one of the nearby windows. Even through the torn sheets for curtains, the room began to take shape. The men peered silently at each other until the nice one spoke. "Please wait here a moment." The two retreated to a back room. I could guess which one had the more heated whispers while I waited.

A reasonable amount of time passed before one returned.

"I'm Ian." The young man held his hand out to shake mine. "He is my father Telfer." Ian pointed to the older man who disappeared into a different room. "My mother and sisters are in the West. They were on holiday when the wall went up. We've been trying to reunite ever since."

Ian's warmth was genuine, and I smiled in return.

"Forgive him. We have gotten little sleep lately."

I nodded as he led me back to the room with the fake cave-in and down the spiral staircase to the hole. Telfer was already there and with mild acknowledgement started to light a handful of lanterns.

"My name is Ella."

"Who are your loved ones on the west side?" Ian laid out a bag of tools from a crate underneath the table.

"My brother Josef and friend Anton."

"Friend?" His lips curved slyly, like he was insinuating Anton could be a lover.

"Yes, a good friend." I grinned back. His kindness was welcoming.

"And you have no family here?" Ian heaved the heavy door aside to reveal the dark opening, and like the night before, my chest pounded rapidly as the tunnel came into full view.

"No," I muttered with an attempt to push Stefan's face aside but failed.

"Here, follow me." With one hand clasping the handle of a lantern, he used his other to pull the dirt cart out before we stepped into the hole that I was too afraid to explore hours earlier. The temperature dipped with every step. In an attempt to conceal my shivering from Ian, both arms folded tightly across my chest. I feared Ian would notice and walk me out. I wanted and needed to see this tunnel. Every three metres or so, wood planks lined the cold dirt walls and ceiling. My hand grazed the sides gently as the opening grew too shallow to stand.

"We're approximately 150 metres away from the goal."

"That means you're barely to *der todestreifen*," I gasped.

"Yes," he whispered, "we estimated at least three hundred to get through the death strip and the second wall from here."

"I thought the progress was much farther." My disappointment was evident.

Ian appeared surprised. "What do you mean?"

"Well, it's been over two years since Klaus . . . I mean Rupert handed this address to me. I hadn't seen them since. I just assumed they were successful and on the other side."

"Why do you keep calling Rupert, Klaus?" Ian's eyebrow lifted suspiciously.

I stuttered, "That . . . was . . . the nickname he had . . . years ago. Remind me what his brother's name is?"

"Lamar?"

"Oh yes, Lamar. I remember now."

"Digging is much harder than it looks, Ella; it is a tediously slow process."

He pointed to the support planks. "These alone take many hours. We scavenge the wood from other buildings."

"Are they necessary?"

"Yes, since our first cave-in nine months ago that took the lives of two of my friends, we're trying to do it right and safe."

"But why choose a building this far from the border? Why not choose one closer and save time? It seems you have added on a year's worth of work that way."

"The border guard are near, but they don't regularly check the insides of these buildings, only the ones at the very front. They believe the same as you, nobody would dig from here. It would take too long."

I thought about that logic. True, it might take longer, but it's possibly safer. "How many people are working on the tunnel?"

"There are six of us . . . well seven if you join, but it is incredibly dangerous, Ella. The border guard are everywhere on the streets, and more than that, informants and spies alone are hard to track. You aren't a spy are you?" he chuckled, half-joking half-wanting to see my reaction.

"It wouldn't be the first time I was accused." My answer surprised him. "Only accused *against* the DDR," I quickly added.

He smiled. "Well, can you help us dig?"

"I . . ." I stumbled on my words. I didn't think it would be that hard to answer, but it was. The first thought that emerged was about the promise I made Stefan to not leave the East, yet that was so long ago, a different time . . . a time when I really believed he still loved me.

Ian watched me carefully. "Is there a problem?"

"No." I shook his hand. "I'm ready to go."

He led me back out of the tunnel and over to the table. Piles of paper remained scattered like I had seen the night before. He pulled one from the group.

"Here, look at this. These are the times we have been most successful. The louder work can be done when the daily noise of automobiles and business is awake; however, the more detailed and precise quiet work is done at night.

"No wonder you're tired. When do you sleep?"

"We don't dig every night. We rotate."

I scanned the paper carefully. "You are sure of these patrol times?"

"Yes." Ian reached for three identical documents. Nothing has changed in six months. They are like clockwork, but you must memorize these times. You cannot make a mistake."

"Do you think it will work?" I questioned once we were back upstairs. "Do you really believe we can get to the West?"

"It has to," Ian said.

"Alright." My voice sounded more confident than my heart felt. "I'll do it."

That night when I returned to Friedrichshain after my shift at Zur, I was met in the main room by Fritz.

"Frit—Lamar!" I had to get used to saying the other name.

"Ella!" Lamar gave me a warm hug. "I'm glad you came."

Rupert fumed in the corner with Telfer. It was obvious which one slipped me the napkin.

"Why me?" I whispered, but it was loud enough for everyone to hear.

"Yeah, Lamar . . . why her?" Rupert grumbled loudly.

"Because . . . Rupert," Lamar responded annoyed, "she's our friend, and we trust her."

"You trust her. I don't trust her."

"Shhh!" Telfer demanded. "This is not the place to discuss this. Let's move down."

The other two members of their digging crew, who were introduced as Jonah and Beti, watched this all play out curiously. They appeared nervous as the exchange continued down the hall.

"Why don't you trust her, Rupert?" Jonah asked a reasonable question.

I studied Rupert carefully with some concern. The original skeptical Klaus had returned, the calm one from the café had disappeared. We crawled one by one through the debris to the room with the staircase, yet I was sure I was the only one who held my breath. *What did I do to make Klaus not trust me?*

Once inside, like those obedient ants at the Franke's house, we walked single file towards the stairway and stepped down. It was there that it became apparent more would be said because everyone looked to Rupert for an explanation. I did too.

His finger pointed sternly my direction. "Because somehow she was detained by the Stasi and let go."

Flushed with heat, my cheeks felt the weight of every eye in the room. The sting of converging tears had begun.

"Is that true?" Ian's calming voice broke through.

I hadn't expected to be interrogated here as well. My nod was truthful. The groans in the room seemed louder than expected.

Rupert continued, "The Stasi don't just let people go . . . they employ them."

Jonah grabbed Beti's hand and headed for the stairs. Ian reached out and grabbed his arm. "Wait, let her explain first. There's no reason to run."

Jonah snapped back, "She shows up here out of nowhere, and now we find out she has a past with the Stasi? That's no reason to run?"

"She has a right to explain herself." Ian challenged me, but Rupert wasn't finished.

"You didn't think I knew about your arrest did you, Ella? After we met at the pub, I checked some things out. The Stasi aren't the only ones with informants." His eyes narrowed in disgust. "You were detained then set free. Why?"

Everyone now faced me. The fear in Jonah and Beti's eyes amplified along with the concern in Ian and Lamar's and evident loathing from Rupert and Telfer. My throat tightened. Very little air managed to seep through as I opened my mouth to speak. Nothing came out.

"Why, Ella! What deal did you make?" Rupert demanded a bit louder. Thankfully, we were at the bottom level where noise was mostly muffled underground.

The tears that had halted at the corners of my eyes now slipped down my cheeks. I walked slowly over to Rupert and lifted up my blouse barely enough to reveal the scars that rippled my waist, the cuts from the glass, the belt buckle imprints, and the permanent discoloration on both sides of my ribs.

"I was arrested by a madman who accused me of being a spy only because I spilled a lousy drink on him." I choked. "He nearly raped and killed me. My release came because a good man sacrificed himself to save me." I moved within inches of Rupert. "I didn't make any deal! I hate the East, the DDR, and anyone associated with it."

The room went completely silent. Rupert stared at the wounds then climbed upstairs without a word. Lamar stepped over and tenderly placed his hand on my arm. The others got to work as if nothing had delayed them.

"I'm sorry, Ella," Lamar whispered. "What happened to you was terrible, and I'm sorry for Rupert's actions. Please stay here and help. If anything, this is where you belong, working towards your freedom."

I nodded, wiping the moisture off my nose, although, the tears had no intention of slowing down. Bringing that memory to the surface in my mind was painful, but to actually speak of it out loud was excruciating. Lamar's hand reached across my shoulder and tugged me in for a hug. He had always been kind to me.

Inhaling deeply, I peeked up and asked, "Can you show me what to do?"

TWENTY

Secret Lover

The next time I worked with Angelika, I completely forgot how she treated me at the club. She seemed genuinely remorseful in her apology, but it was my preoccupied attitude that truly allowed the offense to be forgotten.

The distraction of my new secret consumed my thoughts. It was hard to hide my optimism. The tunnel had become a living thing for me, like it was pumping blood through my veins or oxygen into my lungs. With Stefan's withdrawal, it had become my only reason to survive.

Each day I was assigned a digging shift, I worked harder at Zur to assure I could leave the restaurant on time. My eagerness in my duties and departure did not go unnoticed. One afternoon Angelika met me at the backdoor, one arm draped across the frame, halting my exit.

Her heavily-lined eyes squinted through me. "It's a guy isn't it?"

"What do you mean a guy?"

"That's why you've been happy." Angelika appeared smug in her assessment.

"I'm not happy!" I snapped.

"Well maybe not now," she laughed, "but something is going on."

My cheeks warmed. Small beads of sweat appeared on my forehead. Could she know the truth? She seemed to know everything.

"Ha! I knew it," she cried. "It *is* a man!"

My gaze dropped to my trembling hands. Yes, it would be better if she believed the lift in my step was because of a guy and not the escape plan.

"Yes, you're right, Angelika. I met someone."

"I thought you were engaged?" She craned her neck to see my hand. The ring wasn't there.

"Uh . . it didn't work out."

"Well, what's this new fella's name?" She shed no tears for me. Given how quickly she changed partners, this wasn't a surprise.

"I . . ." sputtering, I stalled. *What am I going to say?*

"I . . . what?" she wailed. "He has a name, right?"

"Yes . . ." My jaw tightened. "It's . . . it's Ian." *I can't believe I just gave the name of my digging partner to satisfy her quench for gossip.*

"Ian?" she giggled. "He sounds sexy." Fumbling in her pocket for a cigarette, she pulled it out and lit it as if completely satisfied with herself.

"He's a gentleman," I insisted, hoping the conversation was coming to an end.

"No man is a gentleman" She cracked the door open with her shoe and blew the smoke out, although, most of it stayed inside. "They only want to get something from you, Ella." Angelika flicked her cigarette outside after only three puffs and picked up a tray of drinks. Her smile went wide as she twisted her head back before she left. "Looks like Ella won't be a virgin for long."

"Angelika!" I chastised.

"Sorry," she snickered as she walked away. "Just kidding." Although, we both knew she wasn't.

Whatever. I can play this game—she needs to stay distracted.

When I got to the tunnel, I saw Ian differently; he had suddenly become my secret lover and didn't even know it. It made me chuckle at the thought of me—Ella, who had never done anything more than kiss Anton and Stefan—having a steamy love affair.

"What's so funny?" Ian noticed.

"Um . . ." I studied him as he faced me. His features were not as defined as Stefan, and he didn't have the physique of Anton, but the kindness in his demeanor was distinctively his: a sense of innocence and goodness and a smile that lit up the darkest corners of this tunnel. *Yes, he would make a good gentleman friend to someone.* "Uh . . . I just remembered something a friend at work told me."

"It's nice to see you smile," he remarked.

"I smile sometimes." I grinned shyly.

"You've worked hard here for over a week, but this is the first time I've seen you really happy." Ian picked up a handful of dirt and tossed it past me into a bucket.

I hadn't realized my facial expressions were noticed. "I'm happy." My proclamation may have been more to convince myself. Each moment away from the tunnel, it truly was all I thought about, but once I arrived here, the conflict began. My actions leading to freedom battled the guilt of leaving Stefan.

Ian's countenance lit up from the single flame nearby. "We have much to look forward to here. Just think about what's waiting for us on the other side."

"You're right." My smile widened with sincerity. "I do have much to look forward to."

TWENTY-ONE

NICE TO MEET YOU, ROMEO

23 July 1970

Dear Ella,

I can't begin to tell you how relieved we were when we received your letter. Josef and I assumed the worst and now we're thrilled you're alive and well. As much as we want you here, we don't delight in your sadness. Please don't misunderstand me, I'm quite angered by Stefan. How could he let you go? What happened, if you don't mind me asking? It puzzles me that anyone would choose to not be with you... you're nearly perfect.

Josef graduated from the Free University and will be attending Law school in two months. He's working as an assistant to my boss, actually. It isn't the most glamorous position, but he's a hard worker and is well liked. He is dating many girls but hasn't settled to one, he may never choose one. He enjoys all the attention.

My professional duties have increased, and I've been assigned the sole lead manager of a high-rise building in the business district. I have nearly one hundred men I oversee and, if things go well, may have the opportunity to become a partner in this company. One owner is retiring within the year and the one who remains is quite satisfied with my contributions.

I've saved a great deal since being here. With so little money to begin with and no need for extras to live on, Josef and I can still live comfortably and use my savings to buy into this company. I'm sure construction will always be my choice of occupation. As you have known since we were kids, I always liked getting dirty.

I know this may sound redundant, but I have to ask now that Stefan is no longer in your life. Do you have any plans to join us? I truly wish you would say yes. We miss you so much.

Please don't make us wait long for a response. Even though we now know you are well and safe, I look forward to another letter soon.

Love Anton

15 August 1970

Dear Anton and Josef
Thank you for your kind words, your thoughts and wishes. It means the world to me. I'm not really sure what happened to Stefan. He stopped writing. He has three years left of his military service, but I know nothing about his post or even of his status. He could even be out of the country. The last letter I received was over three years ago. It's possible he has chosen a different path, one I am not part of.

Anyway, enough of me. I am very proud of you both, accomplishing many great things! Josef, your graduation and pursuit of higher education. I am assured when you find the right girl you will know it! And Anton, I never had any doubt you would be great in any occupation you chose and here you are a manager now, building and instructing others. You always had a greater vision for the future. I don't know what is forthcoming but you must know I love you both with all my heart.

Ella

The muggy humidity of the summer months drove everyone in the group to contend for a turn digging in the coolness of the tunnel, but depositing the dirt was as big a project as retrieving it. To make the process easier and less noticeable, the one storage room in the basement was being filled with the excess clay, but once that reached its limit, we would have to haul it upstairs. By the time the autumn season finally arrived, heat was replaced with rains. Determined to continue, our challenges never ceased to provoke our patience.

While every detail of the system had been working as well as it could under the circumstances, we also recognized the thin thread of fate and how one small mistake could jeopardize everything. Acute alertness and confidentiality was not only a necessity, it was vital to our survival.

"Ella," Angelika caught me before I walked out of Zur one late-September night. "When am I going to meet this mysterious man of yours?"

I laughed, mostly because he was mysterious to me too.

"You always run out so quickly." She grinned slyly. "He must be something else!"

I smiled. "Oh, he is . . ." The tunnel had suddenly become a 'he'.

"Well, when do I get to meet him?" She nudged me with her elbow. "It's the duty of the friend to approve, you know that right?"

My eyebrows lifted, not sure we were really considered friends, and even then I'm not certain I would *ever* let her meet *any* guy I was truly interested in considering what randomly flew out of her mouth. Angelika seemed to read my mind . . . and face.

"I will behave."

I chortled, "I'm not sure you know how."

"What?" Angelika pretended to be offended. "No, really I want to meet him. Let's go out together, the four of us."

"You and Felix?"

"Felix?" Angelika hooted. "Oh my, Ella, that was ages ago. It's Viktor now."

"Who's Viktor?"

"The delivery man." She slid her tongue across her bottom lip and winked.

I scowled. "The guy who delivers our meat from the butcher every morning?"

"Yes, that's him." She beamed. "Tomorrow night, Ella."

"Oh no, I can't tomorrow." I was thinking about how hard we were working in the tunnel.

"I'm not going to let you get out of this. Tell me when."

I knew she wouldn't. I had to figure something out. "I'll let you know."

"It better be soon."

I also knew that it wouldn't be Viktor—it would be the next guy on her list.

"Alright." I kissed her on the cheek and ran out.

The entire walk to Friedrichshain I was heavily distracted. What should I do? If I didn't agree, she might follow me one night and then we would be in trouble. She couldn't keep her mouth shut to save her life. And if she got caught by border patrol . . . the negative consequences mounted. There was no other option, I had to somehow come up with a date. I could ask Lamar, but then I would have to explain why I keep calling him Lamar when I already told her his name was Ian.

"Ian?" I sighed tiresomely.

"Can I ask you something?" We were the only two in the tunnel, and it seemed the best time to talk without his dad or anyone else around.

Ian brushed his dark bangs aside as he turned slightly towards me. Wet dirt left a small trail across his forehead. I wanted to grin at the sight of it, but my chore weighed too heavily to enjoy. I inhaled again, not even sure how to begin my request. Everything felt awkward.

"Are you available?" I blurted. Ian's deep brown eyes widened. *That came out wrong.* I chastised myself silently as I scrambled to reconstruct a logical sentence.

"I mean . . . do you have a girlfriend?" His mouth stretched into a full smile watching me squirm. I put my trowel down and shifted as best I could in the small space. The sole lantern filled the tunnel. "I'm trying to say —very pathetically it appears— that I have a friend who thinks I have a boyfriend, and that's why I'm running off from work every day. She wants to meet him."

"Why me?" Ian was still smiling.

"It was the first name that came to mind. I didn't mean anything by it." I was suddenly grateful for the shadows.

"I'm flattered, but yes, I have a girlfriend."

This surprised me. Why hadn't he spoken of her before, or better yet, why was she not here helping us dig? Why would he leave her behind? Then suddenly everything became quite clear.

"She's in the West, isn't she?"

Ian stopped working once again and nodded.

"What's her name?"

"Chandra."

"How did you meet?"

"At the Free University. I had only been in college a year when the wall went up. If only I had stayed at her place that one night, I would have been able to stay there forever."

"Do you love her?" This was a personal question, and thankfully, Ian took no offense.

"She is everything to me."

"Then I will work hard for you." I patted his hand. "Love should not be separated like that."

"Like you and Anton?"

Astonished, I went still. "What do you know of Anton?"

"When you're down in this tunnel, talking helps pass time. Lamar told me of your friend."

I couldn't be mad at Lamar. He only knew what I told him the night we were hiding at my flat. He never learned of my relationship with Stefan and how my feelings for him were stronger.

"Anton and I really are just friends. We took care of one another in the orphanage." I waited, unsure if I wanted to continue, then the words rolled out effortlessly. "But I fell in love with someone else. One who lives here, a person who I thought I would spend the rest of my life with."

"What's his name?"

I hadn't anticipated the physical struggle it would be to say *Stefan* out loud.

"You don't have to tell me if you don't want to." Ian turned his full attention to me.

"His name is Stefan, and he was everything to me. He was the one who saved me from the Stasi."

"Then why are you leaving?"

It was so easy to talk to Ian that the whole story came out. He listened with great compassion.

"I'm sorry, Ella. I'm sorry that what you went through with the colonel took Stefan away from you." He squeezed my hand. "But . . ." Ian paused, "do you think it's possible that Anton is really the one you are meant to be with, and all of this happened because of that?"

Tears came to my eyes. Would God really put me through all of this emotion, allow me to get close to one person, then tease me and say no, he's not the one? I had absolutely no doubt for years that Stefan was my one true love . . . yet no contact in now thirty-eight months. I didn't know anything.

Ian seemed to sense my pain and grasped my hand again. "I can pretend to be your boyfriend if it'll stop your friend from asking questions."

I smiled, remembering that was what we talked about in the first place. Ian's kindness was a true indication of his character. He would make a wonderful partner to Chandra.

"Thank you very much. It will definitely help."

"Then I'm happy to do it."

"It might have to be a digging night. Can we keep this a secret between the two of us?"

"I'll take care of it, just let me know what night."

The next morning as we parted ways, my respect for Ian had grown. We hadn't accomplished as much work as we should have in the tunnel, but in my mind, learning about Ian and Chandra was well worth the pause, and finally, for the first time in a long time I was able to share my feelings and fears about Stefan.

* * *

The night of our double date arrived. Fairly nervous, I dressed for the occasion like I would have for Stefan. Even though it was a pretend date, it had to be believable. Ian had never seen me dolled up. We changed into work clothes when we arrived at the building every night, where he always saw me messy and dirty. Even when I changed back to my day dress and washed up before I left, my appearance never came close to how I would dress for a night out.

We met outside the club thirty minutes before Angelika and Viktor were to arrive. Grateful it was the same establishment we had gone to when she was with Felix, the idea of familiarity calmed me. Even the rock music revived me.

Ian's black tailored jacket and slacks showed a stylish side I, too, had never seen, and when his eyes caught sight of me with my hair curled down my back over my red dress, his reaction was obvious surprise. We laughed the moment we came together. It was apparent we knew hardly anything about each other and were about to try and convince Angelika that we were in love.

At a quiet table in the back, we took time to get to know each other in case she asked specific questions. It was strange telling my life story to someone I barely knew, but after our talk alone in the tunnel, our friendship wasn't foreign anymore. Ian remained rather attentive and gentle and made it easy to share.

"What is your mother like?" Ian's countenance relaxed when I asked.

"She is kind and loving. She's a seamstress by trade, but rarely charges anyone for her labor. She has a soft spot for those less fortunate."

"She sounds lovely." I hesitated. I didn't want Ian to think I was getting *too* personal, but I really wanted to know. "Why's your father angry all the time?"

Ian sighed. "Mother asked father to join her on holiday in the West, but he refused, saying he had too much work and that he needed my help as well. He owned an appliance business."

Waiting, I sensed he had more to say. Ian's eyes lifted and stared directly at me. "The wall went up while she was gone. We could have all been together, and my father feels the weight of that decision daily. Within a year, we lost the business to the DDR. Shortly after, we became part of the resistance."

"The resistance?"

Ian cautiously peered around the room. "Yeah, we wanted to fight the *monster,* but as you know, it's a beast much bigger than us."

I nodded sadly. "But you're not involved anymore."

"No. It's . . ." He glanced around again, uneasily.

"You don't have to tell me." I swiftly routed back to his family. "I truly am sorry about your mother and sisters. Being separated from those you love is a terrible fate." I exhaled quietly. "We'll be successful, you'll see."

"It has to be—this is the fourth time we've tried an escape plan."

"Four times?" *I guess I'd be angry too.*

"Tell me about Chandra," I encouraged. He beamed. It was obvious this was something he enjoyed discussing, but after only a few minutes, Ian quickly put his arm around me. His forwardness caught me off guard.

"Uh—" I choked, but was cut off.

"Look at the two lovebirds snuggling in the corner." Angelika removed her coat revealing her curvy figure in a tightfitting dress as Viktor hung it on a hook nearby. Smiling, I reached for Ian's other hand, holding it across the table.

As Angelika called for the waitress, I leaned towards Ian's ear and whispered quietly, "I forgot to tell you she can be brash and coarse." He grinned and squeezed my shoulder.

"Nice to finally meet you, Romeo!" She held up a hand like he was supposed to kiss it.

"Likewise, Angelika. I've heard many great things about you." He pulled away from mine and kissed her hand.

"Charming, too!" She giggled and dug her elbow into Viktor like he needed to pay attention.

Viktor, sporting a vivid blue shirt with sleeves rolled up to his elbows, pulled out a long cigar. "Do you mind?"

I motioned *no* even though I secretly did.

"Well, what have you two been up to every night?" Angelika laughed in her usual way. "Ella just goes running from the restaurant. You must be . . . irresistible."

I rolled my eyes. "Let's order."

After the waitress took our orders, I wondered how many times Angelika would embarrass me before we got through this fake ordeal. *Poor Ian.* I would have to explain everything afterward.

"Let's dance, baby." Angelika grabbed Viktor's hands as she jumped to her feet. "Come on, Ella. The last time you were here you loved the music." On their way to the floor, she brazenly placed Viktor's hands on her hips.

I turned to Ian apprehensively. "Would it be a bother?"

He shook his head. "I love to dance."

Taking my hand, he led me to the dance floor as well and surprised me with his natural ability. I enjoyed the music, but it was apparent my steps were not as experienced. When a slow song followed, my rhythm improved. It was much easier to sway slow and steady, especially with Ian as my partner.

Somehow, his skill in making me feel like I was a much better dancer than I really was made the whole experience tolerable. Yet when I allowed myself to see the reality of the moment, a familiar tightening in my chest surfaced. I was in the arms of another man . . . dancing.

Stefan promised to take me to a dance club one day, and as juvenile as that promise was—compared to all the other promises he had made—I still yearned for it.

With each new song, I pushed to free my mind of Stefan. Nevertheless, he seemed to be interwoven into everything I said and did.

"Thank you for coming, Ian," I whispered before he twirled me.

"My pleasure."

Despite the phony relationship, the night turned out more enjoyable than I imagined it would.

"Goodbye, Ella." Angelica leaned in and kissed me on the cheek.

"You too, Sugar." And with a swift pass of her hand, Angelika reached around Ian's backside and squeezed his butt.

"Oh!" He stiffened from her grip.

"When you're done with the nun over there, come see me." She chuckled and put her arm through Viktor's as they swayed, heavily inebriated, down the street together.

"I'm sorry, Ian," I muttered with humiliation. "I'm indebted to you for tonight."

"You don't owe me anything, Ella. It was fun. I haven't been out in a really long time, and sometimes it's nice to forget about all the *Scheisse* that happens around us."

I analyzed Ian carefully. His response to the evening's events was different than I anticipated, kind-hearted and refreshingly positive. I knew we were going to be great friends here and in the West.

Ian walked me home, of course. I wouldn't have expected anything less. He was a gentleman from start to finish, even keeping his cool under pressure from Angelika. I shook his hand goodbye then giggled to myself as I walked up to my flat. There was nothing between Ian and I—our hearts were very much reserved for other people—but the memory of handshake goodbyes left a smile on my lips.

Once again, inside the depths of my mind where loneliness festered, Stefan's image materialized. Still in my dress, I curled atop my bed covers and faced the note that rested on the nearby pillow. Reaching for it for the thousandth time, my fingers brushed against the fading flower picture and words, Ella, you're always in my heart. Stefan.

Pressing it flat against my chest, the vibration of my voice emitted through my clothes as I cried out loud. "Am I Stefan? Am I in your heart?"

TWENTY-TWO

Patrol Change!

8 January 1971

Dearest Lena,
I'm an awful person. Even now as I recognize my error, I can't bring
myself to apologize in person. I know you, more than anyone, can
understand the pain of loss and loneliness from one who was to
be your world and never will. Through tears, anger, and jealousy
I maintained my distance from you. Even when Christoph's fate
was unknown, you stood by me. That is why I don't deserve your
forgiveness or friendship.

Life without Stefan has been hollow. His promises to return, his
letters expressing love and devotion, the ring I stare at a dozen times
a day are all intruding images of a life I will never get to enjoy.
Each day that passes is another step away from him and I can't
do anything to stop it. Sometimes I feel like I'm living in a prison
without any doors or windows . . . no escape. It is confinement I no
longer have the strength for.

I will forever be grateful for your goodness and affection even when
I don't warrant it. Please believe me when I tell you I will be fine, I
have found a way to bring peace back into my soul. May your life and
happiness now be fulfilled with Freddy. He is a perfect mate for you.
I wish you both the very best. Please do not write back. Your letter
might not find its way to me.

Love, Ella

I stared at the envelope for a considerable amount of time. Despite the truth in my long-overdue correspondence, I still felt like a coward. Lena had been such a good friend to me, she didn't deserve this kind of goodbye, but I knew if we met face to face, I would divulge my secret. Only now it wasn't just *my* life I jeopardized, it was six other people. This is the way it had to be done.

January 1971 marked seven months I had been actively involved in the tunnel. Winter was in full swing and in an equal number of months, the tenth anniversary of the wall's creation. For some it represented strength and power. For others it implied deception.

With a renewed sense of importance, the next couple months I contributed all my available time to the digging effort. I worked alongside Lamar, Ian, Jonah, Beti, even Telfer—though he rarely spoke to me. Rupert kept his distance. He didn't warm up to me, but at least he didn't treat me as badly as before.

Our vigilance kept us safe as we remained undetected and out of sight of any prying eyes or border guard—a rarity in a world of treachery—but our meticulous habits and obedience to the patrol times added a layer of immense protection. With an additional fifty metres down, our estimations on distance took us through the center of the death strip and closer to the West.

Forty-four months now and no word from Stefan.

Despite my attempts to erase his memory, every thought circled back to him . . . every turn in my flat led me to something of his . . . his painting, his letters, the dried forget-me-nots that hung from my curtain rod, the sight of him leaning against my counter, relaxing on the floor or lying in my bed. Every time I saw a soldier in the restaurant, I would take another look, wishing it was *my* soldier—if he was even considered mine anymore.

When I walked in those quiet moments to and from Friedrichshain and the tunnel, somehow my mind gravitated to him. Especially when I caught sight of the border patrol who had been quite friendly the first night I found the building last June. He never saw me, but there were times I deliberately arrived early simply to catch a glimpse of his face while making his patrols. The resemblance to Stefan wasn't remarkable, but certain mannerisms when executed, like his smile, reminded me enough about him to satisfy an insane thirst I had. Sometimes I would forget I was counting his steps, and on more than one occasion, came dangerously close to being discovered. It was a risk I needed to be more mindful of.

I knew I had to grieve Stefan out of my life, that I should let it go and not hold onto any hope that he would resurface. His name never showed up on any list of dead or wounded soldiers, and I checked the press weekly. As painful as it was, moving on was essential. Despite my actions, I hadn't committed myself one hundred percent to leaving, and that could put us all in peril. I knew what had to be done, although it didn't come easy.

"The patrol has changed!" Telfer cried as he met Lamar and I at the entrance of the tunnel. Even though the early-March air stung icily, Telfer's face was beet red with drops of sweat dripping briskly from his beard. He gripped his chest as if he was having a heart attack.

"I was well within adequate time, but the guards were suddenly behind me. They commanded me to leave the area, and I did and then entered after they had turned the corner. "The timing is off somehow!" He sat on the stool and nervously flipped through papers on the desk. I placed my tools aside and retrieved him some water from the metal canister we kept in the basement.

"Thank you." That was probably the nicest thing he had ever said to me.

"We need to notify the others." Telfer was understandably panicked. "If one person gets caught, the entire process is doomed, and we could all be executed."

The heavy question lingered. How would we get word to the others before they arrived?

"I can get to Rupert," Lamar said, "and Telfer, you can reach Ian, but Jonah and Beti? How can we find them first?"

"Are you sure it wasn't random?" My inquiry was innocent, yet Telfer gave me the usual glare.

"Fine!" He stood defensively as if I was trying to argue, which I wasn't. "Come!" he demanded, pointing to the paper with the patrol times. "Let's see . . . here, there should be another patrol in ten minutes from the west side to the front."

We followed him to the main area and into the room where I had seen the sheet flutter that first night. Carefully, we waited—none of us making a sound, Lamar monitored his watch. Ten minutes passed, and then twelve, and it wasn't until a full fourteen minutes had passed when we heard the familiar footsteps approaching. It should've brought some relief if the rotations were now fourteen minutes apart, yet the second pair of guards appeared barely three minutes later.

My chest heaved simultaneously to Lamar's wide eyes. Nobody spoke, it was if we were processing the reality of our sudden demise. The times had truly changed. Regardless of whether we could get past the initial risk of people getting caught and the tunnel exposed, the process of learning the new routine could set us back many days—possibly weeks.

I motioned for us to retreat to a back room to speak more openly. "What time are Jonah and Beti due to arrive today?"

"Uh, eight o'clock I believe," Lamar answered as he and Telfer followed. "They work the late shift tonight."

"What about Rupert and Ian?" I took command since Telfer's shock had not worn off.

"They both will be here in less than fifteen minutes," Lamar responded.

"Can you get to Rupert before then?"

"Yes." Lamar grabbed his jacket. "I know the route he takes; I'll catch him down the street."

"Telfer, can you get to Ian before he gets here, as well?"

"Yes." His heavy breathing had finally slowed to a purr.

"Okay, go. You should have time right now since they just passed. Go now, both of you. I'll take care of Jonah and Beti."

"How?" Telfer questioned skeptically.

"I'll figure it out."

Telfer scowled. "How—"

"I will handle it. You need to start trusting me!" And I gently pushed them toward the door. "Meet at Patz tomorrow night at eight."

I went to the basement and retrieved a piece of paper and a pencil and wrote 5:28 p.m., the time the guards had passed. Retreating back upstairs, I waited silently, recording the time of every pass until 7:50 p.m.

I didn't have a solid plan. My one idea was to somehow distract the guards approaching the building long enough to draw their attention the same moment Jonah and Beti were making their entry. It was dangerous, borderline reckless, but we didn't know what direction they came from, and if we chose the wrong one to intercept, they could be caught.

Moving to the front door of the building, I lifted the wooden latch with trembling hands. Opening it slowly, I stepped out into the shadow of the darkened archway. Based on the last two hours' rounds, the guards passed through randomly every three to fourteen minutes. The window of opportunity had decreased by at least two minutes with the change. This was not much time to work with.

Two men in uniform were approaching nearly a block away. Their rifles protruded outwardly from their silhouettes. I knew what needed to be done, but as I stepped into the light, my body shook as coarsely as my hands. I shuffled towards them and within seconds their whistles pierced the calm night with a deafening blast.

"*Halt! Im Namen der Volkspolizei, stillgestanden nicht!*"

I had barely reached the building next door when I froze and raised my hands to their demands. "Please, sir," I begged. I could not see any faces clearly. I could only imagine their thoughts.

"Please, help me."

"*Nicht bewegen!*" was the lone response to stay still, the tone quite unfriendly. I then realized I may have underestimated my plan.

As they got within a metre, my eyes lowered to the ground to appear as innocent as possible. "I'm trying to find someone. Can you help me please?"

"Put your hands down," one man uttered loudly. I did what I was told, and as I peered up, the hardness disappeared.

"You shouldn't be here, Fräulein."

"I know, but this was the last place I saw him. I don't know how to find him otherwise."

"Who?"

"He is border guard . . . like you."

"Border guard?" One soldier still seemed quite skeptical.

"His name is Hans." They glanced at each other and back to me, although their expressions gave little away.

"Why are you looking for Hans?"

"I'm not from this area and met some friends at a café nearby." My mouth curved upward tentatively. "Somehow I got turned around, and Hans once told me if I ever needed help, just to ask any border guard. Since this is the last place I saw him, I came searching for him here."

It was a ridiculous helpless female routine, but it was all I had. My eyelashes fluttered several times before they answered. The groan inside my head was deafening.

"Come." They waved me over to walk with them. "We'll take you to him."

They believe me! It surprised me how much easier lying had become over the years. Papa Kühn had taught me the importance of telling the truth, and I felt my conscience had a clear understanding of right and wrong, but over time those boundaries blurred, especially when danger lurked close by.

"Hans is at the tower tonight." The soldier speaking slung his rifle over his shoulder as if he was about to embark on a pleasure walk. "He hasn't spent much time on patrols lately."

"Oh, really, why not?" I inquired as if I was curious.

"He—Hey, stopp!" Another person who entered the prohibited area caught their attention. This individual, however, darted off in a mad run a separate direction. The other soldier who had remained alert bolted after him. As I watched the confrontation ensue, I wondered what would happen if that person was caught, grateful it didn't appear to be anyone I recognized.

I felt confident that if Jonah and Beti had been near the building when they were supposed to be, they would have seen me with the guards. The length of time and subsequent exit should have bought them the cover they needed.

A few minutes later, the guard who had run off rejoined us empty-handed. A gratifying relief that the person escaped warmed me, but I kept my expression the same.

"Blode landstreicher!" The soldier huffed with exhaustion and continued to breathe heavily until we reached the tower.

"Hans!" The guard with me hollered into his hand-held radio. "Hans, there is someone who needs to talk to you."

"Why me?" his response came in broken syllables.

"She is asking for you."

"She? Okay, I'll be down in a minute."

As I waited, I contemplated what to say.

Within minutes, Hans appeared at the base of the tower then passed through the heavily guarded entryway reserved for soldiers. Although it had only been a few minutes since he had been notified of my arrival, the wait was awkward. Standing this close to the newly reinforced wall brought forth all sorts of emotions. My eyes scanned the masonry detail from the base to its extensive height, and I had to fight to keep my fingers from reaching out and touching it. One could no longer peer over the top without the help of a ladder. Coils of twisted razor wire lined the edges, and although I could not see what lie beyond, the stories told of a viciously designed death trap, nearly impenetrable. For a brief moment my mind felt at ease with the knowledge our escape was intended many metres below.

"Yes?" he questioned the men, not realizing I was standing behind them. "Why aren't you on your patrol?" His demand was cold. The urge to turn around and run bit at my stomach, but my façade wasn't over. I stepped forward.

"Oh . . . Ella?" He was taken aback then turned to the men and spoke more calmly, "Be on your way!"

"What are you doing here?" His question didn't carry the same warmth from when we first met.

"I apologize for bothering you at work." I bit my lip to prevent a child-like snivel. "I should go."

"No, tell me what's going on."

"I came to a café to see my friends and got lost . . . again." I gazed up at him, once more, trying every possible angle to make him feel sorry for me then blurted out. "I came looking for you. I'm sorry. You said if I ever needed your help, I could ask for you, so I did." I pointed to the two guards who had now left us alone.

Hans took my arm gently and walked me away from the wall. It seemed he didn't want us to be mistaken for escapees as well. Once we were a safe distance away, his voice soothed.

"I didn't intend to come across harsh." The softness in both his expression and touch returned. "I have been recently promoted and need to be careful. A lot has changed as of late." Hans noticed my trembling hands and led me to the warmth inside a nearby building. It too was empty but provided the much-needed shield from the unforgiving wind that suddenly arose.

"Why would you be out on a night like tonight anyway?"

"I'm sorry. I shouldn't have bothered you." I moved to leave as he grabbed my arm.

"No, I can help you. I'm glad you found me."

A phony grin filled my face.

"Stay here. I need to grab some papers first, and I'll escort you home."

"Oh, no." I tried to get out of it.

"I insist this time." His eyes narrowed in and trapped mine. "Wait for me." He tipped his hat and left. As I waited, I cursed irritably under my breath. *Verdammt, I did not intend the distraction to go this far!* I weighed the consequences of disappearing to simply resigning myself to an escorted walk home. *Toughen up, Ella. It's only a walk home.*

Once he returned, Hans wasted no time in jumping into conversation.

"Are you from Berlin?" he asked as we stepped off the nearest curb to cross the street. It was a question you would think I was used to hearing, being that I don't exactly look German.

"Yes, I have lived here my whole life."

"Me, too. I love it here."

I glanced sideways at him when he wasn't looking back. Up close, my desire to see Stefan through Hans amplified. By far his half smile carried the most similarity, but I scanned him subtly for other attributes. His hair was very short like Stefan's—along with every other soldiers—but his eyes were dark brown like mine. It could be the uniform and his tan skin or the way he walked. When he spoke, however, it was with a naivety that was far from Stefan's nature.

"Do you live with family?"

"No, I live alone. Do you live with your family?" I returned the question. I figured if the dialogue stayed centered on Hans, I wouldn't have to share much.

"I live with my brother Josef."

"You have a brother Josef?" Astonished, I had forgotten I wasn't going to get personal. "So do I!"

"How come he doesn't live with you?"

"Uh," I took a deep breath, ". . . Um . . . he passed away ten years ago." In a way, I wasn't really lying, but I couldn't tell border guard my brother escaped to the West.

"Oh, that's terrible, Ella."

I hadn't realized we had stopped walking and Hans was watching me. His brown eyes were quite dark; I couldn't even see his pupils. His face, although contoured and firm had softened, the lines in his forehead disappearing. Sympathy filled his face to the point I had to glance the other way.

"I really am sorry to hear that. It must be hard." His hand tenderly wiped my isolated tear away, which startled me. A strange man had just touched my cheek. The last man to do that was Stefan. This would be much harder than I thought. With a step back, my fingers brushed the same cheek as if to undo his action. Hans must've realized how forward he had been and stuffed his hands in his pockets.

"Yes." My answer conveyed more caution. "I miss him very much."

"I'm sorry. I shouldn't intrude."

"It's fine. His memory is important to me."

With a smile, the charming dimple appeared. "Where do your parents live?"

My lips pulled tight. How far was I willing to go with this? We still hadn't moved, and Hans eyes hadn't left me either. I shifted uncomfortably.

"They have passed away also."

His eyebrows curved with concern. "Again I'm sorry." My antsy feet shuffled forward, but he remained still. "I keep asking you terrible questions. My apologies."

I shifted back his direction. His eyes held a warmth that was nearly unrecognizable in my life. It drew me in although my cynical spirit yanked me back to reality.

"It's fine, it's been a long time." I stepped back and nudged him gently forward. "Where do your parents live?"

"They live outside *Torgau*, off the Elbe."

"The Elbe River?" My heart missed a beat.

"Yes, are you familiar with it?"

"I saw a painting of it once. It was . . ." —I couldn't stop my voice from being sad. My thoughts turned to the Fasching dinner and Stefan's artwork— "lovely."

"Yes, it is. My parents like the country. It's where my mother grew up. They visit Berlin just twice a year."

"It must be nice." The conversation slid into what would be construed as an ordinary chat between "friends".

"Why don't you live in the country?"

"I love the city." Hans eyes lit up. "I love being a soldier too."

I frowned but quickly hid it. Who could love being a soldier at the border?

"What do you do for work?"

"I'm a *kellnerin*."

"Where do you wait tables?"

"Zur Letzen Instanz in Mitte."

"I love that place! Their pork is the best in the city!" Simple things seemed to make him happy. "How come I've never seen you there?"

"How do you know you haven't?"

His countenance lifted deviously. "I would have noticed you."

I quickly skipped past his comment. "It's probably because we work the same hours . . . I work day shifts."

"Yes, I have been there at night, but . . ." Hans hesitated. "I might have to change that now." He grinned halfway. My cheeks flushed hot. I couldn't see Hans and not think of Stefan, this was terrible. I grimaced.

"Did I say something wrong?"

"No . . ." I scrambled. I forget how inexperienced I was at hiding my facial expressions. "No, I remembered I have to work early tomorrow, and it's getting late." I studied my surroundings then realized a walk that should have taken a mere thirty minutes lasted nearly an hour—and I had let it.

We turned the corner onto my street.

"I live here." One hand pointed to the building, the other extended for a handshake in an effort to keep him from coming inside. He grinned and met my hand with enthusiasm. Before he turned to leave, he added some thoughtful advice.

"Ella, try not to get lost in Friedrichshain . . . it's not a good place for a woman to be alone, but if it happens again . . . you know where to find me."

I nodded.

". . . and Ella,"

I feared what he would say next, but somehow knew it was coming.

"Maybe we can see each other again. Possibly coffee?"

I smiled but didn't answer the question directly.

"Goodbye Hans, and thank you again for walking me home." I rushed inside as fast as my legs could move. My profound hope was that everything fell into place exactly as it should . . . I would know tomorrow at Patz.

TWENTY-THREE

HANS

"Ella!" Beti met me at the door of Patz and gave me a warm hug. "Thank you! Thank you!" was all she could say. I was the last to arrive having worked later than planned, but to my great relief, all of us were present.

We sat in a tight circle around a back table. It was no secret I had prevented a catastrophe with Jonah and Beti, both of whom watched the entire conversation I had with the border guard from a nearby corner. Then when they received my note, they watched for a break and left. We all realized the small miracle we were blessed with. Things could have gone incredibly wrong at any point, and we all played a role.

"Ella, that was quite brave of you to engage the border guards," Beti gushed in between bites of her Schupfnudel. A piece of the dumpling stuck to her chin.

"I did what any of you would have done, but it didn't even begin with me. Telfer was the one who started it all. Thanks to him, we didn't get caught." I chose not to share the details of what happened *after* I led the border guard away from the building. It was unnecessary, and knowing Telfer or Rupert, they would probably assume there was something more to it than there was, so I kept it a secret.

"Based on those two hours," I said, "their patrols are much more frequent and without routine. We'll need to take time to get them down accurately . . . that's if they're not changed day to day." A few groans went around the table accompanied by nervous fidgeting.

"It's okay," Lamar assured, "we simply need to monitor it like last time."

"It was risky last time. It's risky this time," Rupert spoke up. He was feisty tonight.

"What choice do we have? We can't change locations. We've put too much into this one, and we have less than a third of the distance left." Ian was a voice of reason.

"But if we get caught, it won't matter anyway," Rupert snapped back.

I placed my hand on his arm. "Let's not fight. It won't help the situation." I turned to Lamar. "I realize I wasn't here when you documented the previous patrols. How was it done?"

"Mostly monitoring, observing. Kalle was the one who lived a block away and could see everything from his upper-floor apartment window. That's how we found the location to begin with."

"Kalle?" I questioned. This was the first I ever heard his name. A silence hung in the air. As I peered around, all eyes shifted away, either to their laps or towards something else, anything but me.

"What?" I caught their weak attempt at being subtle.

"Kalle was one of our friends buried in the cave-in," Ian spoke first.

"Oh, I'm sorry." The stillness became awkward.

I respected their quiet observation for another minute then asked, "Well, do we want to keep working under this building, yes or no?" Everyone nodded yes. "Then we have to get the patrols down. Let's take a day to think about it and meet back here tomorrow night with a plan."

As I sat at home trying to devise some ideas, one outlandish thought came to mind. It was as deceitful as it could get. *What if I use my friendship with Hans to find out as much inside information as I can?* I wasn't a spy, but could I be? I had seen enough deceit in my young life to know the basics. Hans seemed like a nice man. Despite his titled duty, he didn't come across as regular border guard. Did I have it in me to use him like that . . . for freedom?

Contemplating my options mixed with possible consequences, my mind toyed with the outcomes. Reaching Anton and Josef was worth the gamble, yet if Hans somehow found out, I could be arrested . . . or worse, killed. Struggling with both the idea and my self-imposed burden, it became apparent I couldn't share the details of my plan with anyone. The risk was too great; the less people knew my intentions, the better. Basically, just me.

Meeting at Patz once again, we were all in agreement; we would do shifts on the patrol. It would be a slow, methodical process——no mistakes. I volunteered for a turn, but I didn't mention anything else.

* * *

It had been a busy afternoon at Zur with many people still on holiday as Carnival was coming to an end, a perfect time for people to travel. Despite the East German restrictions, we still had a lot of visitors from around the globe. Our rapidly declining economy created an advantageous exchange rate for foreigners.

"Hans?" Surprised and pleased to see him at the next table I came to serve, a smile easily emerged. With barely five days since I concocted my plan, I realized its execution might be simpler than expected.

"Ella." He grinned. Out of his patrol uniform, he sported plaid, button-up shirt, and brown slacks. Two friends accompanied him. "I specifically asked for your table," he laughed. "I won't be disappointed, will I?"

"Depends on how well you tip," I joked back.

Throughout the hour, I found it effortless to flirt with Hans. This was all part of the master plan, but I didn't realize it would happen this soon or this naturally.

"Fräulein, what do you recommend?" Hans teased, it was obvious he seized any opportunity to prolong my time at his table.

I playfully went along.

"Well, let's see . . . you might be the kind of person who doesn't fancy spicy things," I kidded. "Maybe a bit more on the dull side." Hans friends nudged him, laughing hard themselves as I continued, "You might want to order the *Goulash* soup and nutbread . . . a simple taste."

"Well, that shows how much you don't know me, Fräulein Ella. I happen to live precariously and would like to order the grilled pork knuckle and fried potatoes."

"Are you sure? It's considered to be one of our more stimulating dishes." I winked. "I'm not sure you can handle it."

He laughed out loud. It was a pleasant sound.

By the end of his meal, it was almost expected we would see each other another time alone and away from our work. Clearly on my mind, I knew this was a role I was playing, but behind the camouflage, it wasn't as awful as I had believed it in my head. I actually looked forward to it.

The following Wednesday night, I faced my closet, discouraged. My earlier confidence leading to this date slipped from my hands to the floor along with my dresses. I needed to get the information for our crew, but now that my strategy was in play, uncertainty prevailed.

Climbing on the bed, I curled my legs inward but remained upright as I studied the crumpled pile. The red dress I wore for Stefan . . . the blue dress I wore for Stefan . . .the yellow one at the park with Stefan and, of course, Katharina's dress she so lovingly gifted me through a letter after I borrowed it to sightsee *with Stefan*! My underclothes were all I wore as my legs uncurled and hung off the edge of my bed. I wilted back against the covers.

Everything has some connection to Stefan! "Why? Why is this happening?" I screamed at the ceiling, unconcerned for my neighbors. *He will never be out of my life or my head!*

My hands overlapped on top my forehead. *Why am I even in this position and what does it really matter what I wear—this isn't even real?* Anger mounted within me. *Why would Stefan do this to me? Why would he make me think we're in love then leave my life entirely without a trace?* For the first time in a while, I reached for my paper and pencil.

19 Mar 1971

Stefan,
Why? Why did you leave me alone? Why would you desert me? How could you express love for me, even ask me to marry you and then leave me? You didn't even say goodbye—don't I deserve a goodbye? My future was supposed to be intertwined with you, good or bad. We were supposed to do it together. We had plans! Remember Cochem? I am now alone and heartbroken.

I don't know if I will ever love another man, I don't know if I ever want to.

My eyes blurred with tears. Large wet drops dotted the paper and smeared the words. The paper slipped from my fingers and sailed to the floor, unfinished. Despite the fire that surged through my veins, I couldn't move. Finding a way to step past this seemed impossible, yet the ticks from the clock in the kitchen expressed an urgency. The date with Hans at Sauers was in thirty minutes. Not close to being ready, and unable to find the strength to go, my reasons became unclear.

Forcing my legs to stand, I went to the sink and washed my face. Although my heart wasn't in it, I knew retrieving information from Hans would help the greater cause. I fussed with my hair until it fell wonderfully to my shoulders, but my will lacked assurance. Out of spite, my hands gripped the red dress and black boots. My intent was to make Stefan jealous even though he would never see me. After a critical scan in the mirror, I strolled out. Physically, I appeared attractive. Emotionally, I was broken.

Hans leaned casually against a streetlamp outside the cafe as I approached. Hoping for a response similar to Stefan's when *he* first saw me, I wasn't disappointed. Hans countenance sparked with delight as I drew near. His hands went to his pockets like an excited schoolboy attempting not to leap for joy. This was the simple part of him I could like. He seemed relaxed by the time I stood before him.

"Ella, I'm . . ." he choked a bit. "I'm glad you came." His hand reached for mine, and with a smile, I let him lead me inside where we found a small table near the back.

"You are beautiful." His eyes rested on me as I took a deep breath. I yearned to hear those very same words out of someone else's mouth. This wasn't going to be as straightforward as I envisioned it in my head.

"Will you order me a lemon tea? I'll be back." The walk to the water closet grew more unsteady with each step. Inside, I leaned heavily on the closed door for support. *I can't do this!* Every time I looked at Hans, a yearning arose for Stefan's baby blues to be gazing back.

This is too hard!

Taking deep breaths, I stepped around the small space in a patterned circle then reached for a towel. Cooling my face with its wet edges, the mirror's reflection caught me off guard. Lines near the tips of my bottom lashes drew new attention. *I'm aging and alone.* The inferno that ignited earlier against Stefan rekindled. Closing the gap, my stare hardened against the woman who faced me. *Whatever happens next, I need to be fully vested or withdraw.* Survival depends on letting him go, his ghost can't control me any longer. This scheme was too dangerous to do half-heartedly. My decision was made.

"Are you okay?" Hans asked as I sat down.

I considered the question carefully. "Everything is good, thank you."

We talked for several hours; it was much more genuine than expected. Thoughts of Stefan emerged only when Hans grinned, which was often, but I would quickly do something to drive his image out of my mind. I managed to slip in several questions about his patrol duties without it appearing suspicious as well.

"With your promotion, do you no longer walk the patrol?"

"Very little. Much of my duties are in the tower now."

"Do you oversee the wall—like the escapees?" My breath ceased momentarily, wondering if I could converse without emotion.

"Yes, however, things have slowed since the latest reinforcement."

"Not too many people try to escape from the Friedrichshain side, huh?"

"Some, but it has gotten more difficult since our new commander arrived."

"Really? How?" I sipped my tea casually.

"Patrol times, strategy, he even recruited various *strabenkind* to watch for unusual activity."

My interest piqued. There definitely was an increase in the homeless present. Who would have guessed they were informants.

"Why'd he do that?"

"His background is intelligence. He's unconventional."

"He sounds clever."

"Clever, yes. Kind, never."

A chill ran the length of my spine. Colonel Anker's image appeared with a shiver. These types of men have no conscience, no mercy. My hand rested over Hans' while I scooted my chair closer. "If I was to come visit you, is there a specific routine you have?"

Hans hesitated. Unsure if this was because the questions were getting more specific or because of my proximity, I waited.

He squeezed my hand and leaned in, inches away.

"Well, we do have a routine. It changes every other day, but for you I would become available at a moment's notice." I cowered under his stare. My heart actually fluttered with his gaze.

What am I doing? My body tilted backward, desperate for air. Hans countenance frowned with concern. Quickly, I refocused and resumed my role. "Well, I might need to visit you sometime." My grin lifted artificially.

Hans raised his hand to get the attention of the waitress. "*Streuselschneken*, first."

I smiled wider, sincere this time. He was still a boy inside.

He ordered two. This helped to keep the conversation going longer, not knowing how many dates we would have.

"How would I reach you if I came to surprise you one day?" My fork dipped into the warm pastry.

"Surprise visits are probably not recommended, but if you do, locate a border guard like last time."

"Are there a lot of soldiers assigned to that post?"

"Not as many as before. The new commander had nearly half reassigned. Mostly the ones with family. He said they tend to be weak."

"But you . . ." I stuttered, ". . . you have a gentle heart, Hans, you don't seem to fit the aggressive character type."

"I'm a soldier, Ella. I protect my country *at any cost.*"

His words sank in. I knew this truth about him and still pursued.

Once a soldier . . . always a soldier. Stefan's face materialized in Hans. Hastily, my watering eyes lowered with a reminder that there was a purpose to my task. I finished the rest of my dessert quickly.

At the end of the night, Hans walked me home.

"You're quiet." Hans held my hand, though it felt different than before. "Did I offend you somehow?"

My head shook no, but my soul shriveled in defeat. All I desired was to get inside my flat fast where I could cry in private. The emotional ups and downs were taking their toll.

"That's good because I would never want to hurt you."

Similar words came from different lips but ended as a lie. My gaze swept to the top of the oak tree in front of my building. Small green buds had begun to sprout. As long as my eyes remained upward, the tears couldn't fall downward.

"Can we meet again soon? Maybe tomorrow?" His voice was both eager and hesitant.

My eyes returned to Hans with a need to decide quite quickly how far this would go, there was still a lot I didn't know. "How about Saturday?"

"I work a long shift that day." Hans played with my fingers as he held my hand.

"That's okay. I can meet you after work, and we can walk." The suggestion was meant to sound appealing but came out weak.

"Walk in Friedrichshain?"

"Sure."

"Um . . ." Hans was serious. "Why?"

"Well . . . I would love to hear more about your job and how you keep us safe," I had to think quickly, ". . . you can tell me more about um . . . protecting the wall. I find it fascinating." My eyelashes fluttered, it was pathetic.

"The wall?"

Nodding, I kissed him on the cheek, my lips lingering longer than necessary. *I kissed someone other than Stefan!* A vigorous stir inside my chest discharged as Hans' arms encircled me, but it was my mouth boldly moving to his that surprised us both. Pressing fervently, I tasted him. The pleasurable mix of heat and moisture coursed through my lips. Yet even intimately connected, my attempt to picture solely him was futile. Silently, my inner scolding reminded me that all this would ever be is a front, a hollow emotion. A means to an end.

"Okay," Hans gasped as we paused for a breath. "Anything you ask, Ella." Holding both my hands now, he continued, "Meet me at six near the tower on Saturday, but please don't get too close to the wall."

"It's a date." I smiled.

Hans moved in once more for another lengthy kiss. I didn't pull away.

TWENTY-FOUR

ESPIONAGE

Saturday was the day before Easter, the Christian holiday. To people all over the world, it was a celebration, a gathering of loved ones . . . to me it was another reminder of why I wanted to leave the East. Although my anger with God gave cause to refuse anything associated with him, the real reason was that it was one more traditional observance to spend alone.

I waited outside the building closest to the tower until Hans could meet me. The weather was much milder than anticipated. My small, brimmed hat was pulled low, barely above my eyes. A light jacket over my dress contradicted my bare knees, but boldness is what I sought, and when Hans reached for my hand, I readily met his as well.

As we walked, my flirtations intensified. It didn't take long to realize Hans would answer anything, especially when I touched him.

"Why did you choose to be a soldier, Hans?"

"During conscript I recognized my natural strength—a gift for stratagem, actually. The colonel I labored under encouraged me to carry on."

"Any regrets?"

He smiled curiously. "What would I regret?"

"I don't know, don't you want to have a family?"

"I can still have a family and be a soldier. I guess I haven't found the right girl, yet." He glanced my direction. Casually, my gaze shifted away.

"What about you, Ella? You're not in the military, don't you want to be married?"

I chastised myself for starting this conversation, knowing full well it would come back to me.

"I was engaged once."

"You were?"

I nodded. "He was a soldier too."

"Stationed where?" Hans didn't hide his curiosity.

"All over. He was NVA Motorieste."

"I see. That's a pretty skilled unit." Hans hesitated, but I knew what he was going to ask next. "What happened?"

"He changed." Shifting anxiously, I didn't want to say anything else on the subject. "Do you plan to be border guard for long?"

"If I continue to promote, I'll get to choose my command."

"Have you ever shot anyone?" The words slipped out before I could control them.

Hans became uncommonly quiet. "Let's not talk about my job anymore."

"I'm sorry. That was inappropriate of me to ask." I truly felt bad.

"Don't apologize. I think many people believe border guard enjoy killing. Not all of us are like that."

As we approached the tunnel building, my arms intertwined tighter, snuggling into his side. We passed one patrol who recognized Hans with a salute. He seemed well respected amongst his comrades.

"Do the soldiers always patrol the same route?"

"Yes, unless there's a disruption or disturbance that requires them elsewhere." The tunnel building was now only steps away.

"Let's turn the other way. This area makes me feel uncomfortable."

Hans chuckled, "Yet it's where you always end up lost, Fräulein." I had hoped he wouldn't remember that.

"... and always rescued by a hero." My hand squeezed his. The flattery was sickly fake but soaked in easily.

As we neared the tower once again, the sun completely disappeared behind the buildings, the lights along the wall now vividly illuminated. Quivering, I was reminded of its dreadful purpose. Hans seemed unaffected and pulled me in tight, his lips dipped into the hollow between my shoulder and neck. They lightly skimmed the surface of my skin below my jaw. The sensation fired goose bumps across my body, and even though he didn't ask, I had no intention of stopping him.

Immediately, the tower light beamed directly on us, blinding us both in our momentary pleasure.

Hans cussed aloud before he guided me away from the wall and the invasive light. "*Scheisse*! He knows it's me! I'm in uniform for heaven's sake!"

"Who?" I questioned.

"My commander." Hans eyes ignited. "Wait for me here, I'll be back."

He left me momentarily and ran to the tower entrance. If this was intended to be a joke, it wasn't funny. My walk across the street was slow. There was very little traffic, and despite the overall decline of the area, it seemed peaceful. I sank to the curb and waited.

After twenty minutes, the outline of Han's athletic physique finally approached. He spit out a whole new set of cusswords then apologized for using them in front of me.

"Ella, my commanding officer is requiring me to work another shift tonight."

"Tonight? Didn't you work all day today?"

"Yes."

"Why would he do that?"

"He is . . ." Hans paused, glancing at a handful of guards nearby. I could tell he wanted to say something else, yet he ended with, ". . . duteous."

"Is he the one who put the spotlight on us?"

"Yes, and then rebuked me for having a woman this close to the wall. He said he should have shot us."

"Would he really?"

"Probably."

Legitimately scared, I scrambled to my feet and started backing away.

Hans followed hastily. "No, Ella, he wouldn't—I'm pretty sure. He's just . . . angry . . . with an intent to make others suffer as he seems to."

"He sounds awful."

"Yeah, his German is flawless, but he came from overseas. He seems to have no mercy."

The way Hans described this man frightened me. Recollection of Anker and how vicious he was—especially his similarities to this commander—made me nervous. This had to be why the patrol suddenly changed and why security was tightened.

"I'm sorry you have to go back to work." My apology was genuine as I leaned in and kissed him on the cheek.

The beam lit on us again. Hans grumbled, "I'm the one who should be apologizing. I won't be able to see you safely home."

"I'll be fine, Hans. Will you?" I chuckled, but it really wasn't amusing.

He still laughed. "I will be alright. I'll see you at Zur."

"Okay." My lips curved naturally as he kissed my hand and walked back towards the tower.

I glanced up at the post. The beam now rotated over the *sperrzone*. The silhouette of the man in the tower was intimidating. I could not see him or his expressions, but felt as though he could see mine. I pulled my hat lower and hustled away.

TWENTY-FIVE

Das Kino

(The Cinema)

"Hans?" I opened my door quite surprised. "I apologize for dropping in, I know we talked about meeting in a few days, but I felt bad about how our walk last Saturday ended."

I stared at him, unsure if I should let him in. My mind quickly scanned a checklist of my flat to make sure I hadn't left any evidence of our tunnel plans out.

"It's fine." I purposefully held my voice steady, my ability to conceal secrets had not been perfected.

"I just . . ." Like a shy school boy, his hands fidgeted with his hat. "I just wanted to see if you would walk with me this afternoon."

I smiled. "That's kind of you." Swiftly glancing back into my apartment, I hoped to see my sweater nearby.

". . . but if I am interrupting, I can leave."

"Interrupting? No, I've been working long hours, though, and my place is a bit messy."

"I don't mind."

"O . . . Okay." Stuttering, I opened the door wider to let him in.

My eyes darted in every direction. I rarely kept the papers out, but I wasn't expecting a visitor either.

"Please come in, but I apologize in advance of its appearance."

"Oh, don't be concerned." He laughed, much more relaxed. "I don't offend easily." In the kitchen, he leaned against the counter the way Stefan had years before. Acutely aware of his form, I fumbled to close the door. It had been a long time since I'd been alone with a man in my apartment. My teeth dug into my lower lip, anxiously. I would have offered him a seat, however, the only one available was Mama's chair, and that was sacred to me.

I quickly scrambled to locate my sweater.

"You have *Immensee*?"

I twisted around to see him at the shelf, touching each of my books. My heart skipped a beat, Stefan's letters were stacked at the end . . . face up.

"Oh. Yes . . ."

"It's one of my mother's favorite stories," he added.

"Mine too." I hurried over, but he had already reached for the tinnie pin and picked it up. He studied it carefully. "Is this yours?" I could sense some doubt in his words. I should not be in possession of a Germanic heritage pin.

"The pin?"

He nodded.

"No . . . not from my family. It was a gift from a friend."

"This should be left to a son. Why would anyone give it away?"

"He . . . um," I stuttered, "He's no longer with us." I inferred death.

"Oh." He readily placed it back on the shelf as I deliberately stood in front of him to block the letters. "I'm sorry you've had so much loss in your life, Ella." He reached for my hand, his kindness authentic.

"Shall we go?" I guided him to the door.

"Yes, I think a walk through the Friedrichshain Volkspark would be beautiful today."

My jaw tightened. *No . . . anywhere but Volkspark.*

Hans pointed the direction as we stepped outside and walked. Grappling with the idea of going to the very place I fell in love with Stefan, I dawdled down the street. My mind fought to create an alternate plan.

Once on Rosa-Luxemburg, we passed a few stores, the Volksbühne . . . then the Babylon!

"Hans," I reached for his arm. "I've never been to *das kino*. Could we go?"

"You have never seen a motion picture?"

"No."

He thought about this for a moment. His eyes flashed around the beautiful sky, and I could practically hear his thoughts about how nice it would be to stay outside. I'd need to work this a bit harder. I slid up next to him, my face within inches.

"It would be nice to be next to you, as well." My eyelashes fluttered, and I smiled. "I was told it's dark in the theater, and well . . . it can be private too."

Hans' countenance lifted, instantly swayed.

"Let's go see." He held my hand and led me inside where a small window on each side of the foyer was occupied by an attendant. We moved to the left where there was no line. The woman told us the picture would not begin for another thirty minutes, but we could go in and watch the news until it started.

I glanced at Hans. "Please, I would love to do this today."

He smiled back then reached into his pocket and pulled out the Marks to pay the employee.

"I was told by a comrade this movie contains a lot of action," he said directing us up the narrow stairs leading to the balcony. Once through the doors, with no other patrons nearby, we had our choice of any seats. Partitions near the front separated every couple of seats in privacy. Hans immediately steered us towards a pair, and I realized he had taken my suggestion to be alone seriously.

"What do you mean by *action*?" I knew little about motion pictures. He held my cushioned seat down and waited for me to sit before he answered.

"*A KLK an PTX* is a spy film on the *Red Orchestra*. Frederick, my comrade, said it features the relationship between the Nazis and Communists."

"With their government?" I inquired.

"No, I believe it also portrays their influence on the people as well, most likely arrests, torture, maybe camps or extermination." His list came quite casually.

Thankfully, the lowly-lit lamps spaced intermittently on the walls kept Hans from seeing my expression clearly. My intent to avoid Volkspark at any cost may have created another dilemma. *Can I actually sit through a motion picture depicting the mistreatment of innocent people by evil men?*

"Okay," I mumbled.

Hans put an arm around me and pulled me in tight next to him. "Don't be afraid. I'm here." His lips brushed my cheek then slid skillfully down my neck. As pleasing as this felt, I grew uncomfortable and turned toward him. At this angle, it forced his lips to withdraw and pull back. I quickly improvised.

"Thanks for bringing me here."

"Like I've said, anything for you, Ella."

I pondered those words as the screen lit up in front of us. A brash sound exploded, and I jumped to the foreign sounds. Hans laughed out loud. The national symbol with the hammer and compass surrounded by a yellow ring of rye appeared on the large, white curtain. An outline of the DDR's borders accented boldly behind it. Precarious music played as a man's voice began to speak.

"Nachrichten aus der DDR ." My eyes grew wide as the news began. I had never seen anything like this. *"2 June movement, which rose from Kommune 1 wreaks anarchy across the West. The name 2 June comes from the date student Benno Ohnesorg was brutally killed by police. West Berlin police are still unable to control the increased bombings and riots organized by extremist groups, such as 2 June and the Red Army Faction.*

"Irish Republican Army claims attacks on a British Yacht Club in West Germany, boat engineer killed in explosion.

"Falkenhöh Border breach attempt ends in fatal self-inflicted accident. The ministry denounces any involvement in the death of Klaus Schulze but insists the safety of both the residents of the border plots and the people's police guard will be protected above any further acts of treason or misconduct."

"See, Ella," Hans whispered, although we were still the only people in the balcony. "Why do people think life in the West is much better? There is nothing but chaos and death with the Amis and Brits."

I listened, although I was sure Hans had probably never been exposed to an ally station in his life. It's simply a matter of perspective. Everything is depicted differently, depending on who is speaking. What I did know and trust were the words from Anton and the freedom he and Josef were privy to. I had seen enough treachery at the Franke's to know whose intentions were more honorable.

"Is it really that bad to want something more?" I proceeded cautiously.

"The DDR is generous; they offer opportunities, advancement, education—all that the West offers—but our people are greedy. Yes, they want more but at what cost?"

"Hans, there are people dying on the streets, not enough housing or food to go around. Is it really asking too much to want a meal?"

"It's not that bad. Many strabenkind have been offered employment—even soldiering—and its refused. It's a choice."

My jaw tightened. For someone quite close to the wall, Hans seemed somewhat ignorant.

"There's always those who believe their life is more valuable than others." Hans steadied his voice. I could see this was a deep-rooted belief. "My duty at the wall is to make sure the people of East Berlin are safe. I have an obligation to keep them from making foolish decisions like this Schulz chap who clearly put our courageous men at risk in an attempt to join a country that only provides its people with lawlessness and mayhem."

I suddenly felt nauseous. Hans continued, "I don't kill people for sport like some of these extremist groups. They are bombing innocent people. The people who come to the border are lawbreakers. They are not innocent people. They're the ones who spread lies and deceits about life here. Is life really so bad here?" Hans gazed down at me. I couldn't look at him and speak the truth.

"Ella?" He reached for my chin and lifted it up.

My head felt light and dizzy. I needed to answer him. Concern crept into his expression, and it was obvious he doubted me.

I need a distraction. Placing my arms around his neck, I drew him close. My lips melted into his, the sweetness transferring to my tongue. He responded by sliding his hands past my waist and tight against my back. The kiss lengthened and another quickly followed. The more I stayed connected to Hans the less I was connected to the screen or the lies that derived from it, but being this close to Hans presented its own predicament.

We took a breath, but our foreheads still rested together.

"Ella . . ." Hans' breath labored heavily as he tried to speak. "Will you come home with me tonight?"

My face remained emotionless. There was no doubt I was attracted to Hans. He was handsome and strong and . . . *the enemy* . . . I stifled a cry. I longed to be held, only *not* by him. Yet every time we were together, my desire for passion and touch allowed it to go too far.

"I can't," I whispered.

Hans appeared deflated. "Why not?"

"I just can't."

Hans didn't push. Above all, he was a gentleman, but I knew I had sent mixed signals.

The music for the movie began, and we both turned forward. Even though Hans still held my hand, the intensity we felt moments ago was gone. Even as the picture developed in front of me, my mind was elsewhere. I started this relationship as more of a duty, but had I let it influence me? Were my feelings for Hans clouding my judgement? My goals? I needed to finish getting the information then get away.

I should have been thrilled with my first experience at the cinema. I had heard you felt as if you were part of a different life or adventure, but as I watched this motion picture play out on the screen in front of me, I winced. All it did was bring the ugliness of lies and consequences to life then reminded me of the dangerous role I was playing.

That night when Hans walked me home, he seemed more distant than before. Few words were exchanged after the cinema, and while he raved about how much he enjoyed it, he was otherwise quiet.

"Thank you for today." I smiled as we reached the entrance to my building.

Hans leaned down and kissed me on the cheek, but a hollowness lingered.

"Are you well?" I hesitated to open this conversation again, but I owed him that much.

He glanced away and then looked back towards me. He wasn't smiling.

"I'm confused sometimes, I guess." He sighed loudly. "I think you like me and then other times I'm not sure."

Exactly why I shouldn't have asked.

I pointed to a nearby bench. "Can you sit for a moment and talk?"

He nodded, and we sat down.

"Hans, I like you—I really do. I simply haven't had a lot of good things happen in my life, and I tend to expect the worst."

He listened carefully as I continued. "Death is a difficult issue with me, and it's a big part of your life and all around us . . . even in a motion picture. I can't seem to get away from it." I surprised myself at how open I was. This was not part of the act.

"Ella, I truly am sad for all of your loss." His eyes softened. "You've had a great deal to handle alone."

"I am alone, and I'm afraid." The *real* Ella was speaking.

His dimple emerged. The slower his smile, the deeper the dent. It was endearing. He placed both hands over mine. "If you would allow me to show you how wonderful love can be, it could change everything. What are you afraid of?"

I shook my head. "I'm frightened about how I feel about you—your goodness, but I struggle with your beliefs . . . especially your job."

"I'm not a bad guy. Yes, I protect the border, but I protect it for people like you."

Reality abruptly hit me . . . .*not for me. From me.*

Hans really did believe what he did was honorable. Was that his fault or the people who taught him? People like his parents? Or people like his cruel commander?

"I need time, Hans. I'm not ready." There was more truth tonight than ever before.

"I understand." His lips brushed my hand briefly.

Somehow, I yearned for his lingering touch. There was too much about this relationship that was wrong, but without doubt, we had a connection.

I opened the door as Hans tipped his hat and turned. "You know where to find me when you are."

I waited at the entrance until I could no longer see the moonlight fall on Hans' muscular outline. He had been nothing but considerate of me, yet during our short time together, I had passed judgement on him many times. I did not deserve such kindness. *Are we really all that different?* The clarity I'd started this mission with was evaporating. With no clear direction of where I stood, or where this was headed, my premise became more convoluted. Did I continue the charade with Hans for information, or had his companionship become an appealing diversion?

TWENTY-SIX

SUSPICION

After three weeks with Hans, I finally felt ready to present what I had learned to my friends and was silently grateful the task was nearly complete. Boundaries had blurred. My longing had become dangerously close to crossing a line, and my original pretense of deception had turned into an emotional attachment, a friendship . . . or more . . . that I had not intended.

Although Hans and I hadn't formerly said goodbye, I now avoided him, more out of fear on my part. He wasn't Stefan or even Anton, but he was kind to me and treated me wonderfully. Had I allowed my heart to truly open up? Despite his obligation to shoot me if he knew my escape plans . . . I believed the possibility of finding happiness with Hans was real, and that frightened me most of all.

Our next meeting at Patz was tonight. I arrived late. A large party came in to Zur ten minutes before my shift ended. I couldn't leave Angelika alone, so I assisted until close.

The moment I took my seat at Patz, I sensed something was wrong.

Nobody spoke.

"What?" I glanced around at all the sour faces. They peered at each other but still no one said anything.

"What's going on?" I questioned. "You're all acting strange."

I motioned to the waitress and ordered Currywurst. I was starving.

"Seriously, somebody tell me what's going on," I demanded. Telfer looked disgusted, but he always appeared angry.

"Rupert? . . . Lamar?"

"Ella," Lamar finally spoke up. "I saw you at a Sauers the other night, kind of cozy in the back. You didn't see me though."

"Okay, well what does this have to do with you guys not talking to me?"

"You were with a man in uniform . . . border patrol."

"Yes, about that. I have some news for you." I reached into my pocket for the papers.

"I bet you do," Telfer quipped sarcastically.

"What's that supposed to mean?"

"I think you know," he added with contempt.

I suddenly realized they misunderstood my purpose. *They think I'm the spy, the wrong kind of spy.* I shoved the papers back into my pocket and felt the hair rise on the back of my neck.

"How long have you been in with them?" Telfer asked with spite in his voice. Although he was the only one talking, the others watched with interest.

"In with them?" I choked the words out. My skin flushed hot. "Never!" I cried louder than I should have. "I can't even believe you would think that." I peered around. Everyone but Telfer instantly glanced down at their hands or the table.

"Lamar . . ." I appealed, "I was getting background info—info we needed."

Lamar shook his head confused. "You were incredibly sweet on him, Ella."

"It was part of the act."

"It looked real."

"Seriously, Lamar? Why would you think it was real?"

"Because we know how much Stefan hurt you," Ian spoke up. He had been silent the whole time.

A sharp sting pierced my chest while tears welled in my eyes. I had shared the most private information I owned, and it was being used against me.

I stared at Ian. "Then you have to know it was all a show, because yes, my heart has always been with Stefan, but as you also know, he left me. He's gone, and all I have now is my desire to leave this place."

I confronted the whole group now. "Honestly, if you guys really want to know what's going on near the building, I could tell you because I practically slept the information out of Hans the border guard, however, since you're convinced I switched sides, I have nothing to say!" I bit my lip and dashed for the door.

Ian followed, regret filled his plea. "Ella. Ella, I'm sorry. Why didn't you tell me?" He reached for my arm. I whipped it away. "Please . . ." he pleaded, "come back inside, and we can talk."

I turned around angrily. "I tried, but it's obvious you all made up your mind about my loyalty." The onslaught of tears continued despite repeatedly brushing them away with my fingertips. Burning with resentment, I reached into my pocket and threw the papers containing all the information Hans had unwittingly shared toward Ian. They no longer meant anything to me. I ran to catch the next bus.

The bus drove on and on as I sat in a mindless stupor. The doors slid open, and I stepped off, staring around bewildered.

I'm in Pankow? How did this happen?

Despite the mechanical movement in my legs, I didn't stop them from approaching Dietzgenstraße. My pause at the Franke residential gates was brief.

No matter what I do, I cannot take the memory of Stefan out of my head. He's everywhere! My feet shuffled past the entrance sluggishly and moved around back. The cemetery loomed nefariously in front of me. The superstitions that rise out of places for the dead and rumors of unfinished business occurring in the dark did not matter to me.

I stumbled to the rock. The grass had grown very high and was not manicured like it had been years ago. The ground was rough and cold as I slipped to my knees, but it didn't hinder me.

"Papa, I need your help," I cried aloud. "Papa, please, I don't know what to do. I'm so alone."

The next hour was spent talking to my father who sadly couldn't talk back. Miserable, lonely, and chilled, I still couldn't pull away. Visions of the Franke's finding my lifeless body lying across my father's grave the next morning crossed my mind, although it might not matter to them in the least. To them, it would be more like a means to an end.

Glancing over to the house, a few lights still lingered in the darkness. I stared at the dark window of the art room. What I wouldn't give to enjoy the memories experienced there; the picnic that changed everything, the dance, the spontaneous paint war, the kiss, the memory of his lips on my neck. It seemed like ages ago and only continued to strain the wounds already carved in my heart.

Reluctantly, I kissed the ground goodbye. "I miss you, Papa."

Once home, the loneliness I felt in every corner extracted what scrap of life I had left within. I grabbed another piece of paper and wrote in big letters:

Stefan, I hate you!

I wrote it twice. On the third attempt, the pencil went through the paper, creating a jagged hole and an unsightly mark on my quilt. Enraged, my hand gripped the pencil tightly until it broke in half. I threw it to the floor then shredded what was left of the paper into dozens of pieces. The desire to break something else consumed me, but I had few possessions as it was. Pressing my head into the pillow, face first, I screamed, then cried. Through exasperated energy, my wails graduated to silence.

The next day at work, Angelika handed me a sealed note. "I found this at the door when I arrived this morning." She shot me a warning glare. "I'm glad it was me who found it."

The last time I received personal correspondence at the restaurant, Conrad scolded me. "Thank you." I squeezed Angelika's hand before I slipped into a bathroom stall to read the simple message. Lamar's handwriting was instantly recognizable. "Please meet us again. I am sorry."

Angered by the night's events, Ian, and this note, the day got progressively worse. I dropped a tray of drinks at the feet of a regular customer, muddled orders, and as expected, received terrible tips. Halfway through my shift, Conrad pointed to the door and commanded I leave until I could perform as expected.

When I arrived home, there was one letter in my postal box. It was from Anton. It should have been a thrill to hear from the one person who always seemed to lift me when others couldn't, but as I read, my spirit—as weak as it was—crumbled.

3 April 1971

Ella,
Stefan is a fool! Hearing the news of your engagement was initially
hard, but over time I have come to accept our lives have changed upon
separation. I hesitate to share my news with you on the outcome of
your break-up. You are my best friend though and I could never keep
anything from you.

   I have met someone. She operates a floral cart near my work, and
Josef wanted to get flowers for his date; that's how we met. It was
like when you and I were together all the time then the kiss. It just
happens, right?

   Her name is Elizabeth. She is German and speaks French and
English fluently. We have been steady for a month. It is a strange
feeling for me to think of someone other than you, but she is good and
smart and can be stubborn too—like you. I can't wait for you to meet
her. Please write soon. Your thoughts are important to me.

Love Anton

The irony of my life was overwhelming. When Ian mentioned maybe
God intended things to end with Stefan because Anton was supposed to
be the path I took, I considered the possibility that he was right. Maybe
even wed and find happiness once again. Now—now I knew that to be
impossible. *God must enjoy seeing me alone and miserable.* My mug of tea
smashed against the wall and shattered into a hundred pieces.

   I spoke to no one the following week. Not that people didn't try. Hans
came to Zur twice, but I refused to serve his table or speak to him. Another waitress told him I needed space, no other explanation given. Lamar tried and even Rupert—surprisingly—but both were given the cold
shoulder. I was done working with others. If leaving the East was something I intended, then maybe I was meant to do it alone.

TWENTY-SEVEN

You're A Man!

13 June 1971

My hands glided across my plaid skirt for the third time. This and the complimentary red blouse were new as of the day before, yet wrinkles kept appearing. Back at the mirror, I double and triple checked my complexion, make-up, and hair then finished with a spritz of perfume Mama G had given me for Christmas the year before she passed. I rarely wore it and doubted it would be noticed, but it seemed like the perfect way to top it all off.

As I passed the small playground at the end of Max-Beer, children were happily playing on the rusted poles and broken balance beams. How nice to be a child—even a child in the Waisenhaus—when life seemed less complicated. Food and friends were about the extent of one's concerns, not life or death.

My pace was slow and relaxed as I turned towards Rosenthaler, the best route for my destination. Hans' flat was next to the *Apotheke* at the other end. I had never actually been inside, though not for lack of invitations. His charming persuasion most likely worked for other girls.

When I reached Invaliden, I still had some time to spare before the assumed meeting. It has been quite a while since the suggestion was made, and I wasn't even sure he would be there.

With the extra minutes, I stepped into the small record store halfway down the block. The door was open and inviting despite the musty, old smell. Upon entry, the ambiance was cozy. Barely the size of my living room, there were three wooden displays that each contained a couple dozen records, and another handful lined one wall. Briefly browsing through the few titles and not recognizing anything, I built up the courage to ask.

"Do you have The Beatles?"

The man working behind a small counter in the corner glanced up and over his eyeglasses. His blond hair was tucked neatly behind his ears and rested against his neck.

"Beatles?" There was a slight shake in his voice. "No, no we don't have The Beatles!"

"Oh." I moved to the other box and flipped through his sections that had been separated by genre. "What about The Rolling Stones?"

He shook his head a bit more aggressively now and peeked at his watch.

"No, no, nothing Brit."

"Biermann?" I threw out the name Mielke had mentioned at Zur.

"No, no none of that." Agitated, the man moved from the corner.

"What about—"

"I will be closing for an hour, can you come back later?" He cut me off abruptly and motioned for me to leave. I hadn't intended to get a rise from him, but he was definitely flustered by my inquiries.

Chuckling as I approached the door, I apologized, "I'm sorry, I didn't mean to upset you." My inquiries were chancy, I shouldn't have been surprised by his reaction.

"No, you didn't. It's fine." He closed the door behind me and not only locked it but shut the blinds. Disappointed, I stared at the now-closed record store windows.

"You are stirring all sorts of trouble up here, aren't you?"

The voice startled me. Although I saw the man sitting on the nearby bench when I first arrived, I didn't expect him to notice me.

"Not intentionally."

He placed the newspaper he had been reading on his lap and chuckled. The wrinkles surrounding his eyes and mouth moved with his laugh. "Don't let Schneider's response bother you," he said, rubbing his gray hair. "He's a bit jittery with everyone. He used to sell all sorts of music until people—" The man gave me an interesting look. "—people suggested otherwise."

"I understand."

He patted the empty part of the bench next to him. "What's your interest in those bands?"

"You heard me?" I asked, astonished that someone as old as this man could hear a conversation in a different room.

He laughed louder. "Oh, anytime music's mentioned, these old ears perk up."

His gnarled hand patted the bench again. "Come, visit with an old man a moment, and we can talk music." I glanced at my watch. With thirty minutes to kill, I smoothed out my skirt again and joined him.

"Where are you going on this fine day, Fraulein?"

"I'm meeting a friend." Friend was incorrect but simple.

"Well, you may just well be the brightest part of their day."

My smile was genuine. An unusual encounter to begin with, this gentleman was intriguing. "So what do you know about music?"

"Music?" His hand gripped his chin as if he was going down memory lane. "What *don't* I know? What do *you* want to know, Fraulein?"

"Ella, you can call me Ella. I actually don't know much. My favorites are Edith Piaf and Ella Fitzgerald.

"Piaf . . . yes, what a delight." His pale blue eyes actually twinkled. "I met her once."

"You did?" My doubt wasn't masked.

"Yes, at the Moulin Rouge in '44. The German occupation of France made it possible for the soldiers to attend her cabaret shows. On record her voice is divine . . . in person, she's an angel."

"You were in the war?"

"Wasn't everyone my age?"

I laughed. Everything he said brought a lift to my heart. "My Papa was also . . . Wehrmacht."

His voice tapered off into a whisper for the first time, "That was a different era."

Despite the momentary silence, it was peaceful, more peaceful than I had felt in quite some time.

I leaned back on the bench and sighed. "My friends introduced me to The Beatles and some songs from The Rolling Stones as well."

"Yes, yes they are good, but have you listened to any bands from Berlin?"

"No, I can't say that I have. I don't go out much."

With one eyebrow raised, he tipped his head to the side. "Why not? You're young! It's always great to be young."

I met his grin but didn't respond. "Are there bands from both East and West Berlin?"

"Oh yes. Both."

"We actually have bands here?"

He laughed out loud again as my face grew warm. My limited knowledge was an understatement.

"There are many talented artists here. Are they restricted? Yes, quite often, but they find a way. You can't stop expression."

"How do you know so much?"

"I'm an old man. I've lived a long time, and I've seen a lot happen . . . and for many years I played the piano and the saxophone."

"Were you in a band?" I had never met anyone who played an instrument. This was so exciting.

"Several, actually. Mostly Schlager and Volksmusik."

"Do you still play?"

He held up his weathered hands "Only if the musicians don't show." He pointed to the pub next to him. "This is my place."

"You own the Nichts tun?"

He nodded.

"Why the name . . . Do Nothing?"

"Because that's what you should do when you go to a pub."

With a smile I asked, "So that's what you're doing out here?"

"Why not? It's a beautiful day, and just think—if I hadn't, I wouldn't have made a new friend named Ella."

I giggled. I most definitely was in need of a good friend.

"I think you should come and visit. We have Volksmusik on Fridays and Ostrock on Saturday nights . . . well most of them. Occasionally, the musicians have a run in with the government and can't quite make it."

"Don't you" —I leaned in for privacy— "Don't you fear someone telling you what you can and can't play in your pub?"

He shrugged. "Are there problems? Yes. Do I fear it? No." He rolled the newspaper tightly in his fist, but when he tapped my shoulder with it, his touch was gentle. "You can't live your life in fear, Ella. You can't control what others do or say, but you can control how you react to it." He winked at me.

Smiling widely, I reached out to shake his hand. "You know, I really appreciate this. Thanks, and it was so nice to meet you, uh . . ." I snickered, "I'm sorry I didn't even ask you your name."

"It's Jörg and you are welcome here anytime."

"Goodbye, Jörg." The walk to the corner was short, and just before my turn down Ackerstraße, I twisted back and waved.

Arriving barely before noon to the makeshift platform, I hesitated. Angry at myself for the way my selfishness exhausted my ability to function, I inhaled deeply, preparing for disappointment. At the very least, I needed to work on being conscious of others, especially him. Was it rational to believe that after all the time he'd been ignored he would still come?

I glanced at the rudimentary platform that had been hastily constructed next to the cemetery wall. Someone had placed wooden boards across several large cinder blocks, giving us barely enough lift to see over the wall but a sufficient distance away to not be a threat.

Unlike the East, safely constructed viewing stations had popped up all over the West for friends and family to catch a glimpse of a loved one. From the ground, I could see very little—the wall rose far too high—but as I slowly took the giant, quite-unladylike steps onto the shaky boards, my view widened.

Because of the condition of the platform, it made sense only a couple bodies could be on it at once. With only one other person present, my timing was right. Once settled, my eyes anxiously met the platform across the wall. Their platform—although also constructed in wood—was much taller, at least a dozen steps to reach its full height, and at the top at least five or six people could be present.

My eyes nervously shifted about their already-full platform. Even if he was there, would I recognize him? Almost instantly, they clicked with a man. We were only ten metres apart, but I squinted to recognize the child he was at eleven. I could hear his cries above all else.

"Ella!!" he shouted. "It's you! You came!" Josef's eyes and simultaneous waves, conveyed his undeniable excitement.

"Josef!" I waved both my hands as tears sprang forth. Finally! Happy tears. "I'm sorry. I should have come so much sooner."

"It doesn't matter. You're here now."

"Thank you for not giving up on me."

"Never, sister. You look older. You've grown up."

"Me?" I cried. "You're a man!" We both laughed at this comment. He really was as tall as I had imagined, and from my estimation, a good two metres! Strong too, broad shoulders, and when he gripped the wood in front of him, his muscles expanded. "Oh, Josef!" I sniffled to keep the tears from disrupting the moment. "I can't believe I'm looking at you. You are so handsome and healthy!"

Josef circled his back to me, talking to someone. The bounce in his shoulders showed his thrill had not reduced. My eyes slowly caught sight of another man rising up the steps. A wave of emotion winded me as an older Anton joined Josef on the platform.

His hand rubbed over his still-short hair just like it used to, but when he rubbed his chin, a neatly trimmed beard now resided there. Other than that, he was the same Anton. *Breathe!* I commanded myself. Scrambling in my purse for a handkerchief, I fidgeted with the fabric nervously then quickly wiped my cheeks, keeping its availability close.

"Ella!" Anton waved. "Ella, it's you!" My heartbeat pounded so loud I was sure he could hear it even this distance away.

"Anton!" was all I could say.

"I'm so glad you came. You look . . . you look really good."

"You too, both of you." My eyes flicked between the two of them. Ten years since my eyes had rested upon them. Ten years! "So much to say." A brief flash went through my brain of all the events that had taken place in the last decade, and although we had written letters, the content was not absolute nor ever would be because of prying eyes.

"Yes," Anton agreed. "Too much." His mouth curved into the widest smile I had seen or remembered. Any hint of the wild, angry Anton was gone. I hoped it hadn't disappeared entirely. His spirit was my salvation more times than I could count.

"And Josef! I'm so proud of you and your university classes—all you've accomplished. You're so smart."

"It's because you insisted on reading to me every night, sister." We all chuckled from the truth.

"How is work, Anton?"

"It's good. I'm in the process of becoming a part owner. Can you believe it, klein Maus? Me, a business owner!"

Our conversation had only begun minutes ago, but my cheeks already hurt from smiling so wide. "I always believed in you, Anton. Always."

"I know." His eyes tore from me and turned to the side. A woman had arrived and stood suspiciously close.

"Ella," he choked a bit, "this is Elizabeth. The one I wrote you about."

My grin faltered enough for me to quickly catch it and force it upward again. *Anton's girl is here?* I wasn't sure I was ready for that. *But Anton isn't mine. He's entitled to happiness whether I have it or not.* The argument in my head was taking precious time from my visit. Two additional people had arrived and paused next to the boards. Even though they were silently waiting a turn, their presence filled me with anxiety.

I turned back to Anton, Josef . . . and Elizabeth.

"Hi, Ella." Elizabeth's sweet voice could barely sail my direction without being overrun by the others on their platform. "It's nice to finally meet you. Anton always talks about his best friend from the East."

She raised her gloved hand in a dainty wave and smiled with perfectly plump red lips. Her flawless, coiffed curls surrounded her pasty white complexion. I bit my tongue subtly. *Best friend from the East?* I silently snarled. *I was his only friend from the East, and at one time, his only girlfriend! And I thought he liked . . . girls like me.*

"Hi, Elizabeth." My tightly clenched fists were pulled behind my back and out of sight. "Josef, tell me what you like to do the most when you're not working."

Anton interrupted before Josef could even speak. "Anything to do with girls, Josef is involved." Anton chuckled aloud and rubbed Josef's long strands until they blocked his sight. When Josef brushed them aside, memories of Stefan doing that same move entered my mind. *Stop!* I warned myself. *This is not about Stefan!*

Josef playfully pushed Anton aside and answered. It warmed my heart to be assured Anton had truly become Josef's family . . . a real brother.

"I go dancing. I love to dance."

"Figures . . ." I laughed. "So what music do you listen to?"

In the corner of my eye I saw Anton lean in and whisper something to Elizabeth. She giggled and kissed him on the cheek. Even from my distance, the red mark left behind could be seen. I shook my head swiftly and centered once again on Josef.

"Anything! Jazz, krautrock, reggae, even this sound called heavy metal."

"H—heavy metal? Reggae? What's that?"

He laughed aloud. "Oh, Ella. I can't get enough of it. One of my favorites is Karlheinz Stockhausen. In fact, I just saw him perform at the Expo a year ago. What about you, sister? Who do you like?"

My face blushed a little, but I knew this wouldn't surprise him. "Edith Piaf . . . still."

Josef grinned like a child again. "La Vie en Rose."

"Yes."

"What happened to our house?" Josef's question exhibited pain but rightfully so, it was our only memories together. He pointed to where our flat had stood five stories up and was now completely unseen from his side of the wall.

I nodded sadly. "Yes, Josef, its gone. It's happened all along the border. Many apartment buildings have been demolished. It's very sad to see.

"The church is still standing."

"Uh-huh, but probably not for long. Nobody is allowed in."

"Yeah, our pastor asked if candles could be lit inside for Advent last Christmas, but the East refused.

"Your pastor?"

Josef stuttered. "Y—yeah. Anton and I go to church most Sundays . . . usually after we check the platform."

"Really?" I was surprised and guilt-ridden. "Which church?"

"Protestant."

This news surprised me a bit, actually it surprised me a lot, knowing Anton, but I immediately realized there was much I didn't know about them now. "So tell me about your house and your friends."

"We live in an apartment building in the British sector. My best friend is Lothar, and we're both studying English. Elizabeth helps us with that." I fought to keep my nose from crinkling as he continued. "It could help me one day when I'm a lawyer."

"That's wonderful." Sorrow crept into my voice. "I just can't believe you have grown up—and without me."

"You should've come with us." His murmur was loud enough to injure me.

"You know I couldn't leave, Josef."

His head lowered as he spoke. "I know." Nobody spoke for a full minute. "Was Papa buried here at Sophien?"

"No, Himmelfahrt."

"I hope to visit him one day."

"He would like that. I go as often as I can."

"Ella?" Suddenly, an eleven-year-old expression appeared opposite me. "Ella, when are you coming?" His voice weakened. I glanced at the guards that patrolled on both sides of me. They weren't necessarily listening to conversations, or at least I told myself that, but they were close. Even the people waiting their turn nearby seemed to loiter with an open ear.

Anton watched us both with intense curiosity. Elizabeth swept her head back and forth between us. She didn't know our bond, but her worried countenance was clear.

"As soon as I can," I mouthed as quietly as possible and still be heard. "I love you!"

Anton cried, "We think of you every day. We miss you."

"I miss you too!" I blew them kisses and waved.

As they were nudged out of the way by others who had waited their turn to visit with their friends and family, my hand extended in a continual wave until I could no longer see their faces. I stepped off the end of the boards with a heavy heart then lifted my head. *No, this was a good day!* I saw Josef—now a man—and Anton. *He is happy. They are happy. I cannot let my sadness take this moment away.* Yet I could not stop myself from thinking of Stefan, triggered most assuredly by the tender sentiments I witnessed from Anton and Elizabeth.

On my return, the same route from before, I paused in front of the pub and the bench that was now empty. With no intention of going home to a lonely flat and dwelling on all that my life was missing, I wanted the way my day had started to continue. I stepped through the doors and walked inside.

"It's my new friend Ella!" Jörg was now behind the bar. Two men with equally aging appearances sat on the stools in front of him.

"What can I get you, my dear?"

"Water, good conversation, and a chance to do nothing."

He laughed. "All three coming right up!" I slid into an empty stool next to the other two men and enjoyed one of the best afternoons I had ever spent in the East.

TWENTY-EIGHT

COMRADE WEITZNER

Throughout the next week, Jörg's words replayed over and over in my mind . . . *you can't control what others do or say, but you can control how you react to it.* Between Stefan vanishing and my friends' accusations, I have reacted in a variety of ways. Emotional, angry, humiliated, vengeful . . . descriptions flowed easily regarding my behavior, yet the truth in his words burrowed deeply and forced me to ask, *Can I really control that?*

I realized part of my struggle in letting Stefan go was that I had too many unanswered questions. I decided to contact his old comrade Edger Weitzner, he was the close friend he mentioned in his letters and had wished I would meet one day. The soldier he served with before he disappeared from my life.

My innermost hope was that maybe Herr Weitzner could shed light on our separation or maybe have an explanation for Stefan's motives, yet no matter what—answers or not—this had to be the end of the road. I could not function believing he was still my future.

As I approached the rundown apartment building in Lichtenberg, it's desolate appearance, magnified by the boarded bottom windows and broken glass, overshadowed any light that battled to emerge from the upper-floor windows. I entered the dark foyer tentatively pulling my purse in tight. The outline of my knife poked through the fabric, offering some assurance accompanied by my increased alertness.

The steps creaked noisily before I arrived on the third floor and located the correct apartment number. The happy screams of a child penetrated through the wall as I snatched a deep breath and knocked. This made me smile, although no one came to the door. I waited, then knocked a bit louder. All noise seemed to stop simultaneously. A television or radio was silenced as whispered voices and quiet creeping commenced. I felt the vibration of feet in motion on the floor we shared but still no answer.

In an attempt to contrast the hard Gestapo knock of the Stasi, my knuckles wrapped ever so gently on the wooden door.

The peephole went dark. Nevertheless, I waited.

After a drawn-out minute, the latch on the door clicked and the knob opened. The distorted curl of a nose was all that was seen through the crack. Scurrying movement sounded behind him.

"I'm searching for Edgar Weitzner." My eagerness was clear.

"Who's asking?" The man's equally disturbed eyebrows now appeared.

"My name is Ella Kühn."

A sudden smoothness evolved across his countenance.

"Ella?" The man's tone transformed to benevolence.

"Yes."

"Ella, please come in! Come in!" he cried excitedly, the door now fully open. "I apologize for being abrupt."

"Thank you." I entered the front room, unable to stop my eyes from scanning the walls for a photograph. As close as Stefan had described their friendship, it was possible it had been preserved in a picture.

"Please, please sit down." He hastily gathered some toys off the sofa and placed them in a basket on the floor. "There is little trust these days."

I nodded my head, understanding exactly what he meant.

"Gretchen, darling, come. Come and meet Stefan's girl . . . remember Stefan, the comrade I told you about? The mortician?"

My head shook subtly, but I caught myself. I didn't want to share more than necessary.

"Ella! I can't believe you are here!" Edgar continued to wave the woman into our room. "How did you find me?"

"Stefan gave me your address once and suggested I meet your wife. I'm sorry it took me this long."

"Don't apologize. Here you are." He was a completely different person than the man who answered the door. "I feel I practically know you already. In the four years I spent with Stefan, you were all he spoke of!"

I smiled faintly.

"Gretchen, will you get Ella some tea? Would you like tea?"

I nodded. "Yes, thank you."

Edgar eagerly talked about the day they met and the training they received, seemingly unaware of my reticence. Gretchen brought us both a cup of black tea. My nods and smiles surfaced at all the right times, but my mind was elsewhere.

While Edgar continued to talk, my hands grew clammy with impatience, so I stuck them in the pockets of my dress as he laughed at something only he and Stefan would remember. It was clear how he and Edgar became friends. He was quite amiable, even growing younger the longer I stared. With his initial wrinkles gone, he appeared much closer to Stefan's age than I believed him to be.

I interrupted him cautiously. "Herr Weitzner? What happened after 1967?"

He stopped mid-sentence, his eyes falling to the mug he held tightly in his hands. The steam suddenly seemed to be his biggest focus. I repeated the question, but this time I added a please.

"Not my place, Fräulein. Stefan should tell you. It shouldn't come from me."

"What shouldn't come from you?"

"Do you want a biscuit with your tea?" He was anxious to move on to another subject.

"No, thank you." I inched closer to him. "Please, Herr Weitzner, I need to know."

Edgar abruptly stood and walked into the kitchen. He didn't tell me why or if he was coming back. I waited awkwardly as several minutes passed. Gretchen and their son appeared without a word. She grabbed the boy's jacket off the hook by the door, put it on him, then they both left.

I stood to leave myself when Herr Weitzner appeared in the room again. "Why do you need to know so badly, Ella?" tension apparent in his voice.

My eyes stung. With my confidence waning, I wiped my cheeks with the back of my hand and sucked in another breath, contemplating my next move.

He stared hard, a roller coaster of emotion. One minute he seemed pleased, the other, distraught, or irate. His reaction to my question frightened me, yet not enough to deter me from my intent.

I stepped closer and raised my own voice to his. "Because whatever happened in 1967 took Stefan from me! Whatever he was called to do, wherever he went . . . it destroyed *us*." My cries came out all at once. I sniffled hard to keep my nose from running while he handed me a hand-kerchief then pointed to the sofa again for me to sit.

Composed again, he asked, "You're not together?"

"No."

"Where is he now?" This query frustrated me.

"I don't know." I wiped my eyes then my whole face. "I haven't heard from him in four years. I don't even know if he's alive! I hoped you knew something."

"Four years?"

I continued to wipe my eyes, the tears a steady stream now.

"That doesn't make any sense." He rubbed his head then inched closer. "That would put your last communication in '67?"

"Yes . . . July."

"That was right about the time we were sent to Moscow."

"So, you really did go to the Soviet Union?" I hungered for anything he could tell me.

Herr Weitzner's eyes clouded over, his pupils fixated erroneously.

"Were you two together that whole time?" I tapped his knee gently. "What can you tell me about him?"

He immediately grabbed my hands. "I know he loves you, Ella. I know that you were everything to him."

Why do people keep saying that? I screamed silently in my head. *How do others seem to know Stefan still loves me, but I don't?*

"If he loves me, why would he no longer have any contact with me?"

Herr Weitzner adjusted uncomfortably in his chair. Whatever it was, it was difficult for him to talk about. "I would be lying if I didn't tell you that the tour to Vietnam took something from us all, and it was different for each of us."

"Vietnam?" I choked out nearly an octave too high. "What are you talking about? Stefan didn't go to Vietnam!"

"Yes, Ella, he did, as well as eighteen members of the company he was put in command of. Only five returned. It was . . ." Herr Weitzner's jaw went rigid. "It was brutal."

My head began to spin. I closed my eyes, but all I saw was uncertainty. Much of what I believed or read about Stefan's whereabouts was suddenly a lie. My hand pressed against my pounding temple. I wanted to prove Edgar wrong. "I read the papers all the time and never heard anything about the Germans or the Soviets involvement with the American conflict in Vietnam."

"You forget, Ella . . . you only read what *they* want you to see."

I felt foolish. I knew the DDR controlled the content, but I also had ways of getting outside news, and if the Soviets had a presence in Vietnam, it had been carefully concealed.

"It was a covert operation. A handful of us were sent to Moscow summer 1967. It was there that after eight months of intensive training we were put on a train to Vietnam. We were commanded to deny any and all involvement to anyone, including the Chinese, on our way to Hanoi." He took a deep breath and continued, "Even though we were colluding with China to strengthen North Vietnam's communist efforts, the aid from the Soviets at that point was mostly military equipment and financial assistance. It wasn't until 1968 that arms, munitions, transportation equipment, metals, and petroleum were provided."

"How did you get through China without them discovering you were soldiers for the Soviets?"

"We were sent under the guise of health aids, chemists, and botanists but we were all combat trained special forces."

I gasped. The stories I'd read about the American conflict were appalling. The death . . . the destruction . . . I never believed anything could be worse than what I lived, but there was . . . and it was Vietnam.

"I had no idea Stefan was involved." Nauseous, I held the handkerchief over my mouth now and mumbled. "He could have died, and I would have never known."

"The Soviets went to great lengths to keep their involvement against the Amis a secret." Edgar's expression grew very solemn. "Lies were what the Soviets did best."

"How did your comrades die?"

"We were assigned to blow up surface-to-air missiles. Our main duty was to disable the Vietnamese and American weaponry, but we were also tasked with advanced recon... spies. Another skill Soviets excel in."

I sipped my tea as he continued. The warmth of the liquid soothed my upset stomach.

"Several months in we were ambushed. Six of us survived the fire fight, but only three of us were—" Herr Weitzner's forehead grew wet with perspiration. He struggled to speak clearly. "Um, taken." His breath was short. He stuttered, unable to finish.

I placed a hand over his, encouraging him to resume. "Please . . . please continue."

"We entered Hell," he finally muttered. His stare remained centered on his hands as they started to shake.

"What was hell?"

"The South Vietnamese prisoner camp."

My countenance didn't hide the horror. "Prisoners of war?"

Devastating images rendered by faces of hate were conjured up in my mind. Anytime war is involved, the sheer numbers of lives that are deemed insignificant and destroyed are magnified. I sniffled once again into the handkerchief, trying hard to stop my sobs.

"How long?" My voice was weak.

"Months."

"1968?" I choked out a cry.

"Yes, through '69."

"How . . ." I wasn't even sure how to form words. "What happened?"

"The Vietnamese . . ." Edgar paused again. "They were inhumane." From his expression, I could tell his thoughts were elsewhere. I couldn't see what he was seeing, but his face wilted in agony. It seemed as if he relived the torment. My attention instantly shifted to Stefan. *This was his horror too.* I wanted to find him, comfort him. Whatever was going on didn't matter, we needed each other.

Edgar wiped his eyes; the moisture came from either sweat or tears. He stood and walked to his window. The curtain blocked the outside view, but he didn't push it aside. He just stared in silence at the maroon-colored drapes.

"How did you get free?" I whispered, afraid I was disrupting his contemplations.

"We took a great risk, Stefan and I. Then ultimately, a prisoner exchange." His back still toward me, he continued, "But we were never the same, Ella. Stefan . . ." He turned around. "If Stefan isn't with you now, it's not his fault."

His words sunk in deeply.

"But you found your way home." I insinuated the possibility that Stefan chose not to return.

"Yes. Fifteen months ago. Moscow initially denied us and any association to Vietnam, but there were several high-ranking officers the Soviets wanted back. We were just part of their deal. Stefan and I were separated after our return. I never heard from him again. I assumed he returned home, but he didn't make contact with me."

My lips pulled tight forcing the bile that built in my throat to retreat. Overwhelmed with the revelation, I held my head to stop the spinning. The mere idea of Stefan having to fight in such a dangerous war broke my heart, but to witness the death of his men, be captured, and live in the conditions he did as a prisoner . . . the burden had to be devastating.

When I came here tonight, I was looking for answers. I never believed those answers would lead me to this. It was far worse than I imagined.

"I'm sorry you had to endure what you did, Herr Weitzner."

Whatever pained him moments ago seemed to fade. His affable side slowly emerged. "Edgar, please call me Edgar. Oh, Ella, I feel like we're practically family. Stefan read your letters to me. Even when we had nothing in prison, he recited all the ones he'd memorized. His every thought was of you."

I tried to smile, but the weight of guilt pulled my mouth into a frown. While Stefan was captive, his thoughts were still of me. I had wronged him beyond compare . . . doubted him, questioned him, even hated him at times. *How will I rectify this, how will I find him and attempt to soothe his angry soul?*

Edgar joined me on the couch once again. "Ella, you must know that if I didn't have my son, my family, and my duty fulfilled, I may not have returned at all"

I let his words sink in painfully. *But wasn't I Stefan's family? His future? Wasn't I enough for him to return to or at least write to?*

"In fact," —Edgar glanced towards his closed front door where his wife and child had departed— "what I told you is more than I have told my wife. I never want to speak of it again."

"Do you have any idea where they would have sent him?"

"They may have kept him in the Soviet Union or sent him to Egypt in their fight against Israel." Dizzy, I wasn't sure I could handle much more.

"I'm sorry I forced you to revisit that horror. It's helped me understand the pain Stefan may be in. I just wish I knew where he is and why he hasn't written." I placed the mug on the counter and asked him for a piece of paper.

"Here's my address. If you're ever in Mitte, please visit me. I know Stefan would have wanted that," I said in a way that sounded as if he were no longer with us. I shuddered at how easy it came out that way. I fought the tears again as I stood to leave.

My hand extended, Edgar reached for it but pulled me into a hug, whispering in my ear, "I don't know of any other man I served with that loved his lady more than Stefan. If he's lost, help him find his way back to you. I know that's where he'd want to be more than anything in this world."

A cry caught in my throat. I wanted to believe him. I hugged him back then departed.

My eyes were so full of tears that I couldn't see the street signs clearly. The emotion that rattled in my head ranged from confusion to sadness to anger. *Stefan asked me to be his and to wait for him, only he was the one who left me. Doesn't he know how I feel about him? Doesn't he know I'd love him no matter what he went through? Shouldn't Edgar's words bring me some comfort? He said that if Stefan could be with me he would.*

Barely to my street, my legs gave way, and I slumped to the curb scarcely past the kinder school. In agony from too many intense sensations, my hands slid over my head, sheltering my face from the overpowering beam of the streetlight above. Confounded, my perception had no direction, no course—a scrambled, convoluted sketch of nothingness.

Edgar's words reverberated through my mind and soul. *—If Stefan isn't with you now, it's not his fault.* Yet, Edgar had found his way home . . . why couldn't Stefan? *—I don't know of any other man I served with that loved his lady more than Stefan.*

In my heart, I truly wanted to believe Stefan still loved me. I wanted it more than air. *— Help him find his way back to you.* How? How was I supposed to do that? By staying here? I most certainly couldn't do it from the West. *—If he's lost . . . if he's lost . . . if he's lost.* The words pounded a steady rhythm in my brain. He **is** lost. But is he lost unintentionally or by choice?

The one thing that was certain . . . leaving East Berlin depended on this precise answer.

TWENTY-NINE

NOTHING FOR ME HERE

July 1971

Edgar's words continued to haunt me through the night. He seemed so sure that Stefan's absence was out of his control. No matter what I tried, my thoughts wouldn't cease. The transition of the blackness turning a deep purple then blue was scrutinized from my bed. Finally forcing myself upward, I heated a cup of tea, the lemon tang tingling my nostrils as I curled up in Mama's chair. *What would you do Mama?* The idea that her spirit still lingered nearby gave me hope that somehow she would guide me towards my next step.

My mind started to whirl, whether by her unseen hand or some other power I didn't know, but almost immediately, ideas began to flood my brain. *What if I searched for him? Stefan must have a trail, a record, documentation of some kind. There has to be a way someone could find out where he is.*

Scrambling to my feet, my tea splashed across my nightgown as I nearly stumbled to the floor. The energy that flowed through my veins was as if someone had shot me with a syringe of the hottest and most caffeinated coffee on earth. Ripping the wet garment off, I couldn't move fast enough, sifting through clothes to find something respectable enough to enter a government building. A dress . . . yes, always a dress, but something more professional than stylish.

Wearing my olive dress and mama's sweater, I set out to catch a bus to the NVA headquarters in Strasburg. As I approached the main building, the large sign out front acknowledged the Volksarmee creed *Für den Schutz der Arbeiter-und-Bauern-Macht* —For the Protection of the Workers' and Peasants' Power. I was here for Stefan, but my grin was for my Papa. Back when the NVA was the Wehrmacht, he had faith in that belief. Immediately upon entering, I was stopped.

"Papers." Soldiers guarded the doorway. The documents that every DDR citizen carried were presented.

"Was bringt Sie hierher?"

"I'm looking for the location of a soldier."

One of the two soldiers couldn't stop himself from smiling, even chuckling. I wanted to sneer and scold him for his thoughts, knowing very well they were inappropriate, but I needed to play the game to get what I wanted.

"Seine Division?"

"He was in the 4th MSD, but sent to the Soviet Union on a special mission."

"Woher wollen Sie das wissen?" The more serious soldier's stare evolved into a glare.

"His comrade told me."

"Es scheint als hätte der Kamerad eine locker sitzende Zunge."

The soldier didn't hesitate to insult Weitzner claiming he had loose lips. "He was only trying to answer my questions. Please, I just need to find someone that could tell me where he is."

"Hier nicht. Wir können Ihnen nicht helfen." Their refusal to assist was followed by their puffed-out chests that nearly rammed me backwards and outside.

"Why can't you help? Can you please just che—"

"Sie müssen gehen."

Discouraged by their dismissal, I stepped away from the entrance and glanced around. There were other buildings, but much like this one, the only identification was the motto, and the access was equally guarded. I contemplated what to do, and just like earlier, a light went on. If I could find the soldiers who helped me when I was at Gustav's, their insight might lead me an easier direction. After Stefan's departure, their information brought a great deal of relief to my restless soul. They should know exactly where to go and who to see.

As I made my way back to the city center and down Friedrichstraße towards Checkpoint Charlie, I realized the border had become further fortified since the last time I had been here. Even the American side swelled with dozens of soldiers. The only difference now was that the buildings on the West appeared significantly nicer than our dilapidated equivalents only a street apart.

I slipped through the front door of Gus' and inhaled deeply. The rich aroma of cabbage and garlic floated around me as I waited until Hilde caught sight of me. She flew from her post nearly knocking down anyone in her path.

"Oh Lord, child, where have you been? It's been ages." Her arms flew around me. I couldn't help but giggle. She reached up and patted my cheek. "It's as if you never age, Ella. You look exactly the same, a vision of beauty!"

"And you, Hilde—" my smile was full "—you are as strong and vibrant as ever, still running this place."

"Chatter, chatter, chatter. That is all women do. *Grünkohleintop* to go!" Gus' familiar rant carried from the kitchen. My laugh, although rusty, could not be stopped. Hilde rolled her eyes.

"Nothing has changed here," she whispered, "except that you are missed. Have a seat, I will be with you in a bit."

I slid onto a bench and casually assessed the room. Nothing really had changed. The three butterfly paintings she had purchased before I left remained exactly where they were nailed in, the brown colored paint, even the sole potted plant that sat on the main window sill had not changed, although the blooming flower inside must be new. I scanned the café. There were two soldiers in a corner and one on a stool, but nobody I recognized. Over the years, we had so many regulars from the military I could practically predict the moment they would arrive.

I thought about this and grabbed a paper out of my purse.

Bauer and Lange —— *every Sunday around 11.*
Group from Charlie's —— *Fridays around 6 pm.*

The checkpoint soldiers showed up like clockwork roughly an hour before my shift ended, but many times I would stay late just to visit. Yet here it was Tuesday afternoon and I couldn't recall anyone regularly appearing at this time, and it'd been a couple years.

"What are you up to, missy?" Hilde sat across from me and motioned to the scratches I had made with my pencil.

"Hilde," Putting the words together, and in the correct order, seemed so difficult. "Hilde, Stefan is missing."

Her glance down at my finger, where the ring no longer rested, caused me to quickly shove my hand under the table. She sighed and motioned for me to meet her hands. Embarrassed that she might think I gave up too easily, I refused. She tapped her fingers then rested them palms up and waited. No words were needed to know exactly what she required. I relented. When she grasped my hands sweetly, her fingers gently rubbed over my fingers and considerably slower over the barren one, conveying a great deal of compassion. She was truly missed.

"Oh, Ella, life is difficult here. Lots of unknowns." Her sigh was loud and foreboding, and she continued, "So many people disappear, so many one-sided questions."

"Yes, with few answers in return."

"Is he still in the military?"

"He should be, his assignment isn't due to end for two years—August 1973—but he stopped writing me four years ago. This is the last letter I received." The July 1967 letter I placed before her was beyond fragile; it had been read, folded, reread, refolded, and pressed to my bosom a hundred times.

Hilde respected its condition as she read.

"This man adores you."

My nose wrinkled, and I held my breath hostage. When the exhale finally came, my voice rose barely above a whisper. "Everyone keeps telling me this."

"It's true." She handed it back, and I carefully placed it in my purse. "This man is most assuredly in love with you." She peered back towards the kitchen where Gus clanked pots together between grumbles. "Believe me, when I tell you that I know."

"I met a comrade of Stefan's yesterday who tried very hard to assure me he would not have left me on purpose." My voice trailed off nearly incoherent. "So I need to find out if he has . . ." I couldn't finish.

"Passed," Hilde answered for me.

I nodded but added, "or just gone away." My cheeks flushed warm and every sensation pointed to a tearful downpour, but nothing came. It was as if I had cried all of my tears out yesterday and nothing remained.

"Officer Wagner, Officer Schneider!" Hilde's shrill call across the room startled me. Her cry turned the two soldiers towards us as she waved them over. My teeth sunk into my lower lip. *What is she doing?*

Both men immediately stood up and walked towards us. She moved to my side and asked them to sit across from us. "My friend, Ella here, needs help." She pointed to me then followed up with a bribe. "Find a way to help her, and lunch is on me." They smiled. Anytime you could get a free meal here was a treat.

"How can we assist you, Fräulein?" Both men wore the insignia of Unterleutnants. The fact that they were officers, even the lowest ranked ones, could definitely help in my search. Earlier, when the headquarter soldiers had criticized me for knowing too much about Stefan's background, it alarmed me enough to be cautious this time. When I didn't speak right away, Hilde took over.

"Her fiancé is missing. We need to find him."

Doubt consumed their expressions prior to an exchange of obvious pessimism.

"I will give you free lunch for one whole week." Hilde stared at them with a look as intense as she could give.

One laughed aloud, "Oh Hilde, it's not that we don't want to help, it's just hard to locate one soldier amongst thousands."

"Two weeks!" she countered. My eyes grew wide. They relied on the business of the soldiers to survive; this was enormous generosity on my behalf.

"Okay, okay, but we need some time." The other soldier finally responded. "We need all the information you have." His request was directed to me.

On the same piece of paper I had written the soldiers, I ripped off the bottom half and proceeded to write Stefan's details. His assignment to the 4th MSD, his mission to the Soviet Union, Vietnam. No longer suspicious, I shared everything Edgar had told me. When the soldiers read the list, the surprise on their faces was obvious.

"Is this true?" the first one asked.

I nodded. "Yes, all of it."

"This may take more time than I thought, but we'll do our best, Fräulein . . ."

"Kühn. Ella Kühn. When would you like me to meet you here again?"

"Give us a week. We have some friends that work in Registers. This seems like a complicated case, but we'll see what we can find and not just because they have the best food here." The soldier winked as he shook my hand. I noticed the small gold band on his left finger, which may have been the key that fostered his empathy.

The other followed suit and said their goodbyes. "We'll see you here next Tuesday at three p.m."

After they left, I reached over and squeezed Hilde quite tightly. She pretended to choke from my grip but hugged me back.

"Thank you, Hilde. Thank you. I can't begin to tell you how much this means to me."

"Oh, I'm pretty sure I know, sweetheart." She smiled and kissed my cheek.

The following week, I endeavored to stay busy and tried not think about the follow-up conversation with the soldiers. I managed to work extra shifts at Zur, located a relatively old book store on Unter den Linden, and read *nakt unter Wölfen* in a quaint café near Monbijoupark that served red fruit jelly. Although I have lived in a five square kilometer radius my whole life, after reading the author Bruno Apitz's description of the Buchenwald concentration camp, my life appeared remorsefully blessed.

When Tuesday finally arrived, my pleasant yellow dress was chosen because it reflected how I wanted to feel, warm and happy. I boarded the U-bahn and arrived at Gustav's a good twenty minutes before three, yet when I entered, the soldiers were already there. The two of them were huddled next to Hilde at the counter.

"Uh-hum." My voice cleared to draw their attention. The men quickly straightened as if a commanding officer had just arrived. When they moved aside, my chest heated, blazing a forewarning trail to my head. Something wasn't right . . . Hilde was sniffling, her cheeks wet. Both men lowered their eyes. All signals led to an outcome I wasn't sure could be shouldered.

"Have a seat." Hilde wiped her forehead and turned the corners of her mouth upward, for show. "Can I get you something? Coffee? Tea?"

"No." My eyes did not flinch as they swung between her and the soldiers. The married one stepped forward, yet he still didn't look me in the eyes. "There is a lot of confusion surrounding your fiancé . . . Stefan Franke."

"Ella, sit down." Hilde's voice was firm. I didn't budge. She shot me a stern warning. I had not swallowed since I arrived, and the lump in my throat only swelled. Somehow my fingers found the chair, and my body followed her direction, although, I kept my hands beneath my bottom to keep the trembling minimal.

"What did you find?" my voice cracked.

"There is no record of him going to the Soviet Union. There are some notes about his training; specific skills, weaponry, promotions, and classified work with an officer named Baust in 1966 through 67."

"What happened after that?" The flatness in my tone proved the necessity to brace myself. Everything felt off.

"His records were red-lined," the other soldier spoke impatiently, no sympathy in his answer.

The married soldier shot him a stern glare then whispered, "Ella, his records are closed after 1969."

"What does red-lined mean?" the words tumbled out.

"It's when they draw a red line through your records."

"Which means?" My own patience grew thin. Hilde moved to my side and placed an arm around my shoulders.

"The last words on Stefan's paperwork before the redline say *Endsieg*—It means—"

"Final Victory." My mouth moved but felt numb.

"Yes."

My hands went to my cheeks. *Am I really hearing this? Is this a dream, a nightmare?* I closed my fingers tightly into fists and squeezed.

"We *generally* see this when a soldier has . . . deceased."

He really didn't need to say it. Everything since I arrived implied bad news. Somehow, I knew. I just knew. Pressing those same fists against my eyes, they slipped with wetness even as they tried to halt it. All the energy that had now been compressed in my fists needed to go somewhere. I slammed them down to the table, startling everyone.

"I'm so sorry." The married soldier placed a paper on the table. "Here's my information if you need anything." Even as he said it, the words sounded foolish. If I needed anything? I NEEDED STEFAN!

My eyes didn't open. There was no courtesies or acknowledgement on their way out. Was I supposed to thank them for destroying my life, crushing my future?

Somewhere between the anger and the sobs, Hilde's hands of comfort found me.

"Hilde! Order's up!" Gus bellowed from the back.

"Not now, Gus!" It was the first time I'd ever heard anger in her voice. Her arms wrapped around me but made little progress against the convulsing that started in my torso and moved through my limbs down to my toes. Every part of my body shook, completely out of control.

"Love," She wiped my hair off my sweaty forehead and pulled my cheek to her chest. The vibration of her voice was felt but not understood. Nothing made sense. Why wasn't his family notified? Why didn't Edgar tell me? Why?

I remembered nothing after that and awoke in the backroom of Gustav's. A light linen had been placed over me as I laid in a corner on the cold tile. The room was dark, but familiar sounds from the café assured me it was still open for business. Moving upright and against the wall, my mind tried to piece the afternoon together. Puffy eyes, swollen cheeks, and stiff muscles shed additional light to my recollection. With somber cognizance, I now knew with probable certainty there was nothing for me here. East Berlin was to be my home no longer.

THIRTY

YOU BELONG WITH YOUR FAMILY

August 1971

"Ella."

My name was called before I reached the table. The familiarity of the voice initiated a cautious approach, then the menu came down, revealing Ian. "How are you?"

"I'm fine." There was no lift in my tone.

"Will you forgive me?" Ian whispered, "It was wrong of us to accuse you."

The bitterness ignited again, only there were no tears. Too angry to speak and too bruised to respond, I bit my tongue. He had taken my confidences and spoiled them.

I started to walk away.

"Wait, please talk to me," his begging amplified.

I circled back to face him and leaned in. "I trusted you, Ian. I trusted *you*."

"I know."

Customers had recently been seated at the table next to Ian, so I moved to take their order, but his cries carried over. "Please, I'm sorry, come back. Anton would want you back."

The spin on my heels was fierce. "Don't you dare say his name!" My rush to the other end of the room could not have been any faster. I tugged on Angelika's sleeve. "Will you please serve Ian?"

Angelika snorted. "My pleasure . . ." With one hand on her hip, she eyed him like prey. On my way to the kitchen, I caught sight of him in a mad dash for the exit.

That evening after my shift, Angelika and I had barely stepped away from the restaurant when Ian appeared again. The darkness covered most of his face, but his distress was apparent.

"Oops, lovers spat," Angelika teased. "Remember my offer, Ian . . . it still stands."

"Please, Angelika, not now," I snapped. I wasn't in the mood for her games. "Walk ahead. I'll catch up with you." She puckered her lips in a smooch towards Ian before she strolled casually down the walk.

Ian didn't take a breath, everything rolling out at once, "Ella I'm sorry about Anton I'm sorry about Stefan I'm sorry about Hans and the whole misunderstanding." He rubbed both hands through his hair. A small streak of moisture rested on his cheeks.

Has he been crying?

"I know we can continue without you, but it doesn't feel right. We're only where we are right now because of all you've done. Come back to us please?"

I remained silent. Ian's decency and sincerity surfaced in his regret. He felt bad, that's just who he was, but I wanted to be angry. Sometimes the only emotion I could control was rage, and there were times I yearned to feel the rawness of it. Today was one of those days.

"Do you know what today is?"

He nodded, but his eyes stared at the ground. *Of course, he knows.* The anniversary of the wall was embedded in our core.

"Ten years, Ian! Ten years since the separation. I am done. I don't think I can do this anymore. I don't belong anywhere . . . everything I have tried has failed. Anton and Josef have moved on, Stefan is . . ." Stammering, I caught myself. Stefan's fate hadn't quite sunk in nor did Ian deserve to know. My heart impulsively beat faster at the mere memory of the soldier's report. "I feel completely alone!" My voice rose louder than it should have. The shadows held many secrets, and not knowing who lurked nearby, my situation could get worse—if that was even possible. Only I was tired of being careful and tired of a lot of things right then.

"*I know* what you're feeling!" Ian closed the gap between us. "Remember, my family is there. My girlfriend is there!" He reached for my hand. "If anyone understands your pain, its me."

"Exactly why the betrayal hurt so much," I muttered.

"I know. I've been beside myself trying to make this right." Anguish spread openly across Ian's face. He scanned the area then whispered, "Life is going to get better very soon. We are only twenty metres away."

My eyes were fixated on his. "Twenty?"

The lines between my eyebrows deepened. "How?" *It's only been four months since I stopped speaking to them. How could they have accomplished that much in such a short time?*

"Several reasons, including your findings."

I fidgeted with the handle on my purse. *They believed me?*

"Don't you want to see it?"

Hungrily, I nodded before I could catch myself. Yes, curiosity tempted me to see the tunnel.

Ian handed me a small piece of paper and said nothing more. Slipped into my purse, it remained untouched until I was safe at home with my curtains drawn and my door locked. It was the new patrol times for this Sunday. Ian wanted me to stop by the next day. Knowing that the patrol times were only good for two days at the most, I had to decide fairly quickly if this was what I wanted.

That night in bed, I held the note in my hand for an immeasurable amount of time. It felt heavy, heavier than a small post should feel, but it was from the weight of the words. The conflict that surfaced this time was less about what had held me back and more about the certainty that if I agreed to go, my decision would be solidified. I would leave East Berlin.

Daylight soared over the tower in Friedrichshain. Even though I would be following a different path to the building, I was driven to this very spot and could not keep my eyes from wandering upward.

The tower itself rested above a cylindrical base that extended at least three or four metres high. Octagonal in shape, every angle bestowed a large window above and a square opening below. With a shudder, I didn't want to imagine what the smaller opening was used for. The outline of people patrolling from above indicated there were two, but no clear answer as to their identity. *Is it Hans? Is it his cruel commander or some stranger?* A month ago, I may have wanted it to be Hans, now the only recurring feeling was indifference.

There were things I missed about Hans. He was sweet, handsome, and easy to be around. The times we were alone, the passion we shared was probably the only honest part of our relationship, but all-in-all he was a border patrol guard who—at the very least—would be obligated to arrest me if he discovered my escape plans.

Shuffling forward and away from the wall, I readjusted my hat and switched the handful of flowers to my other hand. If I happened to be stopped, my excuse was that I was placing these on a relative's grave in the nearby cemetery. It hadn't been too often that I arrived in Friedrichshain during the day, so I came prepared.

After three turns and an alley a half block away, I pulled out the paper Ian had given me then inched closer to the corner. Glancing at my watch, I listened for the steps. As they approached, my body pressed deeper into the ingress of an apartment building until they passed and it was silent again. Stepping away from my sanctuary, I immediately scanned the street and jogged the small distance to the front. Even though my hand shook when I reached for the lever, it only took one quick pull before I was inside.

Tiptoeing through the hallway, I froze, entirely motionless in the entryway of the vast room. The dryness in my throat prevented me from speaking as several eyes fell upon me. *Maybe I shouldn't have come.*

"Ella?" Rupert's voice was not filled with his typical contempt as he approached me. His welcome startled me but his next statement left me speechless. "I'm glad you came back."

My brows curved with confusion. *Is this the same man?*

"Thanks," was all I could squeeze out.

"We're almost free. It's real. It's happening!" Lamar had joined his brother. His typical energy boiled over and resurged my dormant curiosity.

"Come, let us show you." They led me down to the tunnel. Once the door had been removed and the cart rolled out, I stepped inside, lured by my inquisitiveness.

Lamar quickly handed me a lantern before I got too far. Even though I had seen and touched much of it before, the walk felt as though it were the very first time. Pressing my palm against every passing beam, I marveled at its depth. The crew had dug very well in such a short amount of time, and it was nearing completion. At the end, I stopped opposite the black patch of mud that stood between me and freedom—between me, and Anton, and Josef. My desire to rip through it as fast as my hands would move could barely be contained, yet I had to defer. *I'm a guest.*

As I exited the tunnel, I whispered to the brothers. "I'm very happy for you both. What a joyful reunion you'll have!"

"You too," Rupert said, "Come with us."

I analyzed him carefully. There was no hint of tease or malice. His offer was genuine.

"Why would you want me to come when you guys did all the work?"

"Not all the work," Lamar insisted. "You're the reason we were able to speed up the process. Your inside information made a huge difference!"

"It did?"

"Yeah," Rupert added. "It saved our lives."

"Please. Everyone wants you to come." Lamar said.

"Not everyone."

"Yes, everyone." Ian and Jonas had descended the stairs.

My eyes flickered, struggling to comprehend the moment. I resisted the urge to cry. Ian came and placed an arm tenderly around my shoulders. "You belong with your family, Ella."

My eyes skimmed the room. It was a very different sight than the one in the pub months ago. Their excitement and determination exuded assurance while their smiles confirmed my invitation to stay.

I reached for a nearby trowel. "Okay, tell me what to do."

THIRTY-ONE

CRUEL ENCOUNTER

Shortly after 11 p.m. that night, Ian and I departed the building together. He offered to walk me home, and since it was my first visit in this area in a long time, I accepted. Somehow, the neighborhood appeared dirtier and darker.

In spite of my many trips to and from the building, I had not run into Jurek again, but that didn't mean it couldn't happen. He was familiar with the neighborhood and seemed to have a personal vengeance against me. Initially, the belief was due to my association with Anton, although after the last encounter, his hatred for me had become more personal. Ian's presence brought a great deal of comfort.

"Will it be easy for you to find Chandra . . . you know, when you get to the West?" We walked slow and steady. Nothing to draw attention to ourselves.

"Yes, I know exactly where she is."

"What about you?" Ian beamed. "Will you be able to find Anton and Josef?"

"It might take a while." My grin matched his. The idea of freedom had finally sunk in, its reality more tangible than ever before. "I've never been to the West, so I'm not familiar with the neighborhoods. I only hope it doesn't take too long."

"Yeah. I have trouble sleeping at night the closer we get. I can't wait to see her again."

"What's the first thing you'll do . . . besides kiss her?" I chuckled.

"Honestly, Ella, I'll marry her. We don't need to wait another minute. I'll take her to the preacher and marry her."

My chest burned, the longing a familiar emotion.

"I'm sure Anton will be pleased to see you."

"Yes, I suppose he will." My eyes pulled away from Ian's, and my smile faltered.

"Suppose?"

"Anton is . . . with someone," I whispered.

Ian stopped and reached for my arm. "He is?"

I nodded. "It's okay. It wasn't fair of me to believe he should wait. I didn't wait for him when I fell in love with Stefan." His name singed my tongue.

"Yeah, but did you tell him you were coming?"

"No." —I stopped. Not far from Melchior, my eyes flashed across the street. Over the wall, several buildings' windows flickered with a sole candle. The circulated rumor was they would keep the candles lit until the wall fell— "I didn't want to risk it through post."

When I didn't continue, Ian stepped to my side, his expression showed some distress. "What is it?"

With clenched teeth, I fought what pushed to come forth.

"Tell me."

My eyes didn't move from the candles. "Stefan is. . .Aaaooow!" an unexpected blow to my arm caused me to cry aloud. I peered over to see the offender. A man, several years my senior, stumbled away from me, mumbling an incoherent apology.

His hand brushed his tousled gray hair from his eyes as Ian confronted him defensively. "You need to be more careful, sir."

The man wobbled, then twisted back toward us and attempted to bow. His unbuttoned vest and disheveled dress shirt fell open as he gripped his hat and leaned forward. In exaggerated slow motion, he continued headlong into the curb and hit his face.

"Oh." Gasping, I stepped closer and knelt down. The man cursed under his breath, the foul scent of liquor preceding his words. My nose wrinkled at the stench. "Ian, he's drunk."

Ian rushed over and grabbed the man's arm. "Let me help you up."

"Nein!" the stranger bellowed, ripping his arm from Ian's grasp. "*Lass los!*"

Ian let go at the man's request and came to my side. Astonished, we could do nothing but watch as he struggled to get upright. Upon standing, the man's pants were ripped at the knee, but he showed more annoyance towards us than his appearance. "Haut ab und lasst mich in Ruhe," forderte er wütend." he angrily demanded for us to leave him alone.

"Let's go." Ian reached for my arm, but I continued to watch.

Exhibiting very little grace, the man grunted clumsily, wiped the drool off his chin, then brazenly burped. His loose and uncoordinated steps multiplied as he staggered towards the other side of the street. Without deviation, the man headed straight for the wall.

"Sir," I cried in a panic, "please let us help you."

He ignored me and quickened his pace.

My hand flew to my mouth. "Ian,"

Ian yelled for him to stop but was also ignored. The thump of my heartbeat accelerated as the man's silhouette materialized against the bright lights of the border fortification.

"*Bleiben Sie auf Befehl der Volkspolizei stehen!*" The order to halt from the People's Police was followed by a bright spotlight beamed directly on the man, yet he still didn't stop.

Ian yanked me into the shadow of a nearby building, our eyes glued to the scene from the dark. A pair of border guard approached the man, and in between the shrill puffs on their whistles, they commanded him to stop. The drunk man fearlessly shook his finger in their faces and screamed, "Schweine." I turned my head away momentarily, fearing what would happen next.

"Don't look." Ian held a protective stance.

I peeked up at his face. He met my gaze. "I'm sorry. I can't let him die."

I lunged towards the street. Ian attempted, unsuccessfully, to wrench me back before I ran towards the chaos. My eyes watered as I watched the man push one soldier aside and charge the structure. His fingers clung to the cracks in the cement while one shoe rose up in a feeble attempt to scale the wall . . . a wall that was now twelve feet high with razor wire at the top.

"Bleiben Sie stehen!" A swarm of soldiers now descended on him, commanding him to halt.

"Please!" I cried, "Please don't hurt him!" More soldiers converged from all directions. The man didn't stop.

One gunshot rang out and then another until the sound seemed to explode from all over the compound. "No!" I screamed in desperation.

The man dropped lifeless to the ground. A round of bullets continued to hit his motionless body. I slid to my knees less than five metres away, several shots zipping over my own head.

Instantly surrounded by border guard, my hands wobbled upward above my head. The ground felt like thunder underneath me. Through my blurred vision, the man's body curled in a pool of blood that seemed to expand with each passing second.

"*Halten Sie still! Halten Sie still!*"

Despite their demands for me to hold still, I vomited, one soldier slamming my face with the butt of his rifle as I heaved forward. The force rolled me flat on my back. Pain pulsated across my face as blood gushed out my nose. I tried to stop the flow but was warned, once again, not to move. The warm liquid surged freely down my mouth and neck.

"Ella?" A hand reached for me. "What are you doing here?" I recognized Hans' voice. My eyes followed his hand to his face. I had never seen him scared before.

The hollow black tips of several guns gaped within inches of my head. One end shoved me roughly in the shoulder.

"Stop!" Hans ordered as he moved defensively around me in a half circle. The soldiers didn't ease their stance. He kneeled close to me and whispered, "Were you with that man?"

"Hans, leave the criminal alone." One soldier approached crossly. Hans grabbed the man's sleeve and shoved him aside. "I will take care of this, Detlef! Do not forget, I am still your superior!" he shouted with equal anger.

Hans bent down again and whispered. "It's really important for you listen to me if you want to live."

I tried to meet his stare, but tears filled my eyes.

"Don't move," he advised.

More soldiers arrived. Hans stood above me, keeping everyone at a distance.

"*Nehmen Sie sie fest, Hans.*" A set of handcuffs were thrown at him with the demand to detain me. Their sight caused my breath to hasten. Their resemblance to the pair from my interrogation years ago threatened another round of nausea.

256

"Wait. I can question her here," Hans snapped.

"Ella," Hans got down on his knees and leaned over me. "I need you to tell me what happened."

Blood slid down my throat; the metallic taste gagged me. When Hans tilted me forward, bright red drops splattered across my dress from my spit. Wiping the stream, a grisly trail smeared across my arm.

"*Was machst du gerade?*" the angry soldier demanded.

"Don't interfere, I'm getting answers. Back off!" The sharpness in his voice tapered off when he turned to me and whispered. "Please tell me what happened."

I wiped my mouth again and peered up at Hans' worried expression. I coughed. "He was just a man . . . a stranger," I whispered, ". . . a stranger on the street."

"You didn't know him?" He spoke loud enough for the others to hear.

I moved my head back and forth.

"Speak up, I can't hear you." It occurred to me that he wasn't requesting this for his benefit but for those who surrounded us.

"No, I didn't know that man," I spoke louder. "He bumped into me, like he'd drank too much alcohol." I sniffled. "I watched him walk towards the wall."

"You weren't with him?"

"No . . . no, I tried to stop him." My hands, which were now a pasty mixture of blood, sweat, and dirt, shielded my face.

"That's all?"

"Yes."

Hans exhaled loudly in relief then immediately rose to attention. Through my fingers, a pair of shiny black boots appeared, much nicer than the regular guards.

"Detain her!" a new voice demanded. The shiny boots most likely belonged to him.

My breathing accelerated. *I'll never live through another confinement.*

"Sir. She didn't know the man. She tried to stop him." Hans tried to reason.

"Her approach violated the law. Take her into custody!"

Suddenly the world started spinning. I no longer felt like I was part of reality. The tone was vicious, coarse, and cruel, . . . and . . *familiar*. I scrambled to find my feet. The end of another rifle poked against my head, but I needed to know. Dizzy and unbalanced, I swiftly batted the rifle out of the way. The moment I stood to face the soldiers, an intense light shone directly at me, blinding me until I was driven to the ground once again.

The voices went silent.

"Sir?" Concern crept into Hans' inquiry. "Sir?" he questioned again.

A nearby soldier's boot pressed against my neck forcing me flat to my stomach, but I listened intently, suddenly acutely alert, my heart pounding erratically against the cold cement.

"Sir, are you well?"

The shiny black boots moved away. Hans followed. Whispers filled the void, but I could not make them out.

"Yes, sir!" There was a sudden lift in Han's voice. "Thank you, sir!"

Through my altered view, I watched the black boots step farther away and then stop.

Hans swiftly pulled me to my feet. The squaddies who still held their guns towards me exchanged looks of confusion.

"Commander's orders . . . it's over. She's no longer your concern. Clean up the man's body." Hans ordered the men to action then placed one arm firmly around my waist. Pulling me close to his chest, his other arm reached for my hands in an effort to swiftly guide me away.

I peered behind, straining to see the officer. One hand released to wipe the moisture from my eyes, but even with clearer sight it wasn't enough. I stretched my neck further as Hans led me from the wall.

"Don't look, Ella."

I ignored him and tried again. The shiny-black-booted man stood completely still, his back towards us, head turned to the side, the bill of his officer's cap pulled low and close to his eyes. The bright lights near the wall cast an eerie glow against his profile. It was strong and detailed.

Sharp pains stabbed my chest, sucking all air from my lungs. Gasps that spewed intermittently contrasted the whirl in my head. My body fell completely limp.

"What's wrong?" Hans panicked as I slipped to the ground, no longer able to feel my legs. My fingers clenched the front of my dress crudely until my fabric tore. Even when my nails reached skin, I didn't release my grip.

"Please," Hans pleaded, his strength being tested. "We need to keep moving."

"What's your . . . commander's . . . n—name?" I stuttered.

"Please get up."

"Hans!" I shrieked louder. "What is your commander's name?"

Hans scooped me up in his arms and carried me off the street and out of sight of both the lights and the tower.

Nauseous and dizzy, I spied Ian's image a few steps away. Alarm covered his face, but Hans was oblivious to anything but me.

"You need to get home." Hans set me on a nearby bench. "What were you thinking coming here tonight?" Sitting next to me, he tried to pull me in snug to his chest. I pushed back. The force in my hands seemed to surprise him, my stare unrelenting.

"I need to know."

"What?" He sounded frustrated. "Don't you realize what just happened here?"

"I need to know his name!" I screamed.

"*Unterfeldwebel* Franke."

The words cut through me like a dagger. Any semblance of breath was physically wrenched from my chest in spasms. *Stefan is alive and here in Berlin?*

My body and spirit separated somehow, the spirit slid through open cavities and watched from above as my body collapsed, lifeless to the ground. Hans cradled my head before it hit the concrete.

"Ella!" Hans cried, trying to lift me back up. "You need to get out of here! He let you go. You must leave now, or he could change his mind."

Ian came out from the shadows. "I can take her home; she's a friend of mine."

Startled, Hans glanced from me to Ian. "Do you know this man?"

I couldn't speak.

Ian placed a hand on Han's shoulder. "She'll be safe. I promise you."

Hans sounded anxious. "My name is Hans. Please find me after she's settled. This is my post. I need to know she's okay."

Ian agreed.

Hans brushed away the sticky strands of hair from my face, his hand cupping my chin in an attempt to get me to look at him, but blackness had already started to swallow my sight. "Take care of her," he demanded with a simple threat directed to Ian. My eyes closed.

"I will," Ian acknowledged as he took over.

Ian moved easily despite my added weight in his arms. He was young and strong and only had to stop twice before he got me to his flat.

"You will be safe here." He laid me on the couch, a light-weight blanket pressed over me. "Ella?" A kind voice called my name. Moist warmth soothed the back of my hands, then a cloth gently brushed my forehead and cheeks. "It's me. Ian. Please, please talk to me."

My lips parted, a whimper emerging from somewhere deep, but by the time it surfaced, the sound resembled a moan. "Ian . . ." Laboring for more, though, nothing came.

"I'll be back."

Ian left the room . . . I'm not sure for how long . . . but I awoke to his return. With a teacup cradled in his hand, somewhere in my mind I recognized the scent of chamomile, yet unable to respond to the comfort I knew it would bring.

As reminiscence of the evening unfolded and the splinters began to piece together, the pains resurged with forcefulness. Having survived physical torture, loneliness, sadness, terror, and even despair, nothing could have prepared me for what I felt now.

Stefan was alive, and he rejected me.

"Ella," Ian's comforting touch continued to rub my hair. "Rest. I will be close if you need me." He kissed my forehead and turned off the lamp.

The darkness created a blank canvas for my endless gaze. Graphic images appeared. People screaming, dying, being shot, mutilated, or terminated. All by Stefan. Was any part of *my Stefan* left or had the vicious consequence of training men to be killers and being tortured as a prisoner of war destroyed his tender heart? *He killed people for his job. Could his finger have pulled the trigger and murdered that man?*

Queasy, I lurched over the side of the couch, my body retching repeatedly into the canister Ian had left, yet very little spew left my mouth. Exhausted, my head found its way back to the pillow only to be caught in the collision of my thoughts.

Stefan may not have pulled the trigger to kill me, *but I might as well be dead.*

THIRTY-TWO

MY SANCTUARY

Ian's flat became my sanctuary for several days. He kindly notified Zur that I was ill and unable to work. Nobody on the digging crew seemed to question my absence.

"Ella." Ian sat on his coffee table next to the couch. Very few words had been spoken since that night. He pulled the quilt softly over my shoulder while I reclined at one end. "What happened out there?"

Every time my eyes closed, they relived it . . . Stefan's profile, his new post, his job of death . . . one question answered, many more provoked. *Was he forced to be there because of Vietnam? Did he take it voluntarily? Did he even remember me? Us?*

The weariness in my eyes made it hard to focus long, but when I glanced towards Ian, I saw a friend beyond reason. He had cared for me this whole time. While the others had learned of my love for Stefan, they didn't know the depth like him.

"It was Stefan," a mumble inched through. Even though his name had been said a thousand times in my head the last few days, when it finally reached air, my mouth felt as though it was filled with chalk.

"What was Stefan?" Ian hadn't grasped my vague answer. He pressed again, "What do you mean it was Stefan?"

"The other night at the shooting." My eyes followed my hands as they clasped. *Just spit it out, Ella!* My internal rebuke was meant to urge me forward, but it only caused me to stutter, "The . . . the officer in charge . . . it was Stefan."

"I don't understand."

I rubbed my eyes and sat up, crossing my legs. "I don't fully understand it either, but when I heard his voice and saw him . . ."

"You're positive?"

I nodded. The numbness returned.

"How? How did this happen?"

I didn't answer.

"I thought you said he was away from Berlin, a special training or something. This doesn't make any sense. How could he be at the wall?" Ian now paced the room.

"I hadn't told you, but some soldiers researched him for me and recently told me they believed, from his record, that he was deceased."

"Dead? Why didn't you tell me? Why didn't you say something?"

"Ian, please!" My response was out of frustration. Then I stopped myself, remembering what he had done for me. I exhaled slowly. "We weren't talking remember? We weren't friends at the time. I didn't want to believe it. I didn't know what to do."

"I'm sorry." He stopped moving and sat back down. "What a dreadful experience this must've been and now, now to find out he's at the border." His hands covered mine, still shaking in my lap. ". . . but he is alive."

Yes, Stefan is alive.

"There has to be some logic to this. Why wouldn't he contact you?"

My answer made the most sense, "Maybe he doesn't love me anymore."

"No," Ian cried, "you told me the stories—you showed me the letters—there's no way this man is the same person." He knelt down in front of the couch not letting go of my hands.

"The Stefan I knew and loved is gone." Spoken out loud to convince myself, was there truth to the statement? Everything seemed different.

"You should confront him, talk to him. There has to be an explanation."

"I was there. He saw me. He didn't follow me, talk to me, or even touch me. I don't think he has any intention of finding me again."

"Maybe you should rethink leaving." Although his words were filled with hesitation, they carried a great deal of weight.

My mind spun with confusing thoughts and questions. *Stefan is here—here in Berlin—and did not try to locate me. Both Katharina and Lena know I work at Zur and would have told him if he had been home. He chose not to see me, and if he was the reason for the patrol changes, he has been here for at least five months!*

Nauseous, my hands buried my face. What frightened me the most was if I decided to stay behind—deliberately missing the opportunity to leave with the others—then found out Stefan really didn't want anything to do with me, the devastation would kill me.

"Thank you for helping me, especially helping me recover, but I can't sit here anymore."

He helped me to my feet and pulled me in for a much-needed embrace. "I'm sorry, Ella. I'm so sorry."

"I know." I hugged him back then wiped my wet cheeks with my sleeve. "I'll help you finish the tunnel." My fingers pulled my wild hair into a tight braid.

"Maybe you should continue to rest," he suggested.

"Rest is driving me insane . . . he's all I see. I need a distraction."

"Are you sure?"

I nodded, although I wasn't sure of anything.

Within the hour, we were walking towards Friedrichshain.

THIRTY-THREE

Soldier Of My Past

September 1971

The late summer rains made digging a lot more difficult over the next three days. The constant leaking and dripping throughout the finished part of the tunnel created a particularly muddy corridor. When I rejoined the group, progress had slowed considerably.

The good news, however, according to Telfer's calculations, was that we were only a little over twenty metres from the basement of the corner house that his ally in the West had prepared.

"How long?" Beti squealed quietly. "Did you say two weeks, Ian?"

He nodded. "Depends on the weather. It might take three."

"We need to plan the day," Jonah spoke up. "We all need to leave at the same time."

"Yeah, and we should consider caving it in behind us . . ." Lamar suggested, "so we can't be followed."

Subtle excitement floated around the room in different ways; each with their own story, each with their own reasons.

Mine were repressed on purpose. Emotionally torn between Edgar's haunting words, "Help him find his way back to you," and the Stefan I saw: cold, vicious, and cruel. *Can he be saved? If there is the slightest chance he can, is leaving really the answer?*

"We need to call it for the night." Rupert threw his drenched, mud-caked work shirt to the ground at my feet.

"Why?" Lamar questioned, while those who were present waited for a logical explanation.

"We are a foot deep in mud, and our digging just makes the work fragile, plus the cart can't be used. Let's reconvene later this week. It's supposed to clear up by Thursday."

"The sooner we finish, the sooner—"

"We get sloppy," Rupert growled. "Look, let's not be stupid in our eagerness. Telfer assured us his friends are working on the other side. It's going to happen very soon, we just need to be smart."

"Does everyone here understand that you can only bring the clothes you're wearing and maybe one small item in each pocket?"

"Uh-huh." Ian had already prepped me. Anton's tinnie pin would be in one pocket and my dad's pipe in the other. As we parted ways that night, the reality sunk in. Being this close to crossing the threshold into the West should have been exhilarating, but even after I stepped out of the patrol zone, I couldn't force myself to move forward without turning back. My sight beheld the outline of the tower from afar. Its unmistakable image hovered over more than just the wall. *When it comes time to actually take that step, will I be able to do it?*

***

Despite the delay in digging, my return to work was expected as part of our exit plan. We needed to keep our schedules and routines exactly the same up until the moment of our departure. However, expectations and actuality can often contradict each other.

"Ella?" Hans didn't wait for me to make it over to his table; he met me near the kitchen.

"I've been worried about you. I came here twice, and they said you were ill. I also went to your flat but there was no answer."

My eyes remained focused on my task.

He continued even though I said nothing. "I'm glad to see you're healed and back to work."

Glancing up, I offered a faint smile. Hans gently grabbed my arm. "Are you sure you're okay?"

"Yes, I am. I'm just tired."

He grinned boyishly. "Well I'm sitting in the back part of the restaurant. Please come talk to me when you get a moment."

"Alright."

Placing the bottles of vodka back on the bar, I scanned the room then slipped outside to the biergarten.

"Where's Angelika?"

Heather, our newest waitress shrugged her shoulders. "I think she's off today."

My groan was subtle. I could always count on Angelika to get me out of these tough spots. It had been a few months since I had stopped seeing Hans, but only a little over a week since the incident at the wall, and I didn't want to discuss either one.

Hans' nervousness was evident as I approached his table. A fork in one hand and a knife in the other, he twisted them through his fingers, fidgeting.

"Ella?" He sounded surprised I came. In a way, he should've been.

"What can I get you today?" My eyes wanted to look anywhere but at him. I was grateful for his kindness, but troubled. When I saw Hans' face, I saw Stefan's, and everything about that night was devastating.

"You," he joked. Alone and not trying to impress anyone, he was simply being himself—trying to get me to respond. "Can you sit for a minute?"

In an initial scan of the room, I knew we weren't that busy, but I still searched for a reason not to.

"Please?"

That's all he had to say. I slid into the chair across from him.

"I'm sorry about what happened at the border." He placed his hand near the center of the table as if he wanted me to meet it, but my hands remained still. "I'm glad you're safe."

My sigh signaled my surrender. "Hans, you helped me a great deal, and I honestly appreciate it." My voice was calm, yet detached. "I have a habit of always being in the wrong place at the wrong time."

He chuckled. "You really do."

My mouth curved upward, although there was no lift in my eyes.

"Can I ask you something?" he continued, the sound of his foot tapping beneath the table became a distraction.

That was always a loaded question. "I guess so."

"Why did you insist on knowing my commander's name?"

My cheeks warmed. He couldn't see me blush, but I naturally turned away. His hand reached over to my chin and gently rotated it towards him. Our eyes met. "You know him, don't you?"

My head nodded up and down. "It was a long time ago."

He let go of my face and sat still for quite a while as if he was thinking hard.

"He's the one. The soldier of your past, isn't he?"

My lips pulled in tight, and while I tried to *see* Hans, I only saw past him. The rapid blinking began.

Hans watched me fight the tears. "That explains why he let you go."

My teeth released their hold, and my lips gasped a whisper, "No."

"Yes," Hans insisted. "I suspect he didn't know it was you at first, then when you stood up, he froze. He just stopped talking. I thought it was odd, and then he walked away and called for me to release you." Hans wiped his forehead. "I've never seen him show an ounce of compassion towards anyone, ever."

These words finally forced my tears to the surface. Compassion is what made me fall in love with him.

"He must care for you still."

"No." I shook my head dramatically as my hand swiped a runaway tear on my cheek. "No, there's nothing there. I must get back to work. I'll bring you some pork. It's on the house."

As I scrambled to my feet, Hans grabbed my arm. "Ella, I'm glad you're doing better," —his grip softened, although he never let go— ". . . and I miss you."

In a strange way I missed him too. Leaning down, my arms slid over his shoulders and around his neck. The relationship with Hans was meant to be a front, but I mistakenly allowed myself to get too close and to feel. As a result, we both became victims. As Hans stood up, my arms remained in place as he pulled me in closer, his lips resting on my ear. I sensed he wanted to say more, except nothing came out.

When Hans said goodbye, I knew in my heart this was the last time I would ever see him. If all went as planned, I'd be in the West very soon . . . and the East, would become a distant memory. If it failed . . . nothing mattered.

Since the moment I discovered Stefan was in the East, the decision to continue at the tunnel was nearly unbearable to comprehend . . . but I tried to convince myself there wasn't much to leave.

Alone in my apartment, *La vie en Rose* spun on the phonograph for the first time in months. Instead of envisioning my parents dancing around the room as I often had in the past, I saw Stefan and the way he held me the last time we listened to it together. In a way, it had become a farewell song. The shell of him was there, but the goodness and gentleness had disappeared. The music ended, and I turned off the lights. Justifications were all that remained. *No, I won't be leaving my Stefan. If I choose to leave, this Stefan is one I don't know.*

THIRTY-FOUR

MARI

1 October 1971

"Welcome, Adela. It's been a while."

"Yes, I've been quite busy. How is Mari doing?"

Nurse Margret's brow wrinkled unnaturally. "If I didn't know better, I would have thought she was a miniature *kleine Maus*."

I laughed. "Is she too much trouble?"

"No, she's a good girl, but she does remind me of someone I used to know."

"Ella!" Mari's cry reached me before her little body did. She dove into my arms. Her hugs were a dose of delight.

It was such a thrill to see her running. When I first brought her here, her legs had mostly healed, but she had to learn to walk again. Watching her now, my heart leapt at the progress she had made.

"I've missed you. Where have you been?" she scolded me loudly.

"I'm sorry, I've been busy at work and . . ." I paused. I could not mention my after-hours endeavors.

". . . and what?" she demanded. Her hands poised on her ten-year-old hips as if she were an adult.

I giggled. "Nothing is as important as you. Please forgive me."

She kissed my cheek then grabbed my hand. "I want you to meet my friends."

We flew by the hallway closet. Once again, my eyes scanned it as we passed. Speculating, I imagined other mischievous children may have located Anton and my secret room.

Mari waved at one boy and smiled at another as she led me to the day room. She was much friendlier than I had ever been. My social interaction usually began with a fist fight.

As we entered, memories flooded my mind, and all of them included Anton. *How could someone so intertwined in my life be so far away from me now?* My heart ached for my best friend.

Not much had changed since I was here. The crack on the floor where we often stood in line had gotten longer, while the plaster walls and wooden beams—even the sole window—seemed much smaller now. Mari led me to a corner where a group of girls passed a single doll around. Its features were familiar.

"This is my friend, Ginny."

I extended my hand.

"This is Ella. She's my sister," Mari announced proudly, as she easily plopped down next to them.

A twinge of guilt stung me. *If I were truly a good sister, I would not leave her in an orphanage.*

The girls all looked to me with wide eyes. I was positive it was the first time they had ever seen anyone with brown skin.

"I have a surprise for you, Mari." She launched enthusiastically to her feet.

Holding out a small tin of wax colors with one hand, I reached for her with the other and led her out to the back steps. Many pleasant recollections came from these steps; a sprawled-out Anton attempting to draw alongside me was the first to emerge, and my smile could not be contained. I sat on the top concrete step and opened the tin. "Pick one." Mari grinned broadly before she selected bright red then placed the green one in my palm.

"I'm going to teach you how to draw a butterfly."

"Really?" Mari's expression lit up eagerly. "Nurse Margret told me about your drawings. She said you were the best she ever knew."

"She said that?" I questioned, surprised Margaret felt that way.

"Yep. She also told me about your friend Anton."

"What did she say about him?" Curious, my wax held still as I waited for her to answer.

She had already started drawing, heavily focused on a flower petal. "She said he was your best friend, like Ginny is mine."

"Yes. Yes, he is." My mouth curved naturally upward, thinking of how close I was to seeing him again.

We spent the next hour outside in the warmth of an early autumn day, the first in almost a week that didn't end up in a rainstorm. We drew butterflies, flowers, birds, and a figure I could not quite identify, but it was Mari's day and her canvas. When we were done, there was barely a concrete inch not covered by color. It was beautiful.

"Why can't you visit me every day?"

I chuckled; her dirty face was angled up at me, and I saw myself in those eyes. It nearly broke my heart to say goodbye. If plans were successful, I would not be back, and it was too dangerous to even consider taking her. I couldn't risk her young life. Despite it being an orphanage, she would be safer here.

"I wish I could." I reached for both her hands. "Now, do you remember what I've told you?"

Mari nodded readily, but her mouth curved into a frown.

"Don't be sad, little one. What have I told you?"

"That I'm special," Mari whispered with doubt.

"You are *very* special!" I lifted her chin. My nose inched close, then tickled hers. "Don't let anyone tell you otherwise—ever."

"If I'm so special, why doesn't anyone want me?"

My heart pinched. Those same words came out of my mouth once. I needed to find the right answer. My mind reflected back to my own desperate inquiry as a child close to Mari's age, but even if I offered her a suitable reply, she would never stop feeling alone—at least not until she belonged to a family.

"Because Mari, for whatever reason, some of us don't have parents, but that doesn't mean we aren't loved. I love you."

"Why can't we live together?"

Suddenly, I was leaning out my kitchen window as Josef's hand slipped out of mine. I didn't have much of a choice the night he left. *Do I have a choice now?*

It took me a moment to answer. A variety of emotions wrestled within my head: guilt, compassion, fear, even love. Somehow this petite *strabenkind* imprinted on my heavily-guarded heart, and I was leaving her . . . deserting her to fend for herself . . . an orphan in a damaged city.

Knowing what that was like, I despised my circumstances and yet allowed it to happen to her. My lips pulled tight, straining to keep my emotion in check. If she saw me cry, it could instill fear, and she needed to be strong. She needed every ounce of might my spirit could possibly offer. "Oh, I wish we could."

Raising her hands to my lips, I kissed each one. "I can barely take care of myself, sweetheart. I can't afford to take care of a child right now, but maybe someday . . . someday I hope that all changes."

"Me, too!" Her face wrinkled in distress.

Letting go, I slipped my hand in the pocket of my skirt and retrieved a *kinder* chocolate bar. It hadn't been so long ago that I'd forgotten how treats were scarce here. Mari's eyes lit up. She giggled and threw her arms around me. Her hugs got tighter each time we parted.

"Mari," I repeated, "promise me you will never forget how special you are."

"I promise."

After our goodbyes, I ambled down the steps, turned, and drew in one long last look of the Waisenhaus. It represented both pleasure and pain in my short life, and now with memories of Anton, my parents, and now Mari behind those closed doors, my pause overflowed with reverence before I took the first steps in the other direction and towards an unknown future.

THIRTY-FIVE

IT'S REALLY HAPPENING!

5 October 1971

Dearest Josef
I can hardly wait for the day I see you in person, to hold your hands
in mine and talk as if we had never been separated. There is so much
to say. I can't wait to hear your stories of school, friends and even girls
which I understand have been many. It has been hard to picture you
as a twenty-one-year-old man with the image of an eleven-year-old
so deeply ingrained in my memory, but I am sure you are handsome
and strong, much like Papa.

I could not help feeling as though there was a chance my eyes would
behold Josef before he actually received this letter. *I could really see Josef*
soon! Just thinking those words was bewildering. My heart pounded incessantly as each new word emerged on the paper, a minute-by-minute
struggle to keep my pending secret from reaching the pencil.

Maybe you can suggest some books for me to read. I have read the
same ones at least a dozen times each. Oh, how I envy your libraries
and book stores, even the museums you mention. The only drawing I
have done recently is on the cement steps at the orphanage with Mari.

I hope to resume my painting when life becomes — a bit more settled. My friend at work, Angelika, was lucky enough to get to the Centrum Warenhaus at Alexanderplatz the day Herr Honecker gave away 150,000 pairs of these new blue jeans everyone is talking about. Apparently, they came from the West, so they might be something you already know of, but it is strange to see people, specifically women, wearing these pants made of denim material, yet they are the latest fixation here in the East. With little to excite us, you could see why, and people truly seem to love them. I have yet to find the attraction, but I also fancy my skirts. I might never be able to give them up. Well, until next time, my sweet brother, I miss you and love you with all my heart.

Love Ella

The following week, on my way to and from the tunnel, I stalked the tower. This time, a different reason motivated my behavior, with an added necessity of being discreet. Knowing he was close, I yearned desperately for a glimpse of the man of my memory, the man I missed. It was a dreadful game. My mind tried to make sense of the reality. My body craved a glimpse of his face, his movements, his half smile, none of which happened. It was possible Stefan didn't even know how to smile anymore. But could he? If I could reach him somehow, talk to him. When Edgar spoke of their imprisonment and how Stefan recited my letters, even then—even when he was trapped in the darkest of places—his thoughts were of me. Am I turning my back on him too soon? *Can he be saved?* If I were to find a way to get close enough to talk, would he listen? Stefan's callous voice, images of the murdered man, the idea he could hurt someone—even kill someone—scrambled my confidence.

Disappointed and discouraged with myself, I joined the others. Their understandable elation grew with each day, aware we were one day closer to our freedom, but each day also brought a reasonable amount of carelessness.

"What will be the first thing you do when you get there tomorrow?" Beti asked.

My head shook faintly. I really didn't know. Before the incident at the wall, I could have answered her more clearly. Now, my thoughts seemed like a jumbled mass of misgivings.

"What about you, Lamar?" The thrill in her voice amplified and now matched her volume as she went around the room asking each of us different questions. Five of us were present tonight. Rupert and Jonah would meet us before dawn. We had come down to the final hours.

"Sshhh!" Telfer ordered. He understood our risks. "Be quiet!" His demands, although sure, caused his own voice to raise an octave.

"Don't be a grumpy, old man." She got snippy. "I'm rightfully excited."

Something struck the floor above. The thud froze each of us in place. Holding our breath, only our pupils shifting from one to another. All ears extended for further noise, we waited. Nothing came.

"We need to see what that was," I whispered.

Beti whimpered, her eyes the size of marbles. I tiptoed towards her and placed an arm around her shoulders. "It's okay. We'll be okay."

The lanterns were carefully doused, and we sat in the dark for what seemed to be hours, although I knew it hadn't been. If someone was upstairs, we heard no further movement. Lamar took out a small flashlight. "I'll go check it out."

Ian placed a hand on his arm. "I'll go with you."

We watched as they disappeared up the stairs then waited.

The darkness hid the fear I was sure blanketed each person's face. Beti continued to whimper.

"It's nothing," Lamar announced quietly as they descended the stairs several minutes later. "There's a decent wind tonight; I felt the breeze the moment we stepped into the room. I'm sure the draft knocked the board over."

"Did you check the street, Ian?" Telfer's distrust surfaced again.

"Yes, Papa. It was clear."

"And the other rooms?"

"Nobody was up there." Ian relit the lanterns one by one. "We're safe."

The old man paced quietly, momentarily stopping in front of the tunnel. "It doesn't feel right."

"We're nervous being this close to the end." Lamar placed a hand on Telfer's shoulder.

The old man grumbled his discontent. "You continue to work down here, Ian. I'll watch upstairs." Telfer started up the steps.

"Yes. Ella, Beti, and I can finish up." Ian glanced around. "Lamar why don't you go with him?"

Lamar agreed, handing a lantern to Telfer as they went upstairs.

Ian handed us each a lamp, and we stepped through the tunnel. The dampness radiated off the walls. Goosebumps covered my arms and caused my torso to mildly shake. After a considerable walk, we reached the end. A fist-sized hole had been started from the friends on the other side, although, from the silence it was assumed they were now gone. As we peeled away the thick clay, more and more black air appeared. I grew restless, even antsy.

Handfuls of mud were flung behind me until the hole reached the size of my head. Ian stuck a lantern through and placed it on the ground. In the shadow of the light that now danced on the west side, I could see tears trickle down his cheeks. We moved faster. Beti could barely keep up with the piles of dirt. The cart filled twice in a short amount of time, but we didn't stop.

"It's done!" Ian cried. The opening was now large enough for one to slip through at a time. I gaped at the sight before me, hardly able to comprehend its significance.

"It's done." Repeating his words with emphasis, I rested my back against the dirt wall. The sobs came steadily. This was both the most exhilarating and distressing moment of my life. I had no idea it would rip me in half. In my attempt to brush the tears, streaks of mud smeared freely across my face, but I was too preoccupied with my thoughts than to worry about my appearance.

Ian chuckled. "You're a mess, Ella! Anton and Josef won't even recognize you!"

Anton and Josef! I'm going to see Anton and Josef! My countenance lifted at the belief everything could change in a matter of minutes. Confirming the pipe in my pocket and the pin on my shirt, I smirked then slyly picked up a handful of mud and slung it towards Ian's head, hitting him squarely in the jaw. After a gasp of surprise, he broke into loud laughter.

"Can you believe it?" I cried. "It's really happening." I peered at the tunnel we now connected with—right there in front of us.

"I don't know if I can wait for the others," Ian moaned.

"I know," I said, studying the drafty space again before facing Ian. "I think we should go. They'll be behind us in a short time and will know what to do."

Silence filled the tunnel. Each of us shouldered a personal reason to leave, yet we remained stationary.

"I can't leave without my father," Ian conceded with pain in his voice.

Thinking back about the decision to stay with my own dear papa the night the wire went up, I recognized his predicament all too well. My hand squeezed his. "I understand. I really do."

He smiled faintly. "Go see if the others have arrived. I'll finish this up, but be quick. We shouldn't wait too long."

I nodded and crawled out. Beti was waiting in the larger room. She looked drained from pushing the cart, but lit up once I shared the good news. Leaping towards the stairs, she took off without me. Subtle movement was heard above me as I envisioned our final gathering and subsequent departure.

Glancing around the room, the lantern on the table grew weaker but still highlighted the patrol papers scattered nearby, a dusty bedroll curled in the corner for those late-night naps, and a handful of biscuits still piled in a bowl, uneaten. It was hard to believe it was all coming to an end.

Although everything we worked so hard for led up to today, all the "lasts" I was about to experience became suddenly clear. Even the railing on the stairs felt different as I gripped it tightly in ascent. Elation filled my every move. The time to leave had come.

As the lantern below me dimmed, darkness blanketed the top of the stairs; I knew Telfer and Lamar brought lanterns upstairs, yet any trace of them had vanished. Taking the last step upward, the hair on my arms preemptively rose. Even the air smelled unusual. A significant exhale released the moment my foot struck a barrier. *It groaned!* My fingers reached down and pressed against soft tissue—a body!

"Auf den Boden legen, sofort." Through the darkness, a man's voice quietly demanded me to get down on the ground.

What? Who's speaking? I don't recognize the voice . . . what's going on? Puzzled, I slowly straightened to my original stance, but my eyes rapidly scrambled for anything recognizable.

"Auf den Boden legen, sofort." the man's request repeated. His demands were slow to penetrate my senses.

A hard object poked roughly against my chest. My breathing became choppy. The cold metal had to be a weapon.

Flashlights entered the far side of the room. Brief flashes through the dark revealed hints of men dressed in soldier's uniforms. The beam shed enough light for me to see the outline of familiar heads pressed to the floor.

My eyes flickered a quick scan. *Are they dead? Are they breathing? Wait. Yes, I see movement.*

"Ist sie die Letzte?" One soldier questioned his comrades.

My thoughts scrambled. *Why is he asking if I'm the last one?* Suddenly it all made sense . . . *this is an ambush!*

"Auf den Boden legen, sofort!" Again the man commanded me to comply a third time. His voice attempted a whisper, yet his tone grew thin with impatience. The whites of his eyes now glowed. My disobedience to his requests to get on the ground were possibly viewed as defiance.

With added light, the outline of his gun became clear . . . it was pointed directly at my chest. My throat filled with bile. *How can this be happening when we're finally through?* My palm pressed against my forehead, blood pumping through my veins coursed like needles.

Wait! A brief moment of clarity transpired. *Ian! Ian is still below.* My head twisting sharply towards the stairs, I shrieked as loud as I could muster, "Run, Ian! Run! It's border pat—"

One soldier shoved me backwards against the wall as he scrambled down the stairs. I fell to the ground as two more stomped on my legs to get past. My eyes shifted from the stairs to the soldier with the rifle aimed at me. Time stopped, the disgust on his face unquestionable as he chambered a bullet.

"Dafür werden Sie sterben." He pulled the gun up eye level and placed his cheek against it. He had sentenced me to death. A rapid flash sparked next to him. Searing pain pierced my right shoulder. I patted my chest. *He missed my heart?*

Terrified, I glanced up to see a handgun smoking. The bullet came from a different soldier's weapon! Deafening screams followed, possibly Beti . . . possibly me.

The sound of gunshots now echoed above and below the tunnel; chaos ensued. Thunderous reverberation of rapid footsteps mixed hotly with bursts of gunfire. Despite the unbearable sting, my one good hand shrouded my ear to block the horrific noise.

"Go after them!"

I choked. It was *his* demanding voice. The haunting voice in my head.

The soldiers who had been down to the tunnel came running up the stairs, their rifles in firing position.

"Join the others, bring them back alive. I want them alive!" he ordered.

I scanned the room. Lamar sprawled in an unnatural twist. Next to him Beti stared back at me with motionless pupils. My cries rivaled sirens. *They're dead!* A man's hand flew to my mouth and pressed tightly. Face to face with Stefan, I whimpered.

"Don't say a word." Through gritted teeth, his order conveyed wrath.

A warm liquid slowly saturated my shirt. My fingers now covered in blood, I peered down at the stain as a lightness consumed me. My eyes rolled back, and Stefan slapped my cheeks briskly.

"Get up quickly," he demanded. "They'll be back shortly."

"Why . . ." The word slipped out barely audible. Stefan tugged hard and lifted me to my feet.

"Didn't you see he was about to shoot you in the heart? You would be dead now. I had to shoot!"

I knew Stefan was responding to my question plainly, but "why" encompassed more—the four heart-wrenching years since his last letter.

"We need to leave. Now!"

I tried to absorb the idea that the man I loved *shot me* . . . and who really was this man speaking to me with a harshness I hardly recognized from those lips.

Stefan gripped my good arm, kicked the remaining debris blocking the door aside, and led me back to the main room. The blackness began to dissipate to a dismal gray through the broken windows. I continued to stare at this man whose intensity frightened me when I stumbled over another body. I recognized Telfer's brown jacket and let out another distressing cry.

"Shhh! Be quiet!" Stefan's grip tightened. Pulling me close in tow, he hustled faster. "How could you be this careless?" he mumbled, barely coherent. His unyielding touch made it difficult to control my shaking. Weak and confused, I didn't answer.

"My men have been watching this building for several days. We were informed something was amiss." Stefan shook his head angrily. "I didn't know it was you until now."

My eyes blinked fervently, expecting tears, but nothing came despite how much this hurt.

He peered out the large window that faced the rear. "It's clear." He smashed the remaining fragments to the ground with the handle of his gun.

"You need to climb out." He leaned me against the wall and pulled a wooden box over to help with the height.

"Now, Ella." His lips caught my eye as he spoke. *He said my name!*

He pushed me forward. I was faint, so he shoved more than I hoisted, but eventually my body hit the ground outside the building. Jumping easily, he was by my side once again.

With a quick and impatient yank, he lifted me to my feet and held tight as we moved down the street. "Now it makes sense why you were in the neighborhood recently." His unrelenting grip contrasted his breath on my ear as he spoke. Even in anger, I yearned for the graze of his lip against my skin.

"You told me you weren't going to try to leave."

Stopping firmly in place, I snapped. "You told me you would come back to me!" Finally awakened from shock, my emotion unleashed. "You told me that you loved me!"

With no reaction, Stefan's expression resembled stone.

Searching for anything that resembled a heartbeat, I stared intently. Inches from the very image I saw every night in my dreams, the connection could not have felt more foreign. My hand moved to touch his cheek. He quickly turned away then dragged me behind as he increased his speed.

"Go to Katharina," he directed as he checked the surroundings. "Stick to the back roads we used to take through the cemetery."

"Katharina? Why?"

"She'll sew you up. She's your only hope right now, do not . . . " His fingers grasped my jaw, forcing me to look at him. My lips pulled tight in an effort to stifle a cry. The last time we were this close he was kissing me goodbye. I couldn't pull my eyes away. Black streaks infiltrated his blue eyes, and I feared what that meant.

"Listen to me, Ella . . . do not go to a hospital or clinic. They will find you and arrest you. Go! Now!" Once again, my good arm reached to touch him, but this time he elbowed it away. The indent in my bottom lip nearly drew blood.

"Stefan?" I whimpered desperately to a distant and seemingly unaffected man whose sole reaction to my pleadings showed in the rigidity of his jaw. "Please?" I begged for his attention. "I know about Vietnam," I mumbled.

Stefan stiffened, his cheeks flushing red. "You don't know anything!"

I countered nearly as loud. "I know you lost your men and became a prisoner. I know you experienced terrible things, but—" The sting in my shoulder intensified. "—Please, Stefan. It doesn't matter; I still love you."

His stance remained harsh, but a flicker of emotion briefly crossed his countenance. I followed his eyes to my shirt where Anton's tinnie pin rested now covered in blood. "It appears you've moved on fine without me."

I winced in pain. "I never moved on!"

"Hans doesn't seem to know that."

"Don't!" I cried, enraged. "Don't you dare! It's always been you. Only you!" My knees wanted to buckle. I leaned against the building and waited. I wanted answers.

"Everything has changed, Ella." His tone softened in a way that gave me hope. "I'm not that man anymore."

"Yes, you are." I stepped closer to him, his outline glowing from the first spark of an emerging sunrise behind him. "You will always be *my* Stefan."

His eyes studied the ground carefully then his body grew stiff. "I will never be that man again." The bite in his tone returned. I grabbed his sleeve and left a bloody handprint as he pushed me away again. I wasn't ready to let go of any Stefan—new or old—and gripped it again tightly. I didn't let go. The glare was one I hadn't seen in years, since the night of his mother's birthday party. He wasn't drunk now, like he had been then, but the contempt surfaced nearly the same. My breath caught tersely in my throat.

"Then finish the job. Kill me!" —I reached for the gun at his side, the same one that had taken the first shot— "Because I don't want to live this way anymore." He blocked the weapon from me. My words peeped weakly, "I can't live without you." I fell to the road hopeless. I didn't care.

"Go!" he yelled and lifted me limply off the ground. "They'll find you and kill you." He pushed me forward.

"Good," I sobbed as my free hand clasped my soaked sleeve and throbbing shoulder, while the other tried to muffle my cries. I wasn't sure which wound hurt worse. As Stefan moved away, I glanced his direction once more. With no strength and no will, I grudgingly crept along the building walls and inched my way out of sight. Once I believed he could no longer see me, my legs buckled. Between the pain in my heart and the pain in my shoulder, I was paralyzed—nothing mattered anymore. I had no reason to go on.

I rolled to my back. The street lamps and buildings began to fade and despite the glint of the morning light, a blackness spread from the corner of my eyes. Suddenly, I was lifted up, unsure of how or why. But as the person pulled me in tight and started running, my head dropped heavily against his chest. The steady rhythm of movement came from somebody strong enough to move me. *Stefan? . . . Hans? . . . Ian? . . . No, Ian's gone . . . dead?* My eyes closed.

THIRTY-SIX

I WON'T LET YOU DIE!

A rancid smell seeped through my senses and stirred me awake. Propped on my left side atop a cold, steel table, my body shuddered weakly in response. My digging shirt had been removed, and a thin cover shielded my chest. A man leaned over me, his sharp instrument digging stiffly into my skin. The excruciating pain burrowed underneath my skin and detonated in my muscles. My attempts to fight him off were feeble.

"Ella, stop." It was Katharina! Her gentle touch held me down.

I located the familiar kindness in her presence, then convulsed in sobs.

I even saw Stefan in her.

"We need to get the bullet out and it's going to hurt." As she spoke, Edmund poked something foreign into my skin. I shrieked. Katharina grabbed a towel and held it over my mouth.

"Please, bite this. You mustn't wake the family."

Edmund dug the object deeper. My teeth clenched the towel as hard as possible. Tears flowed as Katharina continued to hold me still.

"Now that she's awake, can we give her medication for the pain?" Katharina whispered to her husband. It was apparent she was torn between not distracting Edmund yet calming me.

"Just a little longer," Edmund whispered. Lightheaded, I started to panic.

The sound of a door crashing open startled me, and the towel fell from my mouth. The force with which this person entered was unmistaken.

"What is happening in here?" Herr Franke's angry voice resonated. Edmund froze momentarily as Katharina's father moved closer. "What is *she* doing here?" His volume shook the walls.

Katharina, startled at first, left my side to calm him. Edmund continued to work through it all. The sting of metal still maneuvered painfully inside my shoulder. I thought my eyes would disappear inside my head. Biting my hand; the marks nearly drew its own blood.

"She needs to go to a hospital, Katharina!" Herr Franke demanded.

"She would bleed to death before she got there. Papa, we can fix it."

"She should not be here!"

"Papa, Edmund and I can handle this. Please leave."

Although unseen, the weight of his presence could not be ignored.

"Please?" she begged.

Edmund sighed, "It's too deep; we need to get it from the back. We'll have to make another incision."

Katharina moved to the counter and passed him an additional set of tools. "Try this Edmund, it will make a bigger opening." She returned to her father with equal calmness. "Come, Papa. Everything will be okay." Katharina led Herr Franke to the door and closed it after him.

My head spun wildly. It might have been the bright lights or the loss of blood, but what I really wanted was to close my eyes and never open them again. Stefan's angry voice echoed inside my mind—the rage evident in his touch. That pain was compounded by the realization that my chance of reuniting with Josef and Anton was destroyed. The one plausible answer now was to admit defeat.

"Stop," I whispered.

Katharina and Edmund ignored me as they tried to turn my body.

"Stop!" My demand got louder.

They paused, surprised. Edmund waited, the scalpel held tight in his hand.

"I don't want this."

Katharina motioned for Edmund to continue.

"No." I sobbed.

Katharina held my face with both her hands. Her eyes within inches of mine, "I won't let you die, Ella!" This was a side of Katharina I had never seen. "Keep going." She lifted a syringe and pricked the needle in my arm. "She has lost a lot of blood, Edmund. Hurry, get the bullet out then seal the wound. She's weak. We'll need to give her more blood."

I knew the pain in my shoulder hurt—the scraping, tugging, and pressure—but the sharpness in my chest reminded me of the more painful injury rooted even deeper within.

"I don't want to live—" I mumbled as I dozed in and out of consciousness before the blackness consumed me.

* * *

I awoke on the couch in the office, Katharina in a chair near my side.

Using the pillows for leverage, I tried to sit up, but the intense pain in my shoulder forced me back down.

"Don't move," Katharina reacted to my groan. "You need to rest, it's only been a few hours. It will take a while for you to recover."

The earlier events silently replayed in my head as Edmund entered and placed his hand tenderly on Katharina's neck. I shut my eyelids, unwilling to witness any show of affection, especially since mine had been ripped coldly from me.

"Ella, Edmund saved your life."

"We both did," he added with adoration.

I peeked as he kissed her cheek. My desire to scream dwarfed the muttered thank you. The gratitude was more out of obligation than anything. Dying seemed much more appealing.

My eyes hurt. I didn't want to see Katharina, Stefan's desk, the telephone, or anything in this room . . . everything made me think of him.

Stefan. I was sure they were unaware he was border guard. With the future I'm sure his family thought he deserved, I was positive it would disappoint them.

"Where's the bullet?" I slurred. Katharina peered uneasily at Edmund.

"It's in the other room," he spoke as he stood.

But Katharina questioned, "Why?"

"I want to see it."

Edmund left to retrieve it.

"Ella, what happened?" Katharina scooted closer to me.

I ignored the question. "How did I get here?"

Katharina held a warm mug to my lips and encouraged me to sip, yet

285

it was the way her eyebrows knit together that drew my attention. "You don't know?"

"No." The soothing tea slipped down my dry throat easily. She put the cup down and turned to me again.

"There was a loud knock early this morning, but you were alone on the steps, unconscious. What do you remember?"

I knew I would have to explain the shooting but wasn't sure how much to share. Still, it was Katharina, my best friend. Stefan himself told me to come here. I could trust her.

"I . . ." I scrutinized her husband as he handed me the bullet. Katharina seemed to read my thoughts.

"You can trust him. He's family."

I rolled the bullet around in my fingers. *Stefan touched this. He placed it in his gun; he put it there to shoot someone. How ironic it ended up being me.*

My eyes lowered. "I was shot by a border guard . . . trying to escape."

Her expression was emotionless, neither surprised nor content.

Once again, the door slammed open behind her, and Herr Franke entered the room as angrily as I remembered the first time. He approached the couch and bellowed in every direction.

"Is that true?" Herr Franke must have overheard my confession. "Shot by border guard?"

My eyes flashed between Katharina and Edmund while my heart's pace quickened.

Pointing to me, he cried, "Get out! You cannot be here!"

"Father, calm down. She's injured. She cannot leave." Katharina tried to reason with him, but revulsion flowed easily from his lips. This was not the same man I saw at the restaurant.

"They'll be looking for her, and she'll get us all arrested . . . or worse, killed! I need to call Markus."

"No, Papa, please." Katharina went to him. "Please let us handle this."

Herr Franke grabbed one of Stefan's jackets that hung on a hook nearby and threw it onto the covers across me. His scent was faint. Whether cologne or simply him, the smell made me nauseous.

He yelled through gritted teeth, "She leaves tonight!"

Edmund stood up and put his arm around his father-in-law and whispered in his ear as he guided him gently out of the room. His kindness to the cross old man was impressive. That calming nature would be quite useful as a doctor.

Words failed me. Herr Franke was right. They would be searching for someone who had been shot, and if they had captured the others, they could have given up my identity. Any known associations would be questioned. There was probably little Stefan could do to keep them off course for very long, but even if his feelings for me had changed, he wouldn't let anyone implicate his family.

The image of the bodies on the floor of the warehouse—Telfer, Lamar, and Beti—emerged. Maybe they had caught the others and killed them too, despite Stefan's request. Poor Rupert, who would now have to live without his brother, if he was still alive . . . and Ian . . . my good friend, Ian. All he wanted was to be with his girl in the West. What a devastating turn of events.

Katharina gazed at me and put her own hands over mine.

"We won't let you leave, Ella. Papa is still hurting over Stefan. Even though Edmund and I have taken over most of the duties in the mortuary, there are memories of him everywhere." I knew this to be true in the short time I was here. I hesitated to ask, yet turned to her anyway.

"Do you know where he is?" I questioned apprehensively.

"We haven't had news in years, nothing has changed since we last spoke. We go to every parade, hoping to catch a glimpse of the soldiers, but as you know . . ." —she laughed to herself— "There are too many . . . and they all look alike."

I nodded.

"Ella, he loves you." Her words punctured me.

"Don't say that!" My response was sharp. Katharina's brows raised.

"I know he does. You're the only woman he has ever loved."

"Please," I whimpered into the blanket, "Please don't say that."

Katharina's hand soothed my hair. She would make a wonderful mother one day. When Edmund arrived, the alarm in her voice increased. "Sweetheart, can you get her something for the pain please?"

I knew there wouldn't be anything strong enough for the agony I felt.

When Edmund gave me the shot, I winced. The liquid burned through my system. Relief instantly spread as my body fell drowsy and loose.

"Please rest." Katharina continued to rub my head.

"He's not the s—same per . . . man anymore, Kath . . . Katharina."

"Who?" she asked.

"S—tefan," I slurred.

"What do you mean?" her voice rose anxiously. "Have you heard from him?"

With the closure of my eyes, my body curled like a baby.

"Ella, what do you know of Stefan?"

"He'sbo . . ." —my words overlapped incoherently— "bor . . .bord . . ergua . . ."

"Ella!" Katharina lightly nudged me. She would have to wait.

And wait she apparently did. When I woke later that afternoon, she was still by my side.

"How are you feeling, Ella?"

My stretch instantly triggered a sharp twinge in my shoulder. Everything flooded back.

Katharina lifted back the blanket and peeled the bandage carefully off the wound. The dried blood stuck to the padding and tore a bit. A small leak of bright-red blood trickled down my side. She dabbed it with a cotton ball. The ointment on the ball seared the wound, hurting immensely.

"Ella, you said something strange before you fell asleep. I believe you said Stefan was border guard."

My eyes went wide. "What else did I say?" I was instantly angered at myself. *How could I be stupid enough to let that slip?*

"Nothing else, really."

My mind reeled at how I could fix it. "I probably said a lot of foolish things, Katharina. Edmund gave me a shot, remember?"

"Yes, but do you really think he's people's police?"

"No." I wanted Katharina's memory of Stefan to be as she remembered him, so I added nothing more. She seemed satisfied.

"Have you heard from Josef or Anton?"

"I receive a letter every few months, but I actually saw them."

"Saw them? How?"

"At the viewing platform."

"That's wonderful!"

"Yeah, it's been so long I hardly recognized Josef, but they are both doing well. He dates a lot, and Anton is seeing someone."

Katharina watched me closely for emotion, there was none. I was happy for Anton, but the more I thought about his joy, the more I wallowed in my own self-pity, and that wasn't what I wanted to feel. "Anton is about to be a part owner of a construction company, and Josef is studying law."

She smiled.

Frau Franke appeared at the door. Instantly there wasn't enough oxygen in the room for me to breathe.

"Koen told me she was here." The calm in her voice was eerie.

"She's recovering, Mama."

"I don't care why she's here, Katharina." The erratic side of Frau Franke surfaced, her eyes taking the form of razor-sharp daggers. "I will not allow it!"

Edmund spoke, "She's not strong enough to leave yet, Mama."

"She does not belong here." The truth in those words strangled me.

"Mama . . ." Katharina rose to her feet slowly as if she expected something impulsive to happen.

Frau Franke rushed the couch, anger emanating from her cheeks, which instantly flushed the color of her lipstick. "Is it true?" The question was posed universally, but she glowered directly at me. "She was shot trying to escape?"

Complete silence filled the room. Nobody stirred, either.

Immediately, she reached for my injured arm and roughly pulled me to the floor. I cried out in anguish. Katharina and Edmund lunged forward but stopped when Frau Franke shot a warning glare their direction.

Katharina whimpered, "Please Mama. Please stop."

"You have done nothing but bring misery to this family," she screeched above me, much louder than necessary considering the size of the room. Her grip squeezed my forearm so tightly my skin turned nearly as white as hers.

"Please," I cried weakly, trying to muster strength to my legs. Fresh blood dripped freely to the carpet as my wound started to bleed from the exertion.

"Mama!" Katharina tried to wedge between us. "She lost too much blood; she must rest!"

"She needs to get out!" Frau Franke pushed Katharina aside and dragged me by one arm to the hallway.

My skin burned painfully against the carpet as she towed. Her tug seemed effortless. I hardly had the strength to stop her. Katharina and Edmund followed behind, pleading desperately as Herr Franke arrived in the hall. Frau Franke reached the receiving door and shrieked for her husband to open it. He obeyed as she yanked me through and towards the solid brick steps. With one last shove I tumbled to the bottom.

"You are nothing to us. Never come back!"

My body came to a stop on my injury. A small line of blood trailed my path. Through the onslaught of tears, I could barely see the four images at the doorway. Katharina cried out and ran towards me. When Frau Franke tried to stop her, she physically fought to break loose and reached my side. She pressed the hem of her dress against the wound as I wept. My blood soaked through.

Frau Franke raised her finger our direction and cried, "The guard who shot you should have finished you off."

Heat filled my cheeks. My eyes darted about as Katharina tried to control the bleeding. Edmund joined her. I glanced up, my tongue pressed against my teeth, physically fighting what was to come next.

"It was Stefan!" I blurted between sobs.

Everyone froze.

The weight of the silence burrowed deep until Frau Franke hissed "You lie!"

My head shook. Katharina's hands rubbed my cheeks as if I was delirious, but I turned towards her. "It's true," I whispered.

Frau Franke's anger remained unbridled. "Stefan is not at the border!"

Edmund whispered to his wife, "I need more bandages, she's losing too much blood." He quickly disappeared inside.

My words were meant for Katharina alone. "He shot me to save my life. The other guard was going to kill me."

Frau Franke descended the stairs, her steps heavy and swift. "I don't believe you! How dare you say these things here?" I braced for another attack, though she never reached me.

Rustling from the bushes nearby intensified. Startled, I turned my head as a man approached through the foliage. Nobody moved, even my tears became motionless. Katharina's gasp was the only sound, and while she didn't remove her hand from pressing on my shoulder, I could feel it trembling.

Stefan is here? My mind strained to grasp the rationale. He still wore the uniform of the People's Police. A fairly large blood stain covered one sleeve.

This was the first I had seen him in full light. Earlier, as we exited the warehouse it was only when we were close that there were fragments of familiarity, and even then, his harshness nearly made him unrecognizable, but now his presence confirmed he was not part of my imagination. Stefan was real!

His eyes scanned the scene warily as he maintained his distance. I wanted him to come to me, hold me, and whisper in my ear. I needed to touch his face and soften the hardness that appeared more like his marble statue than a living, breathing human being. *Where is the man I dreamt of all those years? That last loving kiss and embrace and his promise to return . . . where is he?*

"Stefan!" Katharina called to him, ". . . you're injured." She pointed to the blood.

"No, it's not mine." His eyes flashed momentarily my direction then turned to the others.

"You?" Herr Franke descended the stairs excessively pale. "You are . . . ?" He couldn't even finish his sentence as he pointed to the uniform.

Stefan refused to lower his head.

I pushed up on my good arm and struggled to stand but was too weak. In my attempt I slipped backwards. Stefan instinctively lurched forward then reeled back. Evading my gaze, his arms folded tightly as if restraining them. Katharina thwarted my fall and carefully secured me before she rose to her feet. "Stefan?" One hand extended his direction.

"Please . . . don't."

Frau Franke, who finally roused, moved towards him. Stefan stretched his arm out with increasing agitation. "Please stay back!"

I had never seen her face melt with such agony. Her skin turned from red to translucent white. "Stefan—"

"Stop. I simply wanted to make sure you were all safe. Do not call the police, and do not contact Markus, Mother." His eyes narrowed, he knew her too well. "You can't change what happened, but you must keep it contained. Ella can get the medical help she needs here."

Frau Franke stared hard my direction. I was sure she would kill me in my sleep. "Stefan, how did this happen? When did you become border guard? How long have you been in Berlin?" Questions I, too, wanted answers for.

"It's not your concern." His voice was sharp and bitter.

"Not my concern?" she shrieked. "You are my son. Please let me call Markus. He will fix this. You are a Franke, not some lowly *obchladose!*" She pointed towards me as she spoke. "And why protect her?"

I inhaled softly. Although I wanted to know, I glanced down in case he answered, unsure I could handle another tear to my heart. He said nothing.

"Stefan," Frau Franke pleaded uncharacteristically, "come home."

I peered up in time to see him shake his head side to side, but his jaw was set. Never had I seen him this callous. "Do as I say." He was more soldier now than Stefan.

The sting in my heart was nearly unbearable. Reaching for Katharina's hand, I clumsily shifted upright once again. Edmund ran to my side to help. This time when I locked on Stefan's eyes, they beheld me for a moment.

"Stefan, I know there's still goodness in you. You wouldn't have saved me if there wasn't."

It had only been this morning—as I reflected on the shooting—that I recalled the night Stefan told me he was a marksman. He didn't have to miss my heart. I knew without a doubt that Stefan really did save my life when his comrade was ready to kill me. The reality of it all was overwhelming. He stared firmly in my direction.

It was an agonizing moment. Stefan shot me but saved my life. He was standing right here before me, except I couldn't touch him. I pressed my lips tightly together knowing if I said another word, the tears might start again and never stop, but I couldn't just watch him walk away. "Please stay," I whispered.

"I came because . . ." He caught his own words and stiffened once again. "I merely came to make sure you were not turned away." His lips parted as if he meant to say something else, but he never did. Despite his indifference and detachment, this act alone told me he wasn't completely gone.

"However . . ." He glanced behind him as if suspecting he'd been followed. He'd taken a great risk. "This is goodbye."

Our eyes grew wide simultaneously. Herr Franke stepped forward. "For how long?"

I feared his answer before he said it.

"Forever."

"Why?" I demanded angrily.

He stared at me again, no softness in his voice. "I am no longer the man I was before." He spoke firmly and with finality as he skimmed over each person present. "That Stefan is dead to you. *Do not* come looking for me." He regarded me with his final words. "It will only bring you pain."

With that he disappeared behind the gate, taking half of me with him.

Katharina's quiet sobs next to me were contrasted by the vicious words from Frau Franke. "This concession is for Stefan." Leaning in close to my face, every line in her forehead deepened. "When you are healed, never, ever come back here!" She hurried inside the mortuary.

I glanced up to see Herr Franke running his hand through his receding hair line, his expression wrenched in sorrow. He scanned me with an identical loathing then walked away without a word. Edmund lifted and carried me back to the office couch, disappearing to retrieve his surgical kit. The wounds needed to be stitched all over again.

Katharina followed us in. When she came to me, she hugged me lightly. "Why didn't you tell me?"

I stared at my hands. "Who was that, Katharina . . . ? That wasn't our Stefan."

Katharina started to weep again, and this time I joined her.

THIRTY-SEVEN

What Kind Of Life Is That?

November 1971

Although, I had come to accept what happened the night of the tunnel incident, there was no mistaking it altered my life. Not only scarred by a bullet hole, but the murder of three people I cared about . . . possibly more after the shooting started. I never learned the fate of the others. *Were they captured? Killed?*

Since nothing ever came of it, and nobody came looking for me, the only logical answer was there were no other survivors. My greatest loss, however, wasn't so much physical as emotional. Trust was no longer an attribute I believed in.

I remained at the Franke's for almost a month under Katharina and Edmund's care before returning to my flat on Max-Beer. They generously paid rent in my absence and made arrangements with Zur for me to return when recovered.

Despite much to be grateful for, I continued to focus on my shortcomings and inadequacies—all the valid reasons Stefan shut me out of his life. Even while I recuperated in his childhood home, judgement tumbled to *my side* of the mental scale much more than his.

I never saw the elder Frankes after that night. Katharina went to great lengths to keep me safe and isolated. Although she loved her parents and felt an inherited responsibility towards them and their family name, she had been blessed with a natural endowment of love for others, and because of this, it created contradiction.

Stefan stayed true to his word and never returned. The windows had become my solace, partly for sunshine during a dark winter, but also with a desperate hope he would somehow reappear, just as he did the day after the shooting. The habit was insufferable, but I did it anyway.

The greatest fortune—next to the love I felt from Katharina and Edmund—was the friendship I rekindled with Lena during my stay. Moved to the guestroom shortly after my acute care in the mortuary, I was visited daily by Lena. Her gentle nature, constant watch, and fulfilling conversation became the highlight of my healing. With only four months to go before her April wedding to Freddy, she included me in every aspect of her arrangements. I had never seen her happier.

"How are you feeling today?" Lena found me in the art room. Although I frequented the space, I had yet to actually pick up a tool. The idea of painting seemed unnatural in light of the recent events. Painting had always been an expression of joy or love, emotions that currently evaded me.

"I am well. My arm actually moves to here now." I raised it barely past my shoulder for a brief second before it was released. Lena walked to the easel. Stefan's painting of the Elbe River was more of a shrine now than anything else.

She leaned in and narrowed her eyes in examination. "Unbelievable!" Her sudden outburst startled me.

"What?" I moved from the window to her side.

"Have you ever seen this?" She pointed to the grassy landscape next to the water where villagers had gathered as if on a Sunday stroll.

"Yes," I responded flatly. Stefan completed the painting at the height of our courtship. I loved to watch him paint.

"Ella, look!" She pointed to the image of two people having a picnic. I stepped closer and bent down.

My gasp confirmed her discovery. A woman of darker complexion in a bright yellow dress next to a man with shoulder-length, blond hair wearing a familiar brown blazer. He had blue eyes, hers were dark brown, and he was holding her hand. Stefan had painted us into his picture, and I'd never noticed it before. My mouth started to curve into a smile then immediately went flat. Lena squeezed my hand with silent understanding.

"You've told me those closest to Stefan have insisted of his love for you, but I also know your head is filled with more questions than answers right now." She led me to a stool and motioned for me to sit. "You said yourself that you believed he had to shoot you to save your life. That information is incredibly difficult to process, so can you imagine it from his eyes? You know his imprisonment in Vietnam created fears we can't possibly imagine. Now he's assigned to command a wall post where he's required to shoot people, and out of nowhere, the woman he loves has a rifle pointed at her chest."

Recalling Stefan's rejection was like rewinding a movie reel to watch for the hundredth time. "Even if he still cares for me, Lena, he chooses not to be with me . . . what kind of love—or life—is that?"

"Not a complete one," she resigned.

"If he's made up his mind," I swallowed hard. "There's nothing I can do to change it."

"I'm not going to tell you what to do. Only you can decide." She kissed me on the cheek and left me to my perplexity.

THIRTY-EIGHT

BUTTERFLIES TAKE FLIGHT

26 October 1972

Dear Anton,
Again, I have no excuse for my long absence of communication. I am
sorry my esteems are unforgivably delayed. Please give Elizabeth
my regards. You are a good man and deserve to be happy, it is quite
overdue. Please tell Josef I miss him and I'm very proud of his many
accomplishments. He'll make a fine lawyer.

No matter what, continue to look after my baby brother. Although
at 22 he isn't a baby, he will always be my brother. His life and
successes have been a direct result of your sacrifice, care and concern.
For this I may never be able to repay you.

Unfortunately, my efforts to get to you have failed. As you know,
the details are delicate and must not be disclosed. I'm afraid until the
wall comes down, I will always be a resident of East Berlin. I can't
believe we have been apart 11 years. I wish you the best and love you
both dearly.

Love, Ella

One year after the shooting, my body had almost fully healed despite a twinge of pain each time my arm rotated above my head, so naturally I kept it near my side. In a way, it had become a constant reminder of the tunnel and how close we had gotten to reaching the west side. A devastating memory, it joined the likes of many others still rattling around in my head with no solution to eliminating them.

Staring out my own apartment window, my reality had shifted. I no longer saw things the way I used to. The routine of watching the school children or Herr Köhler no longer mattered. Scanning beyond my neighborhood, a binding weight of misery lingered. The fact was that hundreds—possibly thousands—of East Germans desired to leave this country and, at the very least, plotted an escape.

Although the wall was restricted from my view, its presence was certain. The concrete blocks, razor wire, spotlights, trenches, trip wires, and guns—all there. They mocked me, laughing at how close I had come to freedom and how easily it was taken away.

The Western radio recently announced over sixty people had been shot in their attempts to escape the East and many more were imprisoned for their criticism of the regime and their dream of a different life. These statistics I knew were grossly underrated—disappearances, accusations, imprisonment, and death—we may never know the whole truth.

My own friend's names—Lamar, Beti, Jonah, along with Telfer, Rupert, even Ian—appeared in the *Morgenpost* as "missing". The image of Beti's eyes staring motionless at me would never be erased. *She isn't missing! She's dead.* Shot by border guard, now the crime was covered up. I wondered if their bodies had been taken to the Franke mortuary and cremated—all while I rested comfortably nearby.

I should have felt lucky. Somehow, once again, my life had been spared. My thoughts could not rest on this subject without shifting to Stefan. How was it that each time I escaped death he was involved? And why protect me? Why save then refuse me? The more I dwelled on his actions, the more frustrated I felt. What evils had he seen and done? And whatever they entailed, was it possible to believe they were forced upon him and not willingly contrived on his own? He was a good man once. Could he ever find his way back? Was he capable of moving beyond the horrible past?

All the hope I once had vanished. My chance of a reunion with Josef and Anton had been severed, and any possibility of a future with Stefan had shattered. Even with his military sentence officially ending next year, he had made it abundantly clear he wanted no part of my life. This, above all, broke what little confidence I had. Once again, part of me wished that it was really I who was lifeless and silent on that cold warehouse floor. Then I would no longer have to feel.

November marked thirteen months since that night, yet the wounds felt as fresh as the day they occurred. I wasn't sure why I desired to dig up the demons of that night, but they haunted me. I meandered through Friedrichshain with no real purpose, careful not to appear suspicious while two border patrol soldiers passed by. I nodded, but they didn't acknowledge me. I wondered if they knew Hans or served under Stefan. Moving forward, the sound of their steps came to a stop, they probably watched to make sure I was still on my way.

As I wandered close to our building, every possible entry point was sealed off by solid brick and concrete. With the tunnel directly below my feet, it too may have been destroyed. My steps followed the direction of where we dug but stopped quite a distance from the wall. *Ian and I should have left when we could. We should have just left!*

I quickly found myself near the buildings that neighbored the tower. It was here that Ian and I first crossed the drunk man before he headed for the wall. My stare centered on the curb where he tripped and trailed his imaginary steps to his death, a single white cross had been driven into the dirt nearby.

The tower's superior presence intimidated me, only not for the same reasons it would have others. I kept myself hidden in the shadows, mostly fearing to be seen by Stefan, but Hans as well. My eyes trailed the tower from the base to the octagonal top where windows faced every direction. *Is this still Stefan's post?* My mind dangled teasing questions . . . *Will I ever see him again? Does he even think of me?*

Leaning against the wall of the vacant building, my hand grazed the plain surface while my brain played tricks on me. Studying the exterior, I knew what needed to be done here. It would have to be done in the darkness of one night, so when the sun rose the next morning, and the daylight shone across the street, this would be the first thing he would see.

The next night, with fresh energy, I arrived at my designated spot. It was far enough away that I would not be seen as a threat and close enough that my efforts would be seen by dawn. Gently, I brushed the dirt splatters off the wall and set my pouch of small, colored paint jars at the base near my feet. The brush was first dipped into the black jar, and a solid outline of double wings emerged, with a mirror image on the opposite side. My brush strokes took longer since the shooting, but thankfully, my talent endured.

A giant-sized recreation of the butterfly from Volkspark came alive. It was identical to the one that remained on my wrist, comfortably unafraid. It was one of those moments in life that you never forget and never want to.

With the inner lines shaded and detailed with black paint, I reached for the blue, the color of Stefan's eyes. I'm not sure why I continually allowed myself to unearth the pain of seeing him in my head, yet Volkspark was an enchanting memory; it deserved preservation.

I spread the blue liberally in all directions, accenting some areas darker than others. The emotion in the artwork was everything that had been felt, suffered, or experienced since I could remember. In the end, it was a masterpiece over a metre in width and height. Despite the shadows, as I stood back to view it, I knew its presence would have an effect on *someone*.

If my butterflies can't get free, they will definitely take flight in East Berlin.

* * *

Over the next few months, a different abandoned building was picked in each of the bordering neighborhoods, and all of them facing the wall. Pankow. . . red, Prenzlauer . . . purple, Treptow . . . yellow. The butterfly in Mitte was the last, a rainbow of colors, and underneath the artwork was a detailed rendition of the wall. It may be the only way I could experience freedom now or ever.

18 February 1973

Ella!
I saw your design! Josef told me I needed to see something at the
viewing area near Potsdamer Platz. It was the first time I'd been to
the platform in years and there, for the world to see, is your butterfly. I
saw people taking photographs of it. It is the only color reflecting from
the East. It is bold and beautiful, like you! Oh, how I miss you! Seeing
you at Bernauer a year and a half ago was indescribable. We need to
meet more often!

Elizabeth and I are getting married! The date is set for June.
I'm not sure if I will make a good husband, but I will try my best.
I wish you could be here. I hope this news does not bring further
discouragement. I know you said you are no longer with Stefan, and
he is mindless for that. You deserve to be taken care of. Do not give up
on love, it is the greatest thing in the world.

We are also having a telephone installed in our flat. It is common
now here in the West, and with my new ownership at work, I must be
reachable. As soon as the installment is completed, I will send you the
numbers. Can you imagine it? Being able to talk anytime we want to?
Of course, I know you would still have to use the public machines, but
we would no longer have to wait months for news and we could hear
your voice again.

Oh, and Ella, a man came to our home last week. He said he
tracked us through acquaintances. It was very odd at first. He asked
if we knew you then asked if you were alive. I assured him you were
and the relief on his face was remarkable. I know there is much you
probably don't share, but I'm still your friend, Ella. You can tell me
anything. Once I assured him of your status, he urged me to write to
you immediately and tell you thank you. He said you saved his life. He
wouldn't say how, he said you would know. His name is Ian. He also
said that he is with Chandra, the love of his life, because of you. I hope
this news brings some happiness.
Please write soon!

Love Anton

The second part of the letter was from Josef.

Dear sister,

I have met her, Ella. The one! I know at 22 many believe I am too young to know or understand such feelings, but it is real!
I met Heidi at a demonstration against the wall. I have heard people speak of love at first sight and would have never believed it had I not experienced it myself. She is beautiful and extremely smart. I can't wait until you can meet her. I have not expressed this to anyone but Anton, but I do believe she will be my wife one day.

She has a brother in the East, maybe you could find him. His name is Cade Volney. He resides in the neighborhood of Prenzlauer Berg and works as a butcher's assistant. She writes him just like we do. We both keep hoping the wall will be down shortly, and we can have our loved ones present if we do marry. It would not be the same without you!

Anton showed me your butterfly. It is breathtaking. I miss seeing you draw. You are equal in talent to many artists here in the West who make a fair wage with their work. Imagine an income only from your art! I miss you!

Love Josef

I could not decide if my tears were out of happiness or sadness. This letter was full of wonderful news. Anton will be married and have a family someday. Josef, my little brother, in love? A telephone to communicate directly. Of course, they would have to teach me how to call, but to hear their voices! Then the news that Ian made it and is with Chandra. My cries for him to escape succeeded . . . he was not dead! I couldn't imagine a more complete letter in all of the years I received correspondence, so why was my heart aching as though it was crushed? Was it that I feared they had something I never would?

A chance to be with the one I love?

THIRTY-NINE

NUMB

14 July 1973

I stared at the glass.

It was nothing like the fine crystal at the Franke's or even as present-able as one at a pub.

My eyes followed the small crack from the rim to the base, faint fin-gerprints remained scattered along the way. It probably hadn't been washed in weeks—maybe used by his last customer. But it wasn't the glass that taunted me, it was the contents lingering inside.

My sight narrowed, and although liquid doesn't speak, I could hear it laughing.

Lenin's long hair swung forward as he moved around the small space. The back room of the *Kneipe* a few streets away from home was barely bigger than my bedroom closet. I'd only been to this tavern once before and only to find this man.

One thick strand strayed, and when he tried to push it aside, it con-tinued to block his view as he laid his tools out along the counter. He reached for something in a canister and pulled his hair tight in a pony-tail. It was the first time I had seen his eyes; they were so dark they ap-peared black.

"This is what you want?" Lenin held up a wrinkled paper.

I nodded.

"I've seen this before."

"Yes."

"It's yours?" Lenin eyed me suspiciously.

"Yes," I nipped. His small talk grew annoying.

"Lean forward and rest your arm on this." He pointed to the metal armrest where a torn towel had been folded in an attempt to offer some comfort. I moved my body slightly to the right, and pulled my sleeve off my shoulder to expose my bare skin and the scar.

"Oh," Lenin gasped at the sight of my old bullet wound. The skin had been stretched for the stitching, and although it had mostly healed, it was an ugly reminder of a painful night.

He topped the liquid off inside the glass.

"Are you sure you want it there?"

"Yes!" I snapped again.

"It's gonna hurt."

"Pain is relative," I muttered.

"You will want to drink all of this."

I pushed my own hair behind my left ear. Since I had cut it to my chin, there was less to worry about. I no longer cared if it fell down my back or experienced the caressing touch of a man.

Lenin lifted his ink needle and pressed sharply against my skin.

"Remember," I murmured through tightly closed teeth. "The wound must center the butterfly's right wing."

The buzz of his instrument started, and I gripped the chair tighter. With each burning stroke of his tool, my mind checked another person off my list. Anton—Josef—Lena—Katharina—Mari—Stefan . . . another puncture, another severed tie.

The process both physically and mentally was worse than imagined. Tears instantly sprang to my eyes.

He noticed and paused.

"Drink up, little lady . . . it will help if you're numb."

Numb? I've been numb for years.

Today marked the end of Stefan's mandatory ten-year service. This morning as I stared at the "1" on my mirror, the sobs came so unbearably I nearly hit my head on the sink as I melted to the floor.

This day was supposed to be the happiest day of my life—our reunification, our pending marriage, our future—but instead it was as insignificant as my confidence. I no longer knew where I belonged—by far, the greatest loss of my life.

Stefan held true to his words and made sure our paths never crossed. No sightings, no contact. Nothing. I had been erased.

"You okay?"

I absorbed Lenin's question. I wasn't sure if I would *ever* be okay.

The scar tissue around the hole was tender, and as soon as he started the tattoo again, I winced and bit the inside of my cheek to block my scream. My eyes flashed open.

With absolutely nothing left to lose, I reached for the glass. Gripping it hard, much tighter than necessary, my fingers went white with restricted circulation. My hand impulsively shaded my eyes . . . if I couldn't see it, maybe it wasn't real.

The needle stopped. Lenin waited.

The effort to shield my sight from the people who tortured me was weak—even Colonel Anker appeared in his evil silhouette to torment. Rage seeped into my head and coursed with insanity, regret, and shame.

I swallowed the vodka in three gulps, gritted my teeth tightly to fight the bitterness of the taste, and then choked. Lenin reached for a can, afraid I would vomit. My lips pressed firmly together and forced it to stay down. A flame blazed a trail down my throat. Water leaked excessively from my eyes, for reasons I was unsure of.

Twenty-seven years old and my first taste of alcohol.

I tried to convince myself it wasn't as offensive as I had imagined, only that was a lie. One of many I had been naïve enough to believe.

I slammed the glass back on the table, closed my eyes, and motioned to the bottle for more.

ReadMore
📖 Press

Would you like a *FREE* WWII historical fiction audiobook?

This audiobook is valued at 14.99$ on Amazon and is exclusively free for **Readmore Press'** readers!

To get your free audiobook, and to sign up for our newsletter where we send you more exclusive bonus content every month,

Scan the QR code

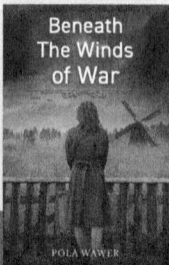

GERMAN GLOSSARY

Nein, bitte nein – No, please, no

Nachrichten für heute – News for Today

Der Stolz Deutschlands – The Pride of Germany

Dem anständigen Soldaten – The Decent Soldier

Dem anständigen Soldaten danken alle landsleute Dem Schützen dankt nur die SED – All Germans thank the honest soldier, only the SED thanks the marksman

Auf den zweiten Mann kommt es an. – It all depends on the second man

Soldat – Soldier

Bäckerei Balzer – Bakery Balzer

Streuselschneken – Pastry

Krapfen – Donut

Brat – Sausage

Danke – Thanks

der Volksarmee – The People's Army

Ja – Yes

Herr – Mr

Ich mache – I do

Fräulein – Miss

Die schönste Frau der Welt bist – Most beautiful in the world

Soldat junge – Soldier boy

Urania-Weltzeituhr – The Urania World Clock is a large turret-style clock, showing the current time in 148 major cities.

Fernsehturm – Television Tower intended to be both a symbol of Communist power and of Berlin. With its height of 368 metres (including antenna) it is the tallest structure in Germany, and the second-tallest structure in the European Union.

Sie ist obdachlos – She is homeless

Es ist egal, sie wird sowieso sterben – Why bother, she is going to die anyway

Was soll's, tut sie da rein – Whatever, put her in there

Welche Nummer wollen Sie anrufen? – Operator, what is your destination?

Hallo – Hello

Bitte bleiben Sie in der Leitung – Please stay on the line

halten bitte – Hold please

Wie kann ich Ihnen helfen? – How can I help you?

Patientenstatus, halten bitte – Patient status, hold please

Was wollen Sie? – What do you want?

Wer – Who?

Es gibt hier niemanden mit diesem Namen – There is nobody here by that name

Entschuldigung, ich habe Arbeit zu erledigen – Sorry I have work to do

Du bist ein Idiot – You're an idiot!

FDJ – "Free German Youth" A political organization used to influence the youth of East Germany into Marxism-Leninism beliefs.

Walpurgisnacht – Walpurgis Night

Auf Freunde und auf Leben und Freiheit! – To friends, life and freedom

An Familie und Freunde – To family and friends

Auf das Leben – And to life

Heiliger Abend – Holy Evening

Komm herein – Come In

Glühwein – Mulled wine

Sankt Nikolaus tag – Saint Nicholas Day

Feuerzangenbowle – Fire Tongs Punch

Außerparlamentarische Opposition – Political Protest movement towards Democracy in West Germany

VEB Deutsch Schallplatten – Music Publisher in the DDR

Halt! Im Namen der Volkspolizei, stillgestanden! Stop on behalf of the People's Police, do not move.

Nicht bewegen – Do not move

Blode landstreicher – Tramp

Schupfnudel – Thick noodle dish with dumplings

Nachrichten aus der DDR – News from the DDR

Was bringt Sie hierher – What is the nature of your visit?

Seine Division – What Division?

Woher wollen Sie das wissen? – How would you know?

Es scheint als hätte der Kamerad eine locker sitzende Zunge – Sounds like the comrade has loose lips

Hier nicht. Wir können Ihnen nicht helfen – Not here, we can't help you.

Sie müssen gehen – No you have to leave.

nakt unter Wölfen – "Naked among wolves" book by Bruno Apitz

Loslassen – Let go!

Haut ab und lasst mich in Ruhe – Get away and leave me alone

Bleiben Sie auf Befehl der Volkspolizei stehen – Stop by order of the people's police

Bleiben Sie stehen – Stop now

Halten Sie still – Hold still

Auf den Boden legen, sofort – Lay on the ground now

Ist sie die Letzte – Is she the last one?

Dafür werden Sie sterben – For that you will die

ACKNOWLEDGEMENTS

There are far too many people to name every single person that played a role in the completion and publication of this second book of the Berlin Butterfly Series, but I am deeply grateful to the many calls, comments, and reviews that have contributed to the success of the series. Thank you.

To my editor Irene Hunt. I don't have enough room on this page to tell you how I feel. You are amazing! Of course, the words "show don't tell" will forever be engrained in my head, and I have nightmares over filter words in my sleep, but seriously, I could not have chosen a better person for the daunting task of shaping and shining this diamond. You truly are talented and have a rare gift. Thank you.

To my husband who continually supports my writing addiction and never hesitates to compliment me and my work to anyone, anytime, anywhere! I love you.

To my second set of eyes, Taylor Moyes. Your belief in me and your love for the story fueled me daily. I could not have done this without you.

To Jennie Durkee, once again your strength and support have helped me become a better person and writer, thank you.

To Melanie Lazcko, as anticipated your German home and culture has helped authenticate the words in the book, Danke!

To those in Berlin Germany who helped make Berlin Butterfly a "factional" experience: Stefan and Marx from the Babylon Theater, the owners and managers of Zur Letzen Instanz Restaurant, and the Berlin Wall Museum for your constant dedication to the memory of the victims from the wall. Please visit their website at https://www.berliner-mau-er-gedenkstaette.de/de/

To my advance team who all play different roles in this process. Aside from their constant words of encouragement, they critique, review, read, suggest, and reread my work. Thank you Dawne Anderson, Wendy Hargrave, Melisa Harker, Brenda Mayberry, Brian Moyes, Susan Provost,

Lani Taunima, Lina Taunima, Nikala Teague and Jody Turpin. I am forever grateful to you for your time, patience, and special friendships!

To the Teotihuacan team at Arizona State University under the direction of Dr. Michael E. Smith and Dr. Angela Huston, thank you for your faith in me as an intern in your department and your constant support and belief in me.

Finally, to the band Skillet. Your talent in music and lyrics was far reaching in my world of writing. Inspired by your words, scenes involving Ella, Stefan, and Anton emerged. Specific songs represented the thoughts and feelings of my fictional characters, bringing them to life in ways that my pen could not reach. Even though you may not know your influence on this story, it has been immeasurable. Thank you.

AUTHOR'S NOTE

My husband made a comment once about the way I speak of Ella as if she is real. In my world she is very real. The emotions, challenges, and heartache she has experienced on the pages, have been long grueling nights for me, many times accompanied by tears and chocolate. Her strength and determination are inspiring and her personality and feistiness, lovable. Recently, I had the opportunity to walk down the street where she lived with the Kühns (Yes, Ackerstraße near Bernauer is still a cobblestone street), meander through Sophien Cemetery, eat pork knuckle at Zur Letzen Instanz, touch the Berlin Wall that would have faced her house and enjoy the beauty of the fairy-tale fountain. As you can see Ella, Stefan, Anton, Josef, Lena, Mari and Hans are alive and have become an integral part of my life. I truly hope they will for you as well.

This second book was emotionally difficult to write. These were some of the darkest times during the Cold War. The stories that are told of successful and failed escape attempts are real. In this book, only the context or characters have been altered and similar to *The Berlin Girl's Choice* (Book 1), the conversations that take place between the factual and fictional characters were created solely for the purpose of storytelling.

Please take the time to visit the Berlin Wall Memorial website at https://www.berliner-mauer-gedenkstaette.de/en/index.html to learn more about the era and both the victims and the survivors.

Berlin Wall: 13 August 1961- 9 November 1989

About the Author

L eah Moyes is a wife and a mother, a former teacher, and a coach with a background in Anthropology. Her best-selling historical fiction novels have won multiple awards and come from unique stories she has stumbled upon around the world. She loves popcorn and seafood (though not together) and is slowly checking off her very long bucket list.

Printed in Great Britain
by Amazon

56828321R00179